T0147123

The Majestic Columbia River Gorge

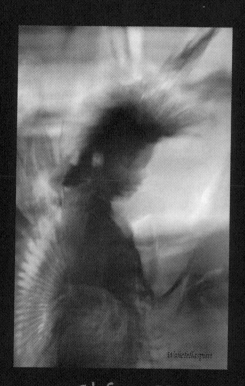

Wawetki.spat

Volume II
From Upon the Shores of En che Wauna
Begins the Trails of All Our Sorrows

These Are To Whom The Great Spirit Speaks

To Those Whom Dream,
She Gives Tomorrow...
To Those That Cannot Hear,
She Offers Diplomacy...
To Those Whom Walk Without Purpose,
She Offers Decision...
To Those Whom Are Impulsive,
She Offers Balance...

To Those That Are Touched In Mind,
She Grants Them Reason...
To Those That Are Unknowing,
She Awards Them Consciousness...
To Those Whom Cannot Walk,
She Offers Them Wings Like the Great Eagle...
To Those Whom Walk in Darkness,
She Gives Humanity...
To Those Whom Cannot Feel,
She Grants Them Perception...
To the Eyes of Blind Men,
She Gives Visions...

The Majestic Columbia River Gorge

From Upon the Shores of En che Wauna Begins the Trails of All Our Sorrows

Volume II

A Fictional Writing and Photographic Guide Through the Valley of the Eagle and Into the Lands of Wah Within the Columbia River Gorge In Oregon and Washington

Author and Photographer
Wahclellaspirit

Rev. date: 10/24/2015

To order additional copies of this book, contact:
Xlibris
1-888-795-4274
www.Xlibris.com
Orders@Xlibris.com
721764

Steven Wronstaff

Contents

Preface

The first edition of the *Majestic Columbia River Gorge* began with our peoples, the Watlalla, owning of the Great Chinook Nation, first arriving upon these lands that we have named Wah, we have chose near Che che Optin, Beacon Rock to be where our village of Wahclella rests.

We fled the land that lies across the sea, and we are now safe from the sharpened lance of those that ruled over our peoples that survived upon the Plattes as the chiefs ruled the land with vengeance, greed, and lust for all the people's property.

Upon arriving within the lands of Wah and the Valley of the Eagle we have been led by the High Spirits as they have taught us of honor, faith, pride, and respect as they have led us to accept each aspect of life that we sit before, or pass upon those trails that we discover ourselves to journey.

Each of our villages have had chiefs pass into the spirit world, and as their souls had then risen before the gates of the Hyas Saghalie Tyee's village, several have found honor to be placed upon the high cliffs of Wahclella.

Our fathers, whom stand proudly upon Wahclella's Wall today are the spirits that lead us along the Trail of Principles as they teach those that have followed in their vision quests to the ways of the Hyas Saghalie Tyee.

There, high above the clear waters, our fathers await those that are called before them, each of our great leaders are honored before our peoples as they have chosen to overlook our lives and lead us safely upon all the trails of these lands named Wah. It is from these same lessons they had followed from the teachings of Hyas Tahmahnawis throughout their lives, and as they offer safe journeys to all those that follow in his way, our lives are led distant from those misguided steps of others upon those trails of which they have blindly chose.

Through our father's teachings, we too can conduct our own lives without worry and regret upon the trails that we will one day cross.

The Land's of Wah have offered our peoples all that we have needed to live without problem, and for this, we are pleased. We have heard the voice of the Spirits that live upon the tall peaks of the Cascades as they have looked down upon us with questioning eyes as we have traversed across their lands without purpose many days. But, as they have addressed our faults without judgment, our people have heard of their message. Today, as we walk in their steps across our lands, we hear what they speak, and we feel what they feel.

Our union with the High Spirits has rewarded us with much worth. From the Hyas Red Cedar to the roots that grow strong in the meadows, to the deer and elk that walk before us and offer their souls and strong spirits so we have meat for our tables, and for the pish that swim thick in our waters that offers us life through the long, cold winters, we offer our respect.

Pish are the cause why our peoples have not strayed far from the Trail of Principles and why we have not sat but have knelt before the Wall of Candor that stands strong beside the tumwata of Wahclella.

We kneel before the feet of our fathers as we have much respect for the lessons they have brought to us that bring warmth to our souls and offer strength to our spirits. From our father's teachings, we have learned to understand the rhythm of the Earth and how each form of life lends themselves into the next, and through their order, comes order to life itself.

Through our preservation for what our High Spirit brings to our tables from the rich soils of his creation, life will not be taken from us, but will increase tenfold with each passing season as we begin to understand all that our Great Father speaks.

Into En che Wauna is brought fresh water from the Spirit's peaks as the snows of winter lie deep upon their shoulders, and as the new season comes, the tears of our Spirits that have fallen from the storm of winter come down from upon their high places. The waters drawn from the Spirits of the Cascades are first cleansed by the Spirits of Rock so En che Wauna will flow to the sea without complaint. Soon, our people's celebration will begin from along the shores of the Big Waters as Pish return to the lands that surround the rivers and streams of their birth.

When the first pish are seen to begin their long journey in return to their rivers and streams from the Big Waters, we dismantle our villages and separate them from the Lands of Wah and go to the great falls of the "Wallamt," Willamette. We are seen to stand upon the high rocks and hope to be the first to catch many pish from our long poles where strong baskets wait to scoop them from the falling water alongside our brothers of the Clackamas, Molalla, and Kalapuyas. Many pish have come from the waters of Wah and those beyond into our brothers nations to only return home many seasons later. We are grateful to our High Spirit to place our canoes upon the waters of the Willamette, Multnomah, and into En che Wauna. With spear and net in hand, we are rewarded with much catch.

Stuchen, as long as our canoes, rise up from the deep waters of En che Wauna. They offer their souls to join with us as they are lain upon our tables in great favor. When each of the new seasons comes fast upon us, great schools of Silver Salmon run quickly to their villages that lie beyond those of our kingdom as they come from the sea. These are the pish that brings much faith to rise up from

11

within us. As we stand upon En che Wauna's shores, our voices can be heard to shout out to all the Good Spirits of our lands in much respect for the right to dream of the tomorrows that will rise up from the light that is extended from Otelagh's, Sun's, gifting hands.

Chapter 1

The First Arrival

I am the son of Bright Wolf. I am named KaKa, Raven, for the black bird whom crosses the heavens. KaKa leads us safely from above the trails of our High Spirits in the Lands of Wah where our peoples have long since journeyed. KaKa is a brother to the great coyote, Hyas Talapus, they both have come to us to share their Great Spirit, and our people are forever grateful.

Many seasons have passed across our horizons since my Grandfather, Nenamooks, Land Otter, led our people safely through the toils that our lives encountered in both the savage winter storms, and the battles wrought between Hyas Pahto and Wy-East above us. Our people prospered through Nenamook's message. He called to the High Spirit and was led in his decisions without fear and doubt. We survived the long, dark battles that were fought between the good and bad spirits, those spirits that dwell among us, around, and within us.

My father, the son of Nenamooks, Towagh Talapas, Bright Wolf, told stories about new people entering into our lands, their hearts told of visions he had seen as he stood high up upon the Great Larch as new people entered into our lands, their hearts darkened by greed. He told of their absence of thought to the ways of the High Spirit, their not understanding the rhythm of the Earth.

As my great father has been taken upon his long voyage to the Village of the Living Dead high above our lands, I am now the leader to my village, and these words I share are the truth.

As the new season brings change to the earth as the cold breaths of winter changes to the warming breezes of spring, we have begun to move many of our villages onto islands that sing chorus to En che Wauna as she leads to the big waters of the west. The new season brings before us the birth of life upon our kingdom's mighty floor as Sun comes to rise high in our sky as it brings warmth to the soils, and soon, shall too come great schools of (pish), fish that will fill the waters of En che Wauna, (Columbia River).

Today, standing along the shores of the Big River, my brothers of the Kawiakum at Kwilluchini, Cathlamet, and their Chief, Tsutho and I throw our nets into the waters in wait to catch the seasons first salmon who will be welcomed upon our tables in celebration of their return. As we stand together in waiting along the shores of En che Wauna for the pish to leap into our nets, many men, dark from Otelagh's rays, hair thick upon their faces, and with no hair upon their heads, wearing only the furs of Mowich and Moolack, appear from behind the smoke, (fog), that settles hard upon the rush of the river.

I have named them, Suyapee for their upside down faces!

As they near the shore, slowly, and with caution, they begin to turn from the fast channel of the river, and with much effort, point their great canim, (canoes), toward us.

My brothers and I gather together and question to who are these new peoples, and from where have they come?

We brace ourselves, grasping tightly to our weapons, ready to defend ourselves if they choose to make war upon us.

As these Suyapee come before us from the fast waters of the Columbia and approach slowly to where we stand along the open

shoreline we wait questioning to why all the sticks that rise high
into the heavens upon our kingdom now stand unmoving through
the absence of wind? We question to why all the voices of the
good spirits that walk amongst us have quickly disappeared from
where we are now gathered, each bird's song lies stilled upon
the trails of wind? We become fearful as wind does not choose
to share its calming spirit before us. Smoke has risen quickly
and without warning from the plane of the great river, it has
swallowed all that lies behind Suyapee's deep canoes.

Suyapee are not brothers of our Nation, yet they come alone,
without spear and without arrow. They smile towards us as they
each raise their opened hands high above their heads, showing no
wanting for battle between us.

Our fathers had spoken vision that one day, coming from the
sea and from the open prairie, there would appear many men
that we had never seen. But as our great leaders spoke of what
they had seen, they did not tell if Suyapee held within them the
Good Spirit, Hyas Tahmahnawis, or the bad spirit, mesahchie
tahmahnawis.

We have many questions to ask of why have these rugged men
taken journey to enter our lands, and as they pull their canoes
upon shore, we too greet them with opened hands as Chief Tsutho
makes sign as he asks; "From what lands, (illahees) have you
begun your long journey as we have not seen men like you come to
our lands in all the seasons we have lived?"

The Suyapee who was sitting at the bow of the first canoe is
named Jean, he is the leader of those that come behind him from
the red, thick smoke, and as he stands from where he was seated
and walks towards us upon the shore he begins to tell of their
long journey. First, pointing towards Otelagh, (Sun), he raises
his arms and drops them from the heavens to his side many times.

15

"Many suns have come and gone during our journey," he tells. He then looks towards the big waters and points north where our brothers of the Chehalis have built villages along the river.

We think Jean tells; "It is there, where the big waters of the river meet those of the sea where the Chehalis capture the spirit of pish as they first return to the waters of their nation.

Jean points to the tree and bush and to the high peaks that rise up and welcome the warmth of Sun upon them, telling us, pleading, so we will understand the land where they have come is alike our own.

Our eyes are quickly drawn to the canoes they pull behind them, each piled high with the spirits of the eena, (beaver), the mink, the (mowitch), deer, the elk, (moolack), the bear, (lolo) and the cougar, (pishpish), the fox, and the great coyote, (talupus).

I stand over the pelts and remember my father telling that a visitor would one day enter our kingdom, share our village's fires, and speak of his many brothers. The vision told for many seasons new people would soon follow in his footsteps, and my father told these people would walk across our lands and see all the High Spirit has gifted us that has awarded us promise to survive upon his lands. These people would first forge trails that would soon lead others to follow after they have journeyed home across the highest mountains and through the lowest meadows, from upon the Big Waters of En che Wauna, and across the smallest streams. It is from these places many pelts of our kingdom's spirits would be taken, and we would soon be left bare before the rush of winter's heaviest storm.

Today, I find myself to ask, "Are these the men of whom my father spoke? Are these the men that wish to take from us and from our lands more than they can use? All that we honor, the meat that is placed upon our tables, to the coats that warm our shoulders as the Cole Illahee, (Cold Winter) comes harsh to our lands, will quickly be lost forever if this is the vision our fathers have once spoken.

As I stand with this man named Jean, and I hear his words, I still have question to his heart as I do not feel his spirit is good. In this, I fear my father's vision has now risen before us this day, and the vision's message has begun to be proven as to be the truth.

I have always been challenged by the thoughts of these men who now have approached our lands. My father foretold they would find fault in our ways and would mock the teachings of my father, his father and his father's father before him. The message of the vision tells that Suyapee would hear nothing of our heart's pulse upon the rhythm of the land. He would feel nothing of our souls, and he would be blind to the witness of our union with life of which our spirits depend, the same spirits that also depend upon us. My father told these men would be quick to thrust their darkened soul upon us if we did not accept the path they chose to take across our lands. Through the cloud of my father's vision, Suyapee's bad spirit would then rise up and make war with all our brothers and take our souls from within us. Sadly, I have been told as they would cast aside our spirits we would be scattered by wind, and we would no longer be found to rest within the village of the Hyas Saghalie Tahmahnawis Tyee.

As we pull our nets from the river we discover them to be empty of Hyas Salmon catch. The bad spirits of the river have left us wanting.

"It is not a good day to stand in this place," I say to those that stand with me. "Otelagh, (Sun), must also be in fear that he shall be sent far from the trails of his lands and all that he has offered as gifts within his kingdoms shall soon lie flattened and dead, and we shall forever be seen wanting the return to the life we once knew."

I again find fear within my soul as Suyapee walks among us. This fear becomes stronger with each new thought, and I sense it is unwilling to release my soul from where it has been imprisoned.

A vision appears before my eyes, I see much sadness spelled before all my brothers and sisters. Suyapee shall bring from deep within his hardened heart, willingly and unthinking, the disease of greed that shall create dark words to be spoken between our peoples.

Sun has passed below the flat waters of the sea as we sit in darkness before the fire of the village and speak of each our own peoples. As it was seen in my father's vision, these men that come upon us spread news their people would one day return to the lands of the north where they had first begun their journey. We are then told it is where the chakchak, (eagle) and kaka, (raven), the great Tkope, (White) and Siam, (Grizzly Bear), the ehkolie, (whale) and olhiyu, (seal), stand high upon their people's totems. But again, I sense their words are not good, as they are not Indian, and they have not come down from where Naha, (Chinook Mother) rests upon the high peak of Saddle Mountain, (Walahoof).

The great drums of all the villages of our kingdom will tonight be heard pleading for guidance from the wisdom of the High Spirits as we are not convinced of these men's good spirit, nor are we sure what we must do to defend given their intrusion upon the trails of En che Wauna within our kingdom.

As there has been prophecy of these new people taking much from our lands of which the spirits have promised to keep our peoples safe beneath their outstretched arms, I must ask of you, my brothers; "Have these new people been told by their own spirits

18

to take life from upon these lands that were first born by the toil and sweat of the *Hyas Tahmahnawis Tyee?*"

"We, the brothers and sisters of this nation, must certainly search for answer to these questions before the day of our fate rises up before us and we have no recourse for our lives direction. All the spirits of our lands may soon be seen no more amongst the waste that these peoples leave behind in their burdensome tracks across our lands. Our own heart and free spirit will be lost to the lands we have promised to keep safe."

I fear one day these same messages that are now spent to the winds shall turn far from the lead of the High Spirit and announce the call to battle, bringing end to our lives as we know it today. Our kingdom, these lands our people have honored, and the lands only we have been called upon by the High Spirit to save for our children's children, shall be lost to all others that will come after we are gone, and they will be seen no more as they were first given to our tending.

The long fingers of the mesahchie tahmahnawis shall then smile upon us all as we wallow in our graves, and it is he that will then take freely of our lost spirit. The bad spirits shall lay our peoples beneath these lands where their darkened souls proudly reign. We shall not be seen upon our lands again once we find fault with the brothers of these men. We will no longer be welcome upon the soils we have long honored before the High Spirits, and our own spirits shall be held as slaves, (elites), beneath the evil one's most lonesome trails.

As this man who steals the souls of those that walk across our lands tells tales, (yiem), of all the lands he has seen upon his many journeys, we find ourselves sitting hesitantly as he speaks that he too is one with the spirits as are our fathers. Though we feel contempt to accept that he is like our greatest leaders, and *that his heart shall not one day stop, we know that all his kind sit high upon their own telecasit, (hillside) as does the evil spirit Tsiatko, he who hunts in the darkness of night. We are easily led to believe their souls shall not rise up before the gates of the Hyas Tahmahnawis Tyee, but shall be taken upon the side of the mesahchie tahmahnawis as they will bring sorrow unto all the souls they pass.*

He is not our brother, (kapho)! He is the brother of the evil one that preys on all that we have been privileged to bring honor and value...

As we sit, sharing the fire of the village with Suyapee, we thank the souls of the sturgeon and silver salmon we had caught many long days ago. We thank the High Spirit for the moolack and mowitch that now sits before us upon the long table. We place cranberry, lavender, and mint upon the meat to add flavor, and our meal is good. With sadness, as we watch Suyapee take from the table all that we offer, he offers nothing to the High Spirits for this gift. My father's vision has come true. Suyapee take much from our table and offer nothing in return. These are the peoples of which my father once told. Men, sitting amongst our peoples as they journey from afar and speak of new lands we have not seen. They take note to all that our kingdom has offered to our people, and soon, it has been told they shall return to our lands with many of their brothers.

Our lands, these lands, shall then become theirs. This has been told for many seasons as a sudden storm shall cover the lands beneath a Red Cloud, then, by the waters of the sea, many boats shall come to our shores, and then from the long praire, many others shall cross our lands in search of making new villages upon those of our own. There will be much change depended upon wind, and as it has long been promised, it shall bring storm to be thrust hardened upon all our peoples for many seasons.

Walking to the shoreline of the river and seeing the spirit's coats tended within their great canoe, many brothers of our village gathered upon the nearest hillside and began to beat upon the great drums. Through the message, I know fear has now begun to enter into all the villages of our lands as the message of my father's vision is now spoken before the long night's fires. Through wind, the message is cast before the villages that stand along the great river, echoed into the lands of the Multnomah, and to my own village. Soon it shall be heard by the Klickitat, and will then spread far across the wind's wailing cry to the lands of the Yakama. It shall then rise high up above the river of the Umatilla and then above the river of the Snake where our brothers of the Nez Perz are now camped. It will not be many days before our message is cast beyond the kingdom of the Great Salmon, and to our brothers of the Shoshone whose villages lie upon the opened prairie as they hunt the Hyas, (Great) Buffalo.

I do not find favor in that one day when these men return to their people as they have seen the treasures of our land, they will offer the coats of our spirits before their village. With closed eyes, I see they will return to march upon the trails of our lands as they cross along the shores of En che Wauna that lead entry into the many kingdoms beyond our own. From behind wide smiles, they shall take the spirits from our kingdoms, and our hearts shall then be separated from our souls with their loss from before our eyes.

But in our fear, we must find honor in the Hyas Tahmahnawis' way.

We sit silently and listen to the speech of Suyapees' leader. In our silence, fear and distrust quickly rise up from within us as we sit unsettled by his words. I sense the battle that has been foreseen shall soon be lent across our lands, and the rise of angered words shall be thrown toward their gathering, and blood shall be spilled upon the ground as we defend what has been honored by all people within the Great Spirit's kingdoms.

As I listen to his dark words, my heart falls heavily within my chest. I sense through my own vision the images of these new people marching forward to the beat of the mesahchie tahmahnawis' taunting drum. From the horizon where Otelagh rises, and from the opposite horizon to where Otelagh finds his bed, I am certain they shall come with much fury...

With closed eyes, I see the soils beneath their march quickly turned toward the heavens. As each day is soon passed onto the next, I see a red, (pil), cloud with great depth forming above our kingdoms. As these new people's march reaches the borders of all the lands we claim, Otelagh shall not spread warmth and offer growth to the plants and to the sticks upon it. These people's numbers shall grow stronger, and all that we have honored, and all that we respect of our land's spirits, shall then be unseen through the darkened mask that rises higher than our own, Hyas Spirit Wy-East, (Mt. Hood).

From Suyapee's most thunderous and demanding step, the good spirits of our lands shall become troubled. The brothers of the beast are drawn tighter to their circle of our lands. Their breaths shall bring the darkness of storm and the cold of winter across all the kingdoms that our brothers have known. With opened arms, I see these peoples offering gifts as they approach us. With split tongues, like that of a snake, these peoples shall promise they have discovered a new and promised land whereupon our people must quickly find our village.

"It will not be the truth!"

By my witness of what is soon to approach before the doors of our villages, I am struck with terror! My soul shakes with fear as I peer, (nanitch), sorrowfully to the flame of our fire, (piah). As I sit, mitlite, (unmoving), I silently plead to the High Spirit for his lead.

This I know shall be the beginning of our peoples' battle to save all the gifts that have been placed upon our lands, but in that fight, I fear our own spirits shall be lost once the call to battle is announced. Once these new people huddle among us upon the trails of wind, disease and death will be brought upon us as they lay claim upon our lands.

This is where I find fear as did my Grandfather! A fear of knowing that we too may not be seen upon these lands again, and our children, and their children after them, shall then too lie silent and lost to the ways of Hyas Tahmahnawis Tyee.

I fear that all that awaits beyond our horizons shall not lend to another tomorrow where we will be able to share Otelagh's pass above these lands, and of the lands chosen of Wah. I fear that as darkness holds taut to the absence of shadow's long cast, we will be blind once again to all that we are, and all that we know today will be lost within the storm that is soon to arise from within the troubled souls of these new people.

"I plead before you most High Spirit; may Otelagh continue to rise in your heavens and smile upon our trails, warming our souls to your ways. Keep us distant and safe from the black soul of the mesahchie tahmahnawis."

Our battle now lies within our own spirits!

The night grows long and the wise owl calls out from the distant stick, (tree). We each rise up with questioning souls, settling to our place within the village. My brothers and I know we must make peace, joined together as one. We know that once these men return upon our trails, war will arrive with much storm. Not between us, but with these people that spill red cloud heavily over our lands.

The screen of the bad spirit shall fall upon us all and bring death to our doorsteps. We will each feel the desperate loss, the eviction from the lands where our souls have settled through the High Spirit's teachings. My question now rises up to the heavens. I plead before the HyasTahmahnawis Tyee and ask; "Is this your way, or is what we envision this night a calling by the daunting mesahchie tahmahnawis for all our soul's surrender?"

My soul is troubled. The silence of the night air resonates within me. If we do nothing to keep these people from taking all that we know, they will not stop. We will have lost. I know if we join arms with the bad spirit and fight to preserve all that the Good Spirit has honored our lands and peoples, we will find our fate to be the same.

Through this vision my heart lies troubled! Through this vision my soul lies numbed!

Through my understanding of this vision, if we accept the orders of Suyapee, all that we may have left to hold within our grasp are memories and the faith one day we will again rise upon the side of the Hyas Saghalie Tahmahnawis Tyee.

"Can we believe one day Great Spirit shall stand us back upon the trails that lead to our lands, to the grounds of our villages? Will our fires still burn in wait for our much longed return", I ask?

In the dead of night, as coyote has journeyed far from the village, and the wise owl sits silently guarding over our gathering at the edge of the meadow, many footsteps, softened by the needles of the Cedar, are heard running swiftly past where I lay. I awaken and stand facing the great river. I peer through the mask of cloud that has settled upon us. Several of the braves of our camp are taking from these peoples' canoes many hides of the spirits they have stolen, *kapswalla*, from our lands. I know, once these thieves take count of their bounty, they shall too call us thieves. We will hear their calling out for those liable for this theft, and the long arm of their weapon shall be quick to discharge upon those who have taken back to what was first taken from the soul of these lands.

Will this be the beginning to the rise of the red sky above us that we have feared? Will this untie the knot that keeps us all from joining the battles that will soon spread across all the lands of the *Hyas Saghalie Tahmahnawis Tyee*?

Will this first skirmish bring war between us, and will the final battle be drawn upon us with swift wing? I know as we cross the lines in defense to our ways, will this war take our souls and spirits far from the *Hyas Saghalie Tyees'*? Will we, those left standing, find our souls emptied beneath these lands where the *mesahchie tahmahnawis* has been known to longingly reign?

Are we, a nation of tribes that spread across all the kingdoms of the *Illahee*, soon, to be set at war?

Shall there soon be more and more of these people, taking all they can carry as the blood of our brothers will be spilled upon the grounds of all our kingdoms in its defense?

I ask; "Will we be left with nothing?"

How will those of our nation still standing, survive? What will we eat? What will warm our shoulders as the cold breaths of winter fall mightily upon us?

These are the dark questions that now spill from my lips that have no answer...

Chapter 2

The Mourning

As Otelagh rises up from the lands where he awakens, the village begins to stir with life. The young boys of the village gather wood for their fires. Young girls gather the berry and esalth, (corn), wappato, (potato), to help their mothers make bread.

Many of the braves of the camp have gathered along the great river, hoping the good spirits of En che Wauna will lure pish into their nets. They hope to have pish drying in Alder smoke, the comforting smell being carried by the warm breath of wind as it sings across our lands. The women and young girls will place the dried pish in baskets covered tightly with mats for store. High up in the longhouse, they shall be kept dry until served during winter's long storm.

I have noticed the four, (lokit), brothers who recovered the pelts are not amongst us. The people of the village have called out for them many times throughout the day and act as if they do not know where they have gone. I choose to believe these brothers will return with the furs once they understand what they have done will bring much harm to their people.

When the Suyapee leader returns to his boat, I fear he will take notice the furs have been taken from him, and peace between us will be lost. I fear the young sons of the Kathlamet will not reappear until these Suyapee go to the village of their own people. As we each listened to the stories spelled of fortune through trade by these new peoples, we each feel numbed by our visions to what will appear one day as Sun is taken from our lands and warmth from our bones.

Knowing these Suyapee will be fortunate to escape our village, and as they may soon be discovered lain within their burnt canoes, unsettles my soul.

As shared to my Father by the great leaders at the Walls of Wahclella, they have taught us to accept those people that are not of our way, and in peace, allow them to pass across our lands without prejudice. These men have journeyed to our kingdom and have sat before our fire. They have told of the many villages where their people sit in wait for their return. I have heard their black words. I know these people await the return of these bearded men with the pelts so they too can find warmth in winter's approaching storm.

Suyapee tell there are many men like themselves that will soon approach our lands in tall ships from the horizon of the great waters of the sea. They tell us they will take many more pelts from our lands and sail back to their villages. They ask that we gather the coats of the beaver, otter, black bear, the mink, deer, and the elk. They ask these pelts be cleaned and brushed many times, and hung high up from the ground as we do with meat and fish. They tell of these people that will come in tall ships and they will want to sit before our fires and offer trade for what will warm their souls through the long winters of their lands.

I ask myself, why do they not hunt in their lands and leave the spirits that walk amongst us to our own peoples? This man takes the coats from the spirits that walk amongst us. These spirits that once stood proudly before us along the shores f En che Wauna and upon the high meadows are left untended to rot upon our most distinguished and honored grounds. I must ask, "What do these men know of these spirit souls? What do they know of our people?

I ask, "Does their High Spirit tell them to take the animal spirits from us and leave only the bad stink, (peshak piupiu), of their remains to rise upon the Chinook's winds and foul the air that we breathe?"

"Do they not understand that we come from the same High Spirit as their people? Are not the heavens above them the same as our own? Do not all people walk the same trails and see with their eyes, and feel with their hearts?"

I stand upon the shore of our great river and hear my father's cry. Many of the fathers of our villages before him stand proudly upon Wahclella's most celebrated wall, and it is there they can be heard joining as one in their wail before the Hyas Tahmahnawis Tyee. Our leaders must have known, as I do today, our tomorrows will be spent in fear below Otelagh's fleeting pass.

All the lands which were seen proud will be hidden behind the dark mask from where Suyapee came. Each mountain, each valley, each stick, and each blade of grass will be hidden behind the red cloud of the bad spirit as it rises from the river's plane and reaches far into the heavens. Where once the song of bird filled the air, and where once the sticks sang from high above us as the Hyas Chinook Wind breathed heavily through their long arms, soon they each will be held in silence...

I ask, "Is this the warning that has been foretold? Do these people bring with them a promise of war upon our nations? Will death spill heavily upon our doorsteps?"

As I stand here, my thoughts lead me to where I have never thought I would be led. I am bewildered by the thought of war with these people. We will lose face before the Hyas Tahmahnawis if we find ourselves following in the ways of the bad spirit. We will lose all the gifts that have been bestowed upon us. I close my eyes and sense the visions of our Great Fathers will soon be fulfilled, and war will fall heavily upon all our nations. A great battle will soon form across all our lands, and our peoples will be left with nothing

The coldest storms of winter will fall upon our shoulders in a single day. Our souls shall be seen no more from atop our own winsome lands. The mesahchie tahmahnawis will soundly hail from high upon the peaks of Wy-East, (Mt. Hood), Pahto, (Mt. Adams), and Lawala Clough, (Mt. St. Helens). He will look down upon the bloodied grounds and his craving for our spent souls will bring him to smile in his victory!

"My Great Father, Hear my cry."

"Hear My Cry!"

("Kumtux kopa kwolan nika cly...")

Chapter 3

The Sun, The Moon, The Stars

From high above the village I hear the taunting of the four braves that have stole the pelts of these men rising up upon the course of wind as they dare Suyapee to follow the trail that leads to where they hide. Their chants speak bravely. They tell Suyapee they stand together in fight for what is first our peoples to cull from the lands, and the coats that hold their spirits close are not to be taken from upon our shoulders. The brother's wails increasingly rise from where the tallest trees stand proudly above their village, and it is well known of their intent as Suyapee look towards them with glaring eyes.

These Suyapee, moving from where they had first made camp the past night are cursing the braves with each step they take. Nearing the shoreline as they walk, their beached canoes come into their view. They look bewildered as they stand in disbelief. Now understanding completely why the loud calls of the four braves, their eyes are drawn from the cut ropes that once held the many furs taut within the hull of their canoes. With loud voice, Suyapee are heard shouting to those that stole the hides from their canoe. The Suyapee leader looks to me with outstretched arms as I am nearest him, he appears as the Hyas Lolo as he snarls and growls and demands to know, "Why?"

As I stand upon En che Wauna's shore and see Suyapee's anger, I wait. I want to ask if he took these spirits without thought before their spirits were taken from their souls? I want to ask, did he listen to the spirit of these animals as they speak of their place within the great forests and upon the waters of our lands?

With tempered voice, Suyapee demands my answer to his question. "Why have our furs been taken," he asks? I know what he thinks is the truth, but I too do not accept his thievery from the lands that were chosen to be our own.

As he questions me once more, I look to the heavens as I point to Otelagh, and with much happiness, I smile...

Suyapee becomes enraged. His eyes are quickly turned to hate. I stand before him but do not listen to his angered words. I raise my arms to the heavens and call out to all the lost souls to which these furs had once belonged. I tell them their spirits shall live forever as they pass from our lands into those of Suyapees. I shout out to Suyapee that one day, the animals will rise up and peer deep into their eyes, and as the animals spirits rise up before them, they will be promised to be in fear for their lives, and as they, themselves, stand unknowing what to do, the spirits of these animals will take from them their souls as their spirits are not good.

I choose to tell Suyapee these spirits that have been taken from our kingdom lived with honor amongst us. I challenge him to cross upon his own lands, and the people he spoke of the past night must find their warmth from the winter's coldest breaths in lands far from where we now stand! I tell him that if he wishes to return before the doors of his village he must leave us and not return before our people. We know now of their bad spirit, and they are not welcome before our fires again.

I kneel upon the ground beside the leader's canoe. I reach out to touch the coats of the lost animal's souls, and as I look up and peer deep into his eyes, I ask Jean; "Did you hear of their voice, and did you feel of their breath?" Again I ask, "Did you sit beside these spirits upon the floor of the forest and first listen to their story?"

I tell him the animals they took from our lands depended upon us to defend them from the evil spirits that wished to take from them their souls and mock of their spirit. As I stand in silence before him and look into his eyes waiting for his answer, the voices of the spirits that lie within his canoe cry out. One by one, and then in unison as they rise up from where they were lain and too ask of Suyapee as he had asked of me; "Why?"

Suyapee stands before me, his eyes drawn to the soils beneath him, not believing what he has just seen and heard! Silence again falls heavy across the land. I know the answer to my questions need not be told as his lowered brow gives proof that he is alarmed and uncertain by the powerful spirits of our lands.

I tell him as he has not dwelt among these spirits, and has not listened to the voice of our Hyas Tahmahnawis Tyee, his own spirit will be lost for all the suns and moons that will pass over his journeys. I tell him because he chooses to kill without thought, he chooses to kill without heart, his own spirit will not rise to the heavens and one day sit beside his father. I tell him that he is not our brother, and he is not welcome before us. These men's souls are as dark as the smoke of the red cloud that has set hardened upon our lands. He has taken life from before us, and he has shown no mercy, and shame does not enter within his calloused soul.

32

I know Jean has not taken upon the High Spirit's trail as have our Fathers. None of the Suyapee have stood upon the sacred grounds the Valley of the Eagle is treasured. They have not walked the trails through the Lands of Wah, nor have they stood before Wahclella's great wall and heard the wise words spoken by our High Spirits. These Suyapee say they are like us, but we know, they are not our brothers, but they are the brothers of Tsiatko that preys on the righteousness of our peoples!

I sense Suyapee shall one day fall from the high place they find themselves to sit as did Pahto's broken stones. They shall be taken by the hand and led by the mesahchie tahmahnawis beneath to where my grandfather once told are only the dens of the Hyas Pishpish and where Klale Lolo dare others to enter and leave their mark.

Standing challenged to my message, I ask Jean to think of my questions; "When you look to the heavens do you not see the sun and moon, or stars? Do you not dream what may lie beyond the light they share? Are you not concerned by what darkness holds within its long arms as it falls heavily upon your lives?"

I raise my opened hands to the air as Suyapee turn their canoe from the shore and begin their journey into the fast waters.

This day, I pray is the last we see of their evil spirit. But I know there will be many more Suyapee who will come hard upon us. I hope he shares my questions to his people so they will know of the Good Spirit of our people.

The Suyapees' canoe passes beyond the turn of the river, far from the sight of our village. The dark mask of red cloud is raised from upon our lands and from the stilled waters of En che Wauna and brings to our souls happiness once again. We see clearly. With faith and trust, our souls shall again walk the trails of our lands with the Good Spirits that look over us with kindness as we follow their encouraging and most needed lead.

Chapter 4

Our Return To Nahpooitle

With the arrival of these men who scout our lands and take much the High Spirits have offered to our lands, a new time has come upon our people. I am blessed by the Earth Mother once again as I look across the river and see red cloud has risen from where it had lain stilled upon our peoples. Many of the deer and elk who lived near where the village stands had since disappeared when Suyapee came upon us. We should have known through the silence of their voice and through the emptiness of the air that our peoples would soon feel this new threat, and we would know through their loss, we are not alone to those that will soon become endangered by the appearance of Suyapee. I must approach my brothers of each of the nations that surround us, and as I sit before them, I will tell of the stories these Suyapee have shared before the past night's fire.

I must warn all those that I pass of these men who come to us from the great waters; how, on their arrival, the red cloud of the bad spirit rose over our lands and settled upon us as it took our sight to what had once lain magnificently before us. How the visions of Suyapee's arrival had come upon us as our fathers shared would come with much regret. All my brothers should be told our lives and all that we have honored for many seasons are now in great jeopardy.

I will tell of the cloud that held strong in the highest trails of the heavens, beyond where our eyes could not see. I will tell them Red Cloud was as thick as the blood of our brothers as it was once spilled upon the grounds by the bad spirits from wars long past. I will tell how the cloud of the bad spirit took from the land the warmth of Sun, and how Otelagh did not shine upon us until these brothers of the Tsiatko, (Demon Spirit), began their return journey to the waters of the great sea. I will stand before each village and speak of the trespass of these evil ones. Then my brothers will remember the visions of our Fathers, and they too will make ready for what is soon to rise up before us.

We of the Chinook Nation must sit beside our brothers of the Clatsop, the (Nusolupsh), the Cowlitz, the Klickitat, the (Pakiutlema), the Yakama, the Paiute, the Umatilla, the Walla Walla, the Nez Perz, and the Shoshone, and speak the truth of these visions to these intruders who are now entering our lands. As we gather at the Spring Festival, Tenus Waum Muckamuck at the village of Wyam, Celilo Falls, (Wauna Wont), "place where echoes falling waters," we shall stand before the council of all our chiefs and we will speak as Shamans to our peoples as we spill the truth from our lips.

From the table where we place our worries before all those that join beside us, we will listen to the chiefs of the villages as they speak of what trails we must journey beneath the hands of the Hyas Tahmahnawis Tyee. My peoples shall take what is good from the words of our fathers, and we must know when to walk swiftly from what is not good and from the foolishness of untruths.

We must unite and become one nation before the great numbers of these trespassers who will soon march in hostility upon our trails. We must be ready. We must together find the measure of spirit within us and heed the warnings spilled by the mouths of savages. We will not be forced to kneel before their heartless ways!

I call out to my five brothers who have joined with me to visit the village of the Kahmiakum and Chief Tsutho. Together we know the importance of this day and why we must gather together as one Nation. We must tell all those we pass what we have seen so they too will know of the change that is soon to join with the harsh breaths of Wind.

A brother of the Chehalis, Ksitilo, whose village is at Chiklisilkh, (Willapa Bay), steps beside me and questions the storm that he too has seen raised from above the waters of En che Wauna and. from upon our lands. I, as he, does not understood all that has been drawn before us, and as I take a deep breath, I think of how I must answer when only emptiness and question lingers upon the edges of my tongue. With much sadness, I admit that I too have no answer of which to offer!

I begin by telling Ksitilo how I asked these evil ones from where they had come. They had pointed towards his village. I ask if he knows of the man, Jean, that sits upon the right hand of the evil one, Tsiatko, and if these Suyapee have taken their places before his village's fires. Ksitilo speaks with truth that he knows nothing of the bad spirit that draws red cloud upon the waters, and that in the village of his peoples, he has not heard word spoken of such men walking in amongst them.

I share of the vision and of the long journey our fathers took at the side of the High Spirit. I ask Kisitilo to take the message of these visions to his father. I tell him as spring comes to the lands, and the leaves return to the trees, when the wildflowers bring color to the ground and spread sweet scent upon the trails of wind, all of our nations shall once again gather beside one another, and we will catch the spirit of Pish at Wyam.

I tell Kisitilo that all the village chiefs will stand upon their stage and speak of these visions before the great fire of Wyam.

As we have now seen the red cloud that our fathers had once envisioned, we must be taken by this same vision and make the long journey to speak of the warning that is now certainly promised to our lands.

We place the gifts of clam, furs, and many shells into our canoes and bid farewell to Chief Tsutho. We point our canoes upon the trails of the river. The waters are high within the channel as they breathe freely from the open mouth of the Great Sea as Wind Spirit pretends to give chase to our passage.

It is a good day. Suyapee is not seen! Warm light is cast down upon the grounds we pass, splintering through the sticks of the forest where the animals of our lands are given safe refuge. We see great numbers of geese, heron, duck, and swan, each basking in the sun. They are all pleased to share of Otelagh's returning warmth. We pass close beside them but they do not take wing. Deer and elk again stand proudly upon the shoreline of En che Wauna as they look out over the waters towards where we pass, and they do not flee.

We are today as one upon our great Earth. Each unafraid, each sharing of Otelagh's greatest gift, life... Each knowing we belong.

Otelagh has passed above our trail for two days before we arrive at the village of the Nusolupsh, Cowlitz, at Kanem. It is from here En che Wauna turns to face the lands of the Cowlitz that have carved the lands by the sacred waters of the river. We have chosen to return to our village by the same route we had come, but first we must again sit and visit with our brothers of Cathlapotle, "Lewis River People", whose village lies upriver upon the Big Island.

When color lies heavy upon the leaves of the mighty oak and fall silently from their branch, the duck and goose shall return to the island lands of Nahpooitle. The fallen leaves offer soft beds for the mowitch and moolack as they gather in great numbers upon the floor of the valley once the snows of winter gather deep upon the high peaks. With the arrival of the storms of winter, when the lands of the Hyas Cascades lie frozen and unbending, when the coats of the spirits of our lands grow long hair, their village gathers within the warmth of the longhouse as their people come to await the return of the new season that brings warmth and new life to rise up from upon the soils of our lands.

As we near where the Cowlitz fish along the shores of the Big Waters, we shout; "Klahowya". I tell them of the message that will be shared at the Potlatch, the gathering of all our peoples in the new season of spring when new life is breathed into all the lands by our Hyas Tahmahnawis Tyee".

We greet the Cowlitz gathered along the shore, and they tell us on the day Suyapee first comes, they too will spread the message from the Great Drum of their village. They have sworn to join with us upon the high rocks at Wyam, and as we all sit at council before the great fire of the village, they will hear our message, and they have sworn to tell of their own.

This night, we will sit before the fires of Cathlapotle and trade pish and clam, oyster from the Long Beach, the coats of mink and beaver they have trapped. We will speak of the bad spirit of Suyapee, and of the untruths spoken in their dark words.

We walk from the river into the village of Nahpooitle and first see the old woman, (lummieh), carrying wild onion, (kalaka), that grows in the meadow. She takes them in her baskets to the longhouse where they will be placed upon the long table in the season that brings rains, (swass), that make rivers upon the low meadows.

The chief of the village is a friend as I have traded with his people many times. He is called Kamilopke by his people, and his kapho, (elder brother), Conchatta, rises up from his place and welcomes our arrival to their village. Conchatta sends his son to call out to the elders to join with us and sit at the long table. Taking a pipe from his purse he tells that we will share of the (wild tobacco), (kinootl), and speak of our trade, (huyhuy).

Coyote is heard to cry out from the edges of the marsh where she lies in wait for her dinner. She too knows of our arrival and is quick to sell her soul to the moon.

We sit before the warm fire of their longhouse, and we all join together and smoke from the long pipe for many hours and make trade for the oyster and clam. Before I speak of the events that have been placed before us these past days, I must remember the wise words that my father shared with me as we sat together high up upon Wy-East, above the white bark sticks that rise to the heavens, and far above the great cedar that have survived all the battles of Pahto and Wy-East.

Great Cedars spirits give witness to many tales of our lands. It is their voice I wish to hear one day speak to all they have seen. These strong spirits have seen the beginnings of Otelagh's potlatch upon our lands as he breathed life unto the soils. They have been witness to the beginning of life as grass, bush and tree had first taken root beneath them, rising up and giving color and shape to our lands. They have grown strong and their numbers thick, offering shade and protection as the cool breaths of winter have fallen, silenting the lips of Otelagh's warming breaths. Otelagh offered the deer and elk, the raven and the great coyote, and all the spirits that today walk and grow freely amongst us the right to live upon his lands. He had breathed life unto them, and they are each his children.

My father once told that if we are to share the visions given with honor before us by the High Spirits, we must first see the message of the vision within our own hearts. We must then feel the words

40

so we can share each of them from what has touched our souls. It is when our heart and soul become as one that our speech shall be heard as words spoken of truth!

The old woman that we had seen earlier again enters into the longhouse and places before us a kalakalahma (goose), which had surrendered its soul to those who had hunted hidden in the tall grass of the marsh.

We thank our brothers for welcoming us into their shelter and we give praise to Hyas Tahmahnawis Tyee for our meal. The kahmooks (dogs), who had lain quietly at our feet take rise from the floor, and with nose held to the air, gather beneath the long table and whine as they await the scraps that will soon fall to the ground. With fast feet, the old woman returns with the kwitshadie (rabbit), and wapatoo (potato and onion), and tsee (bread) with the sweet amota (strawberry), and klikamuks (blackberry), and it was set before us from her large opekwan, (basket).

We have journeyed far against the fast waters of the river, and we offer many thanks to the chief and all his brothers for the rest from our journey. We sit in silence and take from the plate of the Great Spirit until only bones of the goose fall upon the floor. Quick like the fox that runs to hide, dogs rise up from the floor and flee from the warmth of the longhouse as they growl towards one another and guard the scraps they have each gathered.

The night grows long, the great coyote cries again, and we must now lie upon our mats and dream beneath the stars, preparing for the new day for what may hide behind the shadows along our journey. Kimilopke and I walk from the longhouse toward where our beds await us. He asks that before my brothers and I set out for our return to our village, as Otelagh again rises above us, that I join his side and walk through the long meadows that lead to the big lake.

41

Kimilopke says to me with hushed tone; "Raven, I have known you for many seasons. As we sat tonight and took from the table our meal, your tongue was stilled by what lies hidden within your thoughts. I see your eyes have seen much trouble, and I feel there is much that you question for which you have not found answer. When Otelagh again rises above our village we shall walk beneath the Great Oak and allow our hearts to find separation from our worries. There, below the Great Oak who's arms welcome us each day, we will search for answer to where your thoughts have been stilled, and as the dark shadow of the bad spirit disappears before the bright light of the Good Spirit, your soul will be renewed as answer will come to your soul."

My thoughts are of many thanks for my wise friend, for he has seen deep within my soul and knows there is much I have yet to share.

Otelagh slowly awakens and begins to follow the trails of the heaven. We make ready to join ourselves upon the waters of En che Wauna, and we will soon point our canoes to the lands of Wah and to our village of Wahclella. As I promised, before we depart, I will join my friend and walk beneath the long arms of the Great Oak upon the trails of the Talupus (Coyote), leading to the shoreline of the lake where we will sit and speak. We see the coyote waiting for the duck and goose to come within her reach from high upon the ledge to capture a meal for her young pups. Soon, a raccoon comes from the shadows, and with question, watches as we pass beside her. After we have walked some distance we turn to look behind us, and we see she is still standing, watching us as we walk. We call out to her, and only then does she fall upon her feet and follows slowly behind us upon the trail. Suddenly, as we near the waters of the lake we hear a loud scream from the Hyas Heron telling of our approach. She spreads her long wings and soon lands in the distance upon the long branch of a tall Cottonwood. As she rests, waiting, with keen eye, she hungers for the rise of her meal from within the shallows of the lake beneath.

Chief Kimilopke points to the great Oak where he tells that he often sits listening to the spirits of the land as they speak both of their happiness and of their worries. The arms of this great stick stretch further than any other that I have seen. I know with the seasons he has witnessed above the marsh where Muskrat walks, he has many stories to tell of the rhythm of life he has been surrounded.

We sit in silence beneath his welcoming spread, waiting for the animals to come out from where they hide and join their spirits with our own. We are all brothers to this marsh and to the Earth. The Great Oak is brother of the Great Cedar, joining all life together as one beneath their long arms.

Slowly, a dark mink runs into the forest from its den at the side of the lake. A regal buck with many spikes rises up from his bed and stands proudly before us. Birds sing above us and the rhythm of a drummer's beat upon the trunk of a tree shares stories to those who will listen.

Peace has again entered my soul and I begin to tell of what we had witnessed at Kathlamet; "My friend, Kamilopke, several of the braves from my village and many from the village of the Kathlamet stood upon the shore of the Great River, hoping to capture the spirits of the first salmon to arrive in the waters of En che Wauna. We began to gather our nets when bad medicine was cast upon us. The spirit of the Salmon had been taken from their souls. The bad spirit cast them from our nets and they were taken from us as they were chosen to follow the channel of the river as they were swept swiftly to the sea. Their hearts had then been stolen and swept from the waters where they would have begun their return to their homewaters."

"From behind Red Cloud, a cloud as red and thick as we see when the moon is raised in the heavens as a great fire races across the opened plains, came men we first believed without threat from a new kingdom, a new land we have not known. But as they approached the shoreline where we stood in much question, we saw beneath the long pelts of the Lolo, many furs hidden within their canoe. We then knew they were who I have named, Suyapee, as they came upon us behind Tsiatko's dark and mysterious mask."

I told Chief Kamilopke; "The cloud of the bad spirit rose high above their canoes as they came from the waters of En che Wauna. Many clouds formed as one before us and they were soon gathered tightly together as are the baskets our women weave. As quick as a bird flies across the sky light was taken from the heaven, and we stood in darkness unknowing what was to come from the water or from upon the lands before us. Within their souls soon came the battle between what is good and what is bad in Suyapee's spirit. A loud voice was spelled across the lands and in fear, life stopped! The strong smell of threat swept before us. Smoke rose from the great fire just as the one we had seen that emptied our lands of all the spirits that once lived within the golden fields of our prairies. This offered great worry to our souls. Darkness was swept across the land. At that moment it was as if Otelagh had stepped to the side of Moon taking from the land his light and warmth from upon us. The animals of the forests were quick to find shelter from this new storm, knowing their spirits too were then in question of being sacrificed without reason."

I told my brother; "Bad medicine was brought from Suyapee's pouch as it was thrown to the heavens. Darkness fell heavy upon the light of day. Life stopped! The song of birds fell silent to our ears. Trees did not sway to the soothing breaths of the Chinook. The winds too were hushed from their spirited song. Our nets were emptied of their catch as pish were thrust beneath the waters of En che Wauna and swept to the deep waters of the sea. These were not good men as we had first thought. I told Kamilopke; "They carry bad medicine! Their words shall one day bring death to the doorsteps of our villages! I have named them, Suyapee, the brother of Tsiatko, the demon who rises from darkness and craves for all he sees that is good."

Kamilopke hears the worry in my words and sees vision of the bad ways of this demon spirit. My friend becomes like the birds and winds, and he too stands stilled in the absence of life that my story tells. My friend shares my worry! The air above us does not rise, made heavy by fear, by question, by the unknowing of what our tomorrows will place before us once the dark mask of these Tsiatkos brings amongst our peoples.

We both know the questions we must plead before the Hyas Saghalie Tahmahnawis Tyee; "What Good Spirits have we not followed? What have we done? Where have we placed a false step and fallen from the chosen trail you beckon for us to follow in your lead?"

In silence, my heart cries out; "Where will we go when there is nothing? What of our children, and of those children that will one day follow?"

We each must ask; "Will there be children to follow in our footsteps?"

These questions fall as silent whispers from our lips. Great worry and concern comes upon each of us. We look towards the village of the Hyas Tahmahnawis Tyee, and I tell my friend with much sadness; "Soon I fear life will again be held in silenced warn..."

Steven Wanstaff

Chapter 5

Dance of the Deer Spirit

My brothers and I set out from Nahpooitle to return to our village. Near the joining of En che Wauna and the Willamette, as we see the village of the Multnomah I ask my brothers if they choose to visit our brothers of the Kalapuya? I tell them we must trade for the camas to see us through the winter's cold that will soon fall upon us. We are near the valley where the blue flower makes land appear as water and we must hurry to make our choice to what channel we will follow in our return to our village.

Tsemitsk looks to Wy-East where many islands separate the shores of our great river. We notice black smoke rises with great force from within Wy-East, and the bad spirits within him are again chosen to battle those of the good. We do not understand the reasoning for this battle. We speak with one another in hushed tone as we watch with great worry. Dark smoke continues to rise and bellow from within Wy-East. Without hesitation we choose to return to our village where we will sit beside our brothers and sisters and challenge the spirits held within Hyas Wy-East to find peace between them.

My thoughts go to those spirits whose villages lie below Wy-East as it appears they may not have trails to escape as there is much smoke and flame falling from high up upon his steep sides.

The storm that battle brings to the kingdoms beneath Wy-East may suddenly fall upon them and bring sorrow to their hearts. Only with sharp thought and swift hooves will they make their escape and survive the storm that is now wrought sorrowfully upon them.

We take rest upon the long island that stands near the waters of Wy-East, Sandy River. When Otelagh falls from the heavens in the west we shall walk into our village. Upon our return to Wahclella, we must place within our canoes what we need to survive, preparing our escape from the wrath that may fall upon us without mercy. If Wy-East is not battling Pahto, we will take refuge in his kingdom and wait until Wy-East has quieted the spirits within him before returning to our village.

Appearing unaware of what is occurring above the fields they graze, Mowitch feed on the grasses of the meadow at the edge of the tall Sailsticks, (Cottonwoods), and Alder without pause. Otter and beaver swim playfully and without worry in the waters. They will soon find their paths hidden by cloud as it falls thick from the heaven, turning day to night. They too will sullenly become confused as light becomes darkness without warning.

We make camp high up above a barren shore and pull our canoes far from the river's rush. The waters will quickly rise up as the night grows long. We carry the furs and supplies from where they lie and set them close to where we will make our fire to warm us through the long night. It is good to see Great Larch as he stands silent and without the fiery breaths he had once been known to cast out from within his deep bowels.

Great Larch looks over Wah and to those lands where Wy-East's brothers and sisters rise high into the heavens. We are returning to where the greatest spirits of our lands speak clearly, and deem themselves much closer to those of our peoples that have chosen to accept their wise words and accept safe passage across the lands they lead.

We sit before our fires this night and give thanks for our father's guiding hand. We give thanks to the Hyas Tumtum for the gifts of our lands. Each day Otelagh crosses the heavens, we remember his promise before us and give thanks that our people live peacefully and with much prosperity.

Our fire gives us warmth while we cook pish upon the open flame. As we complete our meal my eyes begin to beg to close so they may rest as this day's journey has been long and hard against the fast waters of En che Wauna. I lay upon my bed and yell out to my brothers; "We will begin our return to the waters of En che Wauna as Otelagh is soon to rise, and all those we pass will announce the message telling of our return to our village upon their drums."

As I lie near the warmth of the fire and look deep within myself, I discover myself searching my soul for many answers, remembering to all I have seen these past days.

The water lapping against the shore and the crackle of the fire is all that can be heard. I am finally free from all the day's distractions. Thinking clearly and seeing beyond the scenes that have been cast before my eyes, those swollen and unmoving images that have stayed with me have strained my soul in my understanding to the stories they may spell upon our peoples.

I do not know why the Hyas Spirits chose to lead the Tsiatko before us. I am fearful, and my soul is filled with much question...

I peer deep into the flame of the fire, (olapitski), and wish the mighty muskrat would take my hand and lead me to where my answers would be found so that my soul would again find rest.

Without hesitation, I lay here without thought. There is only silence cast within my ears. I pray the darkness of night is all that will accompany me upon the trails of my dreams...

As if time stood still, and the moon had not moved across the
blackened sky, the smoke spirits journeyed far as they now have
entered upon the trails of my mind. They took from my memory
the thoughts I had shared of the trials of the past days, my
reasoning to the arrival of Tsiatko into our kingdom has now been
lain dormant and unseen.

As though Otelagh had begun to rise from the far place where
he hides at night, a small light rises from the center of the smoke
screen's mask that lies heavy upon the ground across the large
meadow. Though I sleep, I hear it calling out my name, "Raven".

From a distance, the open arms of the trees of the forest offer
their long fingers, leading me within their tight circle. They each
welcome me into the large meadow. I stand from my bed, and I
walk into their gathering to the place where it has been told the
Deer Spirits have been seen to dance.

My eyes open, and the light of day is cast down upon me. I see
the face of Deer Spirit as he prances across the open meadow. On
two legs, he dances. Turning, here and there, he raises his head to
the heavens and rakes the sky with his sharpened horn. He dances
as if upon the emptiness of air beneath his spirited hooves...

"It is here, in the cold of night that I dance," cries out the mighty
buck. "I dance to the memories of the soon dead. From the
celebration of life, death is soon to follow. As this is the way of
life as it has been told from the beginning! Where light merges
into darkness, our spirits will soon be joined. I shall take you
upon a journey where you will see Tsiatko spread bad medicine to
the peoples of all the kingdoms. Life will soon be taken from the
light the Good Spirit has given you, and it will be replaced with
the darkness of cloud as it passes in front of Sun."

"It is not what you see in this dream that you must take with you as you join me upon this journey. It is the message of this dream that shall make you aware of change that is soon approaching. You must be readied to walk when you think to run. You must lead when you think to follow."

"Through Suyapee's unspoken demands, if you do not take from their spirit what is good, and throw out which is bad, your journey upon the lands that you today cherish shall become lost before you. Otelagh's enlightened trails will surrender themselves to the cold of storm's darkened trail, and it shall be spread convincingly across the lands for all the days that we will know."

Tahlkie, (yesterday), and for many days before, we stood safe and far from the wanting eyes of Demon Spirit as he had not yet taken from our souls the teachings of our Hyas Fathers that have been taught from upon the Walls of Wahclella.

Deer Spirit tells; "It is the dark mask of the bad spirit that will demand we lay our souls before his feet, and if we do not comply to his demands, we shall not be seen to walk upon the same trails we have known, or live within our same villages upon En che Wauna's shore. Those trees of our forest whose long arms rise to the heavens and lead us to the village of the High Spirit will not be seen again. We will be taken far from our kingdoms upon these promised lands that Otelagh had offered for our support. In their loss above us, our first step towards the High Spirits village will be held in question. Our souls will lie stilled and unknowing to those that will come after our spirits are drawn beneath the soils of the bad spirit's village."

"You must first cut off your arms to live as it will be by your arrow and the long arms of their weapons that shall cause your peoples to lay upon the grounds unmoving. You must cut off your legs if you wish to walk amongst the Hyas Spirits without creating fault within you."

"If you choose to take the trail of the mesahchie tahmahnawis and take from his many arms those weapons that you choose to fight, you shall be lost from the Hyas Saghalie Tahmahnawis Tyee's path, and you will lose all that you know today as you will then join those promised to the bad spirit's tribe."

"You must not find your fight with their spirit, as the Demon Spirit is most powerful and shall covet over all that we know. The Demon Spirit shall take from our place all that stands upon his way along the march of death that he promises to be held."

"Stand tall, and be proud before them! Raise your heads and smile as you look deep into Tsiatko's eyes, as he will know not what to do! Do not let them take what is yours alone within you! One day, as Otelagh passes above our lands, you will be welcomed to those fires of your villages that yet burn for your return before them. Your souls shall then find rest once more! Make peace within you and you each shall see the light of tomorrow's day, and your souls will journey far from the ways of the mesahchie Tsiatko!"

Deer Spirit jumps high as the light of his spirit leads him far into the heavens. His spirit is then attached to the star chosen by his Hyas Tahmahnawis Tyee. His enlightened trail leads beyond where our eyes cannot see. Through the gates where his new village awaits, he too arrives home and finds rest from the storm that rises from beneath his spirited hoof.

As I wake to Oterlagh's rise from the horizon above our lands, I hear Deer Spirit call out that he is now set free from all that once held back his good spirit from entering within my own! I feel Deer Spirit is now within me, and that we are now brothers to the Earth!

All that Deer Spirit has chosen to offer to my passionate ways as I journey into the lands where I had not yet taken of their trails, shall bind many of our brothers within the Hyas Saghalie Tahmahnawis Tyee's hands. Those taking of our trail shall too be set free as we share of his message!

The last I would hear of Deer Spirit's voice shall offer me strength and lead my journey safely before my brothers. I shall have with me the call of Crow to warn me when I have taken upon the wrong trail. I shall keep close the cunning of Great Coyote at my side, and he shall not allow me to be taken of my soul as the evil spirits approach behind the red cloud's disguise.

It shall be these words that will one day take us far from darkness and from the unknowing of our own spirit's storm within us.

Our Hyas Tumtum will then be heard to speak of his acceptance to our arrival before him as he shouts,

"Klohowya, (Welcome) To Our Lodge, My Brothers!"

Chapter 6

Owing Our Lives To
the Spirit's Lands

We lay our canoes upon En che Wauna, soon passing the village
of Nechacokee where many Tkope Kahloke, (white swans), and
Hahthaht, (duck) swim along the shoreline for protection as the
smoke spirits drop heavily upon the land. Taking light from the
hands of Otelagh, he lies motionless above the darkening loom of
our skies.

Far off in the distance we hear echoes of a great battle fought
between the good and bad spirits below Wy-East's highest bench.

Wy-East's demon spirit has awakened and is angered once more,
choosing to battle the spirits within him for all the forests of his
kingdom, for all the life that walks without fear across his lands.

Many sticks are heard to fall upon the rocky ground, pulled from
the soils where they were long ago given birth. Great boulders
are heard falling and rolling thunderously, crashing across the
land beneath their swarm, some splashing with great force into
the ashen waters of the river that now comes fast upon us from
Wy-East.

Great smoke rises high above Wy-East where the Hyas
Chakchaks, (Eagles) were once seen soaring high above the lands.
Soft ash, first white then black, covers the trails of the forests.
Thunder echoes across the valleys, and then it is heard to return.
Screams lift high above the rising water. Cries of spirits now

entrapped beneath mud and rock while others drown in silent waste; without hope, without escape.

With open arms to all that surrounds us, whether it be good or bad, we honor the High Spirit as it was from his hand that we have been given all that we have. We return before those spirits that shape our lands, those spirits that offer value to our lives. We lend our souls to the discovery of life through the challenges the spirits choose to deliver before our trails.

Great Cedar and Fir rise high above the lands within the Lands of Wah, and we have deep joy for the beauty surrounding us, knowing that we are again joined at the entrance of our kingdom.

Wah, the land where spray from the tears of the spirits falls heavily from their high place, washing over the lands, breathing new life unto the souls they touch. Hyas Chakchak takes wing high above the waters, diving beneath its depths, and with swift wing she rises, tightly clasping to the spirits of pish. These are the lands where the spirits of our people are lifted high before the mighty hand of Otelagh.

We honor Him for what he has placed before us...

As we kneel upon the grounds of his kingdom, we praise him, for he is most powerful and has taken us beneath his shielding wing!

Hyas Otelagh, our people, our village, our great nation... Hear our cry!

"We are home!"

("Kumtux kopa kwolan nesika cly)!

From beneath Wy-East's peak great thunder is cast across the lands as the mesahchie tahmanhawis' powerful breaths blow rock

57

from within him. As they fall from their high place and are heard breaking upon the forest's floor, he releases from within them his warriors so they too may spread across the lands as the bad spirit of Wy-East chooses to rule over the forests and of all the lands owning to his domain. Now, the Land's of Wah, and the Valley of the Eagle, are in great jeopardy of falling before the demands of Tsiatko's dark soul.

From along the trail will soon be heard the growl of the Klale Lolo,(Black Bear), and the loud cry of the Hyas Pishpish, (Cougar), as they will lie in wait to attack our peoples as we wander upon their trails in our escape.

The river of Wy-East rushes before us into En che Wauna as they each join to make one, and many sticks rush before us as they gather in great numbers along the shore of the island. We quickly pass where can be seen mud and sand as they each gather as one and begin to build upon the gathering sticks. A new land quickly rises above the water's maddening race.

With each breath exhaled from the bad spirit's chest, life is taken from the lands that have offered us hope to see the light of Otelagh rising above us each day.

Deer and elk, raccoon and coyote, beaver and bear, they all gather high up upon the peak of the new land, and in their eyes can be seen fear in knowing their villages are not yet safe above the ash of Wy-East's lasting storm.

It is not the fiery breaths of the spirits we fear, it is the absence of the spirit's gifts, Crow and Coyote, who would allow us each to wander across these lands unaided and with reason as we would then become lost upon the very trails we had once found ourselves to be safe.

From the belly of the beast within Wy-East, this land was formed, and as it spewed rock and ash, fire and smoke rose up from within him, and all that we know has been cast in the Hyas Tumtum's grandest image.

It is in that image that we carry in honor each day within us!

This river that runs fast to the sea carries within its course the spirits that offer us life!

Wah, the land we have come to cherish for all our days. The lands we honor each day as Otelagh spreads light upon us to survive what the spirits hail before us to accept. We must find that place within ourselves where solitude and peace brings calm to our souls, and offers depth to our spirits.

These are the lands where our peoples have been chosen by the Hyas Tahmahnawis to extend our long arms in peace and understanding to the ways of the Earth, as they will offer survival upon the lands of our kingdoms, and to our own survival upon them!

Through fire and flood, new life breathes freely again upon these lands. As the bad spirits that hold strong upon their lost trails are consumed within their own baited poach, our lands are washed clean of disease as tears from the high spirit's cheeks fall heavily across them, and our peoples shall survive to share of the sun and moon's new rise!

These are the lands that our souls are offered to walk freely.

In honor to our Great Father's lead through life's challenge, we plead, hear our cry!

"We are home!"

Nearing the high rock that is surrounded by En che Wauna, a dark cloud that promises of death falls from the heavens. Taking from us the sight of our lands as they are lain hidden behind its most terrifying mask. Silence fills the air. Our labored breaths echo as we await the emergence of the mesahchie tsiatko through his deceiving mask.

Day has suddenly turned to night, the warmth of Sun has been spelled to the Cole Illahee of our winter. We each stand bewildered beneath its chilling storm.

We fear the bad spirit awaits to steal our souls, just as he has stolen Otelagh from above us. We fear he too shall take from the heavens wind. We fear the Hyas Eagle shall not rise up above these lands and lead us safely upon his guiding wing.

I ask our fathers in silenced prayer, "What lessons of the Hyas Tyee Tahmahnawis teachings have we not followed that now lends us to each be labored in our journey to our village's longing and warming fire?"

From the center of darkness, I am again reminded of the Dance of the Deer Spirit, its message blazing strong within me. Its message is cast from within me to the spirits that walk beside me, and on to the people for all to witness of Suyapee's most dour deceit.

Unlike the vision shared by Deer Spirit the past night, two spirits rise from where darkness is now drawn, and they each rake their sharp horn to the heavens.

I ask; "If two spirits now come from where one was last seen, is this warning now doubled, and soon to fall increasingly troubled upon our trails?"

"Is this a forewarning that we must be strong and not find ourselves to stray from our father's teachings though these people come upon our lands with threat to our ways? In our faith, we must be assured to witness toward all those tomorrows we find ourselves to want?"

"Does it not share that we must not be seen to sit quietly and allow the lessons of our great leaders to be spent in silenced hope?"

We must prove before the spirits of these lands our strengths, our will, our wanting to survive amidst the treacherous face of those that shall soon walk amongst us.

Our spirits must not stray distant from our father's paths as our fathers had been chosen to sit high upon Wahclella's Wall through their good hearts. It is from there they offer us strength to uphold the ways of Saghalie Hyas Tahmahnawis Tyee. They offer us both hope and faith, and they guide us throughout our lives upon gilded wings that were placed upon their shoulders by the High Spirit as they were led upon their long journey through the gates of the High Spirit's village.

These are the lessons that our fathers share before us this day. As we enter the kingdom where life depends upon the choices we make, our thoughts and our will to survive the storm of the bad spirits upon us must be strong, and in our gathering herd, we shall appear powerful and unerring. We shall gather in great numbers before Suyapee. They will be confused, and in their uncertainty, they will not know from where they should first thrust their pointed and sharpened lance upon us!

All the brothers from each of our nations must look below upon their kingdom from high places, and once the soils turn to cloud above the hardened march of those that want toward us, we each must send warning of their looming and appending approach.

This is the way our fathers have taught us. We welcome all who walk among us with opened arms. It is our way to share the warmth of our fire, to offer mats for them to sit before our tables to share our game and fish, our huckelberry and bread, all giving honor to Hyas Otelagh for all he has given us.

These are our ways!

These were first the ways of our fathers, and their father's ways before them!

We must honor all that we have become as it has been through our great leader's pointed voice that has given us direction in each of those journeys we have been chosen to follow in our lives.

We must honor all that we have become because our lives depend upon one another in our walk upon the trails of the Earth. Holding taut to the visions of our fathers guidance, urging us not to stray from the enlightened paths of righteousness.

We stand tall and peer into the unknowing of what lies beyond the darkness of heaven's gaited light, the place within our minds, our hearts, our souls, where we must first choose hope and discover faith so we may afford to live in peace and see our young grow strong and tall. We must be promised to strive in our dependence upon the virtues held highly within the values of our ancestors.

The heavens, a place held high within us! The place where we journey to the village of Otelagh once the fall of winter reaches our lives. This heaven, where we are taken upon the *Hyas Saghalie Tahmahnawis Tyee's* chosen star. From this heaven, we are promised to see the sun's rise from the horizon of tomorrow's day.

My brothers, we must sit before the fire of our village and speak of the vision I have been asked to share! While we sit blinded beneath the ash of *Wy-East's* darken cloud, the Deer Spirit has once again danced to the deliberate pulse of *Tsiatko's* deceptive drum. We must make our brother's understanding to these people intruding upon us, and even though they daunt their powers to expel from our souls our free spirit, we must desist from joining in the battle that their souls cannot resist.

May the *Pishpish* and the *Lolo* come down from their high places and stand before these people. May they then understand it is not the wish of our people to find fight with those that do not understand our ways!

"My Fathers, I ask that Otelagh rise up above the darkened cloud that now constricts our lungs from breathing life into our souls and into all life before it offers only pestilence and death before the doors of all our villages. We plead the light of day is again cast down upon us, and all our people shall be welcomed to walk without fear, without restraint of our souls, so we will all live in peace and walk beside one another and know we each belong to the Earth Mother, as it is she who permits life to resonate throughout our kingdoms."

"Our Fathers, hear our voices raised to the heavens where you now sit! Fathers, hear our cry! Take from us only the fear of death, and leave us with only the dreams of those tomorrows that will find our spirit joined in your likeness!"

"Hear our cry!"

"Our spirits must stay free from pestilence and far from the disease Tsiatko may soon reek upon all our lives!"

"Our fathers, hear our cry!"

Many days have passed in darkness as we have rested upon the island of the (big rock), Iwash, waiting for the storm to clear. Screams and cries torment the lands beneath Wy-East's flanks, and as great waves break across the shore below, the grounds beneath us shake and tremble with each breath that is expelled from Wy-East's searing soul.

As did the Deer Spirits dance to the heavens, Wy-East's spirit rises, hissing its escape and fleeing capture. Rising high into the darkened and unknowing sky as it forms dark clouds that bring cover to the absence of life within them.

Rain falls heavily across the lands and turns the soils to mud as it flows forcefully across the lands below Wy-East's peak. Cold wind travels across the barren wastelands where sticks once stood proudly bneath Otelagh's raze. Sadly, they are heard echoing in the throes of death as they speed toward the waters of En che Wauna.

Great spears are thrown across the darkened sky, turning night to day, and as swift, day turns to night again.

Sitting beneath the tall firs, we wonder if Wy-East is maddened to these new peoples that will come upon us? Will these people not only wish to take the coats of those spirits that thrive within Wy-East's kingdom, but will they too wish to take our souls and our lives from where our villages join the spirit of our lands?

As the dark clouds begin to lift far into the heaven, the skies begin to clear. Our village calls out our names to again find our seats before the fires of our peoples. We gather our oars and set ourselves upon the swift waters, the moon now shining brightly upon the waves of the river. We can see the fires of our neighbors village, and upon our passing, we call out and tell of our long journey, and to sit with us and hear of our story.

Our brothers offer us shelter from the falling cloud, yet our village calls out louder as we near its brace below the great rock.

We find our pace quickened.

From the floors of the valleys and from atop the high peaks we hear the coyotes call as Moon rises high above their place. It is as though they too welcome us home from our long absence beside them.

Though our Wahkeena has passed on into her spirit world and has been chosen to rest upon the grounds of her treasured lands, we hear her call out to her lost brave. She too is like the soul of the coyote; each night one can listen to her wail as she lies in sadness for her lover's return to the waters of her creek.

Multnomah shines brightly this night from across the far shore where he rises far above the land. From his high place that we cannot see is heard great thunder. The waters of Multnomah's stream plunge fast below to its race into the great river below, and with each torrent comes another and another, each one faster than the last. It seems that each breath taken by Wy-East lends to the rise and fall of En che Wauna, spilling great waves upon its banks as they swell higher than the shoreline's edge.

The princess of Multnomah too cries out as she craves the passion she has held taut within her soul for her young brave. In unison, the daughter of the great chief, Multnomah, and the princess Wahkeena, are heard to cry out.

Sadly, forever in longing mourn...

Chapter 7

From Where Dream Spirits Speak

From the cold of night, we walk into the warm welcome of our village, and with our brothers, celebrate our safe return from Kwilluchini. Sitting again in the comfort of our village and warming ourselves before the village fire, we are grateful.

Kwan Wind, (Gentle Breeze) my wife for many seasons, reaches high upon the shelf and takes from the basket, the cake of camas. She places it upon the table while freshly caught pish is readied above the hot rocks of the fire. We give thanks to the High Spirit, and take cake from the Red Cedar plate.

We each speak of the battle within Wy-East as it is told to us it had begun with the rising of the full moon; when it shone brightly down upon Wy-East and awakened the bad spirit that had slept for many seasons without interuption. We hear as the battle was first heard to rumble across the lands from the high peak between the two spirits of Wy-East, tress were heard to call out with much distress as they were culled from their root and thrown hard upon the ground. The earth began to tremble beneath the great battle between the two spirits as they screamed of their complaint of the other. We are told the sound was even louder than the passionate pounding of the Moolack's hooves we have since become surrounded. The smoke rose thick above Wy-East and bellowed from the bad spirit's pipe as it set down heavily upon his snowy robe. From his flanks was seen a river of mud and water belching and churning from within his opened wound, covering the frozen trails beneath him with mud and rock.

My brothers tell it was like before, many seasons ago, when our fathers spoke of the great battle between Pahto and Wy-East.

As the battle grew fierce with each breath from the bad spirit, birds were not heard to sing. From within the dark heart of the bad spirit, he chose to chase those that had once returned to the kingdom of Wy-East. Now in fear, the animals that lived peacefully within the kingdom of Wy-East were seen to flee hurriedly from his lands, and as the heavens turned from light to dark many times, they were seen to cross the Big Waters. My brothers tell many were seen swimming across the great river. They tell that many of the animals settled along the shore of the river beneath the great rock. Only the great coyote, with a mournful howl, dared to call out to the dim light of the failing moon, and then as moon fell behind the dark mask of the bad spirit, silence was again spilled upon the air.

My brothers tell of great fear within their souls as darkness fell hard upon them, being spelled beneath a sky that swallowed our lands, offering no light to find their way. They could not walk upon the trails where our Spirits had many times led us from the threat and danger of the bad spirits.

As I hear of their story, I find myself angered at their weakness as they choose to allow the unknown before them to bring doubt into their lives even as Hyas Tahmahnawis still stands above us and promises to guide us through each day, through each obstacle that may stand in our way.

I ask myself; "What do they know of fear?"

What do they know of fear when they do not yet know of the darkness that awaits us from the waters of the sea and from across the long prairie? When the bad spirit of the Suyapee's Tsiatko rises up and marches across our lands and demand that

70

all our lands are now his… Then they will know of fear. When we are taken far from our villages, all that has meaning to us, all that we honor, when all that we have known is lost to us, then they will know of fear. When their free spirit is broken by the long arms of the empty soul of Tsiatko, then they will know of fear!

I hear their words, but I am too remembering my vision. I feel great sorrow deep within my heart. I know we will be heard in great mourning. Many brothers and sisters, mothers and fathers, all our children will be taken from our lands. Sorrow will soon enter all our souls, and through that sorrow, doubt will be cast within our spirit. Many will be lost to the Trail of Truths that our Hyas Tahmahnawis has promised our people living beneath his opened hands. From where silence does not draw breath, our people will be seen as the broken tree upon the windswept peak.

Our wail before Otelagh shall be followed with great tears falling from upon our cheeks, spreading sadness across all the lands we were once known. We will not walk the trails of our fathers.

Our long journeys, far from our villages, will be led in deception, as Suyapee shall lead us by force into a new land. As we stand upon soils that have not heart, we shall discover our own souls lost from within us.

It will be upon that sad day our voice shall disappear before our brothers, and we shall not be heard again to speak for many moons.

A great log is placed upon the center of the fire. The flames grow stronger as I look to those that sit within our circle, seeing fear in the eyes of my brothers, lost in their uncertainty. In deep thought,

I watch the dancing flame, and in my silence, I hear the voices of our fathers being cast from across the Big Water. I am reminded of the promise we have taken so we may live in prosperity and in peace. I know the words of our fathers. I knelt before them at Wahclella and have many times seen the wisdom of their ways as I have walked in their steps upon lands that did not offer light to lead my way. This was the last time I stood before the Walls of Wahclella, not long ago. It was that day I knew I must pass down to my peoples what our Hyas Fathers asked for me to remind those of our village of what is Indian way that will keep us safe from the long arm of the mighty Tsiatko as we follow safely in their footsteps.

My father once told of the bad spirit waging war alongside those that took upon his side against the misfortuned, that it is the way of the bad spirit to prey on all those that are weak, those who do not accept the words passed down from their fathers.

Without faith there cannot be hope!

Without hope, there cannot be life beyond the reach of our vision!

We, as mankind, are blind when we lose the gift of belief through the Hyas Tumtum's wise words!

We must not be led astray from the paths of our fathers, but instead, we must be strong and stave off those efforts of the mesahchie tahmahnawis. In this way, our hearts, our spirits, cannot be taken from within our souls!

I raise my eyes from the fire's flame and look deep into the faces of my brothers. I had hoped to see life within them, but instead, there is only the mark of death instilled within them. Silently, I pray to our great leaders, "What must I take from your lessons that will place trust before fear, and how shall I keep the bad spirit from taking those who are easily led from your sacred placement upon Wahclella's Wall?"

As I speak the final word to our fathers, much smoke rises from the fire, settling above the flame. Set free within the circle of the pit where it was first created, smoke begins to wind among where we have each chosen to sit.

We sit stunned!

The fire does not burn what lies upon the ground as it sweeps before our feet. We watch the flame dance before us and ask;

"What is the message?"

Slowly, it swirls in its own wind, it begins to turn toward us, rearing up, and it changes to form the shape of the head of man. Bone white, like that which has lain upon the land below the rays of Sun for many seasons. It peers upon us through dark eyes without emotion, without vision, without life. With eyes that cannot see, without lips and tongue to speak, its silenced forever held. We sit alarmed to the horror that dances before us. We soon realize it is the masked face of death that spells of death to those that do not listen to the words of our great leaders once Suyapee returns before our people.

We ask ourselves, "Why?"

I have not told those of our village of the vision of Suyapee coming behind Red Cloud. Now, watching the masked face rise up before us, I tell them the story, as this is the dark heart of Suyapee's Tsiatko who yearns for all our souls. I tell them this must be bad medicine cast before us from the purse of Suyapee arriving to our village. I warn; "He will soon come upon us with much threat!"

"My brothers, Suyapee will try to take from us our hearts and spill fear within our souls so we will run far from our lands once the red cloud rises above our lands. Many of their people will follow in his steps as they will wish to take all that is the Hyas Tahmahnawis'." "Their weak and venomous souls wish to take all that we know. We must not stray! I promise you, there is no light cast from the depths of the cave where the Tsiatko of Suyapee dwells!"

"Fear not to what rises from the cloud above them as their march is heard to echo across our lands. I say to you all, defeat the enemy as we first join within their ranks, and then, as we learn of their ways, we will take from them what offers them strength through what they believe to be the truth!"

"Tonight, as the Dream Spirit dances, we must join upon the earthen floor and fear nothing. If the Dream Spirit is drawn from Tsiatko's bad medicine, we must rise up to meet him with opened arms, and we must chant to the spirits of our fathers that once journeyed in the same steps we are soon to step. We must keep our souls strong before the grievous soul of Tsiatko as he comes hurriedly upon us."

It was not long after I spoke of joining Tsiatko and not allowing him to steal our souls that we all stood and take our place behind the Dream Spirit, our feet following the paths the smoke spirit led. Through our passage into his world, we raised our heads and stomped our feet. We tell him we fear nothing that Suyapee offers upon the lands our lives depend.

Our good spirit sees we are unafraid to all we are drawn, and he honors our gathering as he first takes the smoke from within us and breathes new breath into our lungs.

Our *Hyas Tahmahnawis'* voice rises above us, and we each hear him speak; "Upon the arrival of Suyapee's *Tsiatko*, I will form the masked face of death the bad spirits had wished to invest within your souls. As it rises from the fire's flame, the mask of death will be seen to rise higher than the tall sticks that find their mark upon the lands."

"Your people shall be forewarned of Suyapee's fast march nearing your villages. They will see their own daunting face rise up to meet them and fear what they do not understand. It will be in their own image their eyes shall see. The dark cloud that rises behind their approach upon you will then be turned from the trails of the heavens and fall heavily within them. In that single moment between life and death, there will be hope restored in all your lives so each of you will have the choice to walk freely upon the same trails across the lands of our kingdom."

"Through the power of your faith, the warmth of your hearts shall not be taken from within you!

Your souls shall not wander into the desert where life wastes upon itself. As long as tears of happiness fall from upon the cheeks of the Good Spirit and fill the channels of our rivers, he shall breathe new life into all that is surrounding *En che Wauna*, and then, there is hope for tomorrow."

"Your spirit shall not lie silent and shriveled upon the parched lands where the *mesahchie tahmahnawis'* darkened soul is known to thrive, but you shall be taken heartily upon new paths as life will again thrive through the gifting hands of *Naha*. Once you step upon the trails where your faith allows your visions to lead, then life will find itself held safely within you."

"This is the vision that I wish you all to be drawn!"

"May it be so!"

Stepping toward the path that rings the fire, we begin to follow where the Dream Spirit walks. Our lives begin anew upon a journey, a long journey to a land where Kloshe Tahmahnawis, (Good Spirit), looks down with much sadness upon our peoples with wary eyes.

Dream Spirit rises up before us and takes the form of man, and from the fire, smoke draws two lines, each twisting and turning from upon the path he had first begun. Dream Spirit warns; "It is from between these lines I lead your souls, you must not stray if you are to remain free of worry and be free of despair".

Dream Spirit tells we will journey to lands we have never seen. He tells that as we journey through the open door of heaven, we will look down upon the land, lands where once the mighty deer and elk stood in the big meadow beyond our count. Here too were the waters of our rivers once swollen each day as pish rushed thick within the river's race, leaping high from the waters of En che Wauna.

Dream Spirit leads us to this land that only the spirits of our fathers have ever seen.

"This is the land of your dreams;" Dream Spirit shares.

Each step we take rises higher towards the heaven. Our feet appear to dance on air, touching the edge of cloud, walking where only the stars of our heavens can be seen as we approach the meadows where our High Spirit's rest. We are told this is the land where the sun never sets, and the moon never falls. Where the stars shine brightly with no end, and where the white tails of stallions are seen to soar across the trails of the heaven as they discover green pasture for our souls.

Dream Spirit rises our spirits higher above the path, guiding our step upon his chosen trail. We dance behind his rhythmic guide. With each step we are promised to see tomorrow's light. We have risen higher from upon the earthen stage our peoples have been drawn. Our spirits have arose from within us all as our hearts have been set free from our mortal bodies. It is as if we are now dancing upon the emptiness of air as we are taken far from the shadowed cloud that looms thick upon our Illahee, (land), and far from the fore warning of Suyapee's grasping hand.

On this journey, our hearts are swollen without complaint. We are set free from all that weakens our questioning souls.

We climb into the heaven and reach out to the village of our fathers that shine bright each night.

The scent of flower and Cedar are carried by the warm breaths of wind, they both whisper between themselves of our arrival. Our names are called in unison by the Hyas Tahmahnawis Tyee as we are led to where our fathers sit. It is from the side of Sun we hear them speak. Our spirits are raised as we now have vision to where we will one day join the kingdom where life never ends.

Formed from a single pebble lying alone upon the barren grounds beneath us, we witness Coyote Spirit born before us many seasons past. Her cries rise up and are heard to announce to Moon they are forever tied by the soils of the Earth.

This vision journey has joined the souls of life before us as we peer down upon our kingdom. We travel through Sun's past journeys and find ourselves standing before the forest spirits, those that thrive upon the driest sands of our deserts, and of those that rise up from the depths of the Great Waters of our seas.

It is here, in the lands of our Illahee, we find our place solidly beside one another. It is here Dream Spirit guides our minds, joins our souls, and where we now become as one.

We dance behind the Dream Spirit's lead, the fire from which it first appeared, lighting the night as if it were day. Our thoughts and hearts are now as one. In this knowledge of the earth, we become strong. Our souls are connected to the Earth in innocence once again just as we were upon the day of our birth.

Though we were chosen to follow in Dream Spirit's dance, and we were honored to grasp a glimpse of the village our fathers now sit, we must remember to follow the lead of the High Spirit. It is through their teachings, and through their vision we may one day be heard speaking to our brothers from the Wall of Wahclella as we too lead them from the dangers that await them from the shadows in their lives.

With the grace of the Mighty Eagle, we soar higher, our sharpened beaks raised to the heaven. Our delighted screams are heard by the Hyas Tumtum! Dream Spirit is taking us upon this journey into the land that we had only pretended to think we knew... A land where we are all as one...the place where the rays of Otelagh shine upon us...to the village that stands safe from evil, and far from the disease of the bad spirit beneath. This is a land distant and remote from any other we have ever known. This is the land where the soul of Great Cedar is seen joined to his mother as they both stand proudly together once again and sway in dance to the gentle Chinook breeze.

This is the land where our spirits stand proud and unchallenged! This is the land where the lost soul of Suyapee can never enter. His steps are untrue, he shall quickly fall upon the hard trail below, broken and helpless as he does not follow in Indian way.

Soaring further and further from the soils of our lands below, grasping tighter to our visage, we are willingly led. How I ask; "Can we not be pleased?"

We wish our spirits to stay strong upon the Dream Spirit's trail. We are free from treading into the dark regions of our lives that lie with fear or wait in question to what lies beyond the next rise of Sun!

This is the Dream Spirit's Trail! Where life depends solely upon its own right to survive...

As we descend back to the soils of the Earth from our vision, suddenly, we rise from where we were seasted and look to the fire, and it is not aflame. There is no smoke cast upon the path where we were just led. We look to the meadow below the great rock, and there are no deer, and there are no elk lying upon its grassy floor. We look to the river and it is sullenly still! Fish are hidden beneath the depths of the Big Waters.

We look to the still, lonely sky...the screams of the Great Eagles are not heard, and their wings are not seen attached to the winds as they were once seen to soar above our lands.

We yearn to hear the call of Great Coyote from the silent valley floor.

The songs of birds lie silent upon the rising breaths of our Hyas Chinook.

We look to the heaven, and Otelagh is once again resting behind the cover of cloud above the sticks of our forests. The moon too fails to shed light upon our souls.

Life is lost from our eyes as we have lost the trail we were just led to the fires of our Hyas Father's village!

I must ask myself and my brothers if they too believe we are lost to the vision we had just shared?

Will we again find the village where Good Spirits dwell within the kingdom where life never ends?

With saddened eyes and broken hearts, we ask; "Where is the trail to the land of our vision? Where has gone the path of the Dream Spirit's Dance?"

I shout out to all my brothers; "We shall again discover within our souls that winsome trail, as it is just there waiting, beyond the rise of tomorrow's sun where our souls have yet to touch."

"We must believe in all our Hyas Spirit's command us to accept as we commit our lives to our own survival. We must first follow their wise words so upon the day our souls take leave of our hearts, and we rise up from upon the soils of our lands, we are taken upon our chosen star. It will be then, as we cross the heaven to the kingdom that holds the village of all our fathers, we will take the sweet huckleberry from upon the arms of their undying bush, and each season will be lived as one beside Sun and Moon. Our souls will then be connected to the heaven and to the Earth, and we will live amongst those spirits that lie in green pastures and drink from pure waters."

Chapter 8

Promising to Take Wing and Fly

The battle within Wy-East's soul has quieted, and life again is welcomed with opened arms as calm has returned to the lands as the spirits have grown tired and have fallen to their mats to sleep.

As the arrival of fall season has brought color to the trees and to the vine that grows upon the river's shore, we begin to make ready for the long winter ahead.

Winter's storm is known to loom just beyond the lands and waters we cannot see. Wind has changed course from which it had come when Sun was high in the heaven, and now, our nights are spent close beside the warmth of our fire inside our longhouse. Moon is hid behind thick cloud that spells of rains that will soon come, and the high peaks have all been taken from our sight. The long winter awaits to spring out from behind its disguise, and to this, we are never pleased.

Once the seasons have shown to begin to change the women of our village have joined with others and have journeyed to the big meadows below Great Larch and below Pahto to gather grasses for the baskets they will make as they sit before the warm fires as winter's storm is thrust upon us. The new season will come upon us in a single breath from the Good Spirit as winter is taken from the lands, but first, the last berries and root are harvested as they are welcomed within the baskets of the children. Upon our return from the high peaks where the sweet Huckleberry awaits, they will be placed on long mats and turned from one side to the other as they dry, then, they too are placed high up upon the shelf beside pish for our meals during the long winter when the lands offer us nothing.

Many men have joined together as we climb the trails that lead to the high peaks, and from behind great Firs we stand stilled, awaiting for the deer, elk, and bear to walk up before us so we will have meat for the winter to keep us strong.

The best skins are first soaked and then scrubbed and scraped with sharp bone with the brain of the animal as it is mixed with water. The skins are washed many times, and as they are cleaned they are stretched, each time, wider and wider. After many days, they became soft like the beaver's coat. The hides are washed for the final time and left to dry upon long beams of Cedar in the open air, and when winter falls upon us with much regret, the furs will warm our souls as they lay across our shoulders and take the chill of winter from within us.

The time to prepare for the long winter has arrived, and there is much work to do. We must walk into the forest and gather much wood for our fires, and we must store it where it will be kept dry from the long fingers of rain and from beneath the deep snow that is certainly promised to arrive.

As we look toward the high peaks of the Cascades, wind has thrust its mighty powers towards the long arms of sticks of our forests. There is much wood laying untended that offers us warmth during the long winter. Cedar and Fir, Alder and Cottonwood have all been culled from the lands by wind's long breaths, and it is where their final cries were heard they now willingly offer their souls for our keep.

As we walk into the forests and along the shore of En che Wauna, slowly we search for the strongest Cedar that wish to join us upon the fast waters of En che Wauna in the spring.

We need much patience as we choose to which we will form from the Cedar's hearts our new canoes as they will contest the fast waters of En che Wauan. The return of spring shall take from the heaven its dark cloud, and snow shall be taken fast from their high places upon the steep cliffs. The river will rise and its current shall become swift, and the great Cedar will prove of their strength as we join together and ply Big River's channel.

Salmon shall then offer color to the river. As they rise up from the depths of the great river to see their kingdom once more before their long journey is complete, the Great Spirit of Salmon's last gift to life on Earth is to the root of plants and to the trees, to the flowers, and to animals to which they will feed. All the kingdoms they have come to return will again be seen green and rich in new life, and life will again begin anew as their gift offers promise for all our tomorrows.

Life begins and ends within our kingdoms as the Salmon return from the sea to breathe life into their own each season. As we stand upon the bank of their waters, we see them smiling, each knowing they have given new life to their own as well as to the kingdoms of their waters. Their lives were vested in the beginning by the High Spirit to return to the same waters of their births, as they surrender their own lives so others may live, Otelagh's smile will rise above us as it was He that gave trust to the pish of these lands.

The Good Spirit has made life easy for our peoples as he has given us much game, tall trees that shelter us from the bad spirit's storm, and streams and rivers where life begins beneath their stilled waters.

We could not have asked for more...

Even as we had walked in the steps of the Dream Spirit and journeyed far from where we stand today, as we reached out to touch the hallowed village where our Hyas Spirits rest, we could not have asked for more. For we had not dreamed to what was more than what we had been gifted across the lands of the kingdoms of our High Spirit before that day.

To honor our lands is to honor our Hyas Spirit's soul, and through his spirit, our lands will be rich, and the trails we follow will be honored for all seasons...

Otelagh breathes life into all that is set before us, and it is He that keeps us safe and leads us from our stray into the bad spirit's den. The darkened dens of the bad spirits, where life is not a condition it wants known to have inhabited within its tainted lair.

The Dream Spirit's dance has taken us beyond the villages we know today, and he has led us to that village that could only have been seen through our dreams.

As we awoke and were faced with a new day, the mighty Dream Spirit has shown us we are only mortals before him. The kingdom where life's village awaits us with opened arms promises if we are to follow his path and honor all that life gives, we too shall one day look down upon the Earth from life's undying kingdom.

One day, as we are taken from upon this Earth and are sent across the heavens upon our chosen star, we will only then step upon that magical land and walk into that village where life never changes, and fear does not prey upon our souls. Then, we will be as one with all those spirits that we have heard calling out our names...

Then too, our souls shall not wander, and our hearts shall not be speared by the bad spirit's sharpened quill, and we will be set free upon that land that we could only dream to share...

"Our Fathers, hear our cry as we make ready our souls for that day when we are called to stand before your judging eyes!"

As we look high up upon the face of Che che Optin, (Beacon Rock), near where our village is raised from the low ground beside En che Wauna, we see warm light cast upon its many faces as it brings color and life to find rest upon them.

Through the long summer it is seen that the trees cry out as they know soon they will have to surrender what offers them color and beauty upon the lands. Each passing day that Otelagh crosses, the leaves that cling to the stick's strong arms make ready to offer themselves to those that wish to rest upon their soften bed as they fall softly upon the grounds beneath. Whispers of the great Chinook begin to pass across the lands, and quickly, it shares of winter's soon storm.

Light from Otelagh passes through the long arms of stick, as he shines bright through each one, it is as if a new gift emerges from where their shadows fall. Reds, yellows, and gold prove of change upon the leaves as they tell of summer's end and fall's approach. Fern and moss cling tightly to their hosts as Otelagh's final pass upon the lands offers warmth upon their souls as they will soon rest until he returns high above their lands.

It is days like today that we only begin to understand the treasure life offers our souls.

Through our respect for the lessons chosen of the High Spirit, we will endure many hardships as we continue to place our own lives before all those others of these lands that lends themselves to the salvation of one another. In their gathering branch, what brings happiness within our hearts shall always be seen by others that will come and pass to our meeting.

Today, I pray the lands will be free of anger and will offer us many sticks upon our search. I know as we journey amongst the giants of the forest, we will discover many Cedar who lie unscathed by their fall upon the soils of the earth. We have always discovered that single, majestic Cedar that calls out our names and pleads to our hearts we take him upon our journey to Wyam across the waters of En che Wauna in spring.

The Cedar Spirits that have spoken our names for all the seasons we have lived within these lands has given us safe journeys, and those canoes of our fathers, and their fathers before them are now with them as they rest upon the site of the Hyas Tahmahnawis' highest village.

From the offering of their souls, we will safely ply the fast waters of our river in the spring. They will see new lands where their brothers and sisters rise high beside the shores of the Big Waters. There, from high up upon the shores of En che Wauna, their brothers and sisters will be seen to wave in the soft breeze, and they will each hear their names whispered as they pass with much honor.

As we gather amongst all our brothers and offer trade for pelts, shiny glass, clam, oyster, and whale from the sea, we shall speak to all those that sit amongst our gathering of the new season as it arrives upon us.

The new season shall come before us all as we shall stand with opened and most welcoming arms to its return!

I remember my grandfather sharing of the stories of Great Cedar and of his visits beneath his welcoming branch. I too have knelt upon his side and shared my own story before him. I feel this day will take me upon his side, and Great Cedar and I shall meet again.

As wind was strong and much rain fell upon the lands, many trees are now lain sadly upon the ground by the floods that fell from the high peaks as they washed the weak from their hold upon the soils. We quickly gather many of the broken arms of those trees we can carry, and as Otelagh is soon to climb to his highest hill in the heaven, we turn from the trails we have followed and return to our village. We each took our own trails to course along the river's bank as we cleared the remains of those broken trees far from where the waters rush past. We pile them higher than the roof of our longhouse, and we are pleased...

Sun has climbed high above us as we sit with those of our village and take from the table the meat of elk. As we sit, we speak together of forming two groups that will walk out in search for the mightiest Cedar's heart. Only the ones that speak loudest of their message, and who promises to be proud as they are seen by many of our brothers of villages far distant than those of our own lands will be taken to form our great canoes.

As we began to venture out along the shore of the river, one group begins to trek west across the land where we had earlier begun this morning. They knew there would be many trees lain waiting for their taking.

The remaining brothers of the group choose to join my side. We climb east toward the cliffs where our peoples fish from above the fast water. It is there where was once formed the bridge that our peoples crossed as we journeyed to the village of the Wisscopam as it stood high up from the river's wash.

At the base of the old bridge were felled many trees from where the ground shook with great force and rock fell from their hold upon the mountain. Quickly, mud was formed from the water that poured from within the rock as both soil and water mixed and raced from the high peak to where they dammed the great river beneath.

From this place we have taken many of those tree's hollowed souls to the shore of our village. We had cut from their trunks what they did not need so our peoples would be seen proudly kneeling within their bows as we coursed the river and fished along each bank of En che Wauna's treasured shores.

As their strong souls offered themselves to become honorable through the shape of the canoes, they were again offered life. We thrust our team before all the land's of the High Spirit's kingdoms in search for the perfect Cedar, and quickly, they each have accepted a new life spent gliding through the channels of En che Wauna as they swept across the waves of the river during our journeys.

Today, as we find ourselves to walk to the bank of the river, there is hope the rains have taken from upon the land the roots of several Cedar that wait to offer themselves for our use.

One day, not long ago, I walked along the river's shore where we now cross. I looked high above to the great wall that was formed from the rock spewed forth from the battle between Pahto and Wy-East. I was called by both Elk and Goat Spirit as they watched over my every step. From the egg of Salmon and from white ash that had once fallen upon our lands from high above the mighty Pahto's bench, their shapes were hardened upon the rock to bring hope that wind will again return to their souls and fill their lungs with life.

I have kept this place where our spirits join together in secret, and I shall never share to where I go to sit and gather the wisdom from our association. I am fortunate they call out my name to sit and contemplate all life beside them without fearing one another, in calm and in silence, I am honored!

There are several days each season when Otelagh rises up to the heaven's highest trail when I find myself yearning to climb upon the cliff. As I sit and listen for their voice to rise up from within them and speak of all they have seen pass before them, I look across the fast waters of En che Wauna, beyond the Big Rock To the east from where Otelagh rises each day, I see islands that offer rest and solace to our peoples for many seasons as they have awaited for their chosen star to take them across the heaven from where they had been sat proudly overlooking the lands where they once journeyed.

Those that have passed on into their spirit world are placed in their canoes raised upon tall sticks high above the soil to be guarded by the spirit of Crow.

Upon each of their canoes are drawn the pictures of their spirit, and in those messages their spirit shares to the Great Spirit so he will remember all that is good within them as he passes overhead and offers peace to enter their souls.

Upon their journey to the village of Otelagh, their spirits shall join and become as one to all life upon the Illahee.

Each of our brothers and sisters are covered in the finest of skins taken from the Moolack and Mowitch as they sit proud within their canoes, and soft pelts from the beaver and mink are placed over them to keep them warm from winter's storm.

Upon each of the great hunter's chests lie bows, and quivers that hold tightly within them the keenest of arrows, and as they guard from the bad spirit's poach, they smile down upon us from the blue waters of heaven.

It is from these islands that we offer our Hyas Spirit their souls to keep.

These are sacred lands!

These are the lands where we do not dare to step!

We have been told from our fathers it is here the spirits shall rise up upon us and bring bad medicine before our doorsteps if we trespass across the Hyas Saghalie Tahmahnawis' most sacred grounds.

It is told, that if we walk fast from the Kloshe Tahmahnawis' lead and join hands with the mesahchie tahmahnawis, as he wantonly stirs the souls of those we have then offended, we will be taken far from the mat that is reserved for those that follow the trail chosen for us all by the Great Spirit Crow.

From that day forward, the light within us shall darken, and as our eyes close, and darkness falls heavily upon us, our last breaths will be drawn suddenly from within our chests.

We will then lie silent without spoken word, and our spirit will become bitter and lost amidst the maize of confusion the bad spirit chooses to lay before those that have unjustly chosen of his lost and lonely trail.

We will not sit beside our Hyas Tumtum once the cold of winter has scoured our hearts from life's warmth, and as we journey into the obscurity of the bad spirit's mind, our souls shall become *frozen and forever suspended throughout Otelagh's passing across the trails of the heaven.*

To those peoples that choose to lie frozen to the ways of the Good Spirit, they will be lost from all those that will come upon the Valley of the Eagle, and their voice shall not be heard as it may have been one day cast out from upon the Walls of Wahclella.

To those of whom have lost faith, and are lost upon our trails in life as we are led by the teachings offered by the Hyas Saghalie Tahmahnawis, they must never have their names or their memory recalled or spoken before the fires of our villages.

Their journey shall last forever alongside the Hyas Klale Lolo, and the memory of their being shall be well hidden within its most inhospitable cave where their bones are scattered of spirit, and where they lie stacked endlessly upon its most desolate and harried ground...

There are no visions telling of what is good in our lives arising upon us from where bad had once taken us captived, and if we allow our minds to follow in what once was, we shall find ourselves forever imprisoned within the Great Bear's inescapable trap where we will lie unmoving for all the days to pass.

Our hearts will then be devoured first by the Klale Lolo, and soon after life has escaped from within our chests, the mesahchie tahmahnawis Tsiatko will take from within our souls the spirit that once promised hope for our lives, and all that we could have become from that day forward will be lost forever in silenced word...

As I look up to the high cliff, I see the ledge where I sit, and I smile as it still draws my name to rest beside the spirits of the elk and goat as they peer down upon our mighty kingdom. One day, I shall find my return to sit beside their Hyas Spirits, and we will be as one again to the Earth, and to one other.

As my brothers and I walk along the river's trail, strong messages flash into my thoughts as we near where Great Cedar stands. Those messages were told by my grandfather as he took of this same walk many seasons past. He joined spirit with all that he was surrounded, and as he sat and listened he came to hear question from all those that walked and flew before him as they came and rested before his feet. With grave concern, they pronounced their dependence towards our people's understanding to their varied rhythms upon Earth's many distinct trails.

I remember that Great Cedar's only asks that we watch over him, and that once the new peoples approach the shores of our lands, his soul shall remain strong and rise high into the heaven. He promises to spread his arms wide below his crown so that life can join upon his side and find happiness beside one another amidst the chaos of confusion that will soon arise before us all.

For many seasons, my grandfather and father had shared of Great Cedar's wish, and as we have heard the story many times, we too understand the significance that Great Cedar holds within his soul as he brings life together in celebration.

Great Cedar is not like any other stick we pass, he is a tree that holds much magic. He too has great soul and powerful spirit!

We have all joined beside Great Cedar as we have passed beneath his tower, and we have placed our hands upon his heart as we felt of his warmth as it rose up from within the sweet scent of his bark.

He asked only to live to see another day before he is asked to lie beside his mother upon the soils where they had both first been given birth.

Through Great Cedar's vision, it is now our people's quest to see that he lives until the High Spirit chooses that his long arms cannot be drawn higher to the trails that lead to the heaven.

Great Cedar is a brother to the soils of the Earth, and through his long life, Great Cedar has witnessed and survived through many changes that have surrendered themselves upon the lands before him.

From the messages Great Cedar has brought forth to our thoughts, our peoples have joined upon his side and offered our support to all life that walks and breathes before us.

As we follow the trails that lead across all the lands of the High Spirit's kingdoms, we do not forget the lessons that he has shared before us. In his memory, and through our understanding of his message, these lands, all lands that we have encountered, are now safe from the pestilence that lies heavy and deep within many men's malicious and darkened souls.

From afar, I now see Great Cedar's rise above the lands along the shore of the river, and his long arms dance as his spirit is attached to the rhythm of his kingdom.

Flowing smoothly, without hurry, as does a small stream in the warm season as it is drawn from the high peaks of our Spirits, this is the dance that he shares with the soils beneath him.

This is the Great Cedar we see each day...

Taking each breath as if it were to be his last, longing for the next to flow across his opened bows, Great Cedar opens his long arms and raises them high to Otelagh as he passes overhead. He offers thanks to the Hyas Tahmahnawis for all the seasons he has been honored to stand free from disease.

Great Cedar is proud and unafraid, and we are pleased that he still rises from the soils that are rich in the knowledge that he shares.

We pass the meadow where my grandfather once sat and listened to the story of life, as all those that joined upon his side told of their concern.

It was as if my grandfather had joined the trail of the Dream Spirit, and through all the voices of the living, he was led through the dance of the Dream Spirit that leads to the village of Life.

My grandfather's feet were taken from upon the soils of the earthen trail beneath him as he was led high above the lands of the Earth, and as he was allowed to stand before the gates of the new land that offers peace to our souls, he entered within the welcoming doors of the High Spirit's own village.

It was there, high above where we stand today, that my grandfather had taken upon the vision that tells of that most magical and spiritual place we have named Life. Unlike where life, as we know it here upon Earth, depends solely upon one another to envision the rise of today's sun, the land of our Hyas Saghalie Tahmahnawis depends solely upon those that thrive beside him to open their eyes and witness to the rise of tomorrow's sun, today…

Life is a magical place!

Life is where peace and harmony permanently exists amongst all those that have been accepted to their seat before the fire within the Hyas Spirit's village.

Life is today.

Life is tomorrow.

Life is beyond those days that we know!

Life is accepting all that the Earth is, and knowing it will always be tomorrow!

As I stand beneath Great Cedar and place my hand upon his heart once more, he quickly settles beneath my touch as my fingers rub his soul and brings to the air, sweet scent.

As we are joined upon one another's sides beside the river's shore, through my vision to where my grandfather had been taken, Great Cedar rose up, and with unspoken word, let out a great sigh.

And all was then held in silence, and I did not understand?

But in those words unspoken that I craved to hear, Great Cedar had seen Sun's rise for the final time here upon the soils beside his mother. Without knowing, Great Cedar's vision had then found its way upon my trail. As he stood proud and gave thanks to the High Spirit, he too was taken from upon the earthen trails and had been led high above from his home to the heaven where he had dreamt to reach higher each day.

Great Cedar's wish had been approved, and all our peoples would dance upon the ground where he stands, and we will be pleased that he is now resting beside his mother without the threat of worry or concern.

Great Cedar's spirit was lifted high into the new land and to the village of Life, from where he stands proudly at the right hand to the chair of the High Spirit. From his chair I hear him calling out my name to one day join upon his side. He asks that I continue to share his story as each Cedar of our forest, each fir, each tree, each plant, each animal, all belong to their own chair within the opened gates of the Hyas Saghalie Tahmahnawis' village.

Great Cedar is still strong as he stands upon the ground beside his mother's grave. As I kneel beneath his covering arms, I wail unto the heaven's trails, so that I, one day, would too, be joined upon his side.

To my brothers that are beside me, I announce that Great Cedar is now our people's Spirit Tree!

The trail of the river will lead us safely to stand beside Great Cedar as we wish to touch the vision shared through the Dream Spirit's Dance. Each season we will gather beside his grave and we will join all our spirits as we walk silently and in remembrance to his sway before our peoples.

Great Cedar's new village will once again lie just beyond our touch, but in our respect for the lands of this Earth within the Hyas Tumtum's kingdom, we too shall one day rise up from our mortality and touch the inner soul where our spirituality shall be seen to thrive for all the days that Sun shall rise.

From where I sit beneath Great Cedar's welcomed cover, I rub the soft bark of his trunk and share of his sweet scent to all that stand in the path of Wind for the final time. I am pleased, as it too rises to the heaven from where Great Cedar stands, and we both are seen to sway with the soft breaths of the Hyas Chinook as our spirits are joined one last time above the earthen floor as we share of our own Dream Spirit's Dance united...

Chapter 9

Klale Lolo's Trap

My brothers and I took the trail towards Beacon Rock, where is heard the song of all those whom have passed when the Table Mountain buried their village beneath huge mounds of rock and tree that were thrown down upon them from where they had proudly stood overlooking the Lands of Wah. The bad spirits chose to rise up upon the surface from beneath the mountain's soils, and as tree and rock shook as the battle brewed with much vengeance, they both had been cast down to the shore of En che Wauna as the bad spirit wished. They each crumbled to the floor of the mountain and to their harrowing deaths, and many trees were swept to the big waters of the sea or were entrapped by rock as En che Wauna was then trapped behind the great wall of debris.

It is upon this trail where many of our brothers and sister's were lain beneath the waste that then formed the bridge of our High Spirit. This bridge offered us safe passage above the trickling waters of En che Wauna to the Land's of Wah and before the entrance to the Valley of the Eagle.

Wind has begun to blow down upon us, and as its breaths come faster and we are challenged to continue, from the high ridge, snow begins to fall and we cannot see beyond the shore of En che Wauna. Now, we have lost the trail we had first come as it has been surrendered beneath the High Spirit's frozen tears.

We climbed far above the shore of the Big River, and as we stepped lightly upon the ground where we thought it was first seen, I heard the call from the voice of Cedar I had awaited.

We walk hurried through the thick forest that brings darkness to the land as the long arms of mighty firs are thrust beside us from the long slope below. As we come to the final turn before En che Wauna's waters, there standing before us, with opened arms, welcoming us to stand with them and hear of their message, stand proudly, not one, but three Cedar. They were brothers, and as their roots were tied together beneath the soils, they asked we would honor them all by honing them into our canoes. They each told that they would honor our peoples with the swiftest canoes to have ever been cast upon the race of the Big River.

The Three Cedar spoke with much promise as they told they would offer safe travel if they were to join with us and be placed side by side with their brothers. They too told if we were to allow them to join together in our journeys, their souls would share of *their mother's strong spirit, and we all would be kept safe above the wanting of the bad spirit that lives beneath the waters.*

I knew as they spoke of their promise to me they would be seen by those upon the shore to be free as are the Great Eagle that pass swiftly above us upon strong and swift wings.

The brothers told they would take us above the water's plane and be seen to fly upon the waves, and our chairs would not be touched by tears shed from the High Spirit's eyes.

Each of the Three Cedar were pleased as they swayed in the wind of the storm that arose above our gathering. As I laid my hand upon each of their strong trunks, we each knew that we would soon be brothers upon the waters of the Great River, and we would travel far together as we each would see much of the lands.

I told them of all their brothers that stood proud upon the many shores that we had traveled, and how they called out my name and waved as wind swept through their arms as I passed. I told them as they were soon to join our party to Wyam, their names would be heard called out from the shores just as were our own, and they would be welcomed upon a new land that they had not yet seen.

Again, as they each swayed to the song sung by Wind as it fell upon us, and as they had heard my wise words rise up from my heart, they felt of my passion to the journey that would soon approach, and they too were pleased...

I held my hand upon their hearts once more, and as my brothers and I began to return to our village, I turned to see their long arms sway in the rhythm of wind. I knew once I returned that we all would be as the Elk and Goat upon the high rock, and we would be connected to the Earth as brothers for all the days that would pass from that day forward.

Slowly, we walked along the river's trail as we spoke of the beauty of our land, and as we came upon each turn, we saw many deer and elk run fast into the forest's hides. They too knew of the coming storm that was promising to reign with much hopelessness for Otelagh's return above the lands.

Wind howled continuously for many days as the voices of those that have chosen the trail of the bad spirit filled the air with their screams. Clouds have clung to the ground and have hid the lands of our kingdom from before us. Much snow has risen before our doors as it has forced us to wait for the skies to clear before we climb out from where we hide.

Each day that we look out to where smoke of our fire rises to the heaven from the center of the roof, cloud has become dark as night as it twists and spirals before our eyes with much anger. We peer towards each cloud that is swept before us, and in each cloud's form, we see the face of Suyapee smiling down towards where we are gathered as he too knows of what he brings within his own spirit that will leave us helplessly trapped.

As we sit in our longhouse and wait for storm to pass, we speak of the three brother's wish that we would take their spirit from the earth as they would lead our hands to shape their forms into our best canoes. I told everyone that sat amongst our gathering that we would soon walk to where our brothers stood, and we would make shelter to keep the rains and snow from filling their souls as we begin to form from their hearts the very best of our canoes.

We chanted to the High Spirit asking him to look over us and to approve of our choice, and he too would be pleased of Cedars, my brothers, and my own efforts as we joined all our souls within the creations we were to be led to shape.

As we prepared to leave to the Three Cedar we knew they had awaited our return for many days, we each gathered our adz, and took from our shelves mauls, chisels, wedges, and placed them all into our packs made from the great bear's tough hide. Bear offered to us the strongest of all hides, and we could carry many tools within the strong pockets our wives had sewn with the bone of elk and deer.

We must take with us many stones to heat in the fire to be placed within the hollowed hulls of the canoes to soften the wood so we can easily cut away the wood we will not need from their strong trunks.

We would collect strong branches to place within the Cedar's trunks once we fill the hulls with water, and as the water has soaked completely into the wood, we would then take the stones from beneath the flame of the fire and place them inside to bring steam into the wood.

We would cut the branches both long and short, as we began to shape the finished cuts we would place them to complete where we would kneel. As each canoe swelled several times, we would again place longer sticks into the sides of the Cedar and heat more rocks in the fire as we place them inside the opened log to hold its shape. Once the canoes are readied for our use, we emptied the water from within them, and we let them dry in the cool breeze. When the wood has dried we take out the cut branches from within them and begin to smooth the rough edges with round stones. This we do many times so both our hands will fold easily along the soft sides of the Cedar, and so we are able to pull into their smooth hulls, pish, into our boats from our nets without rendering them useless by the tears rough edges would bring.

Many days has passed from the day we began to join the spirits of Three Cedar to our own, and as we stood before them, with much admiration as they were completed, Cedar and we were both pleased.

Each of the brothers asked they be taken to the shore of En che Wauna and be placed into her waters so they could prove of their heart, and we agreed. We made ready our paddles and placed them upon our shoulders, but as we began to walk to En che Wauna's shore, we saw the sky had turned threatening with dark, looming cloud.

The sky began to churn and growl with each breath of wind. Louder, and louder, its cries were heard as wind quickly fell upon us from high above where the mighty spirits of the Cascades must be resting nervously as they sit upon their frozen bench and await the bad spirits to rise up from beneath them and spread their pestilence across all the lands.

My brothers and I stand bewildered to the warning that has again shown the face of Suyapee in the sky. We have decided not to take the Three Brothers to the Big River for their first run across her driven wave. Instead, we will wait for a calm day when the Hyas Spirits can watch from their village and see our race is promised faster across the waters of En che Wauna than has been witnessed by any other before.

To this, we have all agreed.

We took each of the brothers and placed them beneath Great Cedar's covering branch. We shared with the three brothers much sorrow, and promised them we would return to take them upon their first run below Otelagh as he shines happily down upon their race before the lands of his kingdom.

Again, I placed my hand upon each of the brothers, and they each breathed heavily beneath my touch. They were saddened that we could not join together on our first run, but each of the brothers told they were proud to be chosen to be taken upon our journeys into the kingdoms of our brothers, and they would stand silent until our return.

The trees of the forest now have begun to sway from one side and then to the other. We discover ourselves in much danger as branches fall heavily at our feet from where we cannot see above us.

Wind whips great white waves to rise up from where the plane of the river once was. Its spray has now reached high above the shore where we hurriedly walk towards the warm fire of our village.

Wind howls loudly, we cannot hear the sticks of the forest scream, and we cannot feel of one another's footsteps upon the rocky ground beneath us as we walk. Wind has promised to take from before us all that we know, and in our loss, we will journey across our lands as blind men without our walking sticks to keep us safe upon the trails we had once been joined.

This storm must be the mesahchie tsiatko of the north coming to join forces with that of the bad spirit we have battled for many seasons!

Wind has taken the trail of Suyapee, and as it spreads its dark cloud over our lands, it now challenges us to stand and face the wrath it lends upon us all. I can see even with closed eyes this has created panic in many of our peoples. I am not afraid, but as I become concerned to what will approach our lands this day, I know I must be aware of all that we are this moment surrounded.

Our trek to the safety of our village is taken with much effort as Wind has taken from us our fast step as it blows hard against us. It is near this place along the trail where I had last seen the large print of Klale Lolo pressed deep within the wet snow a few days past. I motion to my brothers to follow closely and to look around and behind us as we walk. Wind chooses to blow harder each moment we stand. We are defenseless to the onslaught it has chosen to surround us. It takes the sound of our footsteps from our ears, and we must lay caution to what may stand beyond each turn of the trail.

As I lead my brothers some distance from where we had stopped along the snowy trail to our village, here, from above the maddened cries that rise up before us from within the waters of En che Wauna, the trail turns and leads us into the great forest where darkness not only hides all that is good, but too, what is evil from our eyes.

Suddenly, from beyond where I cannot yet see, warm, foul breath sweeps across my face. As if time had suddenly passed without thought to the change from light to darkness, charging from where shadows fall upon the trail of darkness, rising up upon his hind legs, standing taller than my own arms could reach, roars the mighty Klale Lolo. As bear faces me with teeth barred, and huge claws raking the air, he reaches out to take my spirit from my soul. As I step back hurriedly in surprise, my heart stops beating for what seems to be the difference between light of day and dark of night. As quickly as my heart stopped, it rises up from within my chest and begins to pound with the fear of the unknowing to all my tomorrows.

As bear and I stand face to face, I in fear, and he angred, he smells the fear within me as it rises thick before him. I tremble with fear, and the sweat that appears upon my face freezes with the cold breaths of wind. I slowly step back, step by step, slowly without hurry. As he watches me I am certain his charge is now aimed to take from me life and that he would certainly leave no trace that I had once stood where I now tremble in much fear.

Standing before Hyas Klale Lolo I know I must yell out to him to walk from his fight, but as he stands unforgiving to our approach, I motion for my brothers to walk slowly from where we stand. As I yell out to bear again and again, he still stands before me with raking claws and snapping teeth, hungered for his meal.

Slowly, without turning from facing his angered eyes, I step back. Again and again, I step into the footsteps I had taken, and as I came to the turn of the trail and knew my brothers had all escaped, I screamed with much force towards Klale Lolo and dared for him to follow.

I know of this trail and how the creek flows far beneath the covering blanket that hides its place when winter's storm is drawn heavy upon us, and I know my only chance for survival is to run fast and jump across where it is hidden beneath the deep snows of this winter.

As soon as my feet touch the roots of the Fir that lay along the trail, I quickly turn and run. One, two, and three quick steps, and I jump without hesitation or fear of falling into the deep chasm where I too would be trapped. As I reach the opposite side of the creek I am able to catch my balance, and I am able to breathe free from attack.

I turn towards where bear charges towards me. I stand tall with arms raised before bear and scold with loud voice towards his attack upon me. He suddenly stops, and I see his eyes are questioning why I stand stilled before him.

Bear then rises higher upon his hind legs as he mocks the tallest Vine Maple. He growls loudly with dislike to my trespass upon his trail. As he falls heavily upon the ground it shakes beneath my feet. He again charges towards me as the warning of thunder is attached beneath each of his swift feet!

With the vengeance of the bad spirit's storm, he runs fast towards me with teeth popping and claws raking the ground, and then the air with each stride he takes comes fast before me as the wind that comes with storm.

I stand unmoving before him upon the trail, knowing this is my only hope to survive. I raise my arms high over my head, and I chant to the Hyas Tumtum that he will guard over my spirit and honor me with tomorrow.

Again, I begin to loudly scold bear and dare him to join me upon the far side of the bank where I stand waiting, and with the swiftness of the great Cougar, he runs forward towards where I stand. With long arms, he grasps to the emptiness of air as he preys for my soul.

Bear does not think of the creek that is hid beneath the snow as the waters are not heard to flow beneath the snow's deep mound. He runs hurried and maddened to where I stand motioning for him to follow. My voice can be heard across the lands as I laugh out to him as he falls deep into the frozen waters that have now promised to hold his soul within their icy trap.

He cannot rise up and give chase to the fly as he is now like the fish where water is not drawn. He lies floundering within the deep snow.

He is held taut within his frozen trap, and he screams loudly to wind as he admits to his mistake of acting before thinking to where I have led him to his imminent defeat!

He growls and snarls towards me as I peer down to him, and I laugh at his mistake. I tell him that soon his coat shall be drawn across my shoulders, and the chill of winter shall be taken from within me for many seasons, and it is I that will survive to see another day, and not he!

As I look him straight into the eyes as both our eyes meet, he snarls and snaps his teeth once more in hopes that I will honor his strength and allow him to escape the death that awaits at the point of my arrow I have drawn upon my bow. But as I again shout down to him with great pleasure, I tell him that his coat will be worn proudly across my wide shoulders, and I will be pleased. I taunt him one last time as he again snarls towards me, and as he shares his long teeth, I shout out; "I shall take from your chest your heart, and your spirit shall be joined with my own. We will become brothers as I will take from your soul the strength that you possess, and all that you are will be within me, and I will walk upon all the trails of these kingdoms without fear from this day on!"

I tell bear we will walk the same trails, but through the wisdom as it has been taught to me by the Good Spirits, I will be guided across all the trails I am led by the Great Spirit Crow. I tell Klale Lolo I will be protected by the cunning of Coyote as my spirit will remain stronger, and I will be led distant from all his brother's wanting dens.

Then, slowly, as I have notched my arrow upon the vine of my bow, I draw it steadily back until the point of my arrow touches the strong wood of Yew. I steady my aim towards his chest, and as I pull mightily upon my bow's spun vine, without thought, I release my hold to the arrow as it quickly pierces Klale Lolo's now sullen heart.

As bear cries out to those that will listen, his chest heaves with much effort as he takes his last breaths. As I stand over him waiting for his spirit to be taken from within him, I shout out to him that I will savor the flavor that he brings upon my table, and I shall be seen of my wide smile as it was me that has survived our battle!

Bear's chest heaved with much effort one final time, and as he settled unmoving within his frozen trap beneath where I stood waiting, all was then silent as wind stopped, and Otelagh again rose up from behind the bad spirit's darkened cloud, and life was again pleased as Otelagh's warm rays fell hardily upon us once more...

Chapter 10

The Long Winter

Storm has swept across our lands for many days, from the high peaks first came hard rains that have filled the creeks, then, as the waters rushed towards En che Wauna, she too has swollen and overrun her banks. As En che Wauna began to flood the lands, snow then fell heavily for many more days from the high peaks above the Land's of Wah. A great blizzard swarmed before us from the heaven and took from our eyes all the trees and the mighty peaks. Silence fell hard upon our ears. That same silence we know when we walk into where birds do not sing and in the shadows awaits those that hunger for our souls. Once the storm had passed, all life that still survived the frozen breaths of the mesahchie cole Illahee, (bad, cold lands,) whom chose not to hurry towards where their winter beds awaited, were left to move burdened beneath the East Wind's, (S'Lee,) scouring punish.

The land surrounding our village is quiet as snow has fallen heavily upon the land, and nothing moves upon the trails that are now unseen from where we would have earlier placed our step.

As we walk out from our longhouse to gather wood for the fire, each step we take can be heard from far away as the frozen ground is heard to crack and moan in agony beneath our heavy feet.

The cold and bitter face of winter has again found a new home amongst us, and though storm has just begun to reach our lands, we wish the new season would quickly return above us and bring light to the sky, and warmth to our bones.

As we wait the new season, the storms that fall upon us demand that we stay inside the shelter of our longhouse as we gather where the fire glows warm, and where smoke rises from the opened hole to where we watch for change from the sky each day. We look to the heaven with much hope. We wait for the warmth of Otelagh to shine down upon us, but this season is unlike those past, as it is long and harsh, and has taken us prisoner within its enduring reign upon us.

The sky has turned sullen with storm. Each day, as winter teases our hopes with flecks of blue in the sky, it takes hope from our hearts as the chaste of Wind returns and laughs wildly at our disgust. As Wind breathes deep, it is as if it rejoices in our lost hope as it begins anew to its maddening chorus beside that of the Hyas Pishpish's scream upon us.

New cloud has dropped from the high peaks again only to rise up and disappear, and as Wind breathes, cloud falls menacing before us as we sit impatient, waiting once again for winter's merciful hand to take its threat far from our village, and in hope that it will not be drawn again upon us.

On long winter days when we are subjected to the punishment of the bad spirits above us, we sit and make ready for the celebration of the new season at Wyam and at Wishram.

This winter has had many days when we sat together and honed from the shell of the great sea many sharp points for our arrows. We have taken the truest shafts of Yew and have straightened them between two rocks as we soak them to soften the wood so they would bend and not crack or break. Once the shafts are trued, and they promise to find their mark within the heart of deer and elk, we place them to dry high above the smoke of the fire until they become hard.

As we sat working on our new weapons and speak of the season's hunt, each arrow brings closer visions of great triumphs that lie just beyond the next rock, or from behind the next tree where we will take from the land the mightiest deer and elk.

Finally, after Otelagh has rose up above us behind the long winter's cloud and has set many times beyond the Big Waters, we take reed from the marsh we had collected. With the soft bark of Cedar we begin to rub the arrows shafts until they are smooth. We will not be pleased until they are as true as the first horn of young bucks.

We take from the Blue Jay's wing and the Blue Heron perfect feathers, and we place them upon the ends of each arrow. As every feather dries upon their new wing, we place them into new quivers sewn with strips of cedar and vine by our wives from the softest skins from the Mowitch and Mink.

We have told ourselves we will not be caught defenseless and hungry the day we come across the trail of a large elk or deer if it is to stand before us with questioning eyes. Deer and Elk Spirits shall be ours and placed before us upon our long table as we smile to the High Spirit and offer thanks for our reward.

Many of my brothers have made arrows and sharp points to trade at the Great Celebration, and they speak of the meat of the Buffalo and Antelope they wish to make trade.

Today, as we peer out into the sky from beneath the hole of our roof, we see cloud has been taken from the heaven and Otelagh has begun to shine down upon us with warmth and invitation to join together beneath his most welcomed light.

Our spirits have once again shown promise of returning as Otelagh has journeyed to our lands, and our children and the women of the village have begun to make fire within the open pit. Soon it will be time to join together and eat our meal, but as we await for the fire to burn hot, many of the braves of our village and I have chosen to walk to the shore of the Big River.

As Otelagh shines down and spreads warmth to each plant and animal that we are surrounded, my brothers and I have chosen to sit where the skies are free from the limbs of trees. Slowly, from behind the long arms of sticks that line the river, peek out many deer as they stare across to where we sit, and the raucous of the raccoon can be heard as he walks to the shore in search for food. Swimming past us is the great otter as he chases fish in play, and we are all pleased that Otelagh has once again found the trail that leads him to stay high above us.

As I look downriver, I see first a quick movement from behind a large rock, as I slowly turn to look towards to what moves before us I see, slowly peeking out from behind, a white cape draped over the shoulders of a grand elk that stands taller and stronger than any other I have seen. He has great horns that reach longer than a man is tall across its widened brow, and they reach high into the heaven as if they too belong.

Quietly, I tell my brothers to look towards the rock and ask if they too see what takes my breath from me as my heart pounds with great excitement?

Slowly, they each turn and look towards the rock, I can hear their heart's pound in rhythm with one anothers, and nothing needs said in answer as they too sit in amazement and in honor of what stands before us.

It is White Elk Spirit!

I have been told from my father and grandfather that long ago there was a family of White Elk that lived high up where man did not go. They told me this was the land where the High Spirit's of the forest hide, and we should not take their spirit from within them as their hearts must remain strong and their souls free upon the lands they have chosen to run.

"The spirit of White Elk is to be placed beside that of Hyas Tkope Lemoto for all the days that we are honored upon this Earth. These Hyas Elk run where man has not yet walked, and upon the hard trails that rise up to the heaven upon Wy-East and Pahto we must always hear their call."

This is what I was told by my grandfather.

As winter had fallen heavy upon our lands this season, the mighty White Elk Spirit has come down to join upon our side, and it takes from beside the river sweet grass, as he too is pleased that winter is soon to find a new home.

As we stare hard toward the highest spirit of the forest, we take in all that he wants to share of his size and horn, and we each sit silent as we are forced from speaking of our excitement to this great honor.

Hyas Tkope Moolack slowly steps back from the edge of the river as he sees that we stare towards him with great eyes, and as he turns to face us, in a quick blink he takes flight with his fast hoof and disappears within the cover of the forest's sticks where he cannot be seen.

He is a true spirit of the forest, and he is a brother bonded to the soils of the Earth by his inexplicable and defying hoof. His soul has been set free by Hyas Saghalie Tahmahnawis torun far from where man is known to hunt. We will be honored to share of this day to all our brothers that know of the High Spirit of White Elk, and we will tell of his heartiness, and to the proof of his prolonged survival upon the kingdoms we are surrounded.

The spirit of the forest has looked down upon our peoples, and from his high place, as he as approved of our people's worthiness to share in the lands he looks down upon each day, he has accepted our souls to have found peace within our hearts.

As Hyas Tkope Moolack Tahmahnawis has journeyed far to stand upon the shore of En che Wauna, he has shared his eyes before us this day, and we are honored…

Our eyes were torn to look away from the magical hoof of White Elk Spirit, and as he disappeared into the shadows of the forest

116

and has run back into the frozen lands of our kingdom where we could not follow, we still sat unmoving, tireless in our search for his great white cape.

Without speaking, we each knew that he would not return before us, and we turned to face one another, and smiled. We then knew the spirit of the White Elk was told in truth, and we had been honored, and that he was not an enemy that wished to prey upon our village in disguise as would the villages of the Snake.

As the women called out for our return, we joined before the fire of our village and sat amongst one another. I took my seat, and as I sat quietly amongst those of my village that came, I found myself lost in my answer if it were disbelief or in question to what I had seen in each of my brother's eyes?

Many suns had passed since the last day I had heard of the mighty spirit's long journey to our river from the mountain's highest peaks. I knew of Hyas Tkope's spirit as he chose to run free and distant from the lowland's floors where man's heart is not good.

Sadly, this day may be the last we would see of his great white cape spread across his large shoulders, and this may be the last we would see of his great antlers as their beam stretched beyond those we dream to place above our doors from our hunts.

We all raised our hands to the heaven and praised the High Spirit for all he offered us, and we took from the Hyas Tumtum's plate, pish, and the meat of Mowitch. The wild berry and onion gave sweet flavor to the meal, and we were pleased...

As we sat and ate our meal we shared to what we had seen, and those that did not walk to the river beside us were taken through the vision as it was seen through our eyes, and they too were pleased. They too saw the *Hyas Tkope Elk* stand tall and proud before them, just as we were chosen. There was much happiness.

We have each, all my peoples of this village, joined our spirits with *White Elk's* spirit, and have felt of the gift he extends from within his soul by his trust as we have taken upon the trails led by the scream of *Crow* from his high branch above where we have followed the trails that our *High Spirits* lead.

Through the teachings of our fathers, and through the wisdom shared from the *Hyas Saghalie Tyee Tahmahnawis*, our souls have been sent higher upon the mountain, and as we have reached out to again touch the village where *Otelagh* rests at night, we have found ourselves bonded to our father's distant site. One day, we will be seated amongst them, and we will hear them speak once more…

This is where our vision must take us, to the big village that stands mightily above the land where fear is not lent within our souls, and life depends only upon itself to breathe deeply of its own next breath.

This is the vision that has brought ourselves to dream…

We have the vision that one day we may discover our souls rested above the storm of winter's poach, and as we are taken upon those visceral trails to the heaven, the high spirit shall see we have both, hope and faith vested within our lives.

Through our trust and respect for his way, and as we offer support and guard life from being taken by the bad spirit, we may one day rise up and place ourselves upon those grounds, and we may then soon find ourselves to sit before the fires of that same village where our vision has since chosen for us to dream.

It is our dream to dream, as we have entered within the gates of our heaven upon the journey we shared through the Dream Spirit's dance!

Each day we look to the heaven for Otelagh to rise high above us and to warm our souls from this long winter. But it is not his way this season to take from us the chill of winter's storm, so we wait with great patience, and cling to the warmth held within our longhouse for many days as we weather each storm that has been thrust down upon us from the Great Spirit.

When we are able to be free from the Winds of Chinook, and step out and look out over calm waters once again, we are pleased as we have awaited the opportunity to walk to the three brothers of Cedar as we had promised.

As we came upon where we had stood the Three Brothers to rest until we returned, they were each pleased as they knew their initial ride upon the waves of their kingdom had now come. We placed the brothers into the river, and instantly, we were swept across the river's wave by their free spirits, and it can be heard that I shout out to each of them as we sail above the river's wave and share the High Spirit is pleased.

The three brother's dreams have come true, and their wish to be set upon the fast waters has taken them before the shores of a new land as I had promised, and we all are now joined together, not only to the earth, but now to the Big Waters of En che Wauna.

It is along the shores of the Creek to the Eagle, and to the shores of the Lands of Wah that we have chosen to journey, and as the brothers have proven of their heart, we have arrived safely and without threat of falling from their strong frames into En che Wauna's swift currents.

We have chosen to set upon the shore of Wahclella's creek, and as I choose to set out from where my brothers await my return I excuse myself to begin my walk beyond where Munra guards the entrance to the Hallowed Walls of Candor. This is the day I had heard my name called out to stand before our Fathers, and as I kneel before them in respect, I must speak of what we have seen this past season. I must plead for advice so that our souls can be taken far from the eye of the storm that is soon to befall all our nations, and that we be placed where evil will not tempt those that are weak before its beckoning hands.

With each visit into the lands where our father's speak, and before those spirits that stand proud upon the face of their cliff alongside the falls, we find our souls willingly surrendered to their demands through their just words.

We find ourselves honored to stand before them, and as we are taken upon our visions where they lead each of our own journeys, we learn of where our lives will one day be joined. In our team, all our brothers will be free from the deep lines sunk upon one's face where anger and worry has proven to become attached.

One day, when the heaven was clear of cloud, and the breaths of the Cole Illahee were held silent from their loud scream, Otelagh rose into the sky and shone bright upon the land. My brother, Mensitiko and I chose to visit where Elowah's waters fall proudly into her stream, and it was here we stood appreciative to the beauty of many long and frozen spears hung dahgerously from upon the high cliffs. We stood for many hours admiring Hyas Tahmahnawis' creation as we are again bound by the magic the Hyas Tahmahnawis Tyee had promised to share from his purse before us.

As we stood admiring the bright light and colors that were cast through each of the frozen spears, we again discovered why we have found ourselves to honor the lands that our souls have become surrendered.

The High Spirit offers great magic to the kingdom of Wah and to those of the Great Eagle as it is placed upon the walls of their cliff. Each spire glistens with the rainbow's ribboned hues, and they sparkle pleasingly with the light cast down upon them through the giving hand of Hyas Otelagh.

Then suddenly, without warning, shining heartily upon the land, Otelagh brought warmth from within his soul to begin the new season and bring life to blossom once again upon the lands of our kingdoms.

As if spring were placed upon the slightest passing breeze, the chill of winter was suddenly taken from within us. Cloud had too taken change, as cloud separated from their long blanket above us and their spirit was set free into the heaven as far as we could see. They changed into soft white cloud that rested lazily across all of Otelagh's trails, and it reminded us of long, warm, summer's days that reached far into the night.

The warmth of spring's breaths were first blown across the lands, and the whispering of new life was cast down upon the soils of the Earth.

Each plant, each tree, all life that lives and breathes the same air as we, whose souls are tied strongly to one anothers from their birth's beginnings, had then taken from our hearts the troubles that have found themselves to sit hardened within us.

At that moment, our souls had again joined under warm skies, and we each were pleased!

New life beckoned to enter before all creation's opened doors, and as its arrival was lain willingly upon each of Otelagh's kingdoms, through Otelagh's warm hands as they opened before us, rose up from beneath the soils, the new season's first flower.

With spring's arrival, we took upon the trail of the river that will take us to our village, and from upon the highest waves that we were cast, we were heard to shout towards the Hyas Otelagh in welcoming his rise above us as we had become wanting for his return.

Life has again risen from beneath the soils, each blade of grass, each bush, the flower, and each blade of the fern, they have all begun their life's renewal from within the thawing ground, and we are pleased!

Chapter 11

The River Will Run Quick With Silver

As Otelagh has shone down upon our peoples with much promise and has awarded the sticks of our forests new leaves, and the flowering berry shows promise that it too will ripen across the high meadows of the high peaks, we have begun to make ready for our long journey to the village of Wyam.

As we sit upon the side of the night's fire and speak of the day when we will set our great canoes upon the water's wave and find our journey to the Great Chute, we hear, far off in the distant valley, the mourning call of Coyote as she announces her return within the lands of Wah.

From where the waters of our river meet those of the approaching sea, rising up upon the soft breeze that carries the sweet scent of flower, the message arrives from our brother's great drums announcing the return of spring's first run of pish as they have jumped with much pleasure into their nets.

This is the time each year when we are eager for all our brothers and sisters of our village to find seats within our canoes as we make ready for the long journey to the distant village of Wyam. Where we will share celebration and praise the Good Spirits for all the gifts they have honored us throughout the past season.

Only our elders will stay with the village and keep the fires burning as we begin our long trek. Our fathers and mothers wish to await our return within the safety of the village, and once they see us come upon En che Wauna's wave, they will help take from our canoes what we have traded for their baskets, sharp points, and the shell they had sent with us as they complimented our village's finest cache.

It has been this way from the first journey we had taken to our brothers of the Wasco's village as the journey is long and hard against the fast waters.

It is a sad time when our mothers and fathers cannot make the journey beside us, as they too had once taken upon the waters of En che Wauna and journeyed along the great river as they passed below the high cliffs where we will soon stand to take the Hyas Pish as they leap into our nets.

As my peoples have sat and spoke of the journey many years beyond those of my youth, I have heard from many of the Elders they are saddened they cannot visit with all the animal spirits that come out from their hides to greet them as they pass by. I know they will each miss sitting amongst all our peoples, young and old alike, at the Potlatch as we share of the pleasure each day brings to our lives.

This season brings both, good and bad before our tables, and what I must share brings grief to my heart as Red Cloud has come upon us. It allows much question to fall upon us to what we must do, and to where we may have to choose to journey to be free of Red Cloud's storm?

Each new season, when flowers first rise from the earth and bring color to the meadows, pish will soon arrive before us from the Big Waters of the sea and give life to all the forest's creations as they breathe new life into their own and offer the land nourishment. Green grass and flowering bush will sprout up before all the kingdoms and bring happiness to all that breathe the fresh scents that will rise up and touch their souls.

Pish are promised to be countless within the streams and rivers where they first began their lives, and as they return from their journey from the sea, we must quickly take upon our own voyage upon En che Wauna's wave. As we reach Wyam, we will stand with nets in hand and await the pish' rush through the Great Chute, and there, we will fill our nets as they hurdle the falls upon their return to their own villages distant waters.

We must be sure not to be left standing above emptied waters as the light of moon casts its last shadow across the river's course. The pish will continue their mad rush to the Hyas Snake and to the waters of the Hyas Salmon that both run fast and deep as they too await their masses.

125

It is a long journey to Wyam as the river runs fast against us, we will find ourselves taking our canoes from the river as we will be forced to carry our goods and portage for long distances upon the jagged rock that Pahto and Wy-East had once spewed from their troubled souls long ago. In celebration to life, we will find happiness even in our hardship.

We must arrive at Wyam before the Tenus Waum Muckamuck, (Spring Festival), begins. There will be many of our brothers and sisters from villages that sit upon the desert's floor, to those that rise upon the mountain's highest meadows that will be heard calling out in praise to the Hyas Tyee Tahmahnawis for his welcoming of their peoples prosperous stay upon his lands.

Many moons have passed since we last sat before the big fire at Wyam, and as I stand before all the elders and shed light from where Red Cloud had earlier cast its shadow upon the lands of our brothers, I will speak to what we have seen and heard from the mouths of Suyapee. What my brothers and I have witnessed will bring truth to the visions that our fathers had spoken for many season's past, and my message will tell of Suyapee as they come hard upon us in great numbers, and our lands will not be the same again when Otelagh rises from the far lands as the new season comes.

Our brothers will be quick to rise up from their seats before the fire's flame when we tell of the spirit's coats that were taken without thought or notice to how their souls and our own were connected to Hyas Tyee Tahmahnawis' lands.

As we tell of those tall ships Suyapee speaks that will arrive and rest upon the waters of the river, fear will enter into all our brother's hearts as mention of trade for our pelts with these new peoples will not set well with many of those that sit with us that night.

There have been visions shared from several medicine men's purses of our villages that told there would be many Suyapee that will walk across our lands, and they will take all that our lands offer to their own treasures. Our lives will be seen to lose meaning and reason without those spirits that we have found honorable to walk amongst us.

As I sit here along the shore of the river, I must question if trade will be good for our peoples if Suyapee takes all that the Good Spirits offer that keeps our spirits warm in the long winter nights?

With heads bowed, and with each hesitant step we take, our tears shall fall heavy from our eyes! I fear we will not see again our villages standing proudly upon the shores of En che Wauna as our spirits will be lost to the land.

I ask: "Will the Hyas Moolack and Mowitch still dance upon their meadow, and will Great Coyote still be heard to sing to the moon each night?"

"Will our peoples still carry within us the spirit of the land once we are taken from upon it?"

"Will the Dream Spirit rise up before us and still be seen to offer us our dream as we dance in the faint shadow of his steps?"

"When we awake in the morning when Otelagh rises above our village, will we still smile to the heaven and find happiness upon those trails we are then forced to take far from those that we had once been led?"

These questions, I must ask of our peoples as they sit alongside one another at the big fire...

They will not be pleased!

All my brothers will see through my words of the storm that rose up behind Suyapee's canoes, and as it took light and hope from the land, it offered only fear and terror to fill our hearts, and with great sorrow, our souls fell hard from within our chests!

Our souls were then held captive from our spirit as we were sorrowfully led upon the dark trail where we could not see our lands, and we were lost to our way as life as we knew it was then lost behind Suyapee's sullen trap.

Within me now, I feel loss and great sorrow, and I find myself lost upon the Hyas Tumtum's trails.

"What will happen to Wahclella and Elowah," I ask?

"What will happen to the pish that had once been seen to rest beneath Metlako's calling pool?"

"What will we hear of Multnomah's daughter's and Wahkeena's mourning wail?"

I wish I was standing high above upon the Dream Spirit's floor, and he would take me far from the dark scenes I am forced to envision today. I wish we would both be raised high up to the heaven, and free from the pestilence that will soon be drawn upon all our peoples.

I pray that we may find our spirits to soar far above the dark clouds that now rises above us as they raise question to our quest to survive amidst the coming storm.

The questions which rise up from within our hearts and brings sorrow to our souls plead for answer! May they be answered so we may once again find peace within our souls, and through the High Spirit's order, we will find ourselves kept safe and distant from the long arms of Suyapee's darkened Tsiatko.

I am not pleased!

Once we take upon our brother's sides along the high rocks above the channel that leads to the Great Chute, we will find favor in that our nets shall too become full with the Pish Spirit's offering.

At Wyam, we will each praise the Hyas Tumtum for what he has offered all our lives this past season, and we will make trade, and we will dance before the big fire through the night, and life will be good.

But my heart lies saddened as I am now forced to shed good words from the light of day and take our people upon the questionable trail to where light does not shine before the dark cloud that Suyapee came, and I must ask of them all;

"But what of tomorrow?"

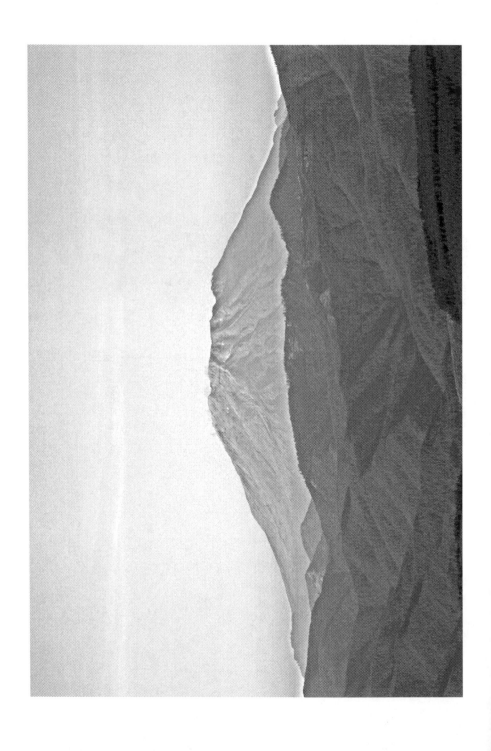

Steven Warnstaff

Chapter 12

Our Journey

As Otelagh is soon to take his daily walk across the trails of the heaven, we have taken our canoes that are laden with supplies to be pulled behind the three Cedar to the shore of En che Wauana. We begin to load baskets for the women, bows and quivers for the men, pelts to make clothes and packs, and many shells and clam from the big waters into the three brother's empty hulls.

Sun as begun to rise above us as the day grows long, and as we have completed to make ready our canoes for the long journey, the women bring to us smoked pish, elk, deer, and camas cake to be placed beneath the soft hides of deer to protect them from the hot sun as we begin.

In each of the family's canoes there are mats for sleeping, hides to keep them warm at night, our bows, our arrows that are held taut within their soft quivers, and we place nets, vines for rope, many weights, and long spears for fishing.

In my canoe is placed our village's great drum. Every village has a great drum that is covered with the sign that offers their peoples power and strength. There are those villages that gain power from the wings of eagles, as they are seen to fly across the bows of their drums. Others villages have honored upon them the long journey of the pish as they too are painted upon their sides as they are seen to jump high from within the waters of the river.

I have seen the cunning of Coyote welcomed upon a drum's frame, as the story shows she stalks her prey from the tall grass of the long meadow as Sun smiles down upon her from overhead.

A drum, I remember well from a village that rests along the still river of the Yakima, held both the feet of the Klale Lolo with its long claws, and the sharp claw of the Pishpish that hung upon its side, and they too added rhythm to the message our brothers wished to share before us as the braves sent song to the winds of the Chinook before the fire at Wyam.

Our peoples have honored the White Elk as it is his image seen promised upon our drum with long horn and white cape stretched across its frame. We have shared of Hyas Tkope Moolack's story as we have been told by our fathers for many seasons. He is known to run across the long meadows that lie high up upon the frozen slopes of Wy-East where we cannot see him, and this makes his spirit strong within the hearts of our people.

We have celebrated Tkope Moolack's approval of our stay upon the Land's of Wah, and as he has stood sharing of our eyes once again this season. His spirit is now seen to join with our own with new color and story upon our Great Drum. Upon the sides of our drum the story is told that he journeys into the lands of Wah from Wy-East, and upon his return into the high peaks above the Valley of the Eagle and from along the shores of En che Wauna where he had last been seen, it is now proven his spirit is still strong as it has been for many seasons.

Our village's people sit before Wyam's fire, and Pitokpl begins to set the scene of our village's successes the past seasons through the beats of our drum, Great White Elk will hear of his honorable place within our hearts. As the Great Drum resonates through all the lands and is swept through the breaths of Wind, it shall bring song to his ears as he stands proud upon the highest telecasit and peers down upon all his lands.

Once we gather to dance and celebrate before the large fire when darkness of night falls upon us, each of our villages will take their drums and spread them across the earthen floor where we are seated before the chiefs of each village that has come to celebrate.

As the spirit of the land swells within our own spirits, so does the rhythm of each drum beats faster. With each new beat, the volume rises to the air and shares happiness across the lands. We give thanks and wail to the High Spirit above as we share before them we are honored to share all the days he has given us. He has gifted us with good health and with good hunting. He has honored us with fish from the waters of En che Wauna as they are lain generously upon our tables throughout all the seasons. Hyas Tahmahnawis brings hope and faith upon us all as we look towards the light of our tomorrows. Life is good across all the lands of his peoples!

We must honor him as he has led our fathers through his teachings as they in turn have directed our lives through their own lessons by the Hyas Saghalie Tahmahnawis. We must prove of our faith to his powers as he offers us safe trails across our lands. We will praise him for all the teachings our Hyas Fathers have taught us as they have led us into the new seasons and have permitted our souls to be guarded from the mesahchie tahmahnawis' taking.

Hyas Saghalie Tahmahnawis will too be greatly pleased!

In every direction from where we sit, each village's song will be heard echoing from the cadence of their drum from the high cliffs behind the village of Wyam. Their song will be spread above the rocks at the Great Chute and attach themselves upon the breaths of Wind. Song will be cast great distance along the river to the peoples that have yet to sit beside us at the side of the great fire as they still are seen to journey through the badlands and down the waters of Kekemahke, (John Day River). Many more villages come from the Towarnehiooks, (Deschutes River), to join with us, and more arrive from above the valleys of the Lemoto Hyas Stone, (Goat Rocks), which are honored to hold the spirits of the Hyas Tkope Lemoto, (Great White Goats).

The announcement of the new season's celebration shall begin to call all those who do not sit beside us as its message travels within the Chinook Wind to those villages we cannot see. To all the peoples of every village that cannot take upon the long journey, our song shall quickly settle upon their ears, and they too will then join in life's celebration as their cries shall join those of our own.

Soon, as our voices are heard to rise up and gather upon the night's air, all the peoples of these lands and those that we have not seen shall become one with one another. Our messages will be sent to the village where our Great Fathers sit, and as they look down and smile upon our gathering, they too will join upon one another's sides before their villages fire, and it will be there they share of the potlatch and hear of our speech that brings honor to their memory.

Given the first call from Coyote as she begins to cross upon her lonely trails, the drums cadence will quickly envelope within our souls. As each drum's measure registers our individuality before all our brothers, our spirits will then bond together, and we will become as one nation below our Great Father's lead.

Our souls shall take lessons from one another's message, and as they are placed within our own spirit, we shall become stronger and wiser as we sit before the Hyas Saghalie Tahmahnawis' table.

Given our many journeys to the potlatch at Wyam, our souls have been invested with the wisdom cast forth from all our brother's messages as they were learned from the last visit we had taken beside them. As the drums of our villages pulse strongly within us, they each bring rise to our faith before our Hyas Saghalie Tahmahnawis as he leads us safely through life's travels.

Even though the dark cloud of uncertaincy arose upon us once Suyapee came upon our shores, we must be assured that our eyes glisten with the promise for all our tomorrows to shine kindly beneath Otelagh's welcoming beam. We must not lose faith that has led us safely upon the kingdom's trails where we each have found our journey.

I have now finished preparing the canoes for our voyage. I sit along the river and peer across the water as I take in all the good spirit has offered us. Though I sit distant from all that I see, I feel the bush and fern within my opened hands. I smell the flower and the scent of Cedar as it drifts before me. I hear the cry of the eagle to his mate as he soars high overhead as she rests with her young upon the tallest branch where she has built her nest. Pish are seen to leap high from the water's plane as they too are pleased to take the fly from the air.

Wind cleanses the air and offers the spray of the tumwata, (waterfalls), to wash over the lands, they cleanse my thoughts and take away my worries that had once, not so long ago, taken me to a place that I could not feel of my spirit.

From across En che Wauna, I hear my name called from the creek to the Eagle, and as I look towards where I had heard its message, I hear Metlako's voice rise up upon Wind. It is from the high cliff she beckons for me to join above her waters once again so we can share pish she has claimed below in her pool.

There is happiness and joy in all that our lands offer to us, and we should all be pleased to sit beside one another without thought of worry and complaint.

This is the way the Hyas Saghalie Tahmahnawis has chosen for us to follow in our lives. Free to invest our souls in all that surrounds us. As we give praise to the opened and offering hands of the spirits owning to the Earth, we should sit in silence and accept the reverance that takes our souls to the place where we dream. That special place where our own spirits will one day stand forever free above where we now sit in question.

As I look down to the water, at my feet, there, hopping from one

rock to another, a small bird dives into the fast waters and returns. From its eyes, the spirits have taken the tears of worry and concern, and in return, the good spirits have filled its heart with peace and joy. Unafraid, it dives deeper and returns, each time, showing favor in his catch that offers him freedom to live another day.

From beneath the waters he dives, I cannot see, but I know life exists even where darkness looms heavy and is taken from the light.

This is the message the High Spirit has offered me this day!

There is hope when we hold tight to our faith, and even as life appears to be taken whole from the light of day, one day, from that same darkened trail we are found to be left standing alone, we will once again emerge unscathed from the unknowing of today's tomorrow.

Life will continue, and life will survive!

We will also survive, as the Good Spirits shall hold us tight within their clasping hands as we walk out to where our souls had not yet ventured!

This message of life and honor must be taken before our brother's own vision at Wyam as we sit and speak of what is to approach beyond the distant horizon in our lives.

In its message lies our faith we will live through all those tomorrows where we had once questioned of Otelagh's return above us.

Our father's have each spoken we should honor all our brothers, and as we gather before our village's fires, we should each rise up in peaceful speech and tell to what disturbs our souls. As we discover new trails to follow in our lives, we will also discover closure to our worries before the bad spirit rises up from beneath the soils of our lands and takes those that join upon his side below to his darkened cave.

The dance of war has not been heard rising from our drums, or seen before the fires of our villages for many long days. Our fathers have shared that we must first learn of the new people's ways that walk in amongst us, and if we are to find ourselves to disagree, then we should take our complaint before their counsel and sit amongst them, and take from the table all that is good.

This is the way of the Hyas Saghalie Tahmahnawis as he leads our lives safely upon his trails. He has been heard to warn we must not venture far from upon them. He has spoken the darkness we have come to fear will fall dishearteningly within us and our souls shall be forever lost if we do not heed his warnings.

Life will then forever be lost to us as we walk blind and deaf to all that our Hyas Saghalie Tahmahnawis is!

We have told our mothers and our fathers the time has come for us to begin the long journey to the celebration. It is both in happiness and sadness that I see in all our eyes as we are driven from the shore and into the fast waters of En che Wauna. Soon we are nearing Che Che Optin, Beacon Rock, that stands tall and sees all that moves across the lands and upon the river's highest wave.

Here, we will place our oars within our canoes and pull them near the shore. The fast waters that breathe here hold much anger as they pass above the fallen sticks and rock of the tall mountains that once fallen from their high place as they filled En che Wauna's waters with their waste.

Here too is where we will have to first take from the river our canoes and portage across the rocky ground as we near the high cliffs. At this point is where once stood land where the trails of our fathers led our peoples safely across the river when they chose to walk to the villages of our brothers. Now, we cross silently upon the lands in respect. There are several villages, many brothers and sisters that lay beneath the waste spent from the broken back of Table Mountain, and as we bow our heads in their loss to us all, we can hear them each cry out as we pass solemnly above where their souls now plead to rest in peace beside their fathers above.

This was a time of great mourning when Table Mountain fell hard upon En che Wauna. Today, it brings great sorrow to our hearts as we step upon the land where they are entombed without soul as they are emptied of life, and it saddens me as their spirits are still held taut within them as they cannot be taken to the Saghalie Tahmahnawis' village upon their chosen star.

When rains fall heavy from dark cloud, it is not safe to follow upon the land beside the river's trail. This is when water mixes with loose soils that have fallen from the high peaks, and as they settle together within the hole left opened from the large rock that once stood half in and half out of the ground, mud quickly turns to sand.

Sadly, it had lain emptied to the Good Spirit's way, and chose to hold within its hidden lair the bad spirit' s wanting poach to all that walked across its beckoning trail.

It was a sad day for our village when a young brave from Two Fists family ran fast along the trail to our village as darkness swallowed light from the trail, and as he was discovered missing from their table that night, his family called out for the Good Spirit to lead him safely to their fire.

Great Coyote was heard to call out for the first time in many moons, and it was then we began to search for his trail through the long night. Each step brought memories of that fateful day when loud screams were heard punishing the lands as Table Mountain fell hard upon our peoples.

As Otelagh fell from behind the far peaks, we followed his tracks until they could not be seen. This was the last we would see of him until the new season comes when the floods of winter are taken from upon the lands of Wah.

Once Otelagh returned and rose high upon the trails of summer's journey, the waters were then taken from the sand and disappeared into the heaven above. The waters rose up to the High Spirit's cheeks, and Otelagh took them behind his dry eyes and waited to offer them upon the soils of the Earth when cloud did not form above our lands and was heard to cry out.

The sands were then changed by the Good Spirit's hand as the broken spirits of rock and tree were taken from the slopes where they had fallen. They were led down from their high place to the sacred spot where our peoples would stand solemnly before them, and here, they would be heard calling out the memory of Two Fists young son.

Two Fists son's spirit now sits upon the side of his grandfather, high up, where he can only fall without fear into the cloud's soft mat, and to where he chooses to lay and dream of the mowitch and moolack's play in the green meadow he sees below.

As he peers down upon us, we will see his spirit held taut upon the Hyas Tkope Moolack Tahmahnawis's mighty shoulders, and they shall be attached to one another for all the days, and they will be seen to run freely across the lands of Wah to where their spirits come together with the Hyas Tahmahnawis Wy-East.

And they too shall smile down upon us…

As we follow the river east we pass many villages of the Clahclellah, Cathlakahekit, Yehuh and Scaltalpe, and as we pass each one, they all come out to share of our long journey. Many of the chiefs I have known for many seasons, and it will be good to see them sit with me beside the fire and hear of the great hunts spoken by those whose villages do not sit along En che Wauna. Those brother's villages are seen to rise up from upon the earth where grass rises tall upon the long meadow where our brothers of the Shoshone and Sioux walk with buffalo.

Today, we have passed many long canoes of the Clatacut as they return to their village, and as they shout out to us in greeting, they raised high from within their long boats, the heads of the Hyas Stutchun so we could see the Good Spirit had taken them upon his side and offered them good catch.

Otelagh has grown long into the sky as he is soon to rest upon his soft bed, and as his last warmth is cast across our lands, we have come upon a small bay where the duck and swan are joined upon its waters under soft, golden light.

Shadows are cast upon the land as we reach the far side of the bay, and it is here that I have chosen to pull from the river our canoes, and tell my brothers and our sisters we will wait for Otelagh to rise from his bed before we join the waters of En che Wauna and begin our journey once again. With much hope and good fortune, we should reach our brother's of the Klemiaksac's village before light falls from the heaven above us.

As I lay here and dream, I see the Hyas Tkope Pish rise from the darkness of the Great River's waters and lead his brothers towards Hyas Pahto where once Pahto's bad spirits fell hard from within him and were quickly swept from the lands far below into the Big River.

It has long been told the White Salmon comes forth to the lands when the moon is full, as it is this night. The White Salmon, Tkope Skaddals, can be seen rising upon the waters of En che Wauna as she leads her brothers and sisters to the waters that come from below Pahto. Tkope Skaddals is seen as clear as the heavens upon a starry night as she swims fast and turns into the river where she was first born.

Soon the kingdom of Pahto will again breathe life into itself, and Salmon will offer new life to take hold within his kingdom. As the soils beneath his flattened crown become rich with Hyas Salmon's Spirit, they will offer great forests for the animals, and sweet huckleberries will grow thick upon their bush and be placed upon our tables with the cake of camas.

Otelagh rises slow in the heaven, and as we rise from our beds, we hear the call of crow as it flies above our camp. He screams loudly towards us with big eyes as he sees food lain upon our table, and with great effort, he demands his share.

Crow lands upon a long branch above our camp and sits restless as he begs, and as I turn to my youngest son, One Who Runs Like Horse, (Ikt Klaksta Hyak Cooley Ticky Kuitan), I tell him to take a scrap from the table and sit quietly as he places it before Crow upon the barren ground.

Crow peers down in silence from his perch watching all that moves within our camp. He judges if he can trust us not to take from his chest his good spirit, and at this, I must sit silently and smile as my son too waits patiently knowing not to why I have told him to wait for Crow to visit upon his side.

When Crow sees that we do not follow him with our eyes, he jumps from the high branch and settles closely to the ground.

Crow waits, still, unmoving, eyes darting from here to there, and back again as he watches all.

As a stiff breeze wiffles through the air, Crow spreads his wings and lands silently with soft wing at the foot of my son.

With questioning eyes, Crow peers deeply into my son's soul. I imagine my son too does to Crows, as Kuitan does not know of Crow's Good Spirit.

Crow still peers deep into Kuitan's eyes as he steps cautiously towards the scrap lain at his feet, and as Crow sees that my son does not move and his spirit is good, with long beak, he takes from upon the ground the scrap. As he raises up from his catch, he Screams!

My son quickly jumps to his feet and runs from our camp, not knowing what has happened to make Crow scream as he knew his own heart was good.

Kuitan became confused and feared that Crow did not find happiness in his offering. Crow then flew to the highest branch of the tree so Kuitan can see him again settled upon it, and in wait for another offering from his hand. But, as Kuitan does not return, Crow sits high upon his perch and is heard to his raucous laugh as only dust can be seen behind Kuitan's swift feet.

Kuitan has not learned of trusting the spirit of Mighty Crow, as it is he that leads us safely across all the trails that we are known to follow as he warns of the Klale Lolo and Pishpish when they come before the trails we are taken.

I too must laugh as Kuitan has again shown he can run fast as the horse, as he is not seen until I call out for him to enter into our canoe as we begin our day's long journey to the peoples of Klemiasac.

Once Kuitan comes out from where he hides and enters into our canoe, he looks towards me with wide and questioning eyes. As I laugh quietly to myself, I must question if he does not trust me too?

Otelagh has shined bright this morning and we have traveled far against the current of the river. We have arrived below our great chief, Wabish Illahee, who stands strong upon the mountain's wall, and where the White Salmon had chosen these waters to be his home. The day has been hard against the current of the river, and we now rest upon the rocky shore where our great chief cools his feet where two waters meet.

Long ago, when war came hard between Pahto and Wy-East, flood from Wy-East's troubled spirit fell hurried from the river of Dog and settled near where the village of Klemiaksac now sits.

For many days hot rock flowed from the high peak of Wy-East, and the waters of Dog and En che Wauna boiled and churned, and brought bad medicine to the air.

It was in that time Wabish Illahee came from within the rock where he is seen to sit as he tired of their battle and to the stink that was carried along the course of Wind to the Big Waters of the sea. He stepped from where the River of Wind meets those of En che Wauna. There, he quickly stepped between where Dog fell into En che Wauna, and he stood strong before Wy-East's flood as Wy-East challenged Pahto's spirit to take battle against him.

Wabish Illahee stepped deep into both the waters of En che Wauna and Dog, and as he made claim to the water's channels where he stood, from Wy- East's opened wound poured fire and then hot rock, and flood soon followed. Bad spirits flowed effortlessly from the high slopes of Wy-East and came down to touch En che Wauna's bed. Steam quickly filled the air with cloud, and the air we breathed was soon filled with bad odor.

As Wabish Illahee stood strong before Wy-East's flood, and drew cold waters to fall over the bad spirits, he cautioned Wy-East of his wish to enter into Pahto's lands where his bad spirit would start fire to the great forests that rose up beneath Pahto's plentiful kingdom.

With great effort, Wabish Illahee brought peace between Pahto and Wy- East, and he cooled the tepid waters of En che Wauna so the Pish of our river would once again swim past as they wished to jump the great falls and journey to their distant villages.

For many suns Otelagh sadly passed overhead as he saw En che Wauna steam with much agony as she was filled with thick ash, rock, and trees. As the sticks swam from Dog in great numbers and were thrown from their high place, they settled deep upon En che Wauna's bed.

En che Wauna cried out with much agony as she became furious as her waters did not flow fast from behind the dam of rock that had swollen upon her. All the trees and bush that stood proud beside her would soon turn brown and die. From the lands soil, life could not exist if breath was not blown into the Pish's young upon their mothers and fathers return to all the creeks and streams from where they had first come.

One day, as En che Wauna sat questioning the High Spirit to what she must do to clear her bed from Wy-East's unwanted approach, word was spread with loud voice to where Wabish Illahee rested. Again he rose up from his seat and began the journey to the entrance of Dog. As he stood in the middle of En che Wauna, he quickly became upset as he saw the waters of En che Wauna stilled behind the dam Wy-East's bad spirit had fastened.

Saddened at her loss, he then stepped down hard upon Wy-East's molten table that was set across En che Wauna's bed, and he released the bad spirit's souls to run free to the sea and wished for them to feel the sting of salt within their opened wounds.

Several seasons passed as great rains fell upon the lands of our enemies, the Paiute, and they filled the Towarnahiooks, Deschutes River, and the Kekemahke, John Day, rivers many times, and they swept clean En che Wauna's bed from Wy-East's molten poach.

The feud between Wy-East and Pahto was then settled as Wabish Illahee was heard to tell each of the brothers he would be seen always upon the high rock at the foot of Wind where he would watch over their lands with a keen and wary eye.

Once the land became settled and only the Chinook Wind could be heard crossing the valleys and peaks, life again appeared happily upon it. From upon the rock that Wabish Illahee came, his loud voice was heard to fall heavily across the lands of the Cascades as he stated to each, Wy-East and Pahto; "From this day, neither of you will approach En che Wauna's bed. The spirits you hold within you will fall silent for all days that Otelagh will look down upon you. If you choose to find quarrel between one another again, as I am the Guardian to En che Wauna, I will then step upon both your lands and they will become like the deserts. Sticks and bush will not be seen again, and all you both have been honored in your kingdoms will be forever withheld from your grasp."

"I will offer birds new forests where their nests can be free of your temper and storm."

"The animals will have new beds beneath strong trunks of mighty sticks where soft fern will lie thick across the forest's floors, and Otelagh will smile down upon them, and he will be blind to where you now stand."

"You will lose all you know, as all life will be free once again from the terror you have both chosen to spell upon them without thought of either yours or their tomorrows."

"The kingdoms to the south and north of your own will become rich in new life, and you will stand unnoticed, and emptied, of your soul."

"Tears from the Hyas Tumtum's eyes shall fall heavy each season upon your slopes, and as your shoulders drop to your knees from their place, they will leave only desolation and disease upon your lands, and life will not be seen again to walk or rise upon them."

"You both shall then be lain before the bad spirit's den, and lost to all those that would one day come before you and join in the celebration of your Good Spirit!"

These were the final words ever spoken by Wabish Illahee as we have not heard he has spoken since that day from our friends of those villages that sit near where he rests upon his chair. These words forced Wy-East and Pahto to join together and make talk at the big table for the final time, and their battle has not been drawn between their lands again. As Otelagh passes into the lands where he is thought to rest, darkness falls as Moon rises each night, and he smiles down upon them with great appreciation. Otelagh feels what comes from the brother's hearts is good, and as their hearts are given to their lands and to those spirits that walk without fear upon them, they have fulfilled the wish he had wanted of both brothers from the beginning, and he too is pleased...

Chapter 13

Rising Cloud

*We have celebrated for several days at the village of the
Klemiasac, and now the time is near for the pish to arrive once
again to our waters as the Hyas Eagles's begin to soar above En
che Wauna. We stand shoulder to shoulder in wait and challenge
one another to capture the first Pish to jump into our nets.*

*The pish' long journey shall bring their schools into our waters
and we will only take from the river what is needed for our
village. The pish are taken from our nets and passed to the
women upon the shore to clean, and then they are made ready to
be lain upon the long bows of stick to smoke.*

*All pish we take from the High Spirit's waters must either be cast
into the fire or placed upon our tables; they must never again
touch the waters from where they came. The Great Father has*

told we must not offer pish hearts to our dogs or they will be taken from us as the bad spirit enters within them. If our dogs are lost to our use, we will walk unprotected amongst our lands. Our lives will be in much jeopardy without their strong nose and loud warning of what lies unseen and ahead upon the trails we follow.

When I sit at the edge of our village fire, and the last light of day is cast down upon our gathering, I will raise my arms to the heaven where our Great Father is seated. Those that sit with me will join in my praise for these gifts that lay upon our plates, and as our wail to the Hyas Tahmahnawis rises up as wind and is cast from within us, our Great Father will certainly be pleased.

Each day we gather at the shore of En che Wauna the numbers of our catch will grow. It will not be long before our canoes will be filled for the long winter ahead. The air will be thick with smoke, and the smell of Cedar and pish will rise far into the lands of the high spirits above the Cascades.

The shelves of our longhouses will be full and we will outlast the ensuing winter's long storms as they fall heavy upon us. We will have much praise for the High Spirit as he has provided and given us great reward. It is a great day when we have taken from En che Wauna what she has offered. Our people will wail to the Hyas Tahmahnawis and dance, offering thanks for all he has given us. The night will be long with celebration.

As the sun of the new day arises, we once again walk to the river and join upon the shore of En che Wauna. As this day has risen above us in good favor, we will make our journey to our brothers at the Wisscopam and celebrate with them at their village of Necootimeigh.

Otleagh shall rise into the heaven with great pleasure as he shines down upon us when the Hyas Potlatch is to begin. There will be many from all the Hyas Tumtum's lands that will sit before the fires of Necootimeigh, they too will have traveled far before sitting at Wyam with us as we all share of our good journeys.

The day the pish call out our names, we will stand upon the high rock of the Great Chute. There will be many canoes seen coming from within the fast waters of the river to join those of us that have arrived. There will be many horse galloping beside En che Wauna's shores as those that come will announce their arrival as great clouds of dust will rise up to the heaven as it trails their swift hoof.

The Wind of En che Wauna will carry our song as we make ready to join one another and give thanks for our full nets. As we meet those we have not seen for many suns, we each will all be pleased with our return to the village to make trade.

Along En che Wauna's rush, we first pass our brothers of Simae Shop standing along the river as they await their call to the Great Chute. Our voices are raised high above the roar of the Big River as we pass, greeting the village people with open hands.

The rays of Otelagh shine down upon us and warm our souls to the morning's chilling breaths. We approach the island of Memulust, Memaloose, that rests quietly alone in En che Wauna's waters. The song of the High Spirit passing softly across the island's sacred lands can be heard settling the souls of our fathers. This is the land of good medicine, where many of our brothers of the Chinook, and several of those of the Yakima have chosen to place their people's remains upon these sacred grounds as they await their calling through the gates of the Village of the High Spirit.

Only the medicine men of our villages are allowed to step upon Memulust. It is only they who may ready the souls of our lost brothers for their long journey to the gates of the Hyas Saghalie Tahmahnawis. These keepers of the dead place our brothers' bodies to sit proudly upon the grounds as they look with blind eyes across the waters of En che Wauna. The keepers are heard to wail to the High Spirit as they work tirelessly in showing the High Spirit their souls are good and worthy of sitting in the long meadow of our father's village. Each of the medicine men ask that he look down approvingly upon those who have passed on the teachings of the land to those who wish to follow in the ways of the High Spirit. When the medicine men have completed their work, they rise up to walk to the shore where their canoes are lashed to the tree's long arms. Those same trees whose arms reach down to the ground and joins life and death together.

Passing slowly along the shore, we stand up from our canoes to look high up upon the hill of Memaloose. Our voice is held in silence as we look across to where our great leaders sit upon the peak of the land. My brothers and I can see those who have passed on into their spirit world, their bones resting proudly, draped in hides of elk and deer and surrounded in their new lodge by paintings of the animal spirits who had once walked amongst them. They each avail their spirit to be captured by the eyes of the Good Spirit so he shall know they have now found rest beneath their lodges of pole and strips of Cedar. Each of them awaiting their chosen star that will take them upon their final journey to the village of Hyas Tyee Saghalie Tahmahnawis.

Though we cannot see their eyes, we know they look across the waters and over the lands from where they took their first steps upon the trails of their lives. Those same trails where their hearts were drawn are now where their souls calmly rest. Soon, the Hyas Tahmahnawis will call out to each who is sitting and waiting *for their ride upon the back of Tkope Kuitan. Their spirits shall rise high above the lands of all our kingdoms as they look down and smile approvingly upon us. They will see we follow those same trails as they had once taken, and they will know their people, our people, have chosen the right trails. And they will be pleased...*

Just like our fathers, we, the new chiefs and shamans of our villages, will one day sit proudly upon the high peak of Memalust. As darkness falls upon our last days we spend upon our Illahee, we shall be seen to rise up from the soils of Memulust in spirit. Rising high into the heavens, our tour of the Illahee shall take us beyond, from those lands where our feet were set upon the treasured soils of the earth. We will sit proudly upon the Hyas Tahmahnawis' Tkope Kuitan, taken upon our ride across the great heaven's trails. We will be set free to live upon the high meadow where the brightly burning fires of the village are seen at night in the heaven as they are surrounded by those that believe in the Hyas Tahmahnawis teachings.

At the edge of the light of darkness, crossing the heaven upon the High Spirit's most notable white horse, with long mane and tail sweeping in the wind on his fast race to the High Spirit's gates, our own Spirit will be finally set free. Our souls will become connected to all those that sit before the long table before us as they welcome our spirit to rise up from within us.

Much joy will be shared as we meet at the eternal fire. We shall be pleased to once again sit beside our great fathers and hear of their wise words. They will speak of the new lands where our new village awaits our entrance through its hallowed gates. These are the lands where our spirits will be joined for all the suns and moons. Our spirits will not step into the unknowing where darkness wears heavily upon our souls.

We have celebrated with our brothers at their village as we have stood beside one another for several long days and cast our nets along the slow waters of the big river.

The pish' long journey shall bring their schools into our waters, and we will only take from the river enough pish that offer us life through winter's long storm. Those others will pass above the Great Chute and take upon their journey into those lands far from our own.

I wish for the head of my first pish to be placed before me when I return to take from the long table, as it offers great flavor to my meal.

As the bright light of day which promises hope in its shadow has been stolen from the mesahchie tahmahnawis' dark soul, it reminds me of the story that tells he wants to take from us all we have known to be good. He chooses to cast his spell upon us as the unknowing of darkness where he chooses to dwell casts question and doubt upon us for a new tomorrow where we may safely follow in our Hyas Tahmahnawis' steps.

The question of doubt that rises from within us stands unanswered, and we are heard to ask once again; "Where does the land of the dream that we have dreamt through the Dream Spirit's dance exist?"

"Where is the land our spirits shall one day be set free to journey across the heaven without fear? Where is the land our souls shall be seen to thrive distant from where we have found ourselves to have placed doubt as it lies heavy within our souls?"

Slowly we paddle along the big river's shore as we take in all that the Hyas Spirit has offered us to witness. From the bright color and sweet scent of wildflowers that rise thick upon the meadow's floor, to the high cliffs, where images of animals and spirits are visible upon the rock where their likeness gives weight to their need to walk amongst us all, we search.

As we pass slowly beneath them, it appears their faces turn towards us as we approach where they rest, and their eyes follow as we again take upon the river's wave and pass beyond their reach from where they watch.

We are each taken in our own vision as we walk beside those animals as we tour their land's many trails. Once their voices fall from the high cliffs and settle within our spirit, we are enabled to envision the stories they wish to share.

One night, as we are gathered before the village's fire, we shall all tell of where their spirits have taken our own, as it will be they who will teach us of their kingdom's many gifts.

From high above En che Wauna screams the Great Eagle as she silently glides across the trails of the heaven and peers down upon us with wide eyes.

She too knows of the great numbers of pish that will soon arrive before us, and she will take food for her young from the Big River. She shall teach them of their ways so they too will return with the new season. As they return above us in the Spring, they will offer the lands their majestic wing, and their soar upon the warm breaths of the Good Spirit will bring smiles upon all our faces.

As we look high into the great Firs, we see many Eagle, sitting quietly as they form thick lines upon the stick's long arms as their eyes pierce through the waters downriver. There they wait to drop from the tall trees with opened wing into the waters of En che Wauna to take pish from within her stream.

We, man and animal, can sense the time to honor the Great Spirit is near. We have all come far to sit where we now rest, and soon, rising from the darkened depths of the Big Waters, there will be silver and red to give color to the mighty river's channel.

Long lines of pish shall await their chance to jump the great falls, and their return journey to those waters where they had been given birth shall soon be drawn unto its completed cycle. They will breathe new breath into all life that thrives along the shores of those lands they have chosen to rest.

The kingdoms will again be rich and green, and they will shine brightly beneath crulean skies. Life shall be gifted by the High Spirit to once again flourish upon those lands as they will share of their joyous song upon the sweet breaths of the Chinook.

They each will offer haven to both the Grouse and Dove, and they will offer cover to the mushroom and to the new leaf and fern, and all the Earth's species shall renew their souls within the villages of their own kingdoms.

Upon those trails where we will be seen to walk, our High Spirit shall see we have honor through their teachings. As we follow in their ways and understand of their pleading to walk amongst all the forms of life in reverence as we take nothing more from upon the Earth than what we plead for our stay upon the High Spirit's lands, he will look down upon us with great respect. He will know we follow solidly behind his lead.

A new sun shall rise above us again, and where we have found hope, and have gained faith, and as kindness is attached to every form of our life's travels through our efforts, we shall be found in favor through all that is good, and in that goodness, life shall be forever known to be great!

As we look across En che Wauna to the river that comes from the snows of Pahto, there are lines of Eagles, spread from wing to wing tip. They are gathered thick upon the trees branch as they watch each movement within the river's narrowed channel. The mighty eagle ready themselves for the first streak of silver to rise up from deep beneath En che Wauna's depths.

There will be many eagle taking from the heaven Wind beneath their strong wing, and they will prove of their placement above all the lands of the Earth as they take from the waters of En che Wauna the first Salmon that rise from the depths above her soft bed.

It is an honor to witness the Great Bird Spirits soar above where we have gathered in wait as they too await their chance to clutch the Salmon within golden talons and sharp beak...

Their appearance in the sky brings much happiness within me, and it offers me hope that we both share of the same dream for tomorrow.

I have followed the Hyas Tahmahnawis' lessons, and our fathers have chosen for me to share them to all our peoples. For the remainder of my life I have sworn before them upon the Wall of Wahclella these lands will stay strong and vigorous beneath Otelagh's pass.

Through our understanding, first from the soil comes grass, and the bush that gives us berry will soon rise high above the floor of the meadow and protect it from Otelagh's bright ray. Then, as tree grows tall above the forest's floor, beautiful fern will be seen to sway in the morning's breeze beneath every corner of tree's long arms.

Each new season that shines bright above us will renew life's cycle as it breathes into itself, and life will again reappear upon the lands that once were deep in the coldest wards of the spirit's frozen breaths.

In our efforts to allow life to breathe freely into itself, much wealth and prosperity will attach itself to that life which exists within our kingdoms.

The Earth's species will be seen to journey across the lands knowing Otelagh will again rise upon the furthest horizon and shine down upon them.

As Otelagh places hope within all the Earth's species, their own tomorrows will rise above them with honor, and he will discover faith's strong will connected within us all.

We will begin to understand that even as the darkness of question lingers above our heads for many days as the dark cloud of Suyapee approaches our lands, happiness will find its stay within our souls. Our spirits will remain strong and understanding before all life's species that find their trails to cross upon our own.

The mighty eagle will be seen for many seasons to look down upon us with approval. If they do not take wing and fly quickly into another land far from our own, we will know we have chosen the right trails to lead our brothers.

The eagle will welcome us from high above En che Wauna's trail and from high above all the lands of the mighty Cascades.

Their opened wing will tell those who see their flight above our lands, our kingdom's spirits are free from pestilence and disease, and they too will cross our trails without worry and complaint.

As we pass slowly below the high cliffs that had offered host to vast forests of Fir, Maple, and Cedar, we have come upon a different land where is now seen to rise upon the open plains, the long arms of great Oak as they offer cool shade on warm days. Sailsticks, Cottonwoods sway peacefully in the calm breeze, and they each offer song to those that are fastened along the river's shore.

Coming forth from the darkness of the trees thick cover, many deer and elk gather in great numbers as they welcome us from along the ledges of the high cliffs where we silently pass beneath.

We see the mighty mountain goat has travelled far from upon the frozen shoulders of Pahto as he stands beside the horned sheep of the high desert. We hear the Hyas Pishpish that lies motionless upon the highest branch of her tree and lends Wind her soft voice.

Klale Lolo knows once Otelagh has journeyed many times across the heaven and has shared warmth and light to fall upon the mountains highest meadows, their long wait for the sweet flavor of the berry that will ripen thick upon its vine before winter comes will set them free. Klale Lolo will then cast himself across all the high peaks, and they will surrender themselves to those lands from where our Spirit's are first heard to speak from the Hyas Goat Rocks.

With the arrival of spring our souls are taken of this journey to Wyam. In each journey, we find ourselves standing before the high walls that lead to the kingdoms of the Chusattea, Klickitat River. It is from high cliffs, and from beneath many falls where loud voice is heard, and they make the calm waters of the Taptat, (Yakama River), welcomed beneath the village of their peoples.

It is here that our celebration begins as we join with all the animal spirits whom have come out to welcome us in excitement for the new season as it is drawn tightly within all our souls.

As many of our brothers are seen to ride fast across the lands which reach out to where the village of our brothers at Wyam sits and waits, the celebration of life shall soon bring happiness and hope amongst us. We will make trade, and we will share celebration with one another.

Man and animal, shall have cause and reason to celebrate the new season as Otelagh has once again spread warmth to the soils, and from the soil rises new life that reaches far into the heaven as they all give thanks for what they have been gifted.

Soon it will be time for all our nations to join upon one another's side and give thanks to the High Spirit, as he too will be pleased with all we have accepted to be surrounded through his vision.

As I lie here, the song of birds have begun to fall silent from where they have chosen their night's nest. Light escapes the last trails of the heaven above me, and it reaches effortlessly into where is soon to be heard the call of crow as he announces the new day as it is soon to rise...

I quickly lose my self as my heart takes upon the trails where the long tails of the High Spirit's great White Horse swiftly course across the sky. They each surrender themselves to the end of their long journeys as they spread far across the wide meadow that heaven holds where I cannot yet clearly see as it is far above from where I now rest.

As the Hyas Tahmahnawis' herd feeds upon the long grasses of their new villages, my soul finds calm through my vision as I find myself to join near their spirit. As I walk amongst the great herd, I know without fear and question, that light will be cast down upon us from the High Spirit's plateau. From within our souls, good will spread across all the lands, and it shall be offered before all those that walk into our villages and share of our fires as we pass the long pipe.

From that day when Suyapee first approached our shores, I have felt fear and question, and as I am unsure to what they bring hidden within their purse, I have sensed there will be great depression and sadness that will enter within us all. I fear our spirit will be lost within us for many days.

Even though Otelagh shall pass above our lands many times, and as he will be seen to smile down upon us with approval, it will be our fight from within our own souls to stay free from Suyapee's plea to take from us our spirit.

In my vision, I have seen Suyapee has learned of the traits of the snake, and they will hide in the long grass and wait to strike upon those unknowing of their silent stalk.

I fear once Otelagh has crossed the heavens for many seasons, and as many battles will have been fought across the lands of the Earth, Suyapee will one day rear back and plunge their long fangs deep within the Earth's soul, and swiftly, they will take from our lands (Mother Earth's) Naha Illahee's heart.

These are the same spirits that give balance between rock and water, between man and animal, and most of all, if these spirits are taken from us, their absence shall bring much worry upon us as they give balance between life, and death...

I have seen the sky above us that was once undisturbed and free from the dark smoke that has since settled upon all our horizons change. It now brings the scream of the Hyas Eagle upon us with great threat that he too is soon to escape these lands before the Red Cloud takes the vision of our lands from beneath him.

Angered with each rise of Otelagh, the land's mightiest bird spirits have begun to fade into the darkness where life does not exist, and as they each begin to fall from their high place across all our lands, we too shall feel of their loss and be taken of our spirit.

The dreadful spirit of the mesahchie tahmahnawis has now invested itself deep within Suyapee's soul as they have begun to demand we follow his lifeless trails that are swollen with disease and death. We must become aware to his immediate threat with much hurry.

Suyapee will take life's spirit from beneath the desert's floor and he will take life from beneath the highest peaks of our mountains. Suyapee will too take life from beneath the waves deepest depths in the sea.

As Suyapee touches the waters of En che Wauna, life will be taken from within her as her waters will soon lie stilled, and her spirited voice forever silenced from beneath where she was once heard to cry out in joy to those who were to stand upon the rock high above the Great Chute.

Suyapee will take and take from all the lands that stand proud today where life is happily attached across their every kingdom.

Through what remains, life shall be subjected one day to lie silent and unmoving below from where the bad spirit's lonely tomb awaits all those that have yet to surrender of their will to stave off the death of their own spirit.

The turmoil of our lives can be seen now thick within our skies as they have begun to fill with bad odor and can be seen heavy with the red haze of fire. It has begun to take life from us and challenge life that wishes to survive upon its lands with disease.

It has begun to manifest itself unyielding within all the many species of life that had once lived freely upon and above the Earth's soils. With much sadness, life today stands in question of tomorrow.

I am surrendered to my vision of what may come of our lands. I remember my father once telling me of the spirit of the Great Buffalo as it was told to him by the great Chief Katchinka, of the Shoshone that lives upon the high plains near the big falls.

As my father sat beside the Shoshone at Wyam, Chief Katchinka explained why the buffalo spirit had risen proudly above all other spirits as they gave their peoples much power over their lands.

The chief was heard to tell the buffalo and antelope were first painted upon their lodge's walls when winter fell hard upon them in the beginning. It is told they gave them hope as the new season came, and they would welcome the buffalo again upon the open plains where thick grass sways in warm winds.

Katchinka said; "As the buffalo journeyed across the open plains where their eyes meet each season, they breathe life into all our peoples through their gift."

As the chief stood up from his chair before the circle, he told those that listened, his peoples would appear strong and powerful before those they did not know as they entered upon their lands and sat before their fires as night fell upon them.

Katchinka told the buffalo brought much happiness to his peoples with their return to the high plains, and the Shoshone would live beyond what the season would offer from upon the Good Spirit's table as the buffalo gave them much.

"The free spirit of the buffalo was alike the sun", Katchinka was heard to say; "As Otelagh rises and travels far across the heaven each day, the spirit of the buffalo too follows the trail of Otelagh and roams freely beneath his warm hands as they feed on grasses that grow plentiful and thick upon the plains where Otelagh shines heartily upon them."

Katchinka continued as he shared of the influence the mighty buffalo posses on their people's lives. He spoke; "As our eyes were first cast upon the buffalo in the spring, and as we saw many buffalo standing from each horizon, we rode slowly amongst them as the swaying breaths of the Good Spirit's voice settled the herd as it blew softly across the golden grasses, and they did not run."

"It was then," Katchinka told; "At that moment, we understood, that both our spirits, man, and buffalo, were quickly joined to one another. We each stood proud and unmoving as we joined upon one another's sides, and we both knew that our peoples would only cull from the mighty herd those buffalo that had yet to rise up to lead their brothers and sisters across the open plains, and their herd would become stronger as their weak would be taken from them."

Katchinka told as their hunting parties followed the trails of the buffalo for many days without finding their spirited hoof, they had many times lost hope and faith within them. Katchinka told they had given up hope of discovering the buffalo's new village, and their spirits fell saddened within them.

Katchinka continued; "One day, as we rode to the highest hill upon our horse we saw great clouds of dust rise high into the heaven. We rode hard, and as we reached the peak of the highest telecasit of the prairie, we looked down across the open plain. There, far below where we sat high upon our horse, free to roam upon the open plain, we saw the great herd once again spread across the rich grasses."

We were quickly drawn to the strong forms of the buffalo below us. This allowed hope to rise up from within our souls, and our spirits were then again raised to the heaven in thanks to the High Spirit.

Life had once again offered trust within our hearts, and we were promised by the Good Spirit to see the rise of tomorrow's light above us as our peoples would be seen proud and in good standing before him.

We sat high up upon our horse and praised the Hyas Tahmahnawis for his gift. He had taken from our souls the darkness from where faith had easily escaped, and from where we had shown our long face. It was from this lonely place where faith had fallen hard upon our spirit, our long faces were not seen again."

Katchinka told; "Seeing the buffalo was like sharing the first and last light of day together as one!"

He said; "To know of the buffalo is like catching the first large Salmon of the new season in your nets, and it is like possessing the spirit of the Great Grizzly after a long hunt when it's last breath has expired as we all stand above him and share of his passing soul."

Katchinka told the mighty buffalo too shared the story of life as they walked amongst their lands and offered their warm coats upon his people's shoulders so they could survive the cold breaths of winter, and their meat and tongue would offer strength and great power to their being.

Through the vision shared from the table of the High Spirits, Katchinka tells that a dark cloud will form across the lands and one day the mighty herds of buffalo shall not be seen again to run free upon the open plains.

"Suyapee will come hard upon us both in great numbers, and from all directions," Katchinka tells.

The great chief continued to speak; "As Suyapee does not see our peoples find honor in their own selfish ways, Suyapee chooses not to hear the spoken word of the High Spirits though each breath that is shared from their lips as they carry wisdom and truth. Suyapee will without thought and regret first sacrifice the Hyas Spirit of the Great Buffalo from across all the kingdoms of their villages."

"The buffalo will quickly be thinned from our lands, and we too will one day be taken from those same lands and left to wander alongside the buffalo upon their most lonesome trails."

Katchinka tells that his peoples and many of our brothers will then be seen to sit high up upon the lands highest peak, and from there, they will be heard to wail as great tears fall heavily from within their eyes.

Flood will be seen to rise high up upon the lands, and everything they once knew, and everything they had once raised their arms towards in praise before the High Spirits will be lost forever beneath its most grievious wake!

Suyapee will take from us our wintered coats and leave the buffalo's souls beside our own to lie untended and frozen upon the lands as winters storms return hard across them.

The mighty buffalo will be taken far from what gave them spirit, as Suyapee shall choose for us each to lie bloodied and lonely upon the tall grasses that once were rich and free from their unapproachable disease."

With a tear in his eyes, my father told that Katchinka had then lowered his head, and with great force, and cried out in question,

"Why?"

My father told as they had sat and listened to Katchinka's vision, they too had lain their heads low before the Good Spirit, and each of those that sat before the great fire rose up from where they sat, and they too were heard to wail to the heaven alongside the Great Chief.

"WHY?"

My father then shared the question Katchinka had asked suddenly rose high up upon the winds and was quickly spread far beyond the kingdoms where we each had come. Then only silence filled the air, and the breath of life was taken from the spirit's voice, and it was easily stolen from our ears.

The silence felt as though the spirit's that walk across the earth had stood stilled before us, and they were frozen in the tracks from which they had once passionately led.

As their voice was not heard, there was emptiness spilled into the absence of air that we now dare to breathe!

Wind did not blow across the lands, and as silence was spelled upon the lips of the High Spirits, they were not heard to speak.

The sun and moon did not draw light to shine down upon us, and as we stood at the edge of heaven's darkened trail, the

Hyas Tkope Kuitan did not find its fast hoof upon the open meadows of the heaven. The unknowing of what was to come before us as we were challenged to take upon our next step created great concern to envelope within all our questioning souls.

The song of bird fell silent from their tree, and happiness did not exist. The call of Great Coyote was not heard to cry out from the valley below or from the high peaks above. It was like she too was taken to those frozen lands of the mountains where her mate had first lost his way and had not found his return.

From high above in the trails of the heaven was heard the final scream of the Mighty Eagle. As we looked to where its cry was heard, we saw, falling from where Otelagh crossed the skies each day, without feather, the lifeless souls of the eagle as their spirit too was stolen from within them.

From within that silenced drawn, life we once knew, did not then exist!"

My father shared all those that stood beside the Great Chief had taken of the same vision, and they all knew of how his spirit fell hard from his soul as his wail touched all those that had heard of his spirit's concern.

My father spoke; "In our confusion, we were then lost to our quest as we knew not to what trails our peoples would then choose to follow if Suyapee brought accusation that our peoples were lost to the good ways of the spirits."

Suyapee told those spirits we had gathered within our hearts were not good, and they would take hope and prosperity from within us."

My Father then shared that life would not be seen as it had been before! He told that darkness and ill health would come upon us, and all we once knew of the land and of its gifts would one day disappear beneath Suyapee's rising cloud.

"Life without deer and the Great White Elk, or life without the spirit of Hyas Tkope Lemolo, or the Hyas Tkope Pish brought great sorrow within us. This is the vision that Suyapee wishes for us to accept without question!"

"Suyapee chooses to take all we have protected throughout our lives from our purses so we are no more than the dried skin of snake that is soon to be unseen in the tall grass upon the High Spirit's lands."

"The dark cloud of Suyapee has now fallen heavily upon our spirit, and we must speak loudly if our voice is to be heard above our own surrender beneath their plunging fangs upon us."

"With course, we must follow the trails set forth before us by our past fathers so our peoples will still be welcomed upon the back of the Hyas Tkope Kuitan as it races for the fires of the village where our High Spirits sit."

"It is not our way to stand upon the side of the mesahchie tahmahnawis and lose our souls as our spirit is taken from within us as we are enslaved by the appalling directions of our enemies!"

I too must ask, "are we not better people than Suyapee if we plead for their understanding and do not draw arms against them even though they wish to take from us those spirits that we have come to accept and have learned to live peacefully alongside?"

"Are we not better peoples if we attempt to find resolution through peaceful talk in those differences that Suyapee cannot

see or accept before they demand we follow their trails as we find ourselves surviving upon lands we do not know of the Spirits that are held beneath the hardened soils?"

We once fled the lands across the great sea and have settled peacefully beneath the Hyas Saghalie Tahmahnawis. It is here, upon these lands, we have found peace and acceptance for all that we are surrounded.

Our peoples were once enslaved by those that took all we had earned in our labors, and as we were left to suffer through our grief, we narrowly escaped across the barren lands where water's freeze, and the sun does not shine with warmth upon the lands for many days.

Our souls were taken from us as we were like the vision spoken of the mighty buffalo without their winter's coat once the cold breaths of winter blew hard across the plains.

But here, the Hyas Saghalie Tahmahnawis has offered us life and free reign across his lands if we follow in his ways.

Here, along En che Wauna's shores, we are surrounded by the beauty of the kingdoms owning to the High Spirit. He has chosen for our peoples to accept through our father's lead and in the understanding of the High Spirit's lessons that peace and compassion quells the anger wrought through the silence of the darkened heart of the mesahchie tahmahnawis.

The bad spirit wishes to rise up before us and threaten war amongst all the peoples of this Illahee. As he brings death and sorrow to settle before all our doors, we must remain strong and vigilant against his many attacks upon us!

"This is not our way to kneel before those that are taken of the bad spirit," I scream!

I ask; "Why will Suyappe follow our every step and take from us all that we have found honorable below you?"

"I ask you Great Father; "Why do I see our peoples forced to walk far from those lands where we unselfishly hold out our long arms, in peace and in the hope it would bring good health to find its long stay within our souls?"

"As we have collected all that is good from within us, and offer to share our spirit before all the lands that we step, why have many days passed pleasingly above us as you have crossed the heaven's trails and smiled down upon us if our eviction is warranted from within the lands of your kingdom?"

I ask; "If our defeat by Suyapee's threat upon us is inevitable, why have you not led their souls to a land far from our own?"

"Have we not followed in your every directive, and have we not stepped where you have first stepped before us?"

I ask; "Were we not right to step within the footsteps where you first led our peoples?"

"Do we not share of your gifts with reverance and acceptance as you have directed?"

"I ask of you Hyas Tahmahnawis, what must we do to follow your enlightened path so our peoples can live peacefully and safely beneath the calling of Crow as he leads us from the evil spirits that are chosen beside the Illahee's many trails?"

As Crow attaches himself to the sky above us and cries out, we are awakened from our sleep as the first light of Otelagh is raised upon the slow waters of En che Wauna.

Once the fire's smoke rises high to the heaven, we join one another and offer thanks to Hyas Tahmahnawis as many pish from yesterday's catch is placed before us. We sit and talk, and I begin to speak of trade for several horse that will allow us to reach Wyam from the trail that follows the Big River.

I motion for Tsemitsk that sits at my side to go to the canoes and gather the Kloh Kloh, Oyster, smetocks, large clam, and Kamosuk, beads, and bring them before us so I can place them upon the soft pelts of the hyas salt chuck nawamuks, (ocean's otter), that I begin to spread out before the village's chief.

As Tsemitsk returns, those of the Necootemigh that sit with us look down at the gifts we bring to their table, and as their moans have quickly risen to the sky, I know they are pleased.

I ask the chief of the Necootimeigh if he agrees to make trade for all we have lain before him, and as he looks down at what we offer him for several of his strong herd, there is question to the number of horse we ask to make trade.

Chief Chemolish smiles towards me and speaks; "My brother that is called and speaks to KaKa, Raven. He who looks upon our lands with wide eyes, you ask for stotekin, eight, horse, and offer me only these lakit tahtlum, forty oyster and lakit tahtlum clam, and many beads I shall not wear."

"I tell you Raven, if you offer from your cache beneath the great elk skin, tahtlum, 10 more pelts, and if they are as soft as these that sit before me, we will each be pleased."

"Then, as we smoke from the long pipe we will walk to where our horse rest upon the meadow, and you will take from the herd the finest horse that stand in pasture wanting to be set free upon the trails that lead to the new season's celebration."

Chief Chemolish does not ask for as many pelts as I had first thought, as I sit and look towards him in disbelief that he does not ask for more than his horse would bring to the table, I quickly look down to the earth as I bow my head, and with low voice, agree.

Tsemitsk walks to the great canoe and takes 10 more nawamuks from our cache,. As Tsemitsk returns, he places them beside those others where Chief Chemolish reaches out to touch each one, and as he accepts those we offer with much happiness, he smiles towards all his brothers that sit with us.

I would have offered Chemolish ten more pelts if he chose to ask, and I too am pleased.

We will have those ten pelts to trade for much we need for winter than what we may have been forced to trade for the horse we will not take with us upon our return to our village.

As I sit and look towards our village I envision our mothers and fathers await anxiously for our return along the shores of the Big River, and as we make trade, we are nearer our return to their arms.

I too can hear the passion of princess Wehatpolitan cast upon the winds as she now rests with child held taught to her bosom on the Big Rock of Che Che Optin. Today, she can be heard of her wail as the wind blows through the rock of Che Che Optin at her side, and her father's call for her return will not lie silent once the winds are taken upon the rocks farthest wall.

We have travelled many days on the river, and to make trade for horse will be good as we will be strong and joyful as we ride upon the last trail which leads where we will take from En che Wauna many Salmon.

We will find much celebration in the games as the best hunters and horsemen will take upon their turn to prove their worthiness before all those that stand and witness of their efforts.

Many of our brothers will gaze towards those that choose to dance long into the night as we sit and smoke kinnik kinnik from the long pipe.

It is a time for celebration for life under the guiding hands of Hyas Tahmahnawis, and as Otelagh passes overhead and shines down upon us, we will raise our arms to the heaven and shout out that we, our peoples, are his, and his alone.

We choose to follow the trails from which the Good Spirit leads, as it is he that brings us good fortune in all that we do.

Chief Chemolish and I sit here at the side of the morning's fire and smoke from the long pipe as we settle our trade. We are pleased we both have to offer what we each ask.

The morning brings good fortune to all, and we are pleased!

As our trade has been sealed, I ask Mentstiko and Tsemitsk to take to the canoes all of which we bring to trade, our food, our nets and weights, and that Pitokpl and I shall quickly return as we take from Chief's Chemolish's herd those horse that will be strong and sure footed to carry our goods.

I assure them both we will pick the best from his herd that will find favor in their free reign upon the trail as we sit high up upon their backs and enter into the village at Wyam. We will be heard to shout out joyfully to our brothers; "Klohowya, may the celebration begin!"

As I had finished my speech, they both smiled as they remembered well the festivities that celebration brings.

Chief Chemolish leads us to the meadow that rests beside the village and points out to the horse he chooses for us to take. I see they are in good health and their legs strong as I run my hand down each one, and I agree.

The chief tells they have run hard along the shores of the river, and their mothers and fathers have climbed into many kingdoms where the great peaks rose high above the valleys as they were joined in the hunt for the Hyas siam itchwoot, (great grizzly).

He told they had last seen the brother of Hyas Tkope Moolack standing proud upon the far ridge as he looked down upon them as they journeyed through the kingdom where the mighty spirit of Mazama had once thrown out the bad spirits from within her disheartened soul.

I have heard from the elders as they were told by their elders, it was long ago when Hyas Mazama threw out the mesahchie tahmahnawis of Llao from beneath her.

Llao was seen to rise splintered into the heavens where the Good Spirit of Skell ruled, and as each season passed into the next, the kingdoms were then in unrest as the spirits battled above them.

Steve Warnstaff

Otelagh was not seen to rise upon the heaven's trails for many days. Each season passed in darkness, and he was seen held in the memory of our peoples behind winter's lasting storm. Otelagh had been taken from above the people, and the huckleberry and camas did not grow, pish were not seen to enter into En che Wauna as they gathered at her entrance where the great waters of the sea breaks upon the lands of the Clatsop.

As the battle between Llao and Skell continued for many seasons, great forests fell from upon their lands, and as the sounds of the Good Spirits fell silent, the Hyas Coyote's call too was not heard.

All the land's spirits were scattered beneath ash that rose up from the great plume above Mazama, and as it spread its waste upon all that breathed upon the lands, life suddenly fell silent beneath its wasteful poach.

Many of the Illahee's animals fell hard upon the ground, and they too were not to be heard again, and their call out to the Hyas

Tahmahnawis to return to their lands were only heard through their silenced thought.

Otelagh had been forced to take upon higher trails across the sky as great smoke rose upon him, and in his sorrow, his final words were heard to promise that he would shine down upon them one day soon, and would offer life to renew itself once more.

All that lived was burnt from their root beneath the soils, or they were cast into the hardness of stone as they lay beneath the hot breaths of the bad spirits as they fell upon them and took from them life.

Steam rose up from the waste left upon the barren grounds, and it was thought the bad spirits had spread bad magic upon them as he shook his stick above the lands as it was then lain emptied and barren beneath Mazama's perilous and heated storm.

We have heard of stories shared by the elders for many seasons of what they knew of the lands of Mazama. They have shared that as our peoples had long ago crossed the lands, they came to the village of Maklaks of the Klamath along the shores of the big lake.

Klamath told they had once, not long ago, seen the forests thick, and the lands plentiful with game, and the kingdom of Mazama had once shone bright with much promise.

As smoke rose thick from Mazama's plume, a great battle ensued. Many days passed as ash and fire swept across the heaven and settled upon the ground. As it spread fast across many kingdoms, darkness fell heavy upon them, and the peoples that lived beneath where the bad spirits fell were held in great sadness.

Skell was seen to chase Llao across many kingdoms in their battle, and as Llao's last warrior fell wounded and dying from the kingdom of Skell, not a single noise was heard as peace had once again settled across the land.

The people that had settled far from the lands of Mazama had not heard the loud voice of Mazama raised to the heaven as battle between the two spirits began, and they would think that day was calm and pleasing as Otelagh passed slowly overhead and brought warmth to the soils of the ground. But in the lands of Mazama, life had quickly been taken from upon the lands as fire and flood rose up from deep within Mazama's soul, and as they each gathered strength in their battle, they swarmed across the heavens of many kingdoms.

The absence of life had instantly created the emptiness of silence to spill upon deaf ears!

As I stand before the chief's herd, Wind has returned upon us, and I am awakened from my toughts. I look out over the lands and toward the kingdoms of the Cascades, it is from this place that I sense when we see the thick red cloud fall from the heaven and settle upon the soils of the earth, only misery and death will soon hold fastened upon all that Suyapee brings within his purse.

"Is this forewarning to the end of our life's long journey," I must ask?

"Is the red cloud that I have seen rise up as Suyapee comes upon us, the end of all we understand?"

Upon the trail of this journey, my mind has set me to ask the Hyas Tahmahnawis for direction, but as each question lies unanswered, my fear for what will become of our lands and to our peoples has swiftly taken hold of my thoughts as it has entered swiftly into my soul.

I sense through this vision's message, Suyapee will one day draw from their long sheath their sharpened blade upon us, and we will then lie humbled and unmoving beneath their hastened charge upon us.

I must ask myself why there cannot be land for us all, and why they cannot choose to live amongst us as our spirits are good?

As we do not wish the bad spirit's drum to be heard cast along their trails and ours, why do they demand that our peoples be seen before all others as the dried skin of shugh opoots, (rattle snake), as it lies unmoving and emptied of life in the tall grass?

If it were not for these visions that have risen from where I could not see, I would not think Suyappe would first choose to spread disease and death amongst us as he begins his long and demanding march through our lands.

I am challenged to look deep into my heart, where was hidden, behind the goodness of our faith, hope that now escapes our hearts as the long faces of our peoples are shown gathered in their own despair! From the purse that Suyapee carries comes bad medicine that has been promised amongst all those they do not care.

Suyapee are the bad spirit's braves that will soon come fast upon our people, and they will choose to make war before they speak of peace.

These peoples that follow in the ways of Suyapee are not held in the Good Spirit's hands. They have not stood before the Walls of Wahclella, and they have not heard the wise words our great fathers speak.

Suyapee are not our brothers!

Suyapee are the warriors of all the bad spirit's tribes that were thrown from the bellies of the Cascades.

There were many warriors spewed out from the depths of the high peaks, and as rock became ash, they splintered into many pieces and settled upon the lands as armies of the mesahchie tahmahnawis .

They were told if they were to take on the face of man as they offered gifts to those they approached, through their disguise, those peoples would then become easily confused as their lands would then be taken from them and it would be ruled by the hands of the bad spirit.

The bad spirits brothers were then promised they would be given new souls that would allow them to live beyond the final rising of Sun, and the dark ways of Tsiatko would return within them and permit them strength to live beyond that day.

They were told the Earth would soon become theirs once again, and they would journey across the lands without challenge. As they dealt misfortune to those they chose, they would be free from our Hyas Tahmahnawis' complaint as we would not be seen, nor would we be heard of our pleading voice.

Again, silence would fill the air across all the lands we had come to cherish, and our souls would be set upon the soil without life attached to our spirit. We would then be lost upon the trails we had been led, and we would lie scorned before all others to see through Tsiatko's most loathing and darkened heart.

As I stand here, with head bowed, I must ask myself; "Why has this vision come to reappear before my eyes?"

I ask; "Why cannot I walk across these lands and find happiness as the new season is upon us with the promise of good catch?"

My Hyas Tahmahnawis, I ask you why, and I plead before you, why not?

With red cloud comes promise of uncertainty and rebellion!

These are not words you led us to believe to be true and good.

I ask you Hyas Tahmahnawis, where will you lead us once Suyappe appears upon our lands and demands that what we have is now theirs?

Our villages are to be seen no more along the Big River as Suyapee will take from our forests the sticks from above us, and it would be those same sticks we wish to sit beneath as their rise into the heavens offered us repose from life's sudden storm.

Those trees which will be taken from upon the forest's floors had once offered shelter from the Cole Illahee's storm, and now, as the land lies emptied from their spirit, Otelagh's hot ray shines down upon the lands and takes breath from the souls of all the plants and animals, and soon, their spirit will be seen no more.

As they each fall heavy to the ground, we shall hear all of their longing cries spilled to the heaven's most lonesome trails.

The lands will become troubled as their spirits will be taken from them, and as they are taken from above us, we too will become distressed!

I ask you Hyas Tahmahnawis; "Where will you then lead us?"

I ask you Hyas Tahmahnawis; "Where will we go where there is heard the voice of stick that can teach us all of how the lands have prospered beneath their rise toward your village from the beginning of Otelagh's first pass across the heaven?"

I ask you Hyas Tahmahnawis; "Where will we go where the spirit of the Tkope Moolack will still run free across the lands and peer down upon us with approving and smiling eyes?"

I ask you Hyas Tahmahnawis; "What waters will you lead us where the Hyas Pish will return plentiful into our nets each season?"

Again, only the emptiness of silence stirred the stilled air about me!

As our Great Spirit stood uncertain to what comes tomorrow from behind red cloud's impending loom, I knew life would soon enter through the opened door where death awaits those who will soon take the trail of the bad spirits.

In their disguise, the chill of Tsiatko's soul will welcome them with wide smiles and with opened arms as his knife is thrust deep within them. Upon the day when our brothers fall back upon the Earth, their souls will not be seen to rest as their spirit will not rise before the gate of the Good Spirit's village!

Through the most harrowing place within my soul where I feel regret, and from where my sorrow is lastly spent, I cry out;

"Why?"

I called out to my younger brother Mesiko, and his two sons,
Olaptin and Pitinka, and as I pointed to the horse the chief and

I had agreed, I told them to take the horse to the canoes and tie them to the trees that stand near the shore of the river. As they passed by where the chief and I stood, I told them we would go to the forest and gather long sticks to tie behind the horse to carry what we bring to the celebration once they return to the fire of the village.

They each agreed, and the chief and I took upon the trail to the village. It was on this walk that I spoke of the visions I had been taken, and of the danger I saw Suyapee would soon bring swiftly upon us.

I told him in my vision I first saw the Hunipuitoka, family peoples hide as the Koa aga Itoka approached their village.

The peoples of the Humipuitoka, as would many other villages, would hide in fright for the safety of their families as the Koa aga Itoka came upon them from the trail of the badlands without warn.

When I was a young boy I was told by my great grandfather where the people's of the Paiute had first come. As my grandfather and I sat before the fire one night when calm was held taut to the lands, this is the story of Paiute that I had been taken to believe.

Long before we crossed the sea, there was the birth of a new land where life did not find their villages yet attached.

This was a land where tree, or plant, or pish were not found to live as great storm fell upon it for many seasons.

Rising far into the sky there were many peaks that spewed the bad spirits from within them. As storm settled over the lands, great floods of mud and ash washed down from the high peaks and swallowed all life beneath their rush upon the valleys.

All hope Otelagh had once wished for his gift of life to become attached to the lands had then become apparent they would be lost beneath the bad spirit's storm.

Many seasons passed. Life began to appear once again upon the land as solitude and quiet was offered to them as great storm was taken from their lands. Hope was then again seen as bush and tree began to appear from beneath its soils.

But in the absence of the Good Spirit's hand from above their rise, death was soon to follow as great rains again fell from the heaven and washed over the lands,. As their hold was loosened, they fell below to the valleys again and again until the valleys began to reach the high peaks of the mountains that had since risen upon the opposite cliffs from where they had first fallen.

As Otelagh passed unseen through thick cloud and smoke, the good spirits who had held tight to the promise of tomorrow were shaken as they fought with much effort, and they felt they would soon be led beneath to where the catacombs of the bad spirit's heart was promised to dwell.

There the Good Spirit's would sit unmoving as darkness fell upon them, and their spirit would be lost within them, and their souls taken by the bad spirit of Tsiatko.

Again, there would be many seasons to pass without storm rising from the bad spirit's hand, and life would once again find prosperity and mix freely upon its many trails.

But as rains were taken far from the land, and great mountains rose up from the west and stole cloud from above them, the land was then lain low beside the tall peaks.

The hot breaths of the bad spirits were then cast down upon the lands, and where rivers once flowed, now lay emptied of life.

This land, where fire first swept across the heavens from the depths of the bad spirit's highest telecasits, and where rain was stolen from the depths of the sea, and flood was spent upon the lands from high up upon the flanks of the peaks where the bad spirit's breathed, has now taken upon new disguise.

Where the lonely and desolate trail of the desert leads to the waters of En che Wauna, the spirits that dwell within the souls of Paiute come upon us with much threat and without promise.

They wish to spill our blood upon the soils of our lands, and as we lie dying and helpless before them, they will take from us all they wish.

This is a long and desolate trail that only they and the antelope would dare to choose, and from along this trail the Koa aga Itoka of the Paiute silently stalk our peoples as they come from the rocks high above the Wahpoos, Snake.

The Paiute wish to take many of our village's peoples from the shores of En che Wauna, and they will sell those that are strong as slaves to other nations that are spread across the lands where they are known to make journey.

The Koa aga Itoka have come many times to steal our women and horse, and we have seen in the pattern of their step they pursue the heels of the bad spirit as only dust from the soles of his feet are left upon the soils as he leads them swiftly across our lands.

It has been told one night, as the bad spirits first approached the villages of the Paiute peoples and sat before their warm fires, they had invested their dark souls within those of the village's warriors through loud cries.

The Paiute were told, if their peoples were to follow the teachings shared of the bad spirit's drum, they would then be led safely through the dark night for all the seasons that would rise before them from that day on.

The bad spirits promised of their safe return through the deep canyons of the desert, and they would offer them safe haven beneath the canyon's high walls and below the waters of the Snake. Once they passed within the bad spirit's dark cave, they would be led unnoticed by their enemies to the sacred lands of the mesahchie tahmahnawis and to the villages that rim the great river of the Snake.

As Otelagh began to rise from the horizon once their pact was agreed, Moon stole the light of day as she swept clear the light of Otelagh from the heaven. Suddenly, darkness swarmed across the lands. Darkness, as thick as a cloud of hornets whose nest was shaken upon the branch of their tree by the long arms of the mighty Lolo, it soon emptied the heavens of life.

The pact between the bad spirit and the Paiute was then forever sealed...

Warning was then lent to all the tribes as Wind fell hard from its high place as it swept across the lands. Message was told of the conference between the bad spirits and the Koa aga Itoka.

As each breath fell sadly upon our brother's ears, notice was given they had both joined as brothers beneath the rising of Moon. From the last breaths that Wind spilled upon them, message was sent the bad spirits and the Koa aga Itoka would gather together, and they would steal into the night to punish those who had been promised much from the Hyas Tahmahnawis' purse.

Many sticks from the forests were suddenly shaken from their hold upon their beds as they fell to the earth, and they were heard to wail with gravest mourning for their sacrifice from their brother's and sister's sides.

Warning was cast across all the lands the bad spirits had joined the soul of the Koa aga Itoka to their own, and they would from that day on be without spirit, and their name would from that day forward be known as Snake.

We would know of them as the Snake that lie in tall grass and hide without warning of their rattle as they wait to plunge long fangs into those that walk peacefully across the trails of their kingdoms.

Snake promises to take from our peoples our souls as they attack our villages, and they promise to leave only our spirits to wander aimlessly upon the lonely trails of our memories.

This is the way of Snake!

One day, as cloud rises from behind Snake's fast race to the shores of En Che Wauna, I have heard both the Yakama and Klickitat tell as the Snake carries within their souls the advent of threat, they will join together with many braves and await to strike with vengeance beyond that of which even the bad spirits and Snake could defend.

The Paiute are known to approach from along the shores of the Towarnahiooks, Deschutes River, or the Keke Mahke, John Day, or from the Atsasuube Huudukwai, Crooked River, where the red willow is taken to make beautiful baskets that carry the bulbs of the Bitterroot from the high peaks of the Ochoco.

These are the big waters from where the Snake choose to come upon us as they wish for blood to be spilled upon those of our villages.

As Snake steals into our lands along the tall grass of the river, the Yakama and Klickitat will sit high up upon the cliff, and as Snake rears up from the tall grass, they will surround them from their high place and set fire to the long grass where they had just sat. The Yakama and Klickitat will lead them to where their spirits cannot breathe. They will take from within the souls of the Paiute their bad spirit.

The Paiute knows of the new seasons celebration, for they were once welcomed inside our circle as we raised voice together to the High Spirits for the Salmon's return.

One night's celebration did not end peacefully as Otelagh rose up from his bed and brought light to the sky as many of our brothers joined in the longhouse as we smoked of the long pipe and spoke of the great hunts we had taken the past season.

As argument began between two braves, blood was soon spilled between a brother to the chief of the Nez Perz, and one of the Paiute who challenged him for Kotchanta, a beautiful woman from the Walla Walla the chief's brother had first shown interest.

The Paiute brave lay upon the earthen floor moaning, and his last breaths were quickly spent. The Paiute that gathered within our circle were then told to leave the lands of En che Wauna and not return as bad medicine had followed them to the celebration.

Many Paiute that sat about the fire were quick to stand with the promise of battle, but as their chief stood before them and spoke that he too agreed there was bad medicine in the air. Paiute picked their brother from upon the ground and quietly followed one another to where they had led their horse in the large meadow to rest into the night. The Koa aga Itoka quickly fled the celebration, their yells were pointed with hate to those that stood at the door of the longhouse as they promised that one day they would return.

Time passed without trouble or war between our peoples. Life was good, but dark cloud was about to fall heavy upon our brothers and their women from the Tygh village that journeyed to Wyam to join in celebration.

The Tygh were stalked from along the long trail, and suddenly, they were ambushed where En che Wauna meets Dog, (Hood River).

Their wives were taken from them, and their goods stolen, and many of the men killed and left bloodied upon the lonesome trail, and those that were wounded and captured were taken to be traded as slaves far away .

As Otelagh crossed the sky for many days, there was blood in the eyes of the warriors of our villages. My father told those that sat with him that night before the big fire, the war they wished would only bring sadness to their mother's doors, and their mother's wail to the Good Spirit once they were seen not to return before them would bring shame upon their family.

We were not warring peoples, and we were not taken to spill the blood of our brothers, but there were many young braves that gave thirst for revenge, and they did not hear the wise words spoken by my father.

Many braves wanting to make names before their fathers and the villages from where they came approached our fires at night. In silence, they first sat amongst us, and as those that came from the furthest villages approached, they spoke of revenge to many of the young braves of our village.

It has been told they preyed upon the souls of the young boys as they demanded they take their bows and quivers in their hands and join the Yakama and Klickitat on their hunt for those Pauite that had taken the peoples of the Tygh.

There was much talk they would bring those that took our brothers and sisters of the Tygh back to the shores of En che Wauna for all to see. There, at the shores of the Big River, they would be hung upon the broken branch of the Cottonwood without hair, and their spirits would be surrendered from within their souls as they would drift through the breaths of Wind to the deepest waters of the great sea.

Their spirit would then escape them, and they too would not rise to the great meadow upon the Hyas Tahmahnawis' Tkope Kuitan's back, and they would not be seen to enter the village where life is good, and where life would not be seen to ever end.

There was much talk between all the braves of our camp, but as my father spoke of the Good Spirit's wish that we do not take up arms in revenge, they heard of my father's wish. Their words fell silent, and word was not spoken again of the battle that would soon ensue.

But in their eyes, my father told he knew they would soon join the Klickitat and Yakima on the hunt, and they would seek their revenge beside their brothers.

Once the full moon rose into the heaven as the village slept, five of the warriors from our village gathered their bows and quivers and stole into the night as they took from our herd their horse. They rode off into the darkness of night along the trail of En che Wauna to join the party at Necootimeigh.

Otelagh rose up from his bed, and in the distance was heard the great drums of all the villages along En che Wauna as they spelled out the beginning of the great battle that was soon to rise up across the lands of the Snake.

Message was sent that many of their village's young braves had taken upon the sides of the Klickitat and Yakima, and they had begun their stalk for those responsible of their ambush in our lands.

My father told he had looked to the heaven for many days, and as his voice was lent to the Hyas Tahmahnawis' village, he asked their young sons and warriors would be offered safe passage across the Badlands. With much hope, they would be seen again welcomed within their villages with their souls untouched for what they were about to do.

My father said that dark cloud did not appear in the sky, and it was sign the Good Spirits had too joined within them, and their journey would be swift, and harm would not come before them.

Many days passed, and word was not spoken if their party had been seen to cross the grasslands of the high plain where the Antelope hide.

As Otelagh passed above us for two days, my father knew they would soon arrive at the entrance of the bad spirit's kingdom where life does not exist, and where the bad spirit of Tsiatko preys upon those that trespass across his most desolate and kingdom.

The Kekemahke, (John Day River), has not offered us safe journey upon her waters as the new season comes upon the lands with much hurry, and the river runs with much hurry.

The snows melt from the high peaks, and as it rushes down from its high place, my father has told travel would not be safe as many sticks would fall from their stand upon the shoulders of the highest peaks, and they would lay in trap beneath her strong waters for those that dared the bad spirits to take them to where light does not shine with promise.

When I was a young boy, I had jumped into En che Wauna. I was held beneath En che Wauna's current by the bad spirit that rose up from beneath her depths, and my breath was taken from me as the bad spirit pulled me beneath her quick currents.

I screamed, without voice, those that stood upon the shore unnoticed to my peril did not hear my cry for help, and only the spirit within me was able to release the bad spirit's hold from taking my soul.

As I climbed up upon the bank of the river, I sat questioning to what had taken me beneath En che Wauna's waters? I only answered to myself that the bad spirit had hoped to place me upon its table to satisfy his need to feast.

As I caught my breath, my grandfather stood over me and scolded me for my foolish play.

I remember him telling me that from where the white water's voice is raised above our own, I must not dare attempt to swim. My screams would rise silent upon Wind's race across the river's wave, and if I were to fall into the fast waters of her rush to the sea, I would be swept to where others cannot see, and my calls would fall silent upon deaf ears. Then I would be lost to my mother and father, to my grandmother and my grandfather for all their days.

We know the Yakama and Klickitat have followed the trail to the villages of the Snake that travels along the cut of the land from the plains of grasslands and across to the Badlands where the bad spirit waits. Danger would loom overhead from the cliffs crumbling edge. Our brothers would find themselves riding beneath towering walls of rock into the kingdom where Snake hides until the light of day is taken from the sky. It is then the Snake comes out to prey upon those that are unaware they are then stalked as they sleep.

My father feared, as did many of the elders that sat with him before the great fire the night the young braves came to gather, that once our brothers were to ride silently beneath the walls of the canyon they would fall victim to the wishes of the bad spirit as they entered into the darkness of the bad spirit's cave. It would be then they would not see Otelagh pass across the heaven again. They would then lie entombed beneath the earthen floor as rock from above would fall and choose their spirits dismembered from their souls within the bad spirit's most lonely tomb.

Then, certainly, the bad spirit of Tsiatko would be pleased as our brothers would be taken from their souls. The mesahchie tahmahnawis would hold taut to our brother's spirit, and they would become slaves to the misdeeds of Tsiatko as he wishes disorder upon all our peoples.

As each column marches behind one another and roars to the ground from upon the high wall, they each would sound out as the beat of the great drum of our village in warning. Each column would cry out in turn as message would be sent to the village of the Paiute and announce their enemies were near.

Those that escaped the falling rock would lose both the element of surprise to their attack upon the Paiute, and by the loss of many of their warriors, they would lend weakness to their grasp of their own souls once they charged into the Paiute's awaiting trap.

The bad spirit's tribe would take upon their horse with strong bows and sharpened points upon their straightest arrows, and they would wait to send hate upon our brothers from where they hide.

The Paiute would then set themselves free amongst our brothers and take all they brought to battle against them, and the Paiute would take from their heads their long hair. The Koa aga Itoka would be heard to laugh in their victorious rout alongside their new brother, Tsiatko.

Sadness would then fall upon all the kingdoms of En che Wauna, and those mothers whose sons were lost to the battle would be heard of their wail to Otelagh for many moons, and life would not be the same as before for many more.

This is what my father had said he found to fear as he sat before the village's fire in the silence of that night.

Many days passed without word of either the parties rout or victory, and uneasiness fell harshly upon the lands of En che Wauna.

Then, as Sun and Moon had travelled both across the heavens many times, came all those that took their revenge upon the Koa aga Tioka to the lands of their birth.

The good spirits were with our brothers, it was told, as they danced to the light of the full moon and asked for strength to be victorious in their battle. As each of our brothers and our mother's sons returned to the shores of En che Wauna, they stood beneath the broken limb of the hanging tree. Many of those villages had heard talk of their son's return and came to gather along the shore of En che Wauna. As their wails to the Good Spirit were heard cast out across the lands, they speared upon the broken limb the hair of the Koa aga Tioka they had taken prisoner.

From that day, talk of their battle did not rise from their tongue.

Peace was again settled within all our souls, and our spirits were lifted once again to the heaven.

And in silenced voice, we were each pleased!

Chapter 14

Kopa Nanitch Alki Kopa Shelokum of Tomolla

"To Look Into Looking Glass of Tomorrow"

It is a good day!

We have set our canoes upon the long sticks, and as the horse are readied for the day's ride ahead, we wish our brothers at Necootemeigh good fishing.

As we ride east from Necootimeigh to where the celebration awaits us, with good fortune, we will enter into Wyam as Otelagh sets upon the horizon.

The trail leads us across golden meadows and across many creeks that begin to give rise to the first Camas along their banks. As the new season brings warmth upon the soils of the lands the low meadows will soon turn blue as a great lake, and upon the slopes of the hill will be seen flower. The color of sun will stain the skies from below where they rise, and the land's table will be spread by Otelagh's most gifted and generous hand.

The women of many villages will walk through the fields and meadows for many days, and they will gather the root of camas for bread and the long leaf and willow for basket.

As my wife, (Gentle Breeze), Kwan Wind, rides beside me along the trail, I look to her many times, and she is seen to smile as she motions for me to look down to the ground towards each plant and to each flower that we pass.

I know it will be soon she asks we journey above Multnomah to the high meadows below the Hyas Larch, and there we will gather the grass and leaf of bear, and taste the sweet nectar of the star flower, tsiltsil tupso, that clings upon the lands of Wah in its many shadows.

I look across the big river and many villages have taken the trail to Tiakluit, Wishram. There is much dirt spread to the heaven behind the hoof of their horse as they hurry to place before others what they bring to trade.

Standing upon the rock above The Chute, many brothers wait anxiously for the first pish to rise before them.

Soon, there will be many villages gathered within Wyam, each set in circle to the village's longhouse as the great fire will burn through the day and night. Life will be busy as we will take upon the high rocks and place our nets where the river narrows between where they break, and the Salmon will jump high to reach what they cannot see.

The spirit of Salmon will be honored as our wails to the Hyas Tahmahnawis will rise higher than the roar of the Hyas Chute where we stand upon planks of cedar above the great tumwata.

We will take from the river those Salmon that wish to fill our shelves for the long winter. As our nets become full, we will, with swift feet, take them to the village, and with much rush, we will return again to fill our emptied nets.

We will fish until Otelagh does not shine down upon the lands, then as we return to our tables and make feast, the great drum of

Wyam will be heard to call out to all those who wish to dance the Dream Spirit's dance in celebration for our good catch before the big fire of the village.

We have taken upon the trail today for as long as it has taken Otelagh to begin to fall from his high place in the heaven. As I stop to look up to where Otelagh passes behind me in the sky, many Eagle have joined the trails of the heaven beneath soft cloud as they are now heard to cry out to the pish they follow with sharp eyes.

Many more eagle rise up from the trees and from upon the high cliff that line the big river as I look to where we had come, and as their majestic wings rise into the hot air and swarm into the land of cloud, they take from the sky, light.

Shadow of their forms fall dark across En che Wauna's waters as the rhythm of Wind is gathered beneath their feathered wing, and with each breath Hyas Chinook steals from the heaven, they are seen to rise and dive as they continue to circle high above.

Excitement has begun to fill the air as many of our brothers from along the river we have seen attached to the trails that lead to Wyam have stopped to look up to the heaven as the cry of Eagle is spread across the lands from above.

With sight of the mighty Eagle and their loud scream above us, we look to one another and smile as Wyam calls out our names to join those that stand upon the high rock.

I know, as I too have stood upon the high rocks in wait for the Hyas Chakchak to rise above our lands in great numbers, those

of the Wasco who see the dark cloud shall come with swift feet. They will take their place upon the cedar's plank, and make ready their nets to take from En che Wauna the first Salmon of the new season.

There will be great feast spread before us all this night. Celebration will bring all that is good from within us and we will be pleased!

I can hear them call out with loud voice from far away as the Salmon first comes to their waiting nets; "Hyas Tahmahnawis, Allow this Celebration to Begin!"

As the trail takes us from the long curve of the river, much smoke can be seen rising far off above the lands.

The scent of Cedar and Fir brought from afar downriver is strong as it burns hot in the great fire of the village.

Many brothers stand with opened arms raised to the trails of Otelagh from the high peak above Wyam as they give thanks to the High Spirit for what is to soon rise up and breathe life into all the spirits whose villages are welcomed upon the soils of his kingdoms.

With much excitement, my soul has surrendered itself to the approaching celebration that our village has yearned since we had last shared of its festival.

I stop and wait for my brother Tsemitan to ride up where I wait along the trail, and as we sit upon our horse we look down to where we have set our nets and spears. Our wanting to fish rises up from within us and we look to one another once more, as we both shout out to all who can hear; "May Our Celebration Soon Begin!"

My brother and I both know that soon it will be us together that stands proud above the great river and takes possession of En che Wauna's gifts, and with effort, we will return to our village with much bounty from our trade at Tiakluit.

Many days has passed over our lands as we have worked hard and journeyed into villages along the great river that we had not before sat. Our wives had gathered the berry, root and had taken many nuts to be placed beside them. The braves of our village were taken to the open waters of the great sea beside those braves of the villages we stayed, and it was there where we first hunted for the otter and seal, and good fortune came to our village.

We had been offered much as the Hyas Spirit had filled our table and our purse for many days.

We have stood upon the highest telecasit beside their memory and have looked into the looking glass where was offered vision to where we would be taken tomorrow upon the trails where the Good Spirit lead.

It was upon this very trail, I have always envisioned our peoples to journey. From the first day I stood before Wahclella, and had taken the message of his teachings within my soul, I knew one day would arrive when we would be known by all the villages as being the peoples who sees all that comes of tomorrow.

This night, as Otelagh has settled upon his bed and Moon has awakened from her sleep, we stand beside the brothers and sisters that came to dance the Dream Spirit's Dance beside us.

Through the vision of the Dream Spirit's Dance we would each discover that celebration brings good fortune to enter within our souls.

Otelagh has risen above us today as it has now for many seasons, and with faith drawn from the souls of the Good Spirits, we know Otelagh will again appear upon the distant horizon and shine bright above us. Tomorrow will come, and we will survive and outlast the bad spirits who are drawn to our souls.

In our free spirit, there may be cloud drawn before our question toward the paths that we often choose to follow, but with faith, the light of hope will bring Otelagh above us with respect. Otelagh will pledge that warmth from his smile will enter deep within our souls, and life will be good, and we will not be seen to surrender our good spirit before the wanting arms of Suyapee's Tsiatko.

Through all that I have seen and thought from that day when I stood with my brothers at Kwilluchini as Suyapee came before us, I am unsure how to address the issue before all those at the big fire at Wyam?

I sense there is bad in the spirit of Suyapee, but as I have faith and hope that they will understand our ways, they will find within their Good Spirit we each can live beside one another without fear.

I question myself now as we near the village and take our celebration to the High Spirit's trails. I ask myself where to begin the long journey of my thoughts to all those that sit with me in council?

I will tell them of Red Cloud!

Then I will tell them of those Pish that jumped from our nets and were cast down to the deep waters of En che Wauna and pushed to the depths of the bad spirit in the sea.

I will tell them of the skins of our spirits as they were piled high upon Suyapee's canoes!

I will tell them Suyapee told they were from a land like our own where the Raven and Great White Bear sits high upon the totems of their lands.

I will tell them Suyapee said they will return before us and make trade for many pelts as were those we made trade for at Tiakluit.

But if Suyapee comes with many men and trades for all the pelts of our animals, what will happen to the spirit of the land and to our own spirit if we cannot find warmth beneath their coats when winter's storm is cast down harshly upon us?

I ask; "What of our souls when our spirits are taken from upon our shoulders?"

I must remind them of the vision Chief Katchinka shared of the mighty buffalo as Suyapee will take their spirts from us, and we will then not be seen as we will be like the dried skin of opoots in the long grass.

As I stood before the Walls of Wahclella our great fathers told of seeing the good trails where all those we pass would go in peace upon their journeys.

I must ask, if those same trails are where Suyapee wants to take us on their own long journey?

Will Suyapee see our spirits are good as we stand beside them and lead them across the trails we have known for many seasons?

I do not have the answers to my question.

I have asked Hyas Tahmahnawis with opened thought so his lead will be the only trail I choose to lead my peoples away from our stray upon the Good Spirit's chosen trail.

I will sit in silence to this quest until the celebration brings question to what we see of tomorrow, and then I will stand and speak to what was and to what is, and to what may be to those tomorrows we have been chosen to dream through the dance of the Spirits.

May my heart be led by the Good Spirit, and may it not be led away from what is the trail that will settle our souls to what is soon to come before us through Red Cloud.

As we near Wyam the smell of fish rises up upon us and brings much happiness to our thoughts as we have come to the end of our long journey.

Golden light falls from the trail of Otelagh upon En che Wauna and quickly spreads the day's last ray upon those that rest within the village.

There is much to see and many brothers to visit, and as we enter into the village to make camp, to those we pass, we shout out; "Klahowa!"

It is like we have come home from where we had first begun our long journey.

We choose the far edge of the long meadow to make our camp, and as we ride through the village we see many brothers and sisters with whom we had sat the past season, and we each smile and wave to one another.

We are again amongst our brothers and sisters, and life is again great!

This is our village!

This is their village!

The air around us is thick with excitement!

Young braves thrust themselves upon the rock to look out over the great chute where pish are soon to come, and they call out to the Hyas Tumtum so he will bring their souls upon us in great numbers.

Women sit as they ready the pish to dry upon the long pole, and others make bread from nut and camas. Many peoples from many villages have arrived and have taken their place in our circle, and as their women take from their supplies the foods they have brought to place upon the table, there is much to share between us all.

The elders of our villages are seen to sit beneath the tree's cover to shade them from Wind that carries much dirt into the sky as they speak of what they have seen these past seasons. They tell of visions that bring both promise and great depression into their villages and to their people.

I have sat with the elders many times at our celebration, many questions rose up and were asked to those that sat beside us in our circle. Each season when we have sat together and spoke to what has been seen in our tomorrows, there is always one question that is asked of all as we speak of the Hyas Tahmahnawis and to the path he chooses for our peoples.

We each take from the table what will bring good before our lives, and we will leave upon the table for Wind to blow far from where we sit which would bring sorrow upon us and take us far from the path the Good Spirit wishes for us to accept without our question.

The celebration brings much happiness and joy to all as we sit amongst one another, and as stories are shared, there is much question to those that have dared to tell tales that could only be seen after we sit before the fire of the longhouse and smoke kinni kinnick from the long pipe.

Laughter soon rises up from where the elders sit as it fills the air throughout the village, and all the people's spirits are again renewed with one another.

We know when the elders are heard to laugh that life is good beneath Hyas Saghalie Tahmahnawis' trail.

Tsemitan and myself take our canoes from the poles that are tied behind the horse and place them at the side of where we will make camp. Each canoe holds many goods and tools we will take across the river and make trade, and these we take from the canoe and set beneath the great robes we bring of the Moolack and Mowitch to trade for the hide of Buffalo.

The baskets our wives had fashioned from the reed of lakes and streams are placed where all can see as they walk by our camp. Our wives are proud as they have weaved the pictures of our lands with colored vine into their design, and they know they will bring much in trade for maize and roots, as well for the fine needle of the porcupine and for the tongue of buffalo.

There are those who will walk among us and smile, and when we do not return to our camp from the high rock, they will take what they wish and leave nothing. We will keep guard through the day and night of what we bring, as I remember the night when loud screams were heard from the wife of a Umatilla as her best robes had been stolen during the day when all were busy with fishing and preparing them for drying.

The young brave of the Tenino that was caught hiding in the high cliff above the village was seen trying to make trade with the son of a Topenish warrior for a long spear. As the boy of the Topenish heard the scream of the Umatilla woman and was told what had been taken from their cache, the young brave came from the cliff and pointed to where the Tenino brave hid.

With much excitement, the braves of the Umatilla gathered below the cliff and the Tenino youth was brought down to the village and forced to stand before all the elders.

As the Tenino stood dishonored before all the elders of the village with head bowed, he was told he would be remembered as a thief for all the days of his life, and he must not join the celebration of the new season as he was not worthy of celebration. He was not welcomed to the village again, and if he were seen near Wyam or Tiakluit, he would be known as the enemy and attacked for he was now brothers of the Snake and promised to the dark soul of Tsiatko.

The young boy did not have to be told what would become of his soul as the peoples of the Wasco held strong to their beliefs that thieves were no better than the bad spirit of the Pishpish, and their souls were welcomed to the sharp point of the spear and arrow.

The young brave was thrown from the village without horse and food, and has not been seen near Wyam from that day.

It is good that he does not come again before us, as we would throw him into the great chute. Stuchen would be served the

Tenino's soul upon their tables from the bed of En che Wauna, and his name would never be heard called out again.

Darkness has begun to fall from the sky and lies thick across the land as Hyas Coyote calls out from the high cliff above the village.

The full moon has again come up from the horizon, and as it shines bright upon the high cliff, Hyas Talupus is seen with head raised to the heavens, and she again cries out.

Each season, as the moon rises from behind the Big Rock above Wyam the first night of celebration, Hyas Coyote only appears upon the cliff above the village. There is told she has been seen for many seasons, and upon Talupus' arrival above our camp she brings celebration as she too has survived the long winter's storms and wishes to celebrate above our gathering through her call.

I have stolen into the night and climbed up to the ledge of the cliff and placed offering for her safe journey across our kingdoms many times, and as Moon rises from the lands of the Shoshone, I climb to where I had placed offering upon the ground for her taking. Each time she comes from behind the big rock, with the paw of her foot, she makes sign of both Sun and Moon as she draws both her and I into our union for all days.

I feel she too is an important part of our celebration, and her place beside me shall always be welcomed. It is Coyote that brings hope and faith to my heart that tomorrow's sun will too rise above the lands we travel and bring prosperity to both our peoples.

The fires of each camp brings much light to the village, and as the feast is soon to end, the peoples of each village take their

Great Drums from where they had lain and begin to space them throughout the village.

Soon, the Spirit Dance will begin, and each village will find themselves taking their place upon the earthen floor before the village's great fire. As we join one another in our dance honoring all we have been honored, we will be seen to raise our arms and bow our heads as we dance within the circle that brings the strength of our souls to join with one anothers. As we stomp the earthen floor beneath our feet, we will find celebration for all that our father, Hyas Otelagh, has offered upon our tables throughout the past season.

This is our celebration as the first Salmon rise up from the depths of En che Wauna, and for the return of the new season as it brings warmth to the lands and the flower's sweet scent as it rises to the heaven.

Celebration is when we see the deer and elk bring their young to the meadow and prove their souls are strong, and their spirits free.

My own celebration brings all these to bare before the High Spirit as I thank him for all he has offered me, and then I find myself to want to sit with Hyas Coyote as we both are drawn to the rising moon of the night.

I call out to all my peoples of my village that has taken upon the journey to join with me at the edge of our camp, and as we are gathered together, I tell them we are to dance together and lead those that sit before us through all we have witnessed this past season so they too will share of our joys and of our sorrows.

We will tell of the cloud that rose up and took light from the sky, and from behind its darken cast came Suyapee. As we step into the circle as we raise our arms and cover our heads, they will know of Red Cloud. We will tell of Suyapee and to all those spirits he had taken from our lands without first hearing of their voice and knowing of their souls.

We will dance the dance of the Deer Spirit as we rake the heavens with our horn, and as we leap high from upon the stage within the circle of those we are surrounded, we will share how we were taken to the Hyas Saghalie Tahmahnawis' village above the lands of this Earth. We will look down upon those that do not believe the High Spirit has told who are soon to be taken from us as they will be led to walk without soul and without spirit upon trails that have no beginnings, and have no endings.

We will dance to the spirit of the Hyas Lolo that had fallen into our trap, and it is upon the fur from his back we will sit when the elders rise up to speak of all that is good, and to all that is bad across our kingdoms.

"Tsemitan, when it is time for me to rise before all the village and tell of what we have seen at Kwilluchini alongside our brothers of the Kathlamet. I wish for you to take upon my side as you are the witness to what many will not believe, and through our vision to what we have seen, they will know that it is the truth."

I am excited as our ceremony awaits us with opened arms as we sit before Wyam's great fire.

Many elders had rose up before the village and spoke of their trials the High Spirit had challenged them as they journeyed across the lands.

Chatsten, of the Nez Perz stood first before us, and as he began, he told of how the winter's storms had brought much snow to the high peaks of the Salmon. He told of thick cloud that settled in the heavens as they were seen to dance from the lowest meadows to the highest peaks for many days, and he told how they carried the cold breaths that brought winter's storm to fall harshly upon them as the voice of Wind was heard to cry out.

"One day," Chatsen stated; "From the valley that rested beneath the sharp peaks was first heard the rush of snow and ice from above, then, suddenly crashing down it took the light from the sky and all the land became dark. We could only hear the cries of the sticks as they fell hard from where they had last stood as they wailed to the heavens, and soon, only the silence of death was heard to rise up from upon the white blanket that was then lain frozen at the foot of our village.

Chatsten told after a few days of the great avalanche the weather was warmed by Sun, and a great flood coursed across the land as much snow and ice was sent from the long valley and was heard of its maddening rush across the lands. As tree, and rock had risen from their beds, they were each swiftly swallowed beneath the waters which could not be held behind the banks of the valley's floors closed hands.

Chatsten then told with sad voice; "Flood took the land's soul from within it as this was the long valley where great herds of Moolack and Mowitch gathered to find shelter and grass. As we looked over to the high meadow, with much sadness, there was nothing left. No trees, no rock, no life stirred upon the fast waters, and soon, we had gathered our peoples and escaped across the valley to find shelter from the storm.

We can only imagine the fear the mighty herds felt as they stood bewildered to what was to come. They had not time to know what trail they could follow in their escape."

As silence then fell across Chatsten's stage, he told how the mighty herds had been swallowed by the bad spirit as he took from them their soul, and now, their spirits lay entrapped within the soils of the bad spirit's tomb.

But even though Chatsen's face proved of great sorrow, he told from the high peak, alone, stood the Hyas Tkope Moolack, strong and proud as he overlooked his lands and the loss of his brothers.

As Hyas Tkope Moolack saw sadness in the faces of the peoples as they climbed up to where his herds had once been seen, he called down to them. From his high place above the village, he promised as winter's storm was raised from where it has since passed, that he would bring his family to settle in their kingdom, and all that was, will then be again.

Chatsten then told how it brought happiness to spread amongst his village, and that through bad came good as their faith brought the Hyas Otelagh to shine down upon them with great favor.

Many elders had taken their place upon the stage as they were chosen to stand before all that listened, and my name was soon called for me to rise up before them and speak.

"Klahowya, My Brothers…

"This is the night I have dreaded to share with you all, as the message my brother and I are to bring before you does not shine bright with either the good or bad of the Good Spirit's thoughts. The Good Spirit has not shown to what direction we must follow when the dark soul of Suyapee's Tsiatko comes before us. I have asked for their guidance to what troubles my toughts, and yet they stand silent and allow me to believe they too do not know what is soon to come before our peoples."

"I fear, with all the trails that we have followed through the Good Spirit's lead, this one single moment, if you choose to call the vision we were taken to be nothing more than what comes today and is not seen tomorrow, will too take light from us."

"I fear as does my brother, Tsemitan, as he and I both stood with Chief Tsutho of the Kathlamet as we witnessed Red Cloud rise up from upon En che Wauna where Suyapee came behind its screen."

"In my vision, my brothers, I fear the approach of Suyapee will lead us onto dark trails where we will not be able to find our way to emerge from his question."

"We may all be lost upon the trails we have always taken across our lands. I know once Suyapee comes with many more of his peoples their eyes will grow wide and they will first offer us little, and then, one day, they will begin to take all that is good we cherish within our souls from us and lead us into lands whose spirits lie stilled and silent beneath the driest of soils."

"Suyapee tells that many more of his peoples will come upon us from their villages as they will arrive in tall ships from the sea. It has been said they will enter the waters En che Wauna, and they will step into our kingdoms and walk the same trails as we as they share our respect for the lands as they too are led by the guiding hand of Hyas Tahamahnawis."

There is much commotion as those that sit with us in the longhouse hear my soul is worried as our spirits may not be seen again to walk the trails that lead us to where our spirits are seen to run free beneath the Great Spirit's village.

I stand patiently and wait for the noise to fall silent from our peoples before I take them upon the long journey my brother and I had sadly seen approach our kingdoms.

I see much worry in the faces of the peoples as they begin to become conscious to the significance of that same vision Tsemitan and I had journeyed as we peered long into the looking glass into all the tomorrows that may or may not rise above our lands.

"My brothers, I have sat upon En che Wauna's shores many times and have seen these Suyapee steal into the night with painted faces that hide the eyes of the bad spirit beneath them. As they come upon us as we sleep, they will take all that we have and all that we know from within our souls."

I ask you; "Where then will our spirits be treasured to walk free across our kingdoms without fear to walk into a land where is seen only the absence of life upon it?"

"Will we be those souls whose spirits walk upon trails with no beginnings and no endings?"

"I have stood before the Walls of Wahclella and have spoken to our Great Fathers who gather proudly upon them as they bring counsel before us. They tell of trails our peoples must follow so we can survive amongst all the spirits that walk upon those same trails we too find our way."

"As I knelt before them at Wahclella, I asked what path would they propose we follow so we both, Suyapee and our peoples, could exist without fear of losing the lands we know today to be free in the spirit of all that lives beneath Otelagh's warm hands each day?"

"I stood before our Hyas Fathers and waited for answer in silence, and in that silence, there was heard nothing but the silence of emptied thought..."

"Our fathers too did not know what was to come though they had spoken of Suyapee for many seasons before I stood before them that day."

"I have been told by my grandfather, Nenamooks, as he stood before the Wall at Wahclella he had been warned Suyapee would one day arrive before us, and we must not draw arms before them as they will come upon us with many of their own villages and take from us our souls and lay us emptied of our spirit."

"My brothers, I have heard one day as I sat upon the peak of Larch, once Suyapee comes and makes trade we should keep peace between us as we will then begin to know to what they will bring to the lands and villages of our peoples. We must wait until we are sure if their spirit is good or if it is bad before we decide!"

"We must know of Suyapee first and to where their strengths and weakness are before we judge their souls and take their spirits from them if they are led by the bad spirit's call."

"If we choose to make trade for the pelts of the beaver and mink, of the deer and elk, or the bear and moose as Suyapee wishes, we must not be sworn to greed, as there will be nothing left upon our lands to save for our own spirit."

"There will not be the call of Coyote to sing to us each night. There will not be the call of elk in the meadow as he cares for his cow, and there will not be seen in the trails of the heavens, the mighty Eagle. She will be seen to dive beneath the waters of En che Wauna and not find pish that once came to her waters. The Hyas Chakchak will too be taken from above us as there will be no food for their young."

"My brothers, if all the spirits that walk amongst us are seen no more upon our lands or in our waters once Suyapee makes trade for all that our kingdoms bare, where will we then go, I ask you?"

"Where will we then go where we may find food and bring happiness to our souls so our spirits are still strong in the teachings of the Hyas Tahmahnawis Tyee?"

"My brothers, if we are to survive amongst these new peoples who will soon come upon us, through my visions, we each must be wise to their ways as we hold strong to our spirit. We must not offer them our lands, but offer to lead them across our lands where they will not be seen again."

"If our spirit is good, then with the hand of Hyas Saghalie Tahmahnawis held firmly above us in all we do to follow upon the path he leads, our spirits will be held safe within our souls!"

Again, there is much question from those that have yet been taken upon our journey, and as I stand with my brother, we hear both, panic and storm!

"My Brothers, there are those that still find doubt in our words. I know, it will be those few that rise from their beds as Otelagh's smile will not be seen to shed warmth across the lands, and they will see nothing they had once known to exist before their longing eyes!

"My Brothers, in your sadness will fall hope from within you. In the loss of hope, faith will be taken from within your soul. In your sorrow, your Spirit will find itself standing alone upon that lonely trail that has been promised to have no beginning, and has no endings!"

As silence then filled the longhouse, I knew then our vision had been heard by all those that sit and hear of our message as we stand before them this night. I know what we have seen through the Looking Glass into all the tomorrows of our lives are now in much question!

From the rear of the Longhouse, coming from the darkness into the light of the fire, rose up Ksitilo, the messenger of the Chehalis I had spoken with at Kathlamet. As he too had heard the unrest of those that sat before us, he knew they must hear the vision from many so that many will become believers into what may be seen of our tomorrows.

Ksitilo stands at the edge of the stage near where my brother and I stand, and I asked him to join with us as he too knew of the vision, and had seen of the Red Cloud from behind where Suyapee came.

Ksitilo stood proud before all those sat before him, and he too called out to those that looked upon him for the first time; "Klahowya."

"My Chief, and honorable father, Kwillikum, has asked me to take upon the waters of the great river and join here at the side of Raven. My father is old and cannot take upon the long journey again, so I stand here beside my friends as I have seen the rise of Red Cloud and those Suyapee that came from behind its dark mask."

"I have taken upon this voyage from where the water's of the sea meets those of the river where my people's village sits, so you can hear my words of what I too have seen."

"As I have sat here in the circle drawn upon the floor, I have listened to the quarrel between you. You ask if this vision is to be

229

the truth, and as I know the truth, I must stand before you and tell you I too had seen the Red Cloud lowered to the plane of the river from the heaven's trails."

"I must tell you I have seen the bad spirit of Tsiatko's Suyapee come upon us from behind its bloodied and painted face. It was not good!"

"As Red Cloud rose up, light did not fall upon us as darkness spilled across all the lands."

"Pish did not jump happily into our nets, but were thrown from them as Red Cloud rose up before us!"

"There were brothers of the Cathlamet that took from Suyapee's canoes many furs, and as Suyapee became angry and swore of their revenge, they suddenly chose to journey in their return to their lands as warning from Raven, and the voice of those spirits Suyapee had culled from the lands spoke of why. Suyapee took upon En che Wauna's wave in fear of our kingdoms strong spirit, and as his canoe was seen to turn at the bend of the river, Red Cloud rose up from where we stood, and followed Suyapee towards the great sea."

"I tell you all, as Red Cloud passed from our lands, the light of Otelagh shone down bright with much promise. Deer and elk, the fox and squirrel, the blue jay and the crow, all came from where they had to chosen to hide. They gathered in great numbers at the bank of En che Wauna's stream as Wind gave song upon the trails of the heaven."

"I too ask you, is the trail where Suyapee came the trail where the Good Spirits had once told they would lead if we were to place within their hands our own, and we must accept where they lead us in safety of our souls?"

"I ask you, have you seen Pish jump from your nets when their spirit had been taken from their souls?"

"I tell you, as I stood beside Raven and Tsemitan along En che Wauna at Kathlamet, the spirit of the land was taken from us. Yes, the spirit of the land was taken from you and I as Suyapee came from behind Red Cloud, and our lands were then held in silence, and in that silence, life was not seen to be drawn upon the soils of our kingdom!"

"This is the truth!"

"I Ksitilo, the son of Kwillikum, of the Chehalis peoples, have seen with my own eyes, what will soon bring trouble upon our tables as they may soon lie emptied from what offers us strength!"

"For those of you who doubt Raven's and Tsemitan's words, hear this and understand. When the day that Suyapee comes again, if you are not ready for what will change about you as you look across En che Wauna and the lands where your villages sit, your soul will not survive before the waste of Suyapee's poach. Your spirits shall then dwell in the darkness of Tsiatko's coldest tomb beneath his highest telecasit."

"We will hear the bad spirit's call to join upon his journey across the lands we had once found promise, and as we march to the rhythm of the bad spirit's drum, he will lead us to a land we do not know or understand."

"He will lead us to a land whose spirits we have never met!"

I too fear the Tsiatko of Suyapee will take our souls and cast aside our spirit, as his greed will force our surrender as we will kneel to his ways, and we will only know of what was, and not to what is today and of all those tomorrows where you have placed doubt!"

"Life will not return as we know it today!"

"Then, as we walk that lonely trail that has no beginnings and has no endings that Raven speaks, our peoples spirits will not be seen again to bring promise before our Hyas Saghalie Tahmahnawis Tyee!"

"Suyapee will own everything we have strived to protect and have found honor in through our acceptance of the many spirits who have chosen to lead our peoples for many suns and moons!"

"Life will never be the same beneath our feet or before our eyes!"

"Silence will fall from the heavens as Wind will not sing of song, and we will only hear the promises of Suyapee spelled upon our ears as winter's long storms rain down upon us as the end of life as we know today is drawn near..."

"My Father, Hear Our Cry!"

"Nika Tilikummama, Kumtux Kopa Kwolan Cly!"

Ksitilo has stepped back from the edge of the circle from where he spoke the wise words that would take question from those that doubt to our vision, and as he now stands beside us, we each offer our hand before him, and we are now certainly brothers to the Earth!

I look to where the elders are seated, and I bow my head in appreciation for this opportunity to speak of the vision that has befallen our trails, and they in turn, bow toward us...

All I can do is hope those that have sat before our speech will tell their peoples of our journey, and to those they meet along the trails they are promised will too hear of what will soon rise above all our lands.

As Ksitilo, my brother.and I leave the circle, we walk to where our peoples sit smiling upon the great fur of bear as they look deep into our eyes.

Slowly they each rise and follow us to where the call of coyote is heard above the high cliff.

Coyote too must have seen the Red Cloud of Suyapee rise up into the skies from the peak she had climbed.

It is my soul that I have promised to our fathers before Wahclella's Wall, and it is through that promise that I would walk where they each have walked, and as I returned to my village and before my peoples, I would teach others to their ways and toward my understanding of how all things matter to one another in our survival.

I have learned well the lessons our fathers have chosen for me to follow.

Hyas Saghalie Tahmahanawis has guided my soul to join his own, and as he has guided me to join arms with all life as we know it, and as I walk in amongst their gathering, we are all then as one upon the Earth.

I have kept my word to the Hyas Tahmahnawis, and as I have followed his lead without question, he has chosen for my gift, the Spirit of Hyas Coyote. Hyas Coyote and I will share of one another's souls again tonight. I will steal into the darkness of night and climb the high cliff as I wait to sit beside her.

I find myself alone, sitting beneath the darkness of night as I await my friend. I rest in the silence darkness brings, and with much patience, Coyote chooses to honor my side as she appears from behind where moon now rises. Coyote brings smile to my face as she too remembers our union to the Earth.

I have brought in my pouch half of my meal of venison that was offered upon our tables from the great feast this night, and as I reach down before her, I place it softly at her feet.

She knows of my good spirit as we have sat here many days before, and she does not hesitate to take her eyes from my own as she begins to eat what I have offered.

Only Wind keeps Coyote and I company this night. It sings song which shares of both our Good Spirits.

Coyote finishes taking what I have offered and she lays her head low to the ground before me, and with her paw, again, she draws the sun and moon as she did the past season when we sat together for the first time.

As we sit together, from high above in the heaven, as if the medicine man had too journeyed at our side from the far mountain and took of this moment Coyote and I had just shared, from his purse he held out two stars, one being for Coyote, and the other being my own. As he threw his hands to the heavens, they each, with swift feet, were seen to run across the heavens until they reached the Hyas Tahmahnawis' village where they found rest in the green meadow.

I will remember this night forever as it brings magic to my soul.

I know when I return to this village next season I will climb upon the cliff and sit before the rising moon and listen for Wind to sing of the passion held within all our souls that have journeyed across the many trails of Otelagh's lands. I will look high up to the heavens, and there, from upon Hyas Tahmahnawis' meadow, with head lowered I will hear Coyote's call as she looks down upon where we had many times sat. That night, as our souls reach out to touch one anothers from where we rest, we both will feel of our spirit, and we will be pleased...

It is from where these stars came where Hyas Coyotes and my soul were first drawn, and it is to where these stars choose to graze in the Hyas Spirit's meadow we will one day soon, meet again...

This would be what I thought to be the last I would see of her. But each night, I hear her call, and I am pleased that her spirit is heard to run free across all the lands of her kingdoms...

Chapter 15

Before Our Peoples Came

The Nez Perz, the Umatilla, the Walla Walla, the Klickitat, the Yakama, the Shoshone, several villages of the Paiute and Tygh, as well as many of the Chinook villages whose smoke rises far into the heaven along the shores of En che Wauna, have all journeyed to Tiaklut to make trade for each of our finest wares.

When light came upon us from above once we had taken our place upon the stage and spoke of Suyapee's question to our brothers, we walked through the village where we began to see pasesse, blankets, that were not from any of the villages we had known. We saw many that were spooh, light, and klale, dark, blue, and others were tewagh pil, bright red. One old woman of the Nez Perz carried tight in her arms a pot that shared the color of

Otelagh, and she said it was called a copper kettle, pil chikamin kettling. Her son had told her a man with a long beard who had traded for the beaver and elk he carried on his pony told him this kettle was to make water hot to cook roots.

The old woman told when her young son journeyed to the Clatsop to see the big waters, there was much trade between the Clatsop and many men from a tall boat that came near shore. She said her son told they were men like we had named Suyapee, tall, and with much hair on their face, and no hair on their head. We were told by the old woman that Suyapee had upside down faces, and they made him laugh in silence as they made trade together.

As I stood and listened to her story, I knew the Red Cloud had again rose up upon our lands as Suyapee had made trade for many beaver and bear skins as they told they would make upon their return. I asked if her son was with the others fishing upon the high rocks, but she stated he had returned to the Big Waters with many pelts so he could make trade for more blankets and for something he said was a long rifle, (youtklut calipeen).

The old woman told her son spoke of a man that came from the tall boat, and as he took him into the sticks, he pointed the long rifle towards a deer and proved this weapon brings much strength to his spirit.

As the old woman told of this story's truth, I saw in her eyes she was in great sadness for what her son was about to do.

The old woman explained, when Suyapee took her son into the tall sticks, he pointed the long rifle towards a mowitch that walked past where they stood. As soon as the old woman held her hand to her ear and placed the other to cover her eyes, she explained there was first much noise, and then great fire, and then, smoke quickly came from within the heart of its bad spirit.

237

As she held her head down in shame she told the spirit of the mowitch was stolen from our peoples, and its soul would wander aimlessly across lands that our peoples would not want to know.

This was the warning that I had seen in my vision to what Red Cloud would bring as Suyapee came upon us in great storm. We would behe same as the mowitch. Our souls would be led by the bad spirit to lands where the Kloshe Tahmahnawis would not dare to enter, and we would be lost to our own souls as we walked blind into the darkness of the bad spirit's den.

Unsettled to what I had heard from the old woman, I took my brothers to the high cliff where we stood and looked out over En che Wauna as we spoke to what was soon to come before our people and to what would take us from our villages.

As we stood and stared towards our village at Che che Optin, I told them I feared Suyapee would march upon our peoples as we were far from where we could protect them from the cold storm that would soon be raised above them. As they stood bewildered to the sudden change they would be left unprotected to what they did not understand. With advisement, I asked my brothers if they would choose to journey to our village and stay with me as I walked to the valley where Wahclella stands and ask of our Fathers what we should do? I told them, I would ask our Fathers advice in order we may safely walk out of whatever storm rises upon us from those that have now begun to come to our lands.

The long rifle the old woman speaks brings much regret within me for it proves that the new people's spirits are strong, and they are willing to kill without first hearing the voice of those they hunt. Suyapee chooses to take from the soils of the Earth what they demand without knowing of the messages that spell of warning through their absent thought to what will come of tomorrow.

We must discover within us to which will bring good faith between our peoples and allow us to walk the trails we are known to journey each day without the threat of becoming like the Salmon the bad spirits stole from our nets.

Our peoples must walk with one hand upon the shoulder of our High Spirits, and sadly, we may yet be forced to take the hand of Suyapee and make trade for all they wish to take from us with the other.

I ask my brothers; "Pitokpli, Tsemitsk, and Mensitiko, do you think they will stop once they have taken all the furs from the backs of our animals? Do you think they will go back to their lands and not return? Or, do you think they will see the tall trees and green grass, or the flowers of the meadows without thought how they each bring song to Wind? Do you think they will build their villages where our own first stood and send us all to those lands that our souls have never been drawn?"

These are the questions that lie before us, unanswered!

Red Cloud's storm is upon us with much question, and in its question rises threat to our existence upon these lands that have offered us much through the High Spirit's most gracious hands.

There was one brave that came from where the distant villages of the Makah has been told to take from the big waters the free spirit of the Ehkolie, whale, with long spears as they sit and rush upon them from within great canoes in the bay that sits waiting for the Ehkolie to arrive. He is called, One Who Walks With Little Hurry, (Ikt Klaksta Klatowa Kopa Lapea Kunamokst Tenas Howh).

He brings with him many furs of the otter and the seal upon his horse's back to make trade, and from beneath the soft hides, he

pulls out from where it was hid, the flesh, itlwillie, of Ehkolie.
He gave us each small carvings from wood of his people's totems
that gave him strength as he journeyed far across new trails.
As he told us of the power of these carvings, I ask if he was to
choose our lands to live, and if not, why would he offer us the
strength and power of those spirits if he were yet to return to his
village as it lay far from our own?

I have chose to call him Tenas Howh as he has asked, and his
answer is spoken from his heart as he tells he will walk amongst
our lands and hear of our peoples stories as he journeys to the sea
where he will see of these Suyapee that we speak. He tells us he
will make trade for the long rifle that will give him much power
over all those he will meet upon the trails that lead to his village,
and he will not need the spirits that hide unseen and lie silent in
stick.

Again, I stand in question to how our peoples can walk away
from all that has given us good fortune. I too question how so
many of our people can take and take again from the hand that
brings the uncertainty of Red Cloud before us as it is the sign
our peoples had been told one day Red Cloud would loom heavy
within our hearts and bring certain closure of our souls towards
the teachings from our fathers.

Tenas Howh had sat at counsel beside us at Kwilluchini, he too
knows of the bad spirit that has come upon us with opened and
welcoming arms.

I told Tenas Howh he could journey with us to our village as it
was along the river's trail to the big waters, and near where the
tall ship rests. I told him my brothers and I too would make the
long journey to the village of the Clatsop and sit with them, and
we would all hear of the stories that Suyapee brings to our tables.

I knew if he were to accept my invitation that I could speak with him to all we had seen and to all that is held within my soul to the change that is soon to come upon our lands along the trails of Wind with much hurry.

As we sat speaking of the great run of pish that had come to our nets, a large Crow called out to us as he flew overhead and landed near where we sat. From within my purse I threw him a small scrap, and without worry, he took it from the ground and flew off into the branch of the tree that stood tall along the river. Tenas Howh too knew of Crow as he told us his peoples were led across their lands by Crow's forewarning cries from above the trails they followed. Then, I too knew he understood of the land's mightiest of spirits.

He and I, at that moment, became quick friends.

As I told him of the story of my son and Crow, Tenas Howh could not hold back his laugh as his voice was raised across the entire village, and many heads turned our way. Those that sat in the camp and had earlier questioned of this brave's heart knew at that moment he was a friend and not like those of the Snake that come before us as thieves in the darkest hours of the night.

Before we began our long journey to our village, we had been asked by several brothers from the Nechacokee, that come from the river of Wy-East, and several braves from the village of Thiakalama that live at the mouth of their river that flows into the waters of En che Wauna, if we would make trade for the Brothers of Cedar. They told us they had seen the three brother's strong will as they flew like the Eagle across the white waters when Wind came from the east as we passed them near the village of Klemiaksac. They each told this had proven of the brother's spirited ways, and they too would make offer so they

would be taken safely to their villages upon the swift waters of
En che Wauna.

As they each quarreled with loud voice over the price they would
offer for trade, I stood from where I was seated, and spoke to
each of them as I stated the Three Cedar and we are connected
through their pleading voice and strong spirits, and I would have
to refuse even their highest offer with much respect.

I am not sad that I had not made trade, though they would
have brought much wealth to our village. Instead, I am pleased,
as all our souls are tied to the kingdoms that lie beside En che
Wauna as we will make many journeys to sit before the villages
of our peoples, and we will speak of this Red Cloud that looms
threatening from each horizon beyond those of our lands.

It is here, in Wahclella, where Tenas Howh, my brothers, and I
now sit before the warm fire of our village and speak of the long
journeys that lie ahead. As we have taken of the wave of En che
Wauna many times, I tell Tenas Howh the journey will be quick
with the current of the river pushing us with great rush towards
the sea, and we will stop many times to visit many villages that
are along its course. When Otelagh has risen above us the fifth
day, we will sit in the village of the Clatsop and hear of their
story and to what Suyapee brings before our tables with trade for
the pelts of those spirits that have given us meat and tools from
their horn and bone.

I know now Tenas Howh has come to our lands from far away,
and I have warned him of Suyapee's Red Cloud, and to all the
skins they had stolen from our lands. As Red Cloud came above
us with much weight, our lives were lain in question as Suyapee
came to our shore from the river. I too want to take upon the
challenge of approaching this tall boat, and to stand before these
Suyapee, but first, it is not to make trade, but I must first see

what they carry within their souls, and I want to feel of their spirit, if it is good, or if their spirits are bad.

I thought back to where Tenas Howh had told us where his village stood, and I ask of him many questions to the lands that separate his from our own, and how his people's beliefs are different through their vision of the Hyas Spirits that rule over the water and the Earth?

Tenas Howh sat silent and searched his soul for answer, after much thought, he turned and looked towards me and began; "The Hyas Ekholie Spirit comes to the waters of our bay in the Spring from far away before Otelagh rises high into the koosah, (sky), when warm waters follow Sun's trail across the heaven from above the waters of the south. In Winter, we see the Hyas Spirit rise up slowly before us from above the waters lowest plane when Otelagh brings darkness from his purse and lays it low upon the Earth longer than he journeys across the trails of the heavens."

"This is the time Otelagh chooses to rest each season," Tenas Howh explains. "We know Ehkolie first comes to our waters as spring brings warmth to the waters, and again, Ekholie returns as kalkala, birds, join together in the sky in great numbers, and the call of keluk, swan, is heard to whistle as they fly south to the lands that hold grass in winter."

Tenas Howh tells; "We hear the call of Ekholie's Spirit as it enters the great bay where our village lies, and as its voice sounds out as elk to their cow, its spirit rushes from the deep waters to touch with its long nose, the heavens. It is then he awaits us to join upon his side from our village as we rush upon him from within our great canoe."

Tenas Howh states with much pride; "This is a great canoe that holds many braves of our village, and it is strong and fast as it rises above the wave of the big waters. We have carved from its nose, the great spirit of Ehkolie as we honor it each day we are seen to make ready for the great race between Ehkolie and our people as we hunt for our prey."

"Ekholie rises many times from below the deep waters of the bay, he offers himself to be joined to our tables. We place our canoe quietly upon the water where big waves will take from him sound of our rush upon where he rises. We row fast to his side and cast out the long spears to join both his spirit with our own."

"The Great Spirit, Ehkolie only pleads we promise him as we thrust the long spear that ties us together as brothers upon the waters of the Earth, his strong Spirit will live forever in our memories. He reminds us that it is he that has chosen himself as our gift, and that through his gift, our peoples will survive through the longest of winter's fiercest storms."

Tenas Howh smiles with much pride, as he has now proven of his promise to Hyas Ehkolie that his free spirit will be envisioned through the story of the hunt, and the Great Spirit's memory will live beyond all the tomorrows that Otelagh will pass above his giving soul.

As Tenas Howh finished telling his story as he and his brothers had hunted for whale, he asked if we had heard of the Thunderbird and Orca's great battles that shook the Earth for many seasons far beyond those of our fathers and their fathers before them? We each told him we had not heard tale of this Orca and Thunderbird, and at once Tenas Howh began to tell the tale.

"There are many stories that hold secrets of how the lands were first formed from the waters of the sea, and these stories have never been shared with peoples beyond the lands of the far northern coast."

"Only our brothers of the Hoh and Quinault have heard of what we know. It has been our choice to share of these stories to those who have wished to sit beside one another at the great fire in their villages when we have gathered for many Potlatch's celebrating the new season, just as your peoples have gathered in Tiakluit."

Tenas Howh began to tell the story his peoples knew well of the Great Spirits, (Hohoeapbess), The Two Men Who Changed Things, who both first came to the Earth from a kingdom far away as they were brothers to both, Sun and Moon, and how they had much power over all there was in the world before Indian.

"From the Winds of heaven there was not sound of the Eagle's scream, as they had not yet been given feathers upon their wings. The cry of Coyote, nor the call of Elk was yet heard, as they too had not come as they had no legs. Only creatures that slithered across the sand like snake carried the spirit of man, and others carried the spirits of animal as they hid behind grass that grew tall and gave protection from Great Sun Spirit."

"When the two brothers stepped down from the heavens onto the sands of the lands, change came to the Earth. When our peoples would come to the Earth, they would not only survive with what they were given, but they would live with much promise as life would become plentiful with many pish and roots waiting to be harvested within their hands."

"Each brother took all the creatures to their village, and there, before the big fire, they took water from the sea, and mixed it with the sand of the land, and in one long night, they gave birds wings, and all the animals strong legs to run. As Sun rose up from the lands far away, they again took the water of the sea and the sand from upon the lands and created leaves upon the tall sticks of our forests, so they would offer shade to the flower and fern, and they in turn would offer all that came to lie upon them, soft beds."

"It has been told there was a thief among all the creatures as he had been caught stealing the catch of fishermen and the meat from those that hunt. As The Two Men That Changed Things had heard of this thief, they took him from upon the land and gave him short arms so he could not reach, and they gave him short legs so he could not run. When they had taken all this creature had, they threw him into the sea, and as he floundered in the waters of the sea, the brothers told him if he wanted to live he must first learn to swim, and then must catch what he eats, and they called him Seal."

"Each day the brothers had seen a great fisher standing upon the high rocks above the waters carrying a long spear. Every time they saw him they noticed he stood with much patience and was ready to thrust his spear into the pish that came close. He always wore the same clothes, and they noticed he wore a round white cape wrapped over his shoulders to keep the cold out. The two brothers formed him from the water and sand to become the Great Blue Heron. His cape became the white feather around his long neck, and his spear became his long, sharp beak."

"The brothers looked about at all the creatures that gathered before them, they saw one that was both a fisherman and a thief as he stole from the sea a necklace of fine shells. The brothers gave him wings and called him the Kingfisher. The necklace of shells that he had stolen was placed around his neck as a ring of fine feathers, and if you stand quiet upon the shore of a lake or stream, you will see him sitting upon the arm of stick. There, as he awaits a fish to rise up from beneath the waters, he will dive headfirst into the waters where he will catch his next meal."

"There were two creatures that could not resist to eat everything they saw, so the two brothers made one into Raven, and his wife into Crow. They both were given strong beaks to tear the flesh from their food, and as they stood together above their meal, the Raven called out Cr-r-ruck, and Crow, Cah! Cah!"

"Bluejay's son sat high up on the arm of the great stick of the forest, and as the brothers stood below him and called out, they asked him; Which do you choose to be, a bird, or a fish? Bluejay's son screamed out that he did not want to be either, and told the two brothers to go away and to leave him!"

"As the brothers both stood shocked he would not choose, and Bluejay had ordered them to leave him alone even though they had strong spirits, they scolded him. Through his bad manners, he would be the mink. Bluejay then saw in the reflection of the water he had now grown a long tail and his colorful wings had been taken from upon his shoulders. He knew then he would have to take fish from the stream or from upon the bank of the river to eat."

"The brothers knew the new peoples who would come to the lands would need much wood, so they made tools to split wood to make their longhouses, and to make bows to hunt. They took the spirit of one creature and turned him into the tree named Yew. Then, as the brothers remembered the peoples would need arrows to place on their bows, they called out for more little creatures, and they made them into the strong glass rock that would be shaped into arrowhead."

"There was one creature that stood out from all the rest as he was fat and red as he lay out in the sun, and the brothers knew the peoples would need soft wood to make canoes, and from its bark, they would make clothes to wear. They each told him he would be honored before all the peoples as his name would be heard called as Great Cedar."

"For fire, the peoples would need wood to place into their pits to cook and warm their souls when winter comes, so the two brothers called out to the old creature that walked slow. They told him that as he was old, his heart had begun to turn hard, and grease did not run fast from his soul, and he would make good kindling as he would offer pitch to their fire. They told him his name would be Spruce, and as his brothers and sisters all grew old, they too would make dry wood and be good for the people's fires."

"The Two Men Who Changed Things then called upon a small creature that stood back from all the rest, and they told him he would be made into Hemlock. He was told as the new peoples took many deer and elk and bear from the lands, they would need him for tanning hides, and their branches would burn hot in the sweat lodges that would take the bad spirits from within the new people's souls."

"Then, as all the creatures but three had been called before the two brothers, there was one that yelled out that he could not be the last to find a new home amongst all the rest. As he was seen and heard to have much temper, he was made into the crab apple tree, and they told him he would only grow sour fruit upon his wanting branch."

"Now, there are only two creatures to pick, and as the two brothers stood before them both, they watched each one to see who they would choose to make into the cherry tree that would bare good fruit and would make good medicine for the peoples from its bark."

"As the two creatures that remained stood before them for a long time, the first that looked away from the two brothers was chosen to be the cherry tree, and the last creature was asked to be the strong Alder that would make hard paddles for the people's many canoes."

"The Two Men Who Changed Things had then formed the Earth as we know it today," said Tenas Howh.

"From the waters and from the sands of the Earth the Two Bothers have created all that we see, and all that we have."

Tenas Howh then sat silent as Hyas Coyote called out to the moon from the high peak behind our village. With much surprise, Hyas Coyote walked in amongst our village and stood before the fire as she looked deep into all our eyes.

Tenas Howh whispered; "She too knows of the Two Brothers, as she was formed from the beginning when there was no grass or tree where she could hide, and yet, her spirit was not seen to run upon the barren ground before the first day when there was nothing!"

In silenced thought, I asked; "Is she the mother of the two brothers?"

"She is a High Spirit amongst us, and one who steals into the night without caution…"

We took our eyes from Coyotes and looked to our brothers as we did not understand why she had come. In that single moment, when we sat questioning of her presence, just as we did when we first saw the Tkope Moolack Tyee, Coyote was like the Wind blown across the loose feather of bird, and she disappeared from upon any of the trails that led to our village.

I ask; "Is this the sister of Coyote that I had sat beside many nights and had shared two stars as they journeyed across the heavens until they both settled upon the High Spirit's long meadow?"

As we sit and look up into the heaven, we speak of the stars that bring light to night. I share with Tenas Howh this is the time we have waited for many seasons as the Good, Kloshe, and bad spirits, mesahchie tahmahnawis' of Lawala Clough, Pahto, and Wy-East have all fallen silent as they have ruled over their lands without much quarrel for several seasons between them.

Tenas Howh; "Otelagh, Sun Spirit, has rose above us for many days and has offered warmth to settle onto the lands. He has shared much appreciation towards us as his kingdoms are seen to flourish with new life as pish from the sea come plentiful into the rivers and streams as they breathe new life unto the lands that rise up alongside the shores where they have journeyed far to spawn."

"Life as we know it today is spent with much joy and happiness, and without worry or complaint."

"Our peoples of the Watlalla who live at our village here at Wahclella, have prospered well. We have joined our spirits with all others that we have passed upon the trails of our lives, and of those that have witnessed life's beginnings. From man to animal, to plant, to pish, to the lone rock that stands tall near where we take from the river, pish, they each hold strong to the soul of the Earth, and we are all connected through the (Kloshe Illahee Tahmahnawis'), Good Earth Spirit's, soul."

"We, the shamans and chiefs of our villages, have all climbed into the long valley, and there, before the Walls of Candor and upon the Trail of Principles, we each have stood before Wahclella and

have heard our father's teachings as they had learned from their fathers, and their fathers long before them. The Hyas Spirits of our peoples have warned us for many seasons, if there is quarrel between us, we should sit before our village's great fires and pass the long pipe between us. They have told that as we sit and hear of our brother's message, we should take away from the Potlatch only what is good, and we must walk away from which is bad. Our fathers have spoken to us with much truth, as this is the way our good spirits will one day grant us to journey upon our own star to the Saghalie Tahmahnawis' village, and there, high up within the heaven, we will be seen to rest upon his greenest meadows."

"We are fortunate we have been gifted to learn from our fathers as they were led by the Hyas Saghalie Tahmahnawis to the significance of these lands that we live, and how each species, from the smallest ant to the largest bear, all are joined together under Great Sun's creation."

"As we journey through life, we find ourselves honored to live here amidst the Majestic Land's of Wah at the shores of En che Wauna and beneath the Hyas Cascades from where our Great Spirit's speak. Through all the teachings that have been passed down before us, we have learned to accept through our faith and understanding that the rhythm of the Earth depends solely on how we each place our next step upon its many trails."

"It is wise we must first ask if we should take the tree or animal, or take from the soil the root or flower from the earth beneath our feet if our needs do not call out for its taking?"

"We must first think if we should pick the lone flower if it is the only one that gives sweet scent to the meadow and brings the bee to make honey?"

I ask you; "Should we take the young buck from the high mountain before he has learned to survive through all the seasons and offer strength and share his knowledge to his young fawns?"

"As I, Raven, our village's Elder, take my peoples upon the trails of life where we find prosperity and live without worry that light from Otelagh's wide smile will not fall upon us tomorrow, those that believe in the High Spirits as I have led them, know the High Spirits will bring much promise upon our lives. Even though we may one day walk blindly and without direction when obstacle stands unknowing before us, there will be light cast upon our trails, and we shall see with great vision, of all those tomorrows that will bring our souls closer to those that sit before the fires at the Hyas Tahmahnawis' village."

"These are good days spent at the right hand of Otelagh as his promise to all our peoples is, and will be forever, the gift of life's promise as we have come to know it each day!"

"But as Suyapee has come before us on the Great River many seasons ago, there, high above us, with faint whisperings of change brought down from the heaven by great tears from Hyas Tahamahnawis through the sticks many arms, we saw Red Cloud rise up to the heaven, and life did not stir."

"From mild, warm breeze, came hard, cold Wind!"

"Both Red Cloud and Wind took light and heat from the land, and as they fell upon us with much threat, they took the sight of land from before our eyes. There, upon the shore of En che Wauna at Kwilluchini, Cathlamet, we stood, bewildered, as pish were thrown dead from our nets. We were left with nothing but emptied thoughts and question to what we may not have followed in the High Spirit's teachings as we had taken upon his

journey. Sadly, as we stood there, lost before the shroud of Red Cloud, we were like birds without feather."

"Many days have passed since that day arose before us, but today, Wind comes from both East and West, and we have become fearful Suyapee is soon to enter our kingdoms as we sleep."

"We fear they will come upon our lands and take the pelts from the backs of the beaver and bear, the deer and elk, the weasel and the mink, each of these to which we have come to honor each day." "Suyapee will bring storm to fall across our lands as they march upon us with much conviction, and all our animal's souls will be emptied of their spirit. In this, we too fear, as Suyapee will leave the lands emptied of soul as all our spirits, man and animal, shall then be taken far from these lands we know."

"The days ahead of our lives are promised of question by Wind as it cries out Suyapee's encroachment upon us is near. Suyapee's arrival upon our lands has been told to our peoples for many seasons through visions wrought before our greatest of Shamans. We have heard one day there will be threat thrown from the bad spirit's purse before our feet with much rush, and we must all be readied to take all that is good from the High Spirit's table and not lose our souls through the black words Suyapee speaks, or from the long arms of his weapons."

"But still," I tell Tenas Howh; "We find question as we look to one another and ask if we will survive when we are taken from the shores of En che Wauna and we cannot take again from her waters pish?"

"Will the Hyas Eagle's be heard to scream still as they fly across the High Spirit's trails when Red Cloud takes the sight of land from below the heaven, and from above us all?"

I ask you Tenas Howh; "Will the spirits that live amongst us today still look upon us with favor, or will they take all that is left from within us as they too mock of our ways?"

"These are the questions that come before us all as change is threatening to march before us like fast Wind upon the open prairie, and it will take us with much force from the lands where our High Spirits rest upon the cliff of Wahclella. As we are swept through many dark visions that show lands where our peoples were not known to have lived, we will be forced to build new lives upon those barren grounds of the bad spirit."

"We are fearful that our High Spirit's voices will lie stilled from their place upon the cliff of Wahclella, and we fear as Wind sweeps across these lands in silenced voice, our faith will too become lost and our voice held in silence from within our emptied hearts. Our lives will then be led upon emptied trails that challenge of meaning and course."

"As Red Cloud is raised from the land and settles in the heaven as it brings Cole Wind to invest within our souls, we find ourselves beginning to question; What of tomorrow?"

"Through this question that has drawn darkness from light, as our father's visions have also spoken one day these new peoples would come upon us in great numbers, the unknowing of the answer lies heavy within us. In this, our good hearts and strong souls may be taken from within us if we do not hold our heads high and remember to follow the words of our Hyas Fathers as we walk upon new trails where life may be hidden from us in the beginning. But, through faith and our understanding to the rhythm of the Earth, we shall overcome, and life shall renew itself before all our lives."

"The Red Cloud brings much warning to our peoples as it spreads across the skies. It tells through its own Wind, if we do not follow in Suyapee's ways as we sit before the fire of our villages and look deep into one another's eyes, all we will see one day will be (Death's Dark Mask), (Mahsh Konaway Yaka Wind Klale Stick Seeowist), in our own reflection."

"This is what we all must fear when Suyappe begins to follow our trails and take all the spirit from our lands...!"

Steven Waverleff

Chapter 16

The Winds of Change

*"Tenas Howh, as we sit here before the fire this night I will
share with you a story that has been held silent from the ears of
Suyapee as they do not know of the great storm that befell our
lands and brought his peoples before us in the days of long ago.
One day, many seasons past, a great storm spread across the
waters of the sea, and a tall boat as we have heard now waiting
for our furs at Knope, was thrown from the waters of the sea and
came upon our lands in many pieces.*

*Long ago, the peoples of the Clatsop had told of a tall boat that
was swept from the sea when storm came upon the lands with much
anger. They have told their fathers tell the storm blew hard with*

much Wind for many days as swass, (rains), fell heavy from the heavens, and many sticks, trees, were bent to the ground and were heard to cry out as their spirits fell from their high place. The spirits, both good and bad, found battle between them. They each threw fire across the skies and announced their anger to those which lived beneath the rumblings they expelled from deep within their souls.

The peoples of the Clatsop knew not what to do as the Good Spirits were suddenly taken from them, and many of their peoples were cast amidst the spinning cloud that takes pish from the waters and sticks from the lands they touch.

The Clatsop knew the spirits were unhappy, but they did not know what trails they had taken that would make the spirits so angry for them to throw great spears upon their lands and shout out with great force so the Illahee would shake with much terror beneath their rising storm. Fear had enveloped within the peoples of the Clatsops as they sat in their longhouses, trapped, like the Great Klale Lolo in the deep pit, where light does not shine with the promise of life within it.

Each day, each night, they were the same, as light was taken from the hand of Otelagh and was spread happily across another land.

Great battles were staged upon all the heaven's trails, and the villages of Knope, Neacoxy, Neahkeluk, Neahkstowt, and that of Necotat were under attack from the spirit's relentless storm. It has been told the waters of all the streams and rivers rose up and swallowed much of the land beneath the high peaks from where they fell, and soon, the waters of the sea met those of the mountains, and the soft sands of the long beach were not seen.

Much question must have filled the minds of the Clatsop as they were heard to ask; "What are we to do and where will we go if we do not have the Big Waters to hunt Seal and catch pish?"

Much worry began to take faith from our brother's souls, and from where they had once believed the Good Spirits would lead them upon safe trails was soon to be lost through the unknowing of what would come of their tomorrows.

As Otelagh returned above the lands and crossed the trails of the heaven, he looked down upon them with much sorrow. Otelagh offered great warmth to be spread across the lands from his soul, and the waters were seen to rise up from upon the lands. As the Clatsop who had survived the storm came out from their longhouses once calm settled across their lands, they looked out to the Big Waters. It was then they have told they witnessed from where the sea and high peaks meet, the waters had been taken beyond the heaven where they could not see.

It was not long before the long beach again appeared as it was, cleared of the lost souls of stick that had fallen into their trap from the spirit's great and mighty storm. They were sent by the Good Spirit to the deep waters where the bad spirit chose to hide his den in the dark, and it was there Otelagh then threw with much anger into the deep waters the sharpened points of stick into the bad spirit's soft bed. Otelagh had hoped the sharp sticks would finally imprison the dark soul of Tsiatko where it could not escape for all the days he would pass overhead.

As darkness settled across the kingdom of the Clatsop that first night after storm had been lifted from upon the lands, there was heard the return of the Great Owls as they called out from the edge of the long meadows. Deer and Elk walked out from where they hid from the battle that was raised above them, and they were heard to rustle the leaves that had then settled softly upon the soils of the Earth. It was told the forests too were heard of their long sigh, as they were pleased storm had been taken from upon them. They each were quickly promising to bring new life to rise up and thrive across all their kingdoms.

Life was returned as it should upon the lands, as all that lived within the Saghalie Tahmahnawis Tyee's kingdoms were gathered in harmony beneath colorful skies that were not threatened by the harsh breaths of bad spirit's Wind.

Through the long night, the Clatsop gathered before the fires of their villages and were heard to shout out to the Hyas Tahmahnawis Tyee as they offered praise before his feet for what he had returned to their people. Happiness and joy lifted high into the heaven and was thick upon the trails where Wind had first come.

Hope had then returned within their souls as they knew tomorrow would bring much to their tables as they journeyed to the Big Waters. There, from along the sands of the long beach, they again would take from the sea what he would offer them to enter into their long nets.

As light from Otelagh's hand began to rise from above the far peaks the following day, Great Coyote was heard to cry out as she was seen to stand upon the high rock above the Clatsop's village and look out over the sea.

She, Great Coyote, has journeyed far throughout all the kingdoms that Otelagh has gifted his peoples, and it was unlike her to stand out where others can see her when Sun comes to the lands. The Clatsop knew, as Coyote called out to them in much warning to what she had seen, they too must walk to the sands of the long beach, and bear witness to what she had announced.

First, the young braves ran out to the long beach and turned south as they, with swift feet, looked over all that stood out before them. They first thought it would be the Great Ehkolie they would find laying helpless upon the sands, but there was none.

Then, an old woman walked slowly from their village, and she saw the young braves had gone their way with much hurry, but as they did not call out, she turned and walked to the north. First she saw what she thought to be a large stick washing upon the sands, but as she came near, she stood questioning with wide eyes to the shape of this stick as it was not narrow like tree, but was wide and split in many pieces, and she first thought; "Good for fire!"

She walked closer, wary of what lived in the heart of this beast.

Suddenly, as her heart could be heard to rise up from within her like the fast beats of the Great Drums when war comes before the fires where her peoples dance, laying helpless and unmoving, and torn from his clothes, a man with open and crazed eyes looked up towards her. A white man with much hair, and she knew he was not one of her peoples.

As the old woman stood unknowing what to think to what lay before her bleeding in the sands of the long beach, two men came from behind where they hid when they saw she had come alone, and they placed this man that was soon dead into a stick that was formed from their forest to hold the furs they come to make trade.

The old woman screamed when she saw them look towards her.

With much question to what she had seen, she ran as fast as an old doe from the sharp teeth of the mighty cougar.

Quickly, there were many peoples of the Clatsop village gathered upon the long beach to see why she had cried out with much fear, and there, as cloud took from the land light, the first Suyapee were then seen by many to come upon our lands.

Many seasons would pass before Suyapee would be seen again upon the waters that mix with those of En che Wauna. But, as we stood at Kwilluchini, we thought they had returned to avenge those that had first come to our shores many seasons ago. The Clatsop had taken those men we have come to call Suyapee as slaves, and they were not seen again by their own peoples.

This was the beginning of the warning of a great storm that would one day fall across all our lands as Red Cloud would soon rise up upon our lands with the gravest of threat upon our peoples.

As my brothers and I stood with Chief Tsutho along the shore of En che Wauna, we had seen of Suyapee's warning cloud that rose up from behind him. We knew the battles between the good and bad spirits would be seen and heard of their lasting storm upon us with much threat once again, and this brings much complaint from all our peoples that know of the Suyapee's promise he would take all the pelts of our spirits from upon our tables.

This night, as we sit at the fire of our village with Tenas Howh, our new friend, I ask you; "We find question where we can journey to find safety from Suyapee's fast march across our lands once they have begun to hunt for those spirits that do not wish to be taken from their villages. As the dirt from beneath Suyapee's quick march makes Red Cloud rise up to the far trails of Otelagh in the heaven, what trails shall we take that will lead to lands where the pish run strong in their waters, and the deer and elk are thick in their herd?"

When we have these answers, then we will know the Hyas Saghalie Tahmahnawis has chosen new lands for us to live. Until that day arrives above us, or the answers we ask lie hardened within our souls, we must make ready for the change that is soon to come upon the Trails of Wind…

Today, those tomorrows we have seen in our visions are beginning to dim with much question. As we have sat before the fire of our village many braves have come to rest beside our fires and have told tale of a tall ship setting in the waters where En che Wauna meets the waters of the sea near the villages of Knope and Neahkstowt of the Clatsop.

We have seen gifts of blankets and beads, axes and kettles offered for the pelts of Otter and Seal, Elk and Bear. We have heard these men who we have named Suyapee plead that we bring in trade all the finest pelts we choose to surrender from the trails of our lands to the villages of the Clatsop where they will be taken to their tall ship and sent to lands of the East where our peoples had first come.

This, I do not see as good, as we would not bring honor upon our peoples as Hyas Tahmahnawis will look down upon us with sad eyes as we take the souls of these majestic spirits from his lands without thought to what may remain upon his trails in all of our tomorrows.

It is to this first tall ship that sits high up upon the waters of En che Wauna along our shores to which I speak, that we are about to find our journey. We ask the High Spirit to keep Crow above us, and the cunning of Coyote within us to warn off what danger may stand before us from behind the dark mask that Suyapee has shown many days before to wear.

We must be certain as we stand before Suyapee that he knows that our spirits are good, or there will be no hope for our peoples to survive amongst them.

We find fear held within our souls that Suyapee's spirit may have been taken by the mesahchie tahmahnawis. We fear he has been led upon different trails through the taunting of the bad spirit's drums.

This, we too have witnessed as we stood upon the shores of En che Wauna at the village of Kwilluchini. It was there when pish leapt from our nets and were seen spent of their spirit, and were quickly washed from the waters of En che Wauna and thrown lifeless back to the sea. Sadness filled our souls as we were left standing with bare hands, torn nets, and emptied bellies. We stood along the shore of the great river as great sorrow filled our hearts. With much question, we could only find ourselves to ask, "why?"

Soon, we will sit before the fires of our brothers of the Clatsop at their village at Knope, and we will hear of their story of these new peoples that come upon us. The day for us to stand upon the tall ship that rests in the bay where wave is taken from the shores has come upon us with much hurry.

When we stand before Suyapee and look deep within his eyes, he will not be able to hide behind the dark mask that we have seen him conceal before his soul.

Suyapee's true spirit will then surely rise up from within them, and as true as the crow flies across the heaven, we will then know..."

Steve Warnstaff

Chapter 17

Crow and Coyote

When Moon, sister of Sun has set into the lands beyond our own to the west, my brothers, Pitokpi, Tsemitsk, Mentsitiko, Tsemitan, the brother of my wife, Mashatah, our new friend from the village of the Makah, Tenas Howh, and myself, have set out upon the waters of En che Wauna as we have begun the long journey to Knope.

The Clatsop do not know we come with much question to what they have heard spoken by Suyapee, and as we walk into their village, their eyes will look deep within our own as they too will question of our silent approach before them. When we sit and pass the long pipe, they will know we do not carry within the three brothers of Cedar, furs and camas to trade, but we wish for our brothers to lead us to the tall ship from where these Suyapee come. We must look deep within Suyapee's souls through their wide eyes, and as we stand before them, we will be certain if their spirit is good or if the spirit they keep within them is the same as those Suyapee that first came from behind Red Cloud.

We had listened to the wise Owl's call throughout the night as he guarded over our village from the approach of all those that hunt during the long hours of darkness. As we rose from our mats, and had placed our weapons and food within the canoes, Crow called out to us with loud voice. As we looked up to where Crow sat upon the long branch of Fir, we saw he looked down to where Great Coyote sat watching all that moved. Both their spirits appeared clearly as they rested before the light of Moon as cloud parted from before them. As we pushed off from the shore of our village, we noticed they both had turned to follow us from along the trail of the high ridge as we began our long journey, and we knew our journey would be safe as all our souls were again connected through our good spirits.

We sit in silenced thought and breathe heavy with short breaths as we are thrown purposely down the stream of the big river with much hurry. Rising from the lands where the Nez Perz's villages stand proud above the waters of the Wahpoos, (Snake), Otelagh has begun to rise up above the high peaks, and as Otelagh climbs higher upon the trails of the heaven, he offers warmth to set deep within our chilled souls.

Storm has not been seen to fall from the heavens for many days, but today, as we journey further from our village near where many rivers meet, cloud has begun to grow thick with much warning. Smoke has begun to rise up from upon both the lands and from upon En che Wauna, and it is as thick as we had seen to follow Suyapee's approach before us many days ago.

I think back to the wise words my father was heard to tell of those less fortunate without sight that could draw from within their souls, great vision. Dark cloud has suddenly settled across the big river, and we are now the same as those blind men my father had once spoke as we are taken inside the dark cloud where we cannot see what lies before us. Only in our faith can we envision ourselves to safely ply the waves of the great river without fear to what may await us. As we become settled to our journey that dwells into the unknowing soul of Suyapee, we sense the sweet fragrance of the wildflower that will soon rise up before us, and in this alone, we know all our tomorrows will pass by without threat of danger through our innocent approach to all we cannot see.

We have placed our trail in the middle of the river's channel, and as we are pushed with much force, we are not wary of what may lie before us that would spill us into the fast waters. As we cannot see what may rise up before us and throw peril towards our long and needed journey, we remember of the Three Brother's oath when we had elected to have them join upon our journeys from the first day we had met. They each promised they would keep the tears of the High Spirit from flooding into where we kneel upon their bench, and all our journeys we were to take together would find us safe from the bad spirit's most plunderous tasks. This too offers us faith we will stand before Suyapee and look deep within his soul without fear to what we may see hidden behind their disguising mask.

As I kneel within our great canoe I welcome what lies beside us upon the river's trail. As I sit back and direct my focus to the loud cries that rise up from behind the emptiness of smoke, my experiences tell me there is much trouble lieing upon the lands we have yet to see. From deep within the dark cloud we hear the call of all the animals, and the whistling of birds that walk and fly across the lands beside us. As I listen to each of their cry, I hear their pleading song wishing we will find safe sanctuary for them all so they too can survive amongst the storm that Suyapee has now begun to bring with swift feet before us. I sense all the animals and birds bring question before the table of life where we all sit, and they tell of their concern of their freedom to journey across the kingdoms they choose without worry and threat.

There is much power in the soul of the bad spirit, and through the weight of the silent and unseen storm we have now become concerned, we will soon be surrounded. We feel with our hearts the bad spirit stands just beyond where we cannot see, and he hides his calloused and senseless being from us as he speaks of good faith and brings reason for the darkness his soul now spreads before us.

As I look over to Tenas Howh, I tell him we have passed the high rock where we had found ourselves to await the storm's pass that fell upon us from Wy-East as his bad spirit rose up from beneath his dark chambers and began to spread great clouds of ash across our lands. I tell him we are soon to come to the river that comes of Wy-East, and to the long meadow where it is now known the Deer Spirit's dance.

I tell Tenas Howh of all I had taken vision of that one night when smoke was taken from the long meadow, and the sticks of the forest bowed before me as their long limbs directed me to where the Deer Spirits waited. I told Tenas Howh I knew well the story Deer Spirit chose to share before me as his message began as he raked the heavens with his sharp horn and cried out with much agony, as if he were being taken by the bad spirit of Pishpish from upon the high cliff. Deer Spirit told that many lives were soon to be lain emptied of life upon the bad spirit's wanting tombs, and many of our brothers would be taken from us through their own absent and misfortuned thought. Those of our brothers that would choose not to walk upon the trails of our Great Fathers would not be seen amongst us again, and their names would be lost forever to our memories.

As Tenas Howh knelt within the bow of the canoe, he took his eyes from me, and in silenced thought, he looked down with great sorrow. I believe though he did not speak of where he had then journeyed, he began to know of Suyapee's storm upon all our lands. He knew then of our people's question to the many journeys we would choose across the trails that we had safely taken throughout all the seasons we had endured beneath Otelagh's gifting hands. As I look over towards Tenas Howh, I tell him; "it

269

is not only our peoples, and our lands that are in grave danger, but all the lands, of all our peoples, that will soon be taken beneath the dark cloud that holds no promise that we will again see our lands emerge from behind its hostile storm.

Tenas Howh, this is the beginning of the dark storm that may never pass! This is the beginning of the dark storm that will take you and I far from our lands and seed us to where life will not grow.

We will hear words spoken from the depths of the bad spirit's soul as Suyapee tells us with straight face that these lands are the promised lands. Suyapee will tell us that we must take the long trail. He will tell us we must leave our villages and take nothing with us from these lands and that we must forget where our souls have become attached to the High Spirits of our lands.

I can hear them today tell us to begin anew where we do not know of those spirits that sit silently amongst the most desolate of lands, where they do not share of promise to our peoples.

Sadness will quickly fall upon our souls, and as our spirit is taken from within us, we will be as the great bear that has fallen into the deep trap hollowed from the soils of those lands that he was seen to once roam free. All our peoples will become lost souls, each walking blindly without faith, taken where the spirit's voices will not be heard to direct us from the evil that awaits to take us from upon the trails we choose. Life will not return to us as we once knew, and we will all be taken within the dark cloud of this storm, and we will not be heard or seen again if my vision of Suyapee brings truth to my father's vision, and to my own!"

Tenas Howh asks; "if Suyapee takes from within his purse the Red Cloud that lies thick across all the lands, and we cannot see what lies before us as we did all the days before today that

270

offered us support and prosperity, why do you question if Suyapee has the heart of the Good Spirit? Would Suyapee not even then be known to be promised to dwell from within the dark soul of the bad spirit and rise up against all that we have known to be good?"

As Tenas Howh had now questioned my thought, I knelt in silence and thought hard to how I have explained this lesson to myself as it was spoken from my Hyas Fathers from upon the Walls of Wahclella. First, I must question myself why I too question if Suyapee is good, or if he is bad?

Our Fathers have told us that they have seen in their own vision the approach of Red Cloud, and from within Suyapee's wide eyes, we would soon see our peoples taken from where we today, stand proud.

As the Hyas Saghalie Tyee Tahmahnawis has also directed us to join hands in peace with all those we pass upon his many trails, I ask; "What trails must we follow if Suyapee's charge across our lands leave us with nothing from where all we once knew offered us life?"

To stand in silence shall permit us no promise to our lands and to what we have known for many seasons, and as quick as the new season comes, we will be no more than a lost memory in the minds of those that will call themselves conquerors over the innocence of our peoples!

From Red Cloud's thickening burden we are surrounded by the cries of all those that live amongst us, all but the snake that thrives lower than the soils of the earth, in deep dens where they await to rise up from the catacombs of the bad spirit to strike madly upon us as we walk! The Snake and Suyapee may soon be known as brothers to the darkness of night. They both will be brothers to the bad spirit who preys upon those that sleep. Soon, I fear we will hear them call out our names, one, and then another as darkness falls heavy across the lands. As Otelagh rises and peers down upon his creation, he will know we will not be seen again upon the lands that he created beneath his saddened and tearful pass.

The dark cloud that we had been held beneath has now begun to clear from above us, and before Otelagh sets in the western sky, we will be near the village of the Cathloptle once again. There, we will sit before our brothers and speak of what we are seeking from Suyapee once we demand to step upon the tall ship that has brought them again before our lands.

We have heard in their strong words, and have seen by their sign, they tell us to lay before them the soft pelt of beaver and fox, and they will offer us much in trade with cloth and copper kettles. It was told to us by Suyapee at the village of our brothers when they first came to our shores, if we were to bring the finest of the furs before them, they will place before us what is called the long rifle and sharp knives in trade. In this, we must first ask; "Once all the animals are taken from upon our lands, what will be left so that our peoples can survive all the winter's storm that will fall hard upon us? We must ask if this cloth they call blankets will keep us warm through winter's harshest storm? We must ask, why do they then demand the warmth of the beaver and fox to be taken from us, and placed before their own people's chairs?

"Will Suyapee then take from us the Hyas Pish that runs fast beneath En che Wauna? Will Suyapee take from upon our lands the Hyas Cedar so we have no brothers whom will offer their souls for us to kneel upon their bench as we follow the Hyas Otelagh to the lands of the East where he awakens each day, or to those of the west where he rests each night? I ask, will

Suyapee take us from upon the lands of which the Saghalie Hyas Tahmahnawis has generously offered us support? Or, from where we find honor before all our brothers through the teachings he has shared to our fathers, as they too are heard to speak to us of our life's long journey from upon the Sacred Walls of Wahclella?"

The river runs high and its current swift. As the heaven has cleared from its threatening storm, many geese and swan have filled the sky above us as their journey has begun early this season. They fly to the south where warmth and seed awaits their arrival from the frigid lands of the far north. I know, as we have passed beside the two high rocks, and have seen the new lands that have been raised from Wy-East's latest storm beside the river that comes of Wy-East, we are near the final turn of the big waters that lead to the village of the Cathloptle at Nahpooitle.

In the fields and marshes that stand magnificently beside us, Hyas Sun shines down and shares to all that look upon them the colors of fall as they each fill our senses with much pleasure. Vibrant reds and bright yellows flash before us from the leaves as Wind turns each towards us as they wave as we pass. Golden fields shine bright with the advance of fall beneath the long arms of Oak. Cottonwoods sing in chorus as Wind soothes their souls, and the mighty Eagle soars high above us as he awaits his next meal. These are what we must protect and honor, before they are each taken from within our people's own, quickly, thinning purse.

When we sit at night and listen to the call of Coyote across the open plains, and from high up within the great forest, she calms our harried souls. As we look to the flock of birds that rise high above us and peer down upon us, we see through great vision from where we stand upon the Hyas Larch, that one day, we too, can take wing and join them as we look across all the lands of our kingdom.

When we walk into the village of Nahpooitle where the mighty White Oak each welcomes us with long arms, they ask we sit beneath their cover and hear of life's many stories by those that approach us from deep within the marsh.

The Hyas Blue Heron, the wisest of all the birds that walks proud across the kingdoms knows first when the land is not healthy. As the frog, the lizard, and the fish are taken from the Heron's long beak, we hear their screams of warning rising up from the high branch along the waters of the marsh where they yearn for life to again flourish beneath them so they too can survive and see of Otelagh's rise tomorrow.

The beaver knows too when life's rhythm is taken from them, as great floods wash over their villages where they were once seen to be connected to the land. I know of this as I stood beside the broken dam of Eena one dark day, and as Eena swam to the shore where I stood, he called out in much pain, as all that he knew was drown beneath the rising tides, and he was then, once again, alone.

When I sit beneath the long arms of the mighty oak and see the great owl sitting restless upon his perch during both, day and night, I know the land is not healthy. I sense the bad spirit has taken from beneath the soils the villages of the mouse and shrew that offers the owl his great vision to see through the thickening darkness of night. Owl once looked over our villages with keen eyes, and he called out to warn us of all those that walk in amongst us as we sleep, but through its absence of warning as my vision tells, it has now made us wary as silence has now filled the night air. We fear Snake is soon to sneak into our longhouses and take our souls from our scalps, and as our spirit's are trapped where the emptiness of air holds the absence of life, we could not dream of reaching the Hyas Saghalie's village high up along the heaven's trails.

All life that is seen to flourish upon these lands offer themselves reason to coexist with one another! Upon them, we each have discovered why we need to give and take from one another so we all can survive the coming storms. I am afraid Suyapee will not understand the rhythm of the Earth as we know it. If they do not sit and listen to all the voices they are surrounded, all that Otelagh has gifted those that do understand to what makes our lands sing in happiness will be lost in Suyapee's senseless and hasty charge across these lands. Suyapee will then choose to steal the breath from Wind in the final battle between good and bad. All we had once known will fall silent from the heaven. We will be seen to walk upon lonely trails where no call will be heard to fall before us from either the good spirit of bird or animal, and we too will be lost forever from ourselves.

There will be no stories told, as there will be no memories of our peoples to be spoken of before the fires of Suyapee's villages. We, of the Chinook Nation, those of our peoples who have thrived with respect and with reverence upon these lands will be taken without thought from upon it. Through these new peoples chief's advice, we will not be recognized for all we have been considered through our honor as we have accepted and respected the rights of all life to walk freely amongst us. As darkness comes thick to cover our souls from light, and we cannot be seen, our voice shall fall forever silent, and we shall be forgotten as if we too were the last breaths expelled from Wind's foreshortened storm.

Though we have travelled far from our village this day, I feel we are watched with keen eyes, just as I had also felt given our departure this early morning. I ask my brothers if they feel eyes staring towards us as they too have looked toward the shores many times. I ask myself if Crow and Coyote have both taken the trail that follows beside the great river that leads to the villages of the Clatsop?

Crow has warned our peoples of danger from above our trails since the first days our peoples had arrived in the Land's of Wah, and as Hyas Coyote and I have become close friends, I have no fear and offer nothing but conviction if they were both to sit beside me. They neither show themselves before me and I miss knowing they are beside us, suddenly, I hear the call of Crow from beyond the highest arms of sticks that line the great river. Crow's cawing is quick to fall silent upon the breaths of Wind, and as silence again fills the voids of Wind, the cry of Coyote soon fills the vacancy of air from where Crow's call was last heard. I sense they too have become close friends. If they have chosen to look over our travels where Suyapee today rests, we shall return safely with word to all our brothers to the east of Suyapee's honor, or to their uncautioned approach before all our peoples. If Suyapee find our people's disagreeing and misunderstood by their own convictions, we will know they will walk amongst us without respect, and they will come upon us with many men armed with the soul of the bad spirit. I fear they shall take what they want and leave only what is useless for our survival upon the lands that will be taken from all our peoples.

Life will not be the same, and we will walk amongst the most barren of grounds, those same grounds where only the bad spirit would not refuse to be taken.

We have rested the night beside the warm fires at Nahpooitle, and have spoken with our brothers to our journey. As we sat before their fire this night, we have taken notice they too had traded for the red blanket and sharp knives. But, as we sat in silence and did not ask to where they came, our brothers did not talk of their trade with either the Clatsop or with Suyapee. Upon our return, before I tell them what I have seen in Suyapee's eyes, I will ask for what they have traded for their souls, and for those *pelts that were not so long ago seen attached to the free spirits of our lands.*

As we rise up from where we slept the night, our brothers have gathered beside the shore of En che Wauna and wish us good fortune as we go before Suyapee. We will take with us much question. Those same questions may lead us to understand of their peoples who will soon come before us with opened hands, and I fear we will all one day bow with much sorrow, as their closed eyes see nothing to all we are.

We are now into our second day of our long voyage upon the fast waters of En che Wauna as she pushes us with great rush to reach the tall ship that brings much question before our peoples and upon our lands. As we are nearing the village of the Wahkiakum on the shore of Cathlamet, (Rocky Beach), rising from beneath the waters as they swim hurried toward us, many Olhiyu, (Seal), gather beside our canoes as they bark out their question to what we have to offer from our cache. We all laugh as they rise up in unison and scream towards us, each, with different song, and with different question.

Tenas Howh knows well of Seal's play, as he scoffs to each of them as they come near the canoe. They each challenge us for our seat, and we must shove them back from the sides of our canoe as they laugh when they reach up to join us. Both, Tenas Howh, and myself, have tired of the seal's play, we look to the deep waters where the current is strong. Suddenly, from beneath En che Wauna's darkest depths comes a large seal, and quickly it jumps high into the sky and lands heavily beside us. With much force, a great wave washes over us. Hurried, we paddle to the shore where we steady our canoe, and pull those we tow behind us from the Big River. Here, upon the rocky shore, we take all that we have brought with us from within their swollen hulls, and our provisions would again be safe and not drown beneath the waters that lie deep within them.

There is first word spoken from my brothers they have not seen within the eye of Seal, fear, as they do today. Tenas Howh cautions that he too has seen the eye of Seal look as they do today. Tenas Howh says he had last seen the look of their lost souls when Ehkolie chased them as prey from the waters of the bay where his village stands today. Now there is question to what may be stalking Seal into the river from the big waters and if they had not begged to find safety amongst us and had not been given to steal from our cache as we had first thought?

We had dried our goods along the bank of En che Wauna as OKtelagh passed overhead, and now we have begun our journey once again. We sit wary of what may lurk beneath us, and from the distance, as we approach with caution, several islands lie along our route as they rest in the center of the Big River, alone and untouched, except for those of our brothers that have been placed upon their soils as they await their turn to rise up and join those in the Hyas Saghalie Tyee's kingdom.

As we come to the big turn in the river we drift towards the slow waters along shore, and there, we begin to see much smoke drift from the west as there appears to be many fires burning near where canoes and huts have been placed for many seasons as the chiefs of their villages awaited their turn to their final journey to the green meadow of heaven. These were our brothers, chiefs, and the leaders of many of the villages who have given us strong memories that remind us of their righteoused ways. They once walked beside us, and as they taught us of the right trails to follow so our salvation would be seen acceptable by the Good Spirit, now, their loss brings both much sadness, but too much happiness, as they will now be joined to their fathers sides high above the lands they so cherished to understand.

As we come upon the islands where they had once rested in peace we see thieves have swept across the islands and have taken from those dead, the spoils of their lives. In their wake, these robbers of graves have lain fire to what remains so those dead shall not have their spirits lifted from upon the Earth, and they will not find rest beside the chairs of their fathers. From the Hyas Saghalie Tyee's great meadow, those that have passed will look down upon us with much regret, and I fear the warning of Red Cloud may soon fall upon us. I fear our great leader's spirits shall wander unnoticed upon the trails of Wind, and they will have no point to where they may claim their souls would one day to rest.

We have seen no Wahkiukum come from their longhouse to welcome us as we step out onto the banks from the big river as we arrive. We have not looked upon their canoes coming to or from one another's villages as we had first seen when we began our return journey to our own village at Wahclella from Kwilluchini after Suyapee had first come.

With sad eyes and with much sorrow, as we stand looking out over the land we see laying motionless and not breathing many of our brothers. Their faces scarred, their eyes staring off towards their fathers above in the heaven. Sadly, there is not the hope for life within them. I sit here unknowing to all that may have come upon our peoples, and I am troubled. I hold my arms up toward the heaven where our Great Leader sits and looks down upon us, and as we are confused to all we see lost before us, with loud voice, I call out, "Nika Saghalie Tyee, ikta mitlite nesika mamook?" "My High Chief, what must we do?"

Though deep within my heart I sense much warning coming from the big waters as Suyapee comes to trade, I know, as my

Great Fathers have led me to understand through their lessons, I must first find within my soul all that is good within those that approach the trails of our lands. My Fathers have shared we may not understand or accept what is presented before us, but if we are to welcome all others into our villages, we must make concessions to live beside one another as we have with the Klale Lolo and Hyas Pishpish. We must accept all life to live and prosper beside us without question. Our Fathers tell us it is not our way to base judgment upon another's path, as their spirit, and may it be Suyapees too one day soon, be as trued toward the same trails in life we are tied.

Tenas Howh has given me much to think with his question, and as we have journeyed far from where we first shared our thoughts to the vision I see of Suyapee, I have begun to find myself to lean differently in my judgment towards them through those same teachings. I tell myself; "If I am to go before those I do not trust without knowing of their intent, then I will never know if their spirit is good or if it has taken the trails of the bad spirit.

In that loss, my soul may not find rest each night that I lie my head down upon the mat. My spirit may not walk in peace amongst them, and as I look towards them, I will show fear and anxiety from within my eyes, and they will know of my true spirit, just as I would know of their own through their wide eyes."

Through our Father's teachings, I have known blind men to see much clearer than I when they have walked upon the many trails where their lives had been led. It is from these same blind men's faith that brings trust to rise up from within their souls as they overcome any doubts that are cast from their mind's wanting scene. As they become attuned to all they are surrounded, they offer faith from their souls to extend out before them, and they know, even through the darkness that is spilled heavily in the absence of light into their eyes, they will not be taken sightless from the trails they are led to follow.

From these men I have learned much of myself, but as I am a mortal myself, and though I am led by the Great Father's teachings, I have discovered my trail across the lands often times confused with those they wish for me to follow. Neither today, nor tomorrow, will I allow myself to become confused or distraught by what I do not understand. From within me, my hope and faith must hold strong to the belief that tomorrow will bring happiness, and the song of bird will be sung softly from upon the tree's budding branch. I plead that Suyapee will too believe our spirit good, and that our spirits will not be led throughout our lives by the many daunting arms of the mesahchie Tsiatko. I too must have faith and not find myself to fear Suyapees' spirit attached to the bad spirit's ways.

I must ask myself if all the voices I have heard call out with concern are from those that too do not understand of the tall ship that brings Suyapee and the Red Cloud that lingers behind them as it is raised before the gates of heaven?

Great concern is lain thick across all the land of our peoples as we approach nearer the big waters of the sea. We have seen Seal's wish to join us in our canoe as they flee from deep within the dark waters of En che Wauna's depths where fear has risen up from within them and they have pled for sanctuary beside us. They must believe Suyapee lurks in wait for their spirit, as does the mesahchie Tsiatko wait for those he preys.

Again, from afar, I hear the call of Crow. Rising high upon the trails of Wind, Crow's cries are heard in attempt to settle the hearts of those that live beneath from where he flies. Crow crosses beneath the heaven and returns time and time again as he flies low over the lands, each time, calling out to those that sit with much worry and complaint as they fear the good spirit has abandoned them upon the lonesome Spirit's trail. They too fear these new peoples have come upon them without respect as they demand to take with them all they see before them. My brothers and I fear there will be much storm lain upon our lands when Otelagh awakes in the morning and passes above the Red Cloud, and when the land cannot be seen through the thick fog that lies heavy upon the lands, we know we may soon walk blindly as storm has once again settled hard upon us. We know this will bring much question to our tomorrows, and with much sorrow, these same questions have no answers."

But as Crow's call insists that we follow his lead, from high upon the mountain top, we hear the return of Coyote's call. She too shares we will be found safe beneath both their watchful eyes. As we look up to where Coyote calls we see her standing upon the highest peak of the mountain that rises beside the waters of En che Wauna. With head raised to the heavens, she cries out to Wind. She tells we must gather together, and from within us, find strength in knowing we will see the rise of Sun tomorrow above this Red Cloud that brings much question to life as we knew it before silence fell harshly from the lips of Wind. She demands we do not find fear in what we cannot yet see arising from upon the horizons across our lands, and we must look deep within our souls before we look into the depths of Suyapee's souls through their most inquisitive eyes.

From where I kneel in the canoe, I again look to where I last heard my friend Coyote call. As I think back to that night we shared upon the high cliff at the celebration at Wyam, I raise high above my head my left hand, and then, I raise up to Coyote my right. I too place the Sun and Moon before her in sharing we are brother and sister to the soils of the Earth and to the big meadow of the heaven. I promise to her we will find honor in treasuring patience and faith for what we do not yet understand and are soon to certainly endure in the beginning of this change that comes before us, and in these, to survive, we must each find honor to live beyond the horizons of today.

Through our understanding that life will always be renewed from the chair of our Saghalie Tyee Tahmahnawis, Suyapee will not take from us all we have within us as they come upon our shores in great numbers and choose to settle upon our lands. They may take from their purse much that we can learn as we walk amongst them, and we in turn may teach them of all we have taken from our Great Father's lessons from upon the Walls of Wahcllela. I have much hope each day will be alike a new birth gifted amongst our peoples, and we will live on forever to see the rise of all those tomorrow's suns our father's speak.

I look to the mountaintop and smile to my friend Coyote, for her words are wise, and from within myself, I know the path she chooses for us to follow is right. I will sit with my friend, Chief Tsutho at Kwilluchini, and we will share the long pipe, and we will speak of our hearts, and before I again step into the souls of the Three Cedar's host, I will walk free from the question that Suyapee brings before me this dark day.

Tomorrow will bring happiness and joy to shine from within me to all those I stand before. To those I ask to lead me to where the tall ship rests, and to Suyapee, where he sits and waits for our furs, they both will know that my heart is good, and my soul cleansed from all that brings darkness before the inception of all that is true.

Forward we ply with new vision to what may lie before us as we walk in amongst those new peoples that have journeyed far to sit beside us at the feet of our village's warm fires. My thoughts go to Chief Tsuthso and to his village. I hope the drums of their village will call out to my friend Ksitilo, and he will join us as we enter the village of the Clatsop as we take our place before those that have come to our lands with opened hands.

We are near Kwilluchini as we begin to follow the last turn of the land where lies the beach I have walked many times while struggling with decision to what had then lain heavy to my heart. With Wind at my back, and with Sun to my face, I walked until Otelagh sat low upon the far horizon and shed light and warmth upon those whom we had not yet met.

The Good Spirit walked with me, just there, in front of me, leading me, offering me the choice of my own decision. But, as I had given my life to the fathers of our peoples who stand immortal upon the Walls of Wahclella, deep within me, I knew they would lead me along the trail I chose, and once I returned, all that troubled me would be lost from within me. My Hyas Fathers have not once misguided me along the trails I had chosen. As I shout out to them for their guidance, they have answered with suggestion I follow the trails where my heart leads to what is right, and far from those trails that offer nothing but wrong to swallow our lives as it would then lead us upon dark trails where we could not see or return.

Life beneath our Great Father's reigns has brought success and wealth to our people's souls. Our hearts warmed by the gifts he has offered from within his hands as he places them each before us all to cherish. The Hyas Saghalie Tyee Tahmahnawis we see in every form that breathes the breath of life and shares of that same breath towards us. From plant to animal, our Highest Spirit is within them as they are each part of his being. Each star we see in the night's sky, to Otelagh's sister, Moon, to each river and stream, to the mountains, to the deserts, they all are within us, and we are within them.

We are all a part of the Hyas Spirit, and through our own spirit, we are within one another as it was from the High Spirit's hands that we were first bore.

I had always thought our peoples had come from the sands of the long beach as the waters of the sea first came together beneath the battle that raged between Wind and Storm. As our peoples rose up from where we once swam with pish, and as we touched the sands of the long beach where Knope now sits, the High Spirit was first heard to call out to us from atop Walawahoof, as Indian.

But one day, my father told me of our peoples and how we have come from the Thunderbird that flew from the south to the north and made nest upon Walawahoof, (Saddle Mountain).

As Thunderbird flew off her many eggs were left untended in the Big Nest, and as Giantess, Wolverine, had given chase to Thunderbird to see where she had chose to roost, she soon discovered her nest high up on the mountaintop. It has been told before the first egg reached the valley below as it was thrown from the nest, it had become Indian. Many more eggs were broke open and thrown down the mountain by Wolverine, and they became the brothers of the first Indian to set foot upon these most sacred of lands.

When Thunderbird returned to her nest, she saw there were no eggs. She quickly flew to where South Wind sat, and they together, began to search for Giantess. They willed themselves to seek revenge upon her for her theft. Many seasons have since past, and they have searched for where she hides in the north *where snow lies frozen upon the mountaintops, but still today, they have yet to find where she hides.*

Giantress is as elusive as the great cat.

Wolverine Spirit is wise and strong.

This is how we have become the peoples of the Hyas Chinook, my father said. We are a proud people that are a part of this Earth, and the Earth is a part of our peoples. We are the same, together. Both our spirits shall live on in prosperity as long as we honor the Heavens above us, and the Earth below us.

This was the story my father had told me when I was a young boy as we walked along the shore of En che Wauna and climbed into the valley where the Great Eagle has been seen to fly from the bowl beneath Metlako. That day, we spoke of all we saw as we walked toward our Hyas Spirit Wy-East, and as Otelagh shone down upon us and smiled, my life began to change. My life changed as does the caterpillar into the butterfly. My youthful views began to diminish, and my thoughts began to demand that I rise up from where my spirit had lain in wait to shine bright before our peoples. As I began to feel the trail beneath my feet, and not only see what lay beneath me, I was reborn to the soils of the Earth, and I became promised to all we were to be chosen by our Great Father.

As my father told me we were one with all that lived upon these lands, I began to hear voice come from all life that surrounded me. From closed eyes, I began to see visions that would one day lead me upon all the trails of our Great Fathers. As change would soon fall upon our lands, this would bring much question to our hearts as we would then have to walk in amongst its gathering branch. Unknowing if the branch we would then be tied would be like the blackberry's long arms where is raised the sharp thorn of disgust?

286

Or, if we were to be tied to the sweet scent of Cedar, and grow tall and strong as we reached high above the soils we were born to touch the Hyas Saghalie Tyee Tahmahnawis' most welcoming meadow?

This has brought all my decisions to have been taken from the trail of righteousness. As I have left behind those trails that cast dark cloud of doubt before us, our peoples, my peoples, all peoples, are now safe from the wishes of the mesahchie Tsiatko. If you choose to follow the trail I have been pointed by my Father's lead, your name will be remembered by all those that come after you as you pass into the Spirit World where the Dream Spirits dance leads to the brightest fires of the High Spirit's village.

My Great Grandfather was heard to speak before those of my village if we were to walk upon the trails as blind men, we would have to first take from within us doubt. The same doubt where we would be taken far from the trails of our lives that would have offered us what was first chosen as one of our greatest gifts, our encouragement to honor humanity through our learned moral principles.

Chief Nenamooks had once been heard too tell if we were to follow closely in the steps of our Great Fathers, we would not need to see what lies ahead in all we may hold within ourselves to question. My Great Grandfather was heard to tell; "We could walk into the darkness without fear, and we would know we would not step from the trail that wills life to be saved distant from the path where death is lent through the error of our judgment."

Through this message, it will allow my mind to remain sharp and allow me to accept Suyapee for whom he is. I shall not walk before them and think their spirit is bad before they prove they are taken far from the morality of life we have been led to understand. If we do see they have shown their spirit to become joined with the bad spirits of Snake and the Tsiatko mesahchie tahmahnawis, then, and only then, will we spell our judgment before them as we ask of them to join beside us in our village and speak of what they wish.

As we sit before the warm fire at night, we will smoke from the long pipe and lead them through the long journey our peoples have been led by the Good Spirit's teachings. If they are chosen to follow in the footsteps as we too had accepted when the Dream Spirit rose up from the fires of our village, and where they led us to dream of the most honorable village of our Saghalie Tyee Tahmahnawis, we will find within Suyapee's spirit, hope. In this hope, we will cry out to the High Spirit with arms raised to the heaven, and ask he will lead them to where they may open their thoughts to the suggestion of change from within their misguided and darkened souls.

Through the changes of Sun to Moon, we will become brothers to the Earth, and all that lives and breathes upon our Illahee will then be free from the ties of imprisonment from one another's conceit.

This is what our peoples must wish before Suyapee. As we follow the trails across the lands of En che Wauna, may we all share respect before one another and know we each belong to the soils of this Earth. "I plead my Hyas Saghalie Tyee Tahmahnawis, may we both find the gift of peace between us that has been seen to be in much question through our visions, and as Otelagh rises above us, may we live on into all those tomorrows we have yet to share.

May it be so today, and may it be so through all those tomorrows when Sun rises before Moon, and as they sit upon their chairs in the heaven and peer down and smile upon us, may they be seen to join together with us, and we each together, shall be as one upon the *Hyas Tahmahnawis Tyee's* Great Earth.

As light comes from where darkness had once settled within our hearts, life too will come from where death may have been closely promised to both our peoples by the hand of the *mesahchie Tsiatko tahmahnawis*. Then, when Sun shines bright over all our peoples, there will be peace and happiness spread across all the lands. We shall know of one another's spirit as life will extend from both our hands, and we will walk beside one another without hearing of either our complaint.

As we climb upon the high hill and look down upon our kingdoms, we will see all those that hid in the darkness of the forest from fear of the passing storm as they will quickly reappear into the light of life.

This is what we wish before our *Hyas Saghalie Tyee Tahmahnawis*. We wish he will allow life to emerge again into the warmth of our light, and as our peoples, all people's happiness returns, it will be spread across all the lands. Our faith and trust will bring shadow to what we had once judged, and life will again be good..."

Chapter 18

The Great Spirit of Chief Tsutho

We look to Otelagh as he has begun to fall below the horizon and is soon to rest upon his bed as his spirit finds its trail led through his dreams to the lands where he will again rise above us in the light of tomorrow.

We turn from the big river, and we point our canoes toward the shore where the village of Kwilluchini stands. Again, we take notice our brothers are absent from along the banks of the river as we walk in from the river, and we see there are no canoes coming from En che Wauna as they would be casting net in hope pish would join within them. We stand with much question as we pull our canoes high up to the bank of the shore, there in line before us sits many canoes of several villages that rest upon the great river. We had not heard the drum call out to those that now sit within the longhouse, and we lay caution to what they may speak.

Silence falls heavy upon our deaf ears, and as we call out to our brothers, there is no answer in return. Dark smoke has fallen from the heaven, and as it has taken the last light from our eyes, it has drawn darkness upon all we had once seen upon the shore. Wind too has been silenced from sharing deep breaths upon the trees that line the hyas waters of En che Wauna. Only smoke from fire in the longhouse brings light of promise to the Wahkiukums and to those brother's spirits that have journeyed to sit with them before the big fire. Their spirits are good, and as they are gathered tightly before the big fire, they will discover prosperity and promise between them as they speak. In this, I have much hope.

We are challenged to approach the doors of the longhouse of our brothers as we cannot first show sign that we walk in amongst them with open hands and wish to sit before their fire as we await the return of Sun before we cross the big river and sit with those at Knope.

I ask Mashatah to stand beside the canoes until we call for him to join us with our brothers, and slowly, we take the trail from the shore as we call out many times toward where our brothers sit.

From the smoke that sits low upon the land, comes the son of Chief Tsutho, Chatska, as he walks to us from the door of the longhouse with head bowed. With sad eyes, he looks up and tells his great father has fallen ill as the bad spirit has lain in ambush upon their lands for many days, and as the bad spirit has chosen to prove of his powers before them, he has taken many of their peoples from them. Chatska trembles with much fear as he tells his father, like his mother, had suddenly fallen lonesome to his bed and had begun to be taken from them in wait to journey to where the High Spirit's meadow sits. Chatska tells us his father lies unmoving upon his bed, and as he speaks to his father, his father's eyes do not open, and his breaths fall silent from his lips. Chatska shares much sadness as he tells his father now lies unmoving in wait for the Hyas Tahmahnawis to take his soul from within him so both his mother's and father's spirit can once again rest beside one another each night.

Great sadness fills my heart as I sense the pain coming from within Chatska's soul.

Chief Tsutho and I had become friends many seasons ago as I had taken my first journey to see the waters of the big sea. As I stand before his son, who is soon to be the Chief to his peoples, I reach out to him and place my hand upon his shoulder. I tell him the High Spirit has held his father's chair before the warm fires of his village for many seasons, and his father would want him to be pleased the High Spirit would call him to sit in the Green Meadow and not find his heart filled with sadness and despair.

Chatska and I stood beside one another in silence as we both thought to his father, then as we both looked towards the sky above, Chatska spoke of all those who had come to sit with his father's strong spirit so they too could take from him all that was good. With a great sigh, he welcomed me into his village, and asked that I follow him as we enter together into the longhouse and sit upon his father's side for what may be his longest and final day.

Chatska knows that his great father and I have been friends for many seasons, and I remember well it was when Chatska was a young boy, he came stumbling from the river with his first catch, a small trout, when I had first met him. In silence, and with hidden smile, I remember well his big eyes. To him, he had brought honor to his father as it was the largest pish caught on that quiet day they shared along the great river.

As I stand beside Chatska I tell him of the honor it would be to sit with his father once more as the Good Spirit awaits his father's soul to rise up from within him. I tell Chatska; "I know your father's spirit will quickly be placed upon the seat of his chosen star, and as it is seen to streak across the heaven, soon my friend, your father, and your people's great leader shall finally sit beside his wife upon the High Spirit's meadow. There, high above you, they both will smile down upon you as they watch with much pride over all you shall do for your peoples.

"Chatska, we must remember not to walk where sorrow's weight takes all that is good from within our memories of those that have been chosen to the High Spirit's village. We must accept that life and death are the same as Sun and Moon. All our fathers and mothers will one day be taken from us, and we must attach our journey in life to the memories we each have shared. We must keep close to our souls all the teachings they have shared before us so we too can become great leaders to all those that look toward us for courage as they choose what paths they too will decide to follow."

I motion to my brothers to take from our canoes our goods and place them upon the high bank where we will make camp for the long night ahead. I tell my brothers I will return when the soul of Chief Tsutho had either risen from within him, or if the Good Spirit had honored him with new breaths where life will enter within him, and offer him much strength to see beyond the darkness of this night. I have much hope he may once again stand before us and speak of where the bad spirit had taken him upon the dark journey where he would then return.

"Chatska, let us go sit with your father, and as we speak to him, may his soul be strong as his spirit will again rise up with much happiness."

Chatska and I begin to walk from the darkness that is spelled from the sorrow of Chief Tsutho's silent and unavoided travel into the light of the longhouse where his thoughts are quelled from our ears. As Chatska and I enter, surrounding the bed of Chief Tsutho that is raised from the floor to bring warmth to his bones, are several chiefs and many friends of his father. Medicine men have come down from their high places to offer Chief Tustho's soul to the Boat Journey upon En che Wauna to the most honorable place of their peoples, the Land of the Living Dead. It is a sad scene to share, but we must remember what comes from the trails of life shall one day too follow that same trail to death.

Many of those that circle the Chief's bed sit in silenced thought and offer him strength from within their own spirit, and others walk in circles as they carry within their hands the Skudilitc which is formed from the Great Cedar where is seen many faces of all those dead of our nation in red and black paint taken from the rich soils of the river.

Standing back from the Elders of our Nation is the Medicine Man, Deshonto. I had met him long ago when I journeyed to the village of Ithlkilak where the White Salmon is seen in the light of full moon. As we look to one another, we both bow our heads with much respect, and it was then I knew without speaking, Chief Tsutho would not be back amongst his people. Calm rose up within me, and as I stood beside the bed of my friend, I spoke to him with silenced voice, and I wished him safe journey to the High Spirit's Great Meadow so he too would find calm as he sits beside the woman he has loved for many, many seasons.

Through the long night, each medicine man rose up, one by one from where they sat. They each walked around his bed as they shook their power sticks of bark of Cedar that was tied with red cloth over the great chief, and they cried out with much sympathy to the *Hyas Tahmahnawis* that his soul would not yet pass.

I looked over to Deshonto many times, and as I took notice he stood stilled to the moments we all shared, I feel he must see great vision to where the spirit of our friend will soon go, and as he stands, alone, he knows of Chief Tsutho's soul. Deshonto knows as I do, the Great Spirit will share before us all to what is good from Chief Tsutho's soul as he passes into the spirit world.

I too look over to Chatska, and as I know of his heart as he watches over all that comes to his father, I am sad this day has come upon him with such regret as he has lost both his mother and father so quickly.

With silenced voice, I call out to the High Father above, and I plead that Chief Tsutho's soul will soon be taken from within him and that his soul will find rest again in the silence of the storm he has become surrendered.

Into the long night, the fire of the village has burned bright as it Offered hope that Chief Tsutho's body would warm from where the cold of winter had fallen upon him. Now, as the night grows long, grave shadows have begun to fill the air where once the light of life was kept lit before us.

From above the trails of the village we all could hear calling out to Moon the cry of Coyote as she sings unto the heaven. As we all heard of Coyote's mournful call and as we turned to each corner of the longhouse from where we each had heard of her cry, we looked down upon our friend as he lay motionless before us.

Suddenly, he rose up from upon his bed and gasped with hope that life would again hold him to the soils of the Earth beside us. Chief Tsutho's eyes opened wide and shined before us with happiness as he then saw his friends had joined upon his side. As Chief Tsutho looked across the room and saw each of his friends look down upon him, a smile formed upon his lips as warmth was again cast out from within him, and as it reached out to touch all those that joined beside him, it gave us each hope he would return from where he had been taken.

In an instant the bad spirit was taken from within him. Chief Tsutho's smile then became hard and unmoving, and he then chose to lie down upon his mat and take easy of his last breath.

It was then, as a star crossed the heaven and spread bright light to shine down through the opening of the longhouse, his soul had begun to prepare itself for his long journey upon the Hyas Waters of En che Wauna where he would join those that too had passed on into the Land of the Living Dead upon the Big Island.

We each stood, some in great mourning, others relieved the pain had been taken from his and our own hearts. From within the longhouse great mourning rose up to those that waited outside as we cried out to Hyas Tahmahnawis to make Chief Tsutho's journey swift and decided without difficulty.

Slowly, we walked to where Chatska stood and placed our hands upon his shoulders, and as we stood with him, we each let him know that his great father was soon to be sitting upon his mother's side, and all that was placed within his father by the bad spirit had been taken from within his good soul.

We each then walked from the longhouse, cloud had then separated from the heavens, and Otelagh once again shone bright across the lands as the dawn of a new day appeared before us.

Life began to walk free from the dark cloud of despair as it had been cast thick over the lands, and much happiness filled the air as song of bird and call of Elk were then heard again to fill the trails of Wind.

"Wawa Mahsie mitlite kopa okoke Hyas Tahmahnawis."

"Praise be to the High Spirit."

Many of those who were together in the longhouse walked to En che Wauna, and there we sat upon the bank as we looked across the water in silence, each knowing, one day, we would be the ones taken upon the Trail of En che Wauna and would be seen of our race to the Land of the Living Dead.

We all knew Chief Tsutho would soon go to be with the High Spirit, and much preparation was needed before he was to be placed to lie within his canoe upon the Big Island where his spirit would await to be chosen to his own star. It will be an honor to witness my old friend journey across the heaven where we would look up and see him make journey for the final time to the lands where Sun and Moon shine down upon him forever as they do not either rise or set. The time had come this day to speak of gathering his treasures that would be placed with him in his greatest canoe as he took upon his final journey upon this Earth he had so treasured.

All those that joined beside me as we left Wahclella for Knope to speak with Suyapee had now come to where we sat, and they knew the Chief had begun his journey into the Spirit World.

My brother, Tsemitan, sat at my side and asked where Chatska had gone? I turned to look toward the longhouse and told my brother; "Chatska, is at his father's side wailing to the High Spirit and pleading his father's spirit will rise up from where he will soon rest on the Big Island."

Tsemitan was a close friend to Chasta as they were of the same age and had played baggitiway, lacrosse, with all the children of many villages for as long as Sun passed over the land before Moon rose and darkness fell across the long meadow. With the rise of Sun the second day, they would return to their game until they tired or a victor was awarded the game. I do not know if they had won or lost the battle they had fought hard between one another. Neither spoke of a winner or of a loser once they returned to the fire of the village. They all smiled and laughed at their greatest feats, so it was with much joy they played the game.

Tsemitan told me he was going to sit with his friend beside his father, and take from his soul the sadness that has taken his hope from within him. As I nodded my approval, he walked to the longhouse and entered through the closed door. When Chasta had again shown his spirit had returned from where his sorrow had led him, both Tsemitan and Chasta walked out into the light of the new day, and they both come to where we sit waiting for them to join us in the celebration of Chief Tsutho's life.

Chasta called out to one of his villagers to take the big drum of their village to the high hill and spread message their father would soon be taken upon the Trail of the Living Dead. He asked for the message to tell his father would soon join those others upon the Big Island as they await their spirits to rise up and gather to those lands where life never ends.

Many people would soon come upon the shore below Kwilluchini to pay their respects before Chatska, and swiftly, many gathered wood for the big fire which will soon be set in the center of the village. This is where all those that come would sit and take of

Pish and Stuchen, Moolack and Mowitch beside one another as we all would then share story of Chief Tsutho's most honorable life and of his passion for his people to live beyond all the next seasons many storms.

Those that care of the dead have begun to come and gather at the door of the longhouse where Chief Tustho rests, and they can be heard to speak of taking his favorite spear and net, the war club he had taken in battle, and his finest robes and pelts to prepare them to be lain beside him upon his journey.

One old man tells he will take the chief's fine bow and long arrows, and with these, he will wash them with soft reed and bring life to the wood. The caretakers of the dead tell they too will collect the shell money, (dentalium), the Chief had saved to trade. Hiis wealth was well known to many of our nation, and the dentalium shall be gathered together in cloth and placed at his feet, and the Good Spirit will know he was wise and good.

Two more brothers came to them, and they took the Chief's canoe from where it was set above the ground between two strong trunks of sticks that had once fallen to the soils where they joined with all the good spirits. From there, the brothers promised they would bring new paint to the Hyas Eagle that flies to the heaven from upon its nose, and the canoe will bring pride to his peoples as those that pass upon En che Wauna will look upon it with much respect. They too speak of taking the sharp horn of Elk to the canoe's bench so water will not gather beneath the great Chief and bring cold to his soul as he awaits his star to rise up before Otelagh where our High Spirit shines with much warmth each day.

As each of the caretakers stood at the door and began to enter the longhouse as they prepared to gather all the Chief's possessions they were to make ready for his voyage, an old man came from the tall mountain and stepped before them. The old man told he had seen vision he was to come down from the mountain and make ready the Chief to be placed into his bed so he can make the long journey upon the channel of the heaven's big waters to the Land of the Living Dead.

As I had heard the old man speak of what he was to do I told Chatska to go to him, and to listen closely of the vision he speaks. When Chatska turned to see to whom I spoke, he rose up with much happiness, and he told me he was his father's brother, One Who Flies With Birds, (Ikt Klaksta Kawak Kopa Kallakala). Chatska told us he lived high up where Indian had not yet touched the snows of the highest peaks of our lands, and it is from there where it has been told he walks beside the Hyas Tkope Moolack. It has been told they have both shared of the same bed, and he has shared of many visions of lands Indian has not seen as his and Tkope Moolack's souls have joined as he has made journey through each of their spirit.

Chatska approached his uncle with opened arms, and they spoke together as if they had not seen one another for many seasons. As I looked to them and watched, I saw Chatska had then understood the difference between sorrow and the celebration of life as his family and friends gave him much strength to see all that was good from what had brought sadness to fall deep within his heart. This I was grateful as I knew then we would soon speak of what we were to do when we approached Suyapee as we sit before the fire with the Clatsop. I will ask Chatska to join with us when his father is at rest high up upon the Big Island, Hyas Tenas Illahee, and once we take of our journey to Knope, we will sit and hear of the Clatsop and what they may see come from within Suyapee's spirit. Then, we will make decision in how we will approach the tall ship, and, if we will talk of trade.

300

The brother of Chief Tsutho told Chatska he would dress his brother in his best Elk skins, Clamon, as he was seen to have wore in protection from the Snakes brother's sharp arrows.

It was there at Que-nett, place of Chinook Salmon, near the village of the Necootimeigh, he had found battle with the Snake as he journeyed to the potlatch at Xia'tixat with several of his braves from Kwilluchini. I remember when Chief Tsutho came upon our village and took his canoes from En che Wauna and sat beside us through the long night. He spoke of his invitation by his friend, Chief Queset, of the Klickitat, as a messenger from his village came to him and placed the short stick in his hand telling of the potlatch and celebration as his daughter's hand was promised to a strong brave of the Assuti, Nez Perz.

As Sun journeyed across the heaven we prepared for the potlatch as we took from our cache, mowitch and moolack that we had brought, and others from the Cowlitz had come and sat before where Chief Tsutho lay. They too placed pish and clam upon the long table at the side of the big fire for the celebration.

When Moon rose up from the east we sat beside the waters of En che Wauna and looked over all the lands, and from the long turn to the west where Suyapee had first come, we see my friend, Ksitilo, as he kneels with his father, Chief Kwillikum. It was not long after we had first seen them come upon us they walked up from the river and gave much respect to Chatska, and it was seen to be good between them. I stood as the Chief and Ksitilo came to me, even though I have journeyed near his village, the chief and I had never met, but as he stood at my side he told he knew of me through the story his son had told of Red Cloud, and I was pleased...

I too told Kistilo's father of the great speech his son shared at Wyam to what he had seen of Suyapee, and how they had stolen light from heaven, and Wind from air. He too, was then greatly pleased...

The Great Drum of Kwilluchini again began to send out message the Great Chief had passed, and from the distance that message was spread to the east. I knew soon all the villages along En che Wauna would hear of our loss, and those who knew Chief Tsutho would come, and there would be much celebration.

When the wise owl was first heard to call out from the meadow this night, several braves of the Cowlitz came to the shore, and they too stood before Chatska and spoke of all that was good of his father.

I knew as the night grew long and Moon journeyed across the heaven that many more brothers would come and celebrate, and it would be time for me and for those that have joined with me upon this journey to stand before them all and bring talk of the vision our Great Fathers had once spoke. If we, as a nation, should take from our lands those spirits we have honored for all our days and take from the hands of Suyapee for what he brings to trade, what will we have left of those gifts the Saghalie Tyee Tahmahnawis has placed before us?"

Many questions arise from my thoughts and they will soon be pointed toward my brother's ears as they hear words spoken that hold much truth.

I will ask them all what is the worth of our spirit and of those spirits that walk beside us each day? Will it be for a knife and copper kettle that Suyapee brings for their trade? When we take water from the stream, and pour it into the copper kettle, is this to warm the water we will soon wash the blood of Suyapee from its blade? Or, will it be to cleanse the blood from our children's bodies as they choose to fight when Suyapee marches with *conviction amongst us and demands that we walk with sad eyes to lands we do not know?*

I will ask what will we do to stay warm and dry when the season that brings rain to fall upon our lands without end begins? What will we do when winter's storm drops upon the face of the tall mountains above our lands, and snows falls deep onto their slopes as Cole Winds are swept upon us with much threat? Again, I will ask, will blanket alone bring warmth to our souls when the pelts of all those spirits that have offered us warmth when winter comes hard upon us are no longer seen to walk amongst us?"

These are the questions I must ask them all, and I will tell my brothers they must answer only to themselves as their answer will be what they will then find themselves to walk for all days and through long nights.

From the darkness calls out more of our nation that arrives to the celebration, it is Chief Shinome and his son, Coshitan, of the Clatsop whose village we were soon to enter upon in the end of our journey. Now, as we sit and speak before all our brothers, we will go to where the big ship that steals the breaths of Wind can be seen, and we will know if Suyapee's spirit is good or if it is bad as we take upon the waters of En che Wauna and speak before them of our decision.

I know if Chief Shinome is to come, then too we will soon see the chief of the Tillamook, and the chief of the Nehalem when Sun rises from his bed. There will be many of our nation's great leaders joined beside one another and they will sit at the big fire. Our talk will be good. From the wisdom shared of our High Spirits before all those who will sit with us, we, as the Hyas Chinook Nation, must all agree to what we must decide.

The canoes of many villages come upon the race of En che Wauna, and as we look out to the river, it is as if the leaves of the old season are about to turn and fall from the sticks long arms. The sight of all our brothers lined across the Great River remind me of the days when Sun stays low in the heaven in the short days of winter. The days when great numbers of kalakala would be seen to rest upon the river's calm, and we could not see En che Wauna push to the waters of the Big Sea beneath their opened wing.

First, to come upon us are the braves of the Clatskanie whose village lies across the banks of En che Wauna from Kuwillchini, and with them, they bring Wapatoo and Camas for the table. They tell us their chief too rests upon his bed and has sent them to stand beside Chatska, and to share before him stories of his great father he has never heard before this day.

Then the Multnomah and the Clackamas come with many people from their villages in one another's canoes. Their friendship has been strong for many seasons between them, and it is good.

Many more come from all around. The Chief of the Tillamook, Nicha, and the Chief of the Nehalem, Hontoo, come to the shore below us, and we see they come together with their wives, the sisters of the Chief of the Clatsop. Each of their wives wear necklaces of shiny glass that looks like sky during the clear and cloudless day. From Suyapee, these too have come before us in trade for the skin of the Hyas Sea Otter and Red Fox.

When En che Wauna is again seen calm from the rush upon her, we hear calling out from beyond where we cannot see those that come with the Great Chief and son of Quesat, Quinto of the Klickitat. They bring many braves with them as they tell they too will go to where Suyapee sits upon the tall ship and offer trade for what they bring. When they stand with us upon the shore of the Big River, they tell they want the long rifle and sharp knife to fight against the Snake when they come as there has been much trouble between them once again. The Klickitat, as well many others will offer hides to Suyapee. They bring with them the Great Cat and Golden Bear they have taken from the high peaks from where legend has been told the Black Feet run from where ice meets snow into the long valleys of their villages as they chase the mighty buffalo from upon the edge of cliff above them.

Through the light of day we have taken the side of Chatska and have spoke well of his father, and we ask him what trails he has chose for his peoples? It will be through the words he will speak before them they will understand of the trails he has been chosen to lead them towards the foot of the High Spirit's chair.

The young boys choose to walk to the long meadow and bring match between them with bow and arrow, and from beyond, where stick's stand tall between us, we hear much roar rise up from where they are gathered. Through the long day, they do not return, and as light has begun to fall from the heaven, and as the fire of the village glows with much warmth, they return to take meal from the High Spirit's hand. The women bring food from the shelf of the longhouse and place it before us all, and we are pleased.

Life is good, and we bring song to the ears of Hyas Saghalie Tahmahnawis Tyee for what he has offered us and to those that rest in the long meadow of the heaven for where they have led us upon the right trail to the feet of our High Spirit.

As we sit I have chosen to speak of the change we have begun to see come upon many of our nations as it has been brought from the hands of those we have yet to know of their spirit. We do not know if Suyapee will ask for more from our lands once they have taken what they first ask, and this creates worry to enter within me, and through my concern, I stand alone and ask for those that sit with me to listen to my words and search their souls for answer to what I speak.

"As I look out to all of you that have come to the village, I see much I have never seen, the blue and red blanket that promises to bring us warmth in the cold winter. Chief Bead that we see worn by the women, and the metal blade of knife we will find with much trouble to bring its blade, sharp edge. I see the bright button and cloth that gives color to the clothes we do not wear. I see the long blade of saber Suyapee tells will bring death to those that stand before its warning, but I ask you, will it reach out to those that bring arrow upon its storm above us from the high cliff? The musket, which an old woman at Wyam had told of her son's story when it was pointed to Mowitch as it made great noise, and as fire was seen to come from within its long barrel, it stole the spirit from the soul of Mowitch. Again, I must ask, does it know of the Mowitch's spirit or hear of its voice as they place honor before us as they offer their soul to be placed upon our table so we can see of Sun tomorrow?"

"I ask you all, is this the way of our peoples? To trade for all we have known to be sacred to our souls, and to make trade for what we have found to favor our spirit when we rest upon the Big Island as these furs offer us warmth before we take the long journey to join beside Otelagh in his village where he shines bright each day?"

"From the sharp horn of deer and elk we make knife, and we make cloth to wear when winter comes from their soft furs. From the Yew Tree we make the strong spear and bow and arrow that takes the soul from Bear so his coat will be worn around our shoulders when the storm of winter does not go from our lands."

306

"Do we need more than what the Hyas Tahmahnawis Tyee offers?'

"This change that comes upon us brings much threat to our peoples and to our ways. Suyapee brings before us gifts we do not need, and as they take all that we have in our lands, our spirits will soon walk lost upon the trails of our fathers."

"Our fathers and we both will be lonely upon our own trails. Our lives will become separated and we will not see of one anothers spirit joined again upon the fleeting stars of our heaven as we yearn to sit in the Big Meadow of the High Spirit's village."

"One day soon, I have vision that my fear will rise up from within me as I will see we are a lost people where we can no longer place our village upon the only lands we have known. We will bow our heads with much shame when we realize Suyapee is like Old Coyote.

Suyapee will take what we hold valuable within our clinched hands without our knowing he stands before us with wide smile and steals all we have hidden beneath clasped fingers."

"We will be seen in great sadness, and we will never return to those gifts we had once given much honor and respect, nor will we be seen again to stand with that same honor or respect offered us once through the eyes of the High Spirit."

"I ask, is this the change we choose to make?"

"Once our voices are taken from the breaths of Wind across our lands, and the sticks are heard to cry out each day below from where the call of the mighty Hyas Tkope Moolack was once cast out across the high peaks where snow lies deep, I ask, Will this be the way you choose to walk the trails we have journeyed for all the travels of Sun and Moon?"

"I tell you, with your opened hand take the fur from your
shoulder and offer it for trade to Suyapee for the blue bead and
button, and when winter's storm falls heavy upon you, take from
them both warmth so that your soul will not freeze."

"These thoughts I offer you as we sit before the big fire and speak
of trade. Let the confusion of what I bring before you not cause
panic and unrest to your souls, but may it keep our spirits strong
beneath the rise of Otelagh for all the days to come."

"We all must remember this as my father had once told me when
he and I walked beside the waters of Elowah and spoke of
our people. When we learn to feel with our souls, we can then
understand the wisdom spoken from our spirit, and then, we will
be as one within ourselves, and to one another."

"This is the High Spirit's way."

"This must be our way, my father told me."

"This is Indian way!"

Steve Warnstaff

Chapter 19

Walawahoof, Sacred Ground of Our Peoples

Chief Tsutho has begun to be taken upon his last trail of his life upon these lands, and he is joined by many of his friends as they follow in silence behind the caretakers that pull his canoe behind their own to the shores of the Big Island. As we sit beside the edge of the shore and look up to where the chief is to lie for the final time, we watch closely to all that is performed through the rituals of our peoples.

As the caretakers place Chief Tsutho high above the land upon two Great Cedar within his most decorative canoe, it gives promise his soul was good before the eyes of the High Spirit. Chief Tsutho's spirit awaits the hand of the High Spirit to lead him upon the sacred trails hidden within the heavens. We know one day soon he would be taken through all the lessons of his life as he began the journey of the Living Dead before being welcomed into the Hyas Saghalie Tyee's village.

Through the long day as Otelagh shined bright down upon them, the caretakers worked steadily, each placing the finest of his arrows into their soft quiver beside the shiny Yew of the bow upon his proud Canam he had worn in battle. They then placed the bag of Dentalium at his feet. The caretakers placed his long walking stick, the Skudilitic, beside him as it gave him much power over the bad spirits when he walked into the land where the bad spirit of Tsiatko awaited to bring storm upon him. Tied to his Power Stick was the feather of the Great Eagle that proved his spirit was strong and free as is Wind. They each proved of his strength before the eyes of our Hyas Saghalie Tyee and they would both show of his good faith.

All the Chief had kept of importance showed of his life's worth was it was set with him where he lay in the great canoe. As the caretakers completed placing all the possessions Chief Tsutho had to offer up to the High Spirit, they covered him in the fur of Beaver and Otter to keep his soul warm from the cold season that was soon to come as he awaited his long journey.

We each knew Chief Tsutho was to leave this life and look down upon us from high above in the spirit world with wish we too would follow upon the trails he and his Hyas Father's have led from our beginnings upon the sacred mountain of Walawahoof, (Saddle Mountain).

One Who Flies With Birds stands over his brother and alongside Deshonto, and they both look down upon Chief Tsutho's soul with much respect. One Who Flies With Birds begins to cry out; "Hyas Saghalie Tyee, take my brother and my friend quickly to the Spirit World where he will be safe from the wanting arms of Tsiatko."

As Deshonto stood quietly and heard Tsutho's brother's pleas to the High Spirit, he then took his Skudilitic and placed it over his friend. As he stood strong and powerful as the Great Eagle, he opened his arms above Tsutho and began to wail to the High Spirit. He then began to shake his power stick uncontrollably above where Tsutho lied stilled to the emotions shared by his calling for the Good Spirit to join them in their acceptance of Tsutho's righteoused life. Both their cries to the High Spirit, each louder and with more sorrow could be heard to echo from across the shores of En che Wauna.

They are certainly promised to become vested deep within the hearts of all the life which clings to the soils of the Earth and to those witnessing from the heaven above our lands.

Much sorrow can be felt through their words as they shout out with much conviction that the Chief's soul is good, and then suddenly, as was the Chief's last breath blown from his chest, there was silence spilled unto all the lands.

Great Coyote's sorrowful call is all that can now be heard fastened to the rising of Moon as she mourns to all those who have been taken from our lands. With silenced wing, Crow sweeps down upon us from the trails of the sky and stands proudly upon the Great Eagle that rises from upon the canoe's shining bow. The Spirit of Coyote and Crow alone shall bring proof before the wanting eyes of the High Spirit that Chief Tsutho's soul is good. Crow's and Coyote's appearance alongside him will enable the Chief's soul to be taken from his body as it will quickly rise up and be joined with that of his spirit. Together, they shall prove Chief Tsutho's spirit is strong. Through Coyote's and Crow's gift, Chief Tsutho shall be connected to the spirits of the lands for all the coming seasons where he now lies peacefully surrounded by all he once knew.

Today brings both sorrow and happiness from within us as we look upon our friend for the final time before we turn from the shore of the Big Island and return to Kwilluchini. Through Chief Tsutho's memory and strong spirit, we shall all walk where he once journeyed, and through his teachings, we too one day hope to take upon the Journey of the Living Dead and touch the High Spirit's meadow at the foot of our Father's village where life never ends.

This night, as we have returned to Kwilluchini, there is little spoken between us as we have chosen to stand in respect for our friend as we look across where Chief Tsutho now rests until the blaze of Sun returns above us once more.

Though the fire of the village glows with much warmth, the light it spreads amongst us is dimmed through our loss. This night will be long in the silence of mourning, and it will offer me chance to think of where my trail must now lead before those of Suyapee.

*I wish to look down upon Suyapee with keen eyes, as does the
Eagle from the high peaks of our mountains as it too watches
all that moves below him. I wish to hear the words he speaks,
to feel the spirit within him. I wish to stand above him atop the
high mountain and cast down before him many questions so he
will know of me before I stand before him and ask of those same
questions I now gather within me.*

*I have been told Suyapee does not leave our lands for many days
once he has come upon us in the tall ship. In this knowing, I must
ask question before my brothers to those that wish to join upon
my side and make the journey to Walawahoof to speak to Naha,
the mother of all our people's beginnings.*

*We must ask Thunderbird to what trail she would choose for us
to follow so both our peoples will survive the change of Wind
as the differences we may be forced to make in our lives will
certainly be blown hard against us with threat.*

*I am ridden with much question, and as I stand here upon the shore
of En che Wauna, I ask in silence how will we both survive beside
one another when it is only we, our peoples, the Hyas Chinook,
that knows of the Illahee's, Hyas Saghalie Tahmahnawis Tyee?*

*I see in great vision as I have made the long journey in spirit and
now stand upon Walawahoof we are again as the Thunderbird's
eggs in the beginning before our steps were first placed upon the
lands. I see clearly Suyapee has come upon us and has taken the
shape of the bad spirit of the Wolverine as he throws us aside from
our lands and hunts all that runs freely upon them. We must be
wary of what Suyapee asks as the darkness of their souls may bring
much gravity to the deceit that may lie well hidden within them.*

*Though, we know Suyapee will come upon us with much storm,
and there shall be many who will make lodge beside our own,*

313

we must not let them see we carry the long knife in our defense to our customs or to what we know to be the meaning of life. They do not carry within their souls the teachings of our Hyas Fathers with them, and what is important to the High Spirit is not important to where Suyapee's hearts lie. If these are the same Suyapee as the first we had met last season, then they too will not have heart to know of all that lives within our kingdoms.

We shall make trade and accept what they offer, but we too must be strong in our beliefs. We must not let Suyapee take all the spirits from our lands that we treasure. We must not lead them into where our spirits are strong, and into those places where the sacred spirits of the Tkope Moolack and Tkope Goat are held in the highest esteem within us. We shall bring honor to the Hyas Elk and Goat, and as we will be alike the Great Coyote, through our disguise, we shall smile upon Suyapee as they pass blindly beside us as they will not know of everything that casts light upon our souls and brings honor and strength to our spirits.

Through the light cast upon us from Otelagh in the heaven, we shall remain strong and vigilant beneath the opened hands of our High Spirit. As the light of all our tomorrows are cast pleasingly within our souls, life's trails will be evident to all whom give honor and praise to the Hyas Saghalie Tyee for what he has awarded those who have promised themselves to have followed his footsteps across the lands.

We must be assured our people's spirits will be the last to stand upon the battlefield in protection to our beliefs when Suyapee's spirits are drawn tight within the wanting arms of mesahchie Tsiatko. We must make choice when to concede to their wish, and when to make demand before them when we see their spirits are leading them into the darkened heart of Tsiatko where light shall never shine bright with promise.

This must be all our people's wish.

We are a proud people, an understanding people to all that lives and breathes. But, as we stand before those who wish to take from within us our honor, many of our peoples will accept the sacrifice of their souls. Again, as in the past, when the grace of Sun did not shine down with warmth upon us, when battle between our brothers of the south where the Spirit of Shasta and Lassen looms high above their lands were joined by many of our own brothers in their grievious battle, sadness was soon spilled before all our doors.

Word fell hard from the bad spirit's drum that our peoples had been seen to lie lifeless and bloodied upon the evil spirit's grounds. As dark cloud arose above us in great mourning, our wail to the High Spirit for Sun to bring good to the lands once more could be heard cast out for many days as we awaited his return above us.

I see with vision cast from the looking glass our brother's blood will be spilled without pause in defense to our ways, and their voices shall fall silent forever before us. They will yearn to join their souls with the High Spirit's village as they plead he will understand and accept their choice to make battle with these peoples. Even through the darkness war brings to all mankind I see clearly our peoples will be the last of those to stand proudly upon the same telecasits where the bad spirit is soon to rise up from beneath the lands he has proven to reign strong and free from fear.

Suyapee will be swept clear of his travels through the Journey of the Living Dead beneath his own Red Cloud where they will soon discover themselves to suffer upon the trails that have neither a good beginning or ending. Wind shall take from within them their spirit, and as they have chosen to be swept far from the Trail of Righteousness our Hyas Saghalie Tyee has led our peoples, their spirits shall become mired in their confusion for all days.

This is my vision as Great Thunderbird has arose within me and has spoken with much truth to the days we will soon see arise before all our tomorrows.

Life will only survive if we make our stand when it is necessary to teach those unaccustomed to the ways of the land's own spirits, the same spirits that brings balance to all living things.

As the change of Wind brings separation between the spirit of the Earth from the ways of the Hyas Saghalie Tyee, it shall blow hard against us all and bring much question to where we cannot lay answer to why it comes.

We must remain strong and vigilant through our Hyas Father's teachings. One day, I pray that Suyapee will too know of the spirits of our lands, and there will be calm spread across all the kingdoms as Wind's harsh breaths will fall silent from upon us. That day, we each shall be pleased to walk without the threat of further storm falling upon us as we share the trails that rise up from upon the shores of En che Wauna. Then, the warmth of Sun shall invest itself fully within all our souls as our hopes will bring much needed strength to our faith.

We will then each be pleased to walk beside one another as our smiles will bring understanding to both our ways, and in this, we shall each survive all the winter's storms that will fall upon us. As the new season brings new life to our lands, we shall be seen by the Hyas Saghalie Tahmahnawis Tyee to stand in good faith before him, and he will allow us to survive beneath his long arms and strong hands.

Sun will course across the heaven and shed light beneath his travels, and Moon shall shine bright through the long night and take the trail from the feet of the mesahchie Tsiatko as he will then hunt abated for his longing quarry.

The battle between Thunderbird and Wolverine shall then end, and they too shall live beside one another without further threat.

Red Cloud will part from the heavens, and peace will reign down upon us with much favor, and we all shall be set free from the onset of war, and our spirits will not linger again where sadness looms heavy within our souls.

As we stand upon the high peak and peer across the lands beneath us, we shall be pleased with all that we have gathered within our purse from the hands of the Hyas Saghalie Tahmahnawis Tyee. There, just beyond the furthest horizon to the east where the mighty buffalo run free beside the antelope upon the long plain of golden grasses beneath the blue of heaven, light will again emerge from the darkened sky of night. As we gather nearer the gate of our High Spirit's village where hope and despair had once met with much conviction, we shall feel the gift of warmth upon our faces, and we shall bear witness to the promise of all our tomorrows as Sun rises and welcomes us all to a new day.

In this, we must consider without question we are to accept faith within our souls...

Steve Warnstaff

Chapter 20

In Trade We Decide

Many days have passed since we returned to Kwilluchini from the Big Island where Chief Tsutho awaits his spirit to rise up upon his chosen star. We know the *Hyas Saghalie Tahmahnawis Tyee* has felt our loss in our brother's passing as he took the darkness that was spilled heavily to each corner of the longhouse when Chief Tsutho was taken from his final breath. It was then when silence filled the air the *Hyas Tyee* allowed us each to find happiness in knowing of our friend's kindred soul and great spirit. A passing star crossed the heaven and as it brought warmth and hope to our spirits, *Hyas Saghalie Tyee* demanded our peoples welcome Chief Tsutho's soul to be taken safely upon the Trail of the Living Dead and be found connected with his spirit for all to witness. As the threat of change could be felt approaching throughout the kingdom, we were pleased that Chief Tsutho would not bear witness to the coming change of Wind across all our lands.

As Sun coursed across the heaven and Moon grew dim with light as Sun passed before her, we were reminded that Chief Tsutho was the final chief to hold guard over our kingdom from the table of our elders. Soon, change would fall upon us without warning, and our peoples must be readied for what Wind shall bring before us as it sweeps across all the lands. The air is heavy with concern, and as I sit before many of our peoples that have come to the village in honor of Chatska's great father, I choose the words that may spell my worries of what is soon to approach our lands before

322

them. It is before the fire of the village we each form the circle where we speak through the long night of truth.

I have raised question of my reason to stand before Suyapee as I share of visions that have sadly taken me upon a trail where our peoples will soon stand fronting where they cannot see beyond the darkness that lies just beyond the shaft of light where the light of hope was once promised. With great measure to the messages I have shared before my brothers through my strong words, many have still spoken well of trade with these new peoples who come to our lands. They tell Suyapee brings much to our tables that we have not seen to this day, and trade is good.

The Klickitat find honor in battle, and through their many wars, they do not show fear of these new peoples that have been seen in our father's visions to march upon us with quick step and without regard for those spirits that hold us each safely upon the soils of the Earth.

We too hear the choice of the Chehalis as they gather upon the sides of the Klickitat and wish to trade their furs for the musket with Suyapee. Yet the question they ask that brings worry to their souls has now left them standing alone in the darkness of this night as they know not what to expect through the visions I was chosen to spell before them. Now they must sit and ponder what will come of their peoples if Suyapee does come with much storm across all our lands and take from the forests the souls of Cedar and Fir, and take from the waters of En che Wauna the Salmon?

"What will happen to the Hyas Huckelberry," I ask? I tell them through my vision the bush from which comes the fine berries will soon be taken from the mountain top as they will trample all the lands we have honored through the greed that is vested within their souls.

I ask them; "Have you seen the Red Cloud form across the lands as Suyapee came from the waters of En che Wauna in the new season? Did you too see them stand upon our lands as darkness and cold was swept before our feet as it challenged us to understand the storm that had led their path before us?"

"I tell you all, we must question if Suyapee will raise the Red Cloud of despair upon our peoples as our lands will become theirs?"

I ask them; "What if our villages were then to lie silent and unwelcomed to us as the fires where we sit tonight will not be lent the flame raised from the High Spirit's hands once again?"

Again, I ask; "What will come of our longhouses where the cold of night was once taken from our bones as we slept peacefully upon our mats and covered with the same furs you now wish to take from your own people's shoulders to make trade?"

The Tillamook, Nehalem, and the Clatsop, all have spoken they have made trade with Suyapee, and as Suyapee have welcomed them with opened arms, they have not found quarrel between them for what they ask in trade for the warm coats of the land's great spirits.

As I sit and listen to their stories, I have told them; "It is not the price Suyapee offers in trade that should bring worry to us all, but it is the cost to all our peoples when Suyapee cannot be given what he demands. When there are no more deer and elk that lie in the big meadows, or the bear, or the golden cat, or the fox, or beaver, or the otter that plays in the river's streams to take from our lands, what will they then demand for us to set before them?"

Yet, as I ask this questions of my brothers, they do not understand what brings much worry within me from what I have seen in my visions, and they choose to know not to what I speak of my father's vision before me.

They wish to trade what has brought honor to their souls and had once given strength to their spirits for colored cloth, bright beads, and for the long arm of the musket that takes the spirit from mowitch before first hearing of their voice's plead to join upon our tables.

My brothers; "I fear Suyapee offers the long arm of the musket so we can take all the animals from the forests and from the waters that run fast and clear. As the last of those animals stand before us, we will not hear of their pleading voice to once again be able to walk free and safe from our own greed, and as their voice falls stilled upon the trails of Wind, there shall be no more seen before us that choose to walk beside us on the trails of our lands.

I fear that Suyapee will be pleased when the long barrel of the musket places each of our brothers against one another. I sense that as we cross one another's trails in search for that last elk or deer, or lay trap for the beaver and otter, we shall become one another's prey for what we do not need."

Sad days are soon to come upon us, and my brothers cannot envision the dark skies that loom heavy just beyond where we can today see. As I sit and listen to each of their worries and complaints, and to each of their wishes, with great sadness, I must bow my head in silenced thought. I am surrounded by many that favor trade, and those that carry with them furs, outnumber those that have too become wary of Suyapee and what they may bring upon us.

I know we must all agree to make trade so our peoples can remain strong beside one another. Even as my visions begin to bring before us all dark days through the truths my Hyas leaders have *seen, soon, all that will come upon us will covet the land with the stench of disease and death. As my peoples sit before the fire and raise up their strong hands as they choose to agree to trade with Suyapee, I fear I am now condemned by my own vote as I too must agree with those who vote for trade as they outnumber those others that feign from what will soon come.*

As Sun rises across En che Wauna the third day, we have agreed to take the brother's of Cedar upon the waters of En che Wauna and sit beside the tall ship. There, at the bay where the smoke rises from the village of the Tillamook, we will tell Suyapee of all our decision.

Through their eyes, may they see our spirits are good!

I pray our peoples will be saved by the hand of the Hyas Saghalie Tyee Tahmahnawis once Red Cloud rises from the trails of our lands. As the light of life dims before us, I pray we will be safely led to those trails that will deliver us far from the wanting poach of the long muskets that have been offered in trade for what Suyapee cannot take again from our lands.

There will be no more to take from us except our own souls from our spirits once Suyapee becomes displeased as he sees we hold out nothing within our emptied hands that once held furs that gave balance to the sticks of the forests, to the waters of the lakes, to the rivers, and to the many streams of our lands. From the heavens, the Hyas Eagle's scream will fall silent across all the lands as he will look down upon us with sorrowed eyes, and he too will begin his long journey to a land we do not know. That day, we will know what is lost from the treasures we have taken for granted, as our absence of thought to what we have dreamed shall be forever drawn into the emptiness of darkness for all our tomorrows.

Suyapee will not understand, and as we tell them we have nothing left to bring before them, they will cast our peoples aside and march towards a new land, and there, they again will take all that gives honor to those lands. I wish Suyapee will then find themselves to squander in their own filth through what they will leave behind in their maddened craze across our lands once they begin to return to their tall ships. May this be their punishment as their spirits have shown they find themselves to want selfishly for all that can be presented before them without first feeling the heart of those lands they seek out to covet in their storm.

May the swamp where the Hyas Heron speaks from the high branch swallow them all when they do not see where once ran cool waters from the high peaks that now lies their trap beneath the soft crust of tepid soils. We must have hope they will not be seen again as Earth will swallow them without worry, and their souls will then join that of the mesahchie Tsiatko where great men do not dare to dwell.

"This is my wish," I cry out to the High Spirit many times as I stand at the shore of En che Wauna and listen to my message's echoed across all the lands we can and cannot see. Then, with much hope, that same message will be heard beyond the borders of our kingdoms, and far beyond those kingdoms, so all our peoples will know the storm has begun to approach our lands and we must remain strong beneath the guiding hands of Saghalie Tahmahnawis Tyee.

"In the end," I shout out; "We must have faith we will survive the onslaught that will come hard upon us, and as we stand strong above the graveyards of Tsiatko and take back what is ours as we witness Suyapee's army swallowed beneath the same soils they had earlier crossed, our lands will once again be ours. Suyapee do not know of our lands, or of those bad spirits who wish to take us all prisoner behind the gates of the catacombs where life does not exist, and where the warmth of Sun is misplaced before the cold and distempered night."

"In the sadness of silence, we fear we will not again know of the promise sung by the calming breaths of Wind which were once spelled across our land. As those days come upon us through the rise of many Suns and Moons, we will stand alone upon the trail that allows the absence of hope to infuse within our souls."

I have asked of the Klickitat and the Chehalis if we can join them as they go to the tall ship to make trade so we can sit and speak with Suyapee before we too return before them and bring the finest of our furs and salmon. Chief Quinto and Chief Kwillikum have agreed to place several of their furs within our canoe as we begin to journey to the waters where the tall ship sits.

Our nation knows of three legends that has been told of the Big Rock that stands in the wake of En che Wauna. One has been told that Chief Tuluaptea's son had begun to cross the Big River to sit beside the Chief of the Clatsop's daughter without bearing gifts to offer her Hyas father for the honor of his daughter's hand. This brought much anger to the Spirit Tamamous as it was custom to offer the finest furs to be lain before her father for approval before his visit would be looked upon with the greatest of respect.

As the young brave began to cross En che Wauna from near where Kwilluchini sits, the Spirit of Tamamous shook the power stick he held tightly in his hand above the young brave. Dark cloud and much Wind fell upon him from the heaven, and quickly, the young braves canoe was swallowed beneath the race of the Big River where it was sunk deep into the bed of En che Wauna.

His memory remains as the rock we see before us off into the distance. We see him sitting in his canoe, unmoving, without life, without spirit. It has been told when our peoples journey to these lands without bearing gifts, they too will be found turned to stone and marked for all to look upon as they pass beyond this point, (Pillar Rock), on their journeys to the villages of the peoples that live by the mercy of the storms at sea.

The second legend speaks of this rock once living at the Great Falls as he was once an ancient animal god to the lands and to the peoples that resided along the big river.

One day, a sad day for our peoples, Rock Spirit made a choice to build a dam that would keep pish from passing this spot of our great river. One day, after many seasons, the Great Coyote journeyed into the lands of the Wasco where the mighty Chinook are now seen to jump willingly into our wanting nets. It was there Coyote took from the river the big rock that Rock Spirit had built for his own selfish reasons to entrap the spirit of pish. As Coyote asked of Rock Spirit why he kept pish from passing the great falls of the river beyond his dam, he was told he could not willingly set the pish free from beyond the reach of his wanting arms. But he too was heard to tell Coyote it was not intended to take pish from the Wasco's or from their brother's tables beyond the Great Falls, but as he did not look straight into Coyote's questioning eyes, Coyote knew this was not the truth.

As Coyote mocked of this answer by the Spirit of Rock, he took him from the waters and carried him far downriver upon his strong shoulders. It is here, across from the village of our brothers, the Wahkiukum, at Skamokowa, that Rock Spirit was told to stand alone, forever. His punishment for his selfishness and greed would bring the salmon in many numbers as they would school beside him, and the many pish would be heard by him alone to laugh and nibble at the plants that attach themselves upon the soles of his feet as they passed where he now stands.

Coyote knew the hardship of the peoples whose villages stand beyond the Great Falls when pish did not run thick in their waters, and they were left with little to eat but the meat of deer and elk, and root from the meadows and from the flooded plains that lie along the rivers. It is because of Coyote the Nez Perz are able to catch pish in the big rivers of the Imnaha, the Snake, and the Salmon. Much bounty has again returned to the lands as the soils have become thick with new grass and bush, and with new leaf upon the tall sticks that line the waters of their lands. There, upon the far waters of the rivers and streams is shown much promise the spirits that come to the waters will again return with many numbers.

There is one story that has told the rock is the body of a chief who had lost his mind and as he walked amongst his brothers, he stood before them and spoke as if he was awarded to sit upon the chair of the Great Spirit, Speelyei. The chief knew he could not be harmed by any mortal threat that is lain upon the Earth, and as he chose to prove to many that stood upon the shores of En che Wauna he could walk on water, the Great Saghalie Tyee turned him into stone.

The Hyas Tahmahnawis Saghalie Tyee called out to those that watched the old chief, and there, in the big waters, our Great Spirit has turned the old chief into the weathered rock that will remain here until the storms that come upon him with much force wash his bad spirit from our waters. As his hardened soul crumbles into the waters of En Che Wauna, he will be sent unaccompanied to the depths of the great sea where the mesahchie Tahmahnawis of the Squid and the Kloshe Tahmahnawis of the Ehkolie can be heard sharing in their great battle for his broken and misguided soul.

Chapter 21

Our Calling From Atop Walowahoof

As we pass the Spirit Rock that lies alone in its wake within the Big Waters of En che Wauna, we row faster and faster as we steer our canoes further from the place where the bad spirit calls out our names. Fearing the legends of our peoples, we strive harder to row against the rush of waves that wash over us from the depths of the great river.

Otelagh follows swiftly from the trails of the heaven above us as our pace is quick to reach Knope. In his mighty powers, we have faith our journey will soon end without loss to any of our brothers that have joined our race to the sea. As we push harder and with much conviction to what lies ahead, I am assured we will be rewarded for our efforts and we will soon sit before the fire of Knope and gather warmth from the chill cast out from upon the breaths of Wind.

As we look across the great peaks that border En che Wauna, we see Crow sitting upon the high Fir, crying out as he watches over us. I know Coyote must not be far away. With a loud scream from Crow, I look up to where I last saw him resting, Crow lunges from the long arm of Fir and circles above our canoe. Nearer he comes, circling, demanding our attention. As he nearly settles upon my shoulder I hear him call out my name. Without pause to his cries, he demands I follow him to the Great Peak where the mother of our peoples, Naha, calls out for us to sit beside her and hear of her plead. Naha calls out with much urgency as she demands we listen as she shares how all our *peoples may still prosper beneath the Red Cloud that has begun to swarm with much regret across our kingdoms and upon our lives.*

I had envisioned this day may come as I saw through the long glass of tomorrow I must stand above all our lands and watch over the Big Waters where Otelagh rests at night.

Naha calls out my name through the tongue of Crow. Louder and louder, I hear her cry; "Kaka, Raven, come to me and sit beside me so I may shoulder your worries, and so I may take from your heart doubt that creates the fear you bear within your soul for tomorrow's uncertainty."

I look towards Tenas Howh and motion towards the shore where we must take ourselves from the river. Where we must begin to follow the trail where Crow leads us to the high peak at Walowahoof. With much haste, we make our final turn and suddenly from behind the Cottonwood tree, smiling towards us with kind eyes, awaits my old friend Coyote. She is pleased our souls are again joined.

I call out to my brothers to continue their journey to Knope, and once we have climbed Walowahoof and have spoken with Naha, Tenas Howh and I will again join them. With raised hands, we depart from one another. When Sun has risen and his sister Moon has cast hope within us once again, we will join together, and we each will be able to look into the eyes of Suyapee with much better understanding and with much respect for one another's peoples.

It is my wish and prayer to the High Spirit we will both be welcomed beneath the pass of Otelagh once the spirit of Red Cloud that offers doubt to swell up within us is sacrificed from both our people's question.

As I stand upon the bank of En che Wauna, Coyote steps down upon the loose soils and paws the soil to form the shapes of our bond. From where Sun was first formed by the patterns of her paw, soon rises Moon beside her brother, and Coyote's and my own bond are gratefully renewed. There, as she and I stand beside one another in happiness to meet again, hope is again cast out from within me for our tomorrows. Coyote looks deep into my soul as she stands before me with questioning eyes. I sense she feels the sorrow I had not so long ago been surrendered. Coyote understands my fears. Coyote knows of all my thoughts, and as she walks to me with head bowed, she brushes against me to bring happiness once again to my sullen heart as we become bound together again by the love we had gathered between us once before. The bond we share tells that Sun and Moon shall always travel across the heaven above us, and as Crow shall join her as they lead our way safely through the kingdom of the Tillamook to the high peak of Walowahoof, our spirits shall remain strong and vigilant to our purpose.

It will be there, high above the lands of the Chinook, our people's beginnings, we shall take from our mother's heart the agony and despair the battles that rage within us bring. We shall share of her highest table, and we shall honor her as we sit and comfort her, and it will be good between us.

Tenas Howh and I have begun to enter into the unknowing the darkness of the forest lends to our souls. With each step we take behind the lead of Coyote and below the cry of Crow, we become one with all we are surrounded. As faith enters within me our journey shall find us safe, bright light shines from the hands of Otelagh and warms our souls as it breaks through the mottled sky above. From each greening fern and budding flower that clings to the soils of the forest, we hear their voice calling out to us as they open to welcome us along our fast march.

Sweet breaths blown softly from the Great Cedar cascade down upon us from each limb, and there, just above us, sits the woodpecker, (Kokostick), as he taps out the message we are soon to come before many of those that have yet to gather hope and faith within their souls for peace and to the promise of life beyond the passing of Sun overhead today.

Each form of plant and animal that shares of our Illahee too knows of our kingdom's frailty beneath the Red Cloud that has now begun to form thick below the cast of Sun. They have all welcomed us within their own kingdoms, and as we approach where they rest, I shout out to them I will listen to their worries, and I will feel of their hearts, and once I return, I will carry within me the knowledge that will lead us safely into all those tomorrows we today hold in dire question.

I am first hesitant to promise them as Red Cloud looms dark over our lands and takes from the soils warmth. But I have much hope that Wind will not allow Red Cloud to settle above us for many long days, and as we find prosperity in the new seasons that will come, the despair of darkness will be taken from our souls. At first, I fearerd Red Cloud would take the life from the forest and from within our waters, but in my faith, I am committed before my own questions as I speak to each of them of hope and perseverance.

"Hyas Tahmahnawis, hear my plead, and let me not promise to what is not absolution to the truths I seek!"

As Sun rises above the lands of our kingdoms upon this, the second day of our journey to Walowahoof, Tenas Howh and I now stand beneath the high table that sees all that moves across our kingdoms. It is there, just there, that our people's mother, Naha awaits for our spirits to meet. As we peer up to the high table, we see cloud rise and fall upon it. As Otelagh battles with the bad spirits that come from behind the tall ships from the Big Waters, he sweeps the heaven clean and whisks cloud to distant lands we cannot see.

Tenas Howh and I both look to one another and begin to climb upon the ledge of Walowahoof as we have no fear of the stones the bad spirits have loosened from their hold above us as they cascade to the valley floor beneath.

Climbing higher and higher we begin to hear Naha cry out for us to join upon her side before Sun is taken from the lands and Moon rises. She tells the bad spirits have promised soon to rise up from the depths of our waters and from beneath our lands to prey upon our people's lost souls.

With much worry, Naha pulls us quickly into her opened arms as she urges us to reach her side. With each step, with each hand, we climb higher upon the bench where our peoples had first come.

We have risen with great rush to step upon the High Table where Naha awaits us, and as we look down to the Big Waters, Wind can be heard to scream out with much force as it spreads terror to the lives that cling to the soils beneath. Much sadness fills our hearts as we witness great waves break upon the long beaches, and many longhouses are seen punished upon the high rocks as they are swept into the depths of the sea.

Cries lift up to where we stand and we are forced to watch all that begs for the High Spirit from below us. With much sorrow, those who had once found peace upon the soft sands have lost everything to Wind's assault upon their lands.

As we look down upon the forest Wind blows hard upon the mightiest of sticks, and there, sadly, many are swept from the floor where they once stood proud as they gave shelter to those that shared of their strength. Wind's breaths suddenly have fallen silent, and as we peer down to what remains of our peoples villages, those cries that had been cast upon us are now held in silence, and they are all lost from our mighty nation. There is nothing that would tell of our brother's good will or to their praise of the High Spirit for what he had chosen for them to hold.

In silence, Tenas Howh and I look out over the clouds that linger upon the plane of the sea, and we witness the threat of dark cloud as it looms heavy along the horizon. Quickly a long line of darkness approaches the shores of our lands, rising higher and higher as it nears to meet the trails where Sun shall soon have to maneuver in his pass across the heaven. Far out, beyond where the waves do not reach higher than the rocks below us, we see it is there, where Otelagh's bed waits for him to rest, and where storm appears promised to reign free upon the kingdoms of the sea. In this, we fear, as Otelagh shall not rest as Sun shall become unsettled, and so shall our lands beneath his angered and fiery throes!

Tenas Howh and I begin to gather wood for fire to warm us through the long night ahead. With the rush to sit with Naha we have chosen not to bring with us pish and berry, so we will sit beside the fire upon Walowahoof and gather within us the strength of our spirits, and we shall then become one with them all.

From the heart of our spirits we shall take what nourishment they offer for us to gather within us. We will soon journey to our brothers that walk the lonely sands of the beaches below us as they search for those that have been swept to the deep waters. As we come upon them we will share before them the wisdom gathered from our potlatch. Life, we pray, will once again be renewed into their souls with much hope.

I sit here, alone to my thoughts as I see why this hyas peak was chosen for the birth of our peoples. I look out to the far waters of the sea, and as I turn to each point that is cast out from where I sit, I am able to envision all the lands of our people's kingdoms. From the sands of the sea to the high peaks that rim En che Wauna, our peoples have called this home for many seasons. With the leadership of Hyas Tahmahnawis we have lived and prospered beneath Otelagh. Life is good. Life beside our Great Fathers has brought plenty to our tables, and we have not to this day felt fear within us for those tomorrows that are now soon to be upon us with much storm wrought through its unanswered question.

As I raise my arms to the heaven and to the Hyas Tumtum I cry out! "Why have you brought despair and doubt to our peoples? Why have you brought storm to each corner of our lands as we cannot walk beneath the clear sky that casts warmth to the soils that brings life from beneath them so they too may join us beside the trails we share?"

Again, I cry out with much worry and question!

As I stand quietly and peer out to all I know, from the silence that is not cast upon Wind, my cries soon rise up and are shared to each corner of the lands for all our peoples to hear. With great sorrow, I have seen through the looking glass of tomorrow our lands have begun to change with the turn of Wind, and as change falls heavily upon our lives, my question demands answer from Hyas Tahmahnawis how our peoples can live besides these Suyapee who demand all that we have through trade for what we do not need? Much sorrow has gathered within my soul, and as tears fall heavily from within my eyes, storm has begun to darken the skies above heightened waves that now sweep unending upon our lands with great threat.

The battle I have feared has now begun!

Crow lands beside us from the high branch, and as Coyote now lies beside me with head bowed, there is much urgency for the lesson's answers we seek. Angered once again by the approaching storm, through the vision cast down upon me by my fathers, Wind begins to call out to our peoples from behind the veil of cloud. In terror, as I see all that is prevalent beneath me through the eyes of our spirits, I cry out to them to run to shelter from the onslaught of Suyapee's bad spirit as their tall ship emerges from within the dark cloud that lies thick upon the sullen waters of our sea.

Suyapee comes again with more men as they had promised! Bringing with them much threat to our lands as Red Cloud rushes upon us, they come fast before us. I again find fear as Red Cloud takes from us the sight of the promising meadows of our High Spirit in the heaven above, and we will not find the trail that leads our souls safely upon the Journey of the Living Dead once the Good Spirit calls for us to join beside him.

I believe the spirits that hide beneath the deep waters of the sea too have cast Suyapee from within their kingdom as Wind gathers fully upon their bellowing sails as they enter into the mouth that opens wide to the sea where flows into it many rivers.

There, below in the waters of the Tillamook, The Land of Many Waters, swallowed by their own cloud that follows their approach, hidden from the village of our brothers, they strike fear within all our people's souls as they come upon our brothers from behind the thick shroud of cloud that sits motionless upon the stilled and lifeless waters they are surrounded.

From high above the lands that reach out to the bay of our brothers of the Salish, a battle ensues along the mouth of the

Salmon River. We see with much sadness quarrel has brought three men, one Suyapee and two braves to be left stained upon the ground. In much sadness their souls have been emptied from the ways of the High Spirit.

I raise my arms to the heavens and cry out to the High Spirit; "Why have you taken the freedom from our souls as we must now run from our own lands to find safety from the approach of these peoples who come with much threat to our ways before us?"

"My Fathers, why have you taken from us choice in living our lives as we once knew it beneath the giving hands of your Fathers?"

With much conviction, I scream out in much agony as I know our defeat awaits before the long arms of Suyapee's charge before us if we do not find answer that will keep peace across our lands as they begin to build villages beside our own.

As Otelagh is seen to cross the heaven, Tenas Howh and I sit waiting, waiting for storm to come upon us again without faith of mercy.

From above where I sit, I hear Naha's cries to our great fathers above as she too waits with much sadness to become enveloped within the rise of Red Cloud's shame. Louder and louder her pleas rise up to the heaven, each wanting and begging for the salvation for her children.

As I sit with her upon the nest of our people's birth, I bow my head as I tremble with fear of the unknowing to what may lie ahead.

From blind eyes I must seek the light that will shed hope and faith across our lands. From deep within my soul, I question what trails I must take as my fathers have not chosen for me to be led. My peoples are now promised to stand upon trails that have neither beginnings or endings! Life as we once knew it is not to be the same again. All we have, and all we could be is now held in the absence of our Hyas Tumtum's voice from above. Through his absence, our souls have become challenged as we have begun to wander questionably through all the seasons of our people's once promising past.

Where hope and faith had once stood strong within us each day Otelagh passed above our lands, today I see, with much sadness, they are both now taken from within us. As we lose hope and surrender beneath Red Cloud's approach, I fear we shall be seen no more. Our peoples shall soon become the same as those spirits seen in visions by our fathers and brothers that have told of the mighty Buffalo that now reign free across the golden plains as they will one day be quickly taken by the long arms of Suyapee from upon the trails of the prairies where the tall grass grows.

Soon, I fear, we shall be seen scattered by the same long arms of Suyapee's weapons, and we will be taken from the lands of our births. As we lie unmoving and stained upon our lands, and as our spirits cannot take of our next journey, those of us who will survive shall be placed behind the veil of cloud where no man can see our struggle or hear our wanting cries.

I ask; "Where shall we go? What shall we do when we can not see or feel of our land's soul we had once not so long ago been favored to know?"

From my eyes shed tears of sorrow as they gather flood from within me. From the soils beneath me, now rises up new life as the greening bud of flower reaches high to touch the warmth of Sun. Yet I find doubt heavy within me as I question; "Will the sadness that is soon to be spilled heavily within us take from us vision of promise toward all our tomorrows as we may not be able to share of the new season's gifts?"

Otelagfh passes above seven, (sinamoxst), times, and as storm has settled, we see the tall ship turn from our lands and join the cloud that had brought storm upon us with much conviction as it journeys from where it had first come. Without haste, wind blows hard upon their sails, and they disappear from upon the horizon in much hurry. Our brothers come again to their village from where they had chosen to hide from the long arms Suyapee had brought to bare upon our lost brother's souls. From the silence cast across the lands is now heard their longing and most chilling wail for the brothers who have fallen.

As Otelagh passes slowly overhead and peers down upon us and sees of our sorrow, I ask; "Is this the last I will see of new life shared upon our land as the dark, cold cloud of misery consumes our souls?"

Otelagh reaches out to touch my shoulder and his warmth is cast down upon me as he comes from behind cloud where all can see his raised brow as he finds question to why I weep. I look up to him and thank him for his love as it is again showered over me. It was then, as I lowered my eyes from the heaven his voice was heard to shout out with much force as he requested my answer; "Raven, why have you come to sit beside Naha upon Walowahoof if you have no faith?

Raven, I tell you to remember this story; "From the eyes of blind men they too seek the trails beneath their feet through their faith as they do not fear being taken from upon them. Though they seek vision, they see all from the light of their faith as it lies before them clearly and without obstacle. They must always be devoted to their faith, this will allow them to walk safely across the trails of our lands without worry, or, through the deception the bad

342

spirit wills upon those who are not confident, their minds and souls will wander forever in darkness, and those shall be lost to themselves and to us forever."

"Place within your eyes light that emerges from the ends of the long course of darkness, and as you too walk in their steps without casting doubt within you for what lies ahead, hold out your hand and feel the soul of the Earth. As it calls out to you from beneath its soils, your answers to all your people's tomorrows shall await you. Cast from within you which rises up from the soul of the bad spirit, and you shall be rewarded with faith, and through faith, you shall be granted from the soul of the good spirit to the gift of confidence that will lend you strength to lead your peoples safely across the lands of your kingdom even though the storm that promises to bring change to Wind cries out with much threat."

I kneel before Otelagh, and with much thankfullness I look up to him and seek out his guidance so I too shall become strong and bring hope and promise to my people as I had told them upon my return I would carry within my purse to share before them.

As I bow my head in shame, Naha has chosen to touch my soul as her mighty hand lifts my heart from beneath the soils of our land where I had allowed it to fall with much hopelessness. It was there, hidden from the eyes of my brothers where I allowed my soul to be lain lingering within the darken cave of the mighty Lolo. As Naha reaches deep inside my soul she takes the hurt from within me. As my strength is returned, I stand upon Hyas Walowahoof where I can see all below me, and I cry out: "Father, forgive me for I have brought shame before your table. My spirit had fallen from the trails you have led me safely for many seasons, and as I had chosen to walk without vision and hope through the coming of Red Cloud as the rising storm was beginning to be cast deep into our souls, I too have brought shame to our peoples!

Father, forgive me, and as I find journey amongst our peoples, I will share with them your voice so they too will have vision as does the blind man. As that day comes, they will see of your mighty hand above us all as we walk with you and share of your message to all those we pass upon our kingdom's trails. My message before them will bring excitement and promise towards a tomorrow blessed beneath the rays of Otelagh as you walk amongst us!"

With solemn thoughts again rested within me through the vision shared from my father, I now sense hope and feel empathy towards our people's plight as change is now soon to be strewn across our kingdom. I know we shall endure those changes which will come about us even though they may demand we be taken from our lands. But we shall not be taken from the power and influence of the spirits who have created these lands or from those that have led us safely upon the trails through the wanting of the bad spirit's poach.

As we honor our father's spirit, we shall always keep them within our souls as we walk with them and speak with them as they bring pride to our peoples. We shall always honor them as they promise reason through those same visions they share before us as they mold our people's beliefs through their teachings.

From within the dark cloud that has gathered across the lands which tells of great legions at their ready to come upon us with much rush, I know there is hope we will walk amongst their great armies and share of the wisdom our father's speak. With faith, I can see beyond today once again, and in those tomorrows, there is life promising to rise up just beneath the trail of Otelagh as he will once again smile down upon us.

I listen to the rush of Wind upon us as Tenas Hogh and I stand upon the peak of Walawahoof, and as message has entered into my heart, I must go to my peoples and tell we must offer the pelts of our spirits to Suyapee for what they offer in trade. I know now this will bring peace to our lands, and we shall hear our father's voices without fear of their absence as we walk with excitement for what tomorrow shall share.

"Father, hear my plea for peace!"

"Father, hear the song cast out from our people's souls as we begin this journey alongside Suyapee and once again bring joy and promise unto the lands of your fathers!"

Chapter 22

The Fire That Burns Within Us

Our journey from Walowahoof to Knope was not long as we took the trail down the mountain that leads to the Big Waters. As we walked beneath the tall firs and mighty Cedar of the forests that gave life to the land, we soon turned from the bay where the tall ship had sat quietly before Suyapee were seen to come upon our shores.

Each stick of the forest were heard to breathe freely without pause to what Wind was soon to kindle across their bows, and as we stepped from upon the peak of Naha, their long arms directed us to where our brothers awaited our return. Life was again renewed. As we walked beneath the protection of our forest, their promise to uphold the heaven from falling beneath our feet offered our souls to rise up from within us with much hope.

As we walked praising our Great Spirit for what he has given us, the voices of each plant and animal were each heard to call out as we passed before where they lay. From the waters that flowed gently into the rivers, we passed where pish were seen to jump and touch the long arms of Sun and were heard of their chorus sharing a joyous song. Rising to the crown of the mightiest fir and beyond to the heaven, their song was cast up to the High Spirit so he too would know of their heart and of their faith he would bring warmth to their souls and blow breath to their lungs so their youth may live beyond the day when Red Cloud comes upon us and Wind promises to blow hard against us.

We must not fear what we cannot see even though the message of change is soon to come upon us with much question. We must persevere in order we will be seen as honorable and forthcoming to those that find question in our ways. Fear must be cast before the feet of the bad spirits, and we must follow the sweet scents that reign down upon us from the mighty Cedar that rise up alongside the cliffs of Wahclella where our lessons have been cast out to offer us perception to the righteous paths where our fathers have led their sons for many seasons.

My father once sat with me and told me of fear. He spoke of days he too had journeyed as he did not know of what was to come towards him from the unseen horizon. I sense those days he had questioned is now upon us. My father told when fear invests itself within one's soul, all that is good is quickly lost in all its confusion.

"Much warning must be lent to ward off the storm we would then bare within us," I remember him telling me.

He told we would fall from the trail of the High Spirit and muddle upon trails that would not cast light upon our lives. He then shared through its absence, the darkness of shadow would take us into lands where we could not envision our return as the

347

Good Spirits would not be heard calling out to us to follow. He shared they would be gathered high above the telecasit where we would then be lain beneath in deafening shame.

One day, as wind and storm had ceased their battle between them, our peoples came out from the safety of their longhouses and walked along the long beach. It is here, where we stand, today, a tall ship was first witnessed to come ashore. It was lain broken as a great battle between both good and bad spirits of the sea had consumed its soul. It was here where we stand today, Suyapee was seen first by our peoples many long seasons ago. From where our peoples had come to walk along the long beach where the tall ship silently rested, we have begun to see smoke rise from the village of our brothers. It is just there, beyond where we cannot yet clearly see Knope calls out our names.

It is good we have come safely from the high peak of Naha so we can sit with our brothers and speak of the High Spirit's hope for our peoples. Tenas Hogh and I shall sit and gather warmth within us and we shall take from the table of the Good Spirits. We will both stand before the fire of the village and share of our journey to those who wish to know of our travels, and to the vision we both have seen from within the cradle of our people's birth atop Walawahoof beside Naha.

I will tell them how the Good Spirit spoke to me as he said to listen to the earth and take from it the lesson it would share, and then, with faith, I would be able to lead my peoples through the trials we would soon be faced with the change of Wind across our lands. I knew as I sat at the foot of Naha and took her hand, she and I were again joined to the earth as our souls had been touched through the trial I had accepted. As I stood upon Walawahoof and looked out across all the lands, across the big waters, I knew, with Naha's soul laden within me, I would be able to walk without fear before Suyapee.

From the soul of the soil was heard a scream for our peoples to hold patience and fortitude before the unseen and unknown trails we will soon be faced to travel. We are a proud people, and as we encumber the lessons of our High Spirit and cherish those lessons of our fathers, we, as a people united, shall stand proud before their charge. We will walk amongst Suyapee with much welcome. Suyapee will then know of our peoples as we choose not to find battle with them but to make trade and offer them comfort and warmth before the fires of our villages.

From the spirit within us, we will tell Suyapee of our people's spirits and how they have formed the land and have brought good to our kingdom. We will share with them how each spirit brings promise of life from another, and how we are all connected by the Hyas Tumtum as he looks down upon us with much appreciation as we follow in his ways.

Through that thought, I still question how Suyapee believes they will not be held accountable for what they take from the lands as they do not give back to the land, or to those peoples that find their promise upon the soils, or within the waters of their kingdoms each day?

I ask; "Father, shall we take from our lands the coats of animals and trade them for what we have not held in our hands yesterday or today? Once we do not see those spirits who once walked amongst us as we place them before the tall ship of Suyapee, will the offspring of those spirits return once again before the storm of winter comes? Or, will we walk across the lands of our peoples without the call of bird or the whistle of Moolack high up on the greening slopes of our great spirits? Will the cry of the Great Eagle be heard to scream out to us from the trails of heaven as she looks down upon us with hope, or will its shrill be always silenced as it looks down upon us surrounded by the misery stemming from our own disgarce?

I ask you father, how must we bring balance to the lands and to our souls if we are to make trade for all the Eena and fox, for the deer and elk, for the mink and coyote, or for the spirits of pishpish and klale lolo if they will not return to walk upon those same trails we have become surrendered by your will?

What will we do when we cannot walk amongst the spirits that speak towards us from the grounds of our kingdoms? Our solace shall be swift in its escape from our souls, and as we become excited and anxious for their return, they will not find comfort in us as we would have then been known to have traded our souls for the offerings of their spirits.

Our people's will take upon the face of the bearded ones that come upon us as they offer nothing to the land as they take all from upon it without first hearing of their joyous song. We will become like Suyapee, poachers of life without retaining refuge for our souls. Our absence before the teachings of our Most High Spirit shall allow the cold of winter to envelope our souls even as the warm rays of sun screens across the soils of the lands beneath our feet.

"Father, as Otelagh peers down upon our peoples, he will see we are no longer worthy of his kindness. As we have taken all that once had touched our lives and brought us wealth in the knowledge that life breathes from the breaths expelled from his own spirit, we have forgotten we are all connected to the soils of the Earth. We shall fall hard upon the lifeless sands of the deserts within us. We will become lost for all days in our misery. In our despair, we shall not be seen by others the same again as protectors of Otelagh's many gifts to the lands of our kingdom.

To those that will one day come before the entrance to the kingdom of Wah, they will not find our people's warm and welcoming fires, nor will they hear our joyous song. They will not find the lands cleansed from the bad spirits wanting hands."

"We shall be no more..."

"We shall fall hard from the trail of honor we once held through our perseverance in the understanding of goodness and sacrifice we had chosen to will unto our lands so others may survive and walk amongst us as winter's storms come and pass. As the new season returns above us, there will only be the dark clouds of misery to lay our heads as we dream."

"What must we do my father, what must we do?"

"My Father, from our souls I fear we will only find apathy where once empathy was held taut within our hearts. As we find ourselves to walk the trails of our lands we shall not hear your calling, nor will we feel again the warmth of our kingdom's soul beneath our feet or across our brow as Wind shall fall silent one day and not return with the breaths of the Good Spirits."

"I ask you Father, lead us, your peoples, to where our salvation awaits us with opened arms. Lead us to where we will be afforded the right to be seen one day sitting upon the greening meadow of our Saghalie Tyee's village. We must look down upon the kingdom of Wah with reverance in knowing we had not taken journey beside the call of Red Cloud. Our people's spirit must not be banished from our lands or taken from our beliefs as Wind brings change to all we know and understand."

"We must hold strong to the lessons of your Fathers, and we must follow in your footsteps. We must be able to hear your calling so our souls will not be taken by the bad spirits that lie in wait for our submission before their soiled feet."

351

"We must be strong in the eyes of your Fathers, and we must not walk from their lead, nor should we accept the calling of our names from the desert where the Hyas Pishpish who have survived the storm has promised to cross our lands in wanting for our souls. Through our belief and faith in the Hyas Saghalie Tyee, we shall always be kept safe from entering the bellies of those that lie silently in ambush as they await hungered for their next meal."

"My father, may the cries of our spirits be silenced forever upon the Trails of Wind, and may we not find ourselves glowering in shame for what we are about to do."

Sun and moon has risen above the Lands of Wah and above the Valley of the Eagle without further storm to fall upon our lands. New leaves have begun to cling to the arms of their hosts as great numbers of pish have returned before us as they swim hard against the fast waters of En che Wauna.

It was not long ago our peoples and our lands had come under threat when we journeyed to Knope to meet with those that came from the sea to make trade. But as Sun sets upon the horizon as the new season promises of good across our lands, a time of change has begun.

Our villages have gathered together before the fires that have brought warmth to the night, and as we sit and speak, there is word our peoples have begun to trade in great numbers with Suyapee.

The village of the Clatsop welcomes all that come and make offer for the furs they bring. The Clatsop tell those who sit before the big fire they are friends of Suyapee. Through trade, they can bring much to their purses if they alone challenge the price for trade. It is told those of our brothers of distant nations who have come from lands far away are hurried in their return to their villages, and they have agreed to settle for what price is offered for their goods without haste.

With the best furs of the otter and beaver trade for the musket is good. The Klickitat and Yakama know they will take the Mowitch, Moolack and Lolo from the forests and deserts without effort. The deer and elk would soon know they were chosen to be taken without respect of being first heard of their pleading call, and in disgust, they would turn and charge upon those that stand alone without cover. Those that hunt as does Suyapee, without heart, would then be joined with the soils of the Earth beneath the spirited hooves of those they had once so honored.

There are those we do not like that come to make trade with our peoples, and others like those we call Myers, Bishop, and Gray, are promised to return with the rising of the New Moon, and as each new season brings leaves to the sticks wanting arms, they will bring to us much we do not yet hold within our people's purse. We have traded well for the furs of Otter, Beaver, and Fox. From within the purse our peoples carry, there is much that calls out for us to offer others so they too may share in the wealth we have acquired through our labors.

I sit alone this night before the big fire of our village at Che Che Optin. Once my brothers had taken the trail to where their mats await for them to become attached, I look around our village and see the blanket, the kettles of copper, and long rope. Hung before the door of our longhouse strands of bead welcome others to enter into our house where our spirits are strong.

Our homes are filled beyond the days of long ago as pish swim eagerly into our nets, and now, as they lay drying in the smoke of Alder that spreads sweet scent across the lands, life is good...

The snows cling to winter like a child to his mother, and as rains of spring have fallen from the heaven as tears from mothers of new born children, Saghalie Tyee has offered us much in Camas and Wapato, and reeds to make baskets. Our peoples have begun to trust Suyapee more each day we sit and speak with them before the fires at Knope. There, they speak of their lands and we share of our own.

Many days have passed as we had gathered at the village of Knope where the tall ships come. Trade for the spirit's warm coats are accepted with the Dentalium that have been offered to Suyapee from our brothers of the Nuu-chah-nulth Kingdom, the (Nootka), the brothers of the Makah, whose villages lie to the north along the Big Waters. Much happiness is shared by all as the shell that comes from the lands where Otelagh rests upon the flat waters brings great wealth to our village.

Much happiness has been shared by all our peoples for we have each gathered much through the gifting hands of our Hyas Tahmahnawis Tyee. As Otelagh passes over us each day we welcome his warm smiles from above with great favor. Life as we know it today is good between all our spirits, and we are pleased...

Though with much sadness I find myself to sit and question why we have been offered good fortune when it has been told through visions that our lands will be swept clean of our villages. Our peoples will one day lie unmoving upon En che Wauna's banks as our souls will be lain to waste as we are taken from our lands by these same peoples that now sit with closed smiles as they await to strike fear within our souls.

I ask of my father where our peoples may have taken a different trail that would have led us from the greed which has become swollen within us?

In the silence brought by my question, I fear my father's voice is held with much sadness as we have chosen to trade for the souls of our kingdoms. We were once connected to the lands of our

Earth, and we were once seen to walk without fear along the trails of our lands. Now, our own souls are soon to be sacrificed from within us. When others walk into the Lands of Wah they will see only of our misery. They will know of the disgrace we have left behind in our tracks for others to recall of our people's history upon these great lands.

With heads bowed toward the heaven we wail to the High Spirits. The great Otelagh passes over us from behind the Red Cloud that is now wrought by our own greed for the blue bead, the sharp ax, and the musket that steals of our kingdom's greatest spirits. With the change of Wind's breaths blown down upon our peoples, Wind spreads across our lands as it changes all that we know. It promises to take from us all that we may have once become.

Our peoples must ask of the High Spirit why Suyapee have chosen our lands to take of its spirit, and once they take from our hands all that Otelagh's kingdoms offer, will they be seen to take upon the journey of Sun and return to their peoples?

We ask; "Will Suyapee leave us squatting upon barren grounds once they come upon us the final time when there are no spirits of which to cull from our lands? Will we be seen wanting for the return of life beside the stilled waters of our lakes and rivers where we once knew life to abound plentifully beneath each day?

We ask, will Suyapee come with many men and make villages where ours once stood without respect for the life they are surrounded? Will Suyapee take from our forests the ancient sticks that share story of our kingdom's great past? Will all we have known from our beginnings upon these magnificent Lands of Wah pass in silence as the stories are taken from our souls and displaced where no man can hear of their words or be felt through our yearning hearts for our return to our homes?"

In this, I must cry out!

As you sit beneath the Great Cedar and the tall Fir, fear the dark message that has come upon our peoples as our names are called out in silence from the walls that tower above Wahclella. Soon, our Hyas Father's voices shall be stilled from where they were once heard shouting out to those that would listen as they knelt beneath their calling.

As the Winds that bring change has begun to blow hard upon us with much force, all we knew of life yesterday as Sun rose up from his bed has begun to be taken from us as Moon rises silently through the unknowing darkness of night. In our error, we must fear we shall all be left only to wander within our kingdoms with the absence of those spirits that spoke to us of love and understanding.

We must too fear once the Sea Otter is taken from the Big Water, and their brothers from our rivers, they will not bring comfort to our souls as we have watched them play from the first day we came to stand upon these majestic lands. We must fear as Eena is taken from the waters of our lakes and ponds, the waters will not gather upon the lands and offer new growth to the soils, and they will become dry and parched like the deserts where the Hyas Saghalie Tyee's tears do not fall.

We must fear as the spirit of elk is sacrificed from our mountains the air will lie stilled as Moolack will not call. From the silence of the high peaks will be heard the scream of Pishpish as it will then come before the entrance to our villages and our souls will quickly become their quarry.

Great Cedar had once shared from the smallest to the largest plant and animal, you must know they each offer balance to the lands. It is that balance we must respect so the order of life will survive as we will each endure the storms which will fall heavily upon us as winter comes hard upon us all.

In the absence of thought by our wanting, the wisdom of our High Spirit has begun to escape from within our souls. We too have become alike the bearded ones we have named Suyapee.

Our people's have chosen to take upon the trail of bitterness in our allowance of those spirits we have chosen to sacrifice without the need for meat, or for the warmth these furs bring as the cold of winter's lasting storm falls upon us without hope of end. Our souls are undeserving to the gifts offered from the hands of our Hyas Tahmahnawis. As we sit in dishonor before him, he sees we have quickly taken upon the bad spirits trails. Now, the stench of death looms heavy around and above us, and we know not what to do as the Red Cloud has settled upon the lands and shows no ending from where it had once begun.

In disgrace, I kneel upon the soil where once rose up in all his majesty, Great Cedar. Beside the shores of En che Wauna, I am heard to cry out to my father.

"What have we done?"

Why has the spirit of Suyapee brought to our villages what would lead us to walk from our father's ways and choose for us to wallow in our own disgrace?

Father, I ask, what have we done?"

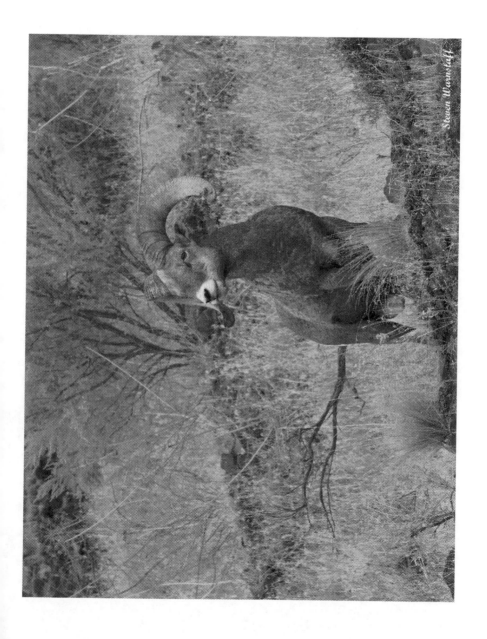

Chapter 23

From the Journeys of Wind Has Come Change Upon Our Lands

Life has been busy as I look across the fast waters of En che Wauna each day as many canoes pass swiftly before our village.

Trade between our people has taken place now for many days without cease. From the distant villages of the Nez Perz, the Klickitat, the Yakama, and of those of our nation that stand proudly to be called Chinook, there are many that have joined their souls to the waters of En che Wauna. They have each chosen to journey to Knope where the big ships rest and where Suyapee await our peoples to bring them furs that will offer warmth to their people's shoulders and to take cold from their heads.

Each day as Sun rises there is no end to those that choose to trade as they journey to the bay beside the Big Water. As our neighbors pass before our village, there is heard word of good fortune spent towards their peoples, and as each of my brothers call out with much joy, I must bow my head in their unknowing and blinding shame as tears fall heavily from the deep trails that are pronounced upon my own, now weathered cheeks.

I know soon there will be nothing left for others to find sanctuary beneath the Great Cedar and tall Fir. As those people we have not yet seen walk in amongst us and enter into our kingdom from their lands, they will not know of our peoples. As they look to the high peaks where our Hyas Spirits rest, they will walk without the voice of wisdom or to the character the High Spirits have lent to our peoples. Their souls will one day be lost forever in the silence drawn from within their own shame.

With much sadness, as darkness envelopes my soul to what is to come to our lands and to my peoples, I fall to my knees as I am taken by the vision spent before me by the High Spirit to where our lives will soon be chosen to lie in the end. As I look towards the heaven's trails, I see with much sadness the storms of all our winters fall heavily upon our shoulders without the hope for the new season's return.

Again, I cry out to my father; "What have we done?"

From high up within the heaven, great clouds form and swallow the lands beneath their swarm. I am reminded by the darkness that is drawn across the lands by my memory of many geese and duck that took light from the sky as both our villages gathered together and walked along the shores of the big lake near the village at Cathloptle as we celebrated in our hunt. We each stood in silence as great flocks flew just above the trees and across the open meadows. As they swept above us, great wind fell from the sky upon us, and light was not cast below upon the soils.

Today, it is seen by those that look to the clouds the darkness we are now enveloped brings much sadness as we know of warmth and promise with Otelagh's crossing above our lands. These clouds warn of storm as they pass with much hurry across the heaven. Wind comes hard across the lands as each cloud passes before us. From our lands life is not seen, and the voices of those living are not heard to cry out for us to find favor in their calling.

Again, our souls are lost upon the paths which now lead us blindly to what is soon to come.

The memory of our brothers when they were heard to shout out as they passed beside Che che Optin towards Knope not long ago fell heavy upon my soul. They were last known to be far from their villages and would soon long for shelter from this rising storm. Sun has not been seen for many days as he has journeyed to another kingdom where their peoples have long awaited his return. We shall not know of our brothers for many days. These clouds we see today lie low before us and spell much threat to those who are yet sitting upon the open meadows and upon the rushing waters of En che Wauna and have not yet taken to the cover of their wintered house.

The warmth summer brings has been taken from the lands as the cold of winter has returned once again. We sit idle as we have been taken from along the waters of En che Wauna through the battles fought between Wind and Storm. We await anxiously for the new season to come upon us. As each day slowly passes, with much hope, we cry out to the Hyas Tahmahnanwis Tyee so Sun shall soon be seen to rise up from the horizon and cross the

Big Waters of En che Wauna. Then, our lands will unfold in Otelagh's most welcomed warmth as life will begin anew across our kingdoms. Life will soon be seen replenished before all those who have sat with much hope and survived the test of winter's promised storm.

One night as Wind called out with great mourning I sat before our great fire in the center of our longhouse. It was there, I first spoke to my brothers and sisters of my village. I began to take them upon the journey our peoples will soon be faced. I was told to share with them the vision the Great Spirit shared with me as he drew upon the heaven the sad scenes where our people's will one day march upon the lonesome trail that leads far from the lands we have always known to prove of our promise upon them.

Darkness fell before my eyes as my great fathers shared of this vision. There were scenes of our villages falling to the ground and crumbling as there would be no one left to raise the fallen Cedar's soul from where they once stood proudly. From the thick of the forest would be heard the cries of all the spirits who had been known as friends amongst our peoples. They too will know of our absence as the bad spirit of the mesachie Tahmahnawis would be seen to rise up from the darkness as he will steal the light and warmth from day.

The spirits of our lands will find themselves walking amongst the waste left in the trails of Suyapee. Those spirits who had once walked before us will now only run with fast feet to find safety from Wind that has brought desecration to our lands.

It is Suyapee who have promised to their High Spirit to quickly bring change upon the land as they will come with many and take all that we know from upon it. They will demand we walk upon lonesome trails that do not bear witness to the wisdom of the Hyas Tahmahnawis Tyee as he too has chosen to walk free from those lands that burn beneath the rising of Otelagh. There, just beyond the slopes of the great Wy-East, in the lands where Snake first comes and hides in the tall grass, lies dieing the lands we will be seen to march in the greatest of our sorrow.

Though the day my Great Spirit called out for me to sit with him from atop the Great Larch was long ago, I, to this day, envision with great mourning, battles which shall bring blood to pour out upon the soils first as streams and then to rivers. War will soon come hard across all our lands, and in the end, those that come fast upon us will take our peoples to those kingdoms we have been told that are near the shores of En che Wauna. The same lands which we are chosen to accept will offer us little as the only tears that fall from their spirit's eyes will dry beneath the razing of Sun. Upon the fervid sands of those lands spirit's depriving souls, we shall be left standing in disgarce, alone.

We will be worse than geese when the cold of winter freezes the water and settles hard upon our lands once Suyapee takes our peoples to the kingdoms of the desert. Our spirits shall not be seen attached to the shores of En che Wauna, and as we cannot take wing and fly, we will not be seen of our return to rejoice in the warmth of the new season again. Our souls will then be lost to those trails that had once offered us heart and courage, and we will then walk alone into the darkness of our souls.

Our lives will be drawn to the forest's floor as are the leaves of the sticks when wind blows hard upon them in the end of season. With much sadness, I tell you this, as the new season is heard to sing with much happiness once new life returns to their wanting arms, through our memories, we will not hear of their song as we walk with much sadness with bowed heads in our loss.

"My Brothers; My Sisters!"

"From our mother's womb we first entered into the lands of our kingdoms where our souls are now surrendered. As we looked to the heaven from our mother's backs as they carried us with much effort in our cradle boards across the lands, they searched for root and berry each day. It was then, from our mother's backs, we were first seen to reach out to touch the light cast from the great village's many fires high above in the heaven. Those same fires have been told would one day lead us across the Hyas Tahmahnawis Tyee's meadow to where the Village of Life awaits us all to sit with one another. As we are taken from within ourselves, our souls will wander alone and without spirit, and we shall be lost to the memories of all those that will come after our spirits are lain beneath their feet once Wind lies unsettling upon our lands."

"We have been told of promises which will bring good to all our villages if we followed in the steps of our fathers. From high above, just beyond our reach, we have seen the Great White Horse that carries our fathers to the High Spirit's meadow. It is there our father's souls rose up from where they sat resting on the Big Island as they awaited their final journey to sit before the High Spirit's Council.

Here, in the end of our days upon this most beautiful and magnificent Land of Wah, sitting high above us, a land that offers our soul's repose from the trials we have been selected to journey throughout our lives, lie our strong spirits through our acceptance and following of our father's teachings from upon Wahclella's greatest wall. As we near the day when cloud comes to cover our eyes and cold lies heavy within our hearts, we shall, without fear, be taken upon the Journey of the Living Dead. We will then find rest before the day comes when our souls take upon their final journey and rise up to meet with those of our fathers, and we shall all be greatly pleased...

From high above where only travels the fleeting stallions across the heaven, we hear our names spelled out upon the trails that follow Otelagh across the sky. It is there, where love first finds itself wanting to reside within our hearts. This is where we each have felt the warmth of light from Otelagh's gifting hands as it settles our souls and brings reason to our hearts as it shares of hope and faith for better tomorrows to reign down upon us. This is the kingdom where is heard spoken only the truth towards our people's visions. It is there where we discover peace across our lands through the truths of those good visions. It is those truths that promise to sound out with much conviction from within us to all those that come to sit at our village.

With opened arms we shall reach out towards one another knowing there is the power within us to take from our souls the disease of uncertainty and question that reigns free within us. We shall cast out what troubles our souls from within ourselves as we look towards the light of the heaven that speaks of truth and resonates in reason.

There will be a day, the day which will be remembered by all those who will follow in our steps across these lands. The day when Otelagh shall shine down upon us, and as his light warms our souls, we too shall spread warmth from within us and share it before all the peoples. This day, the heaven above shall unfold its mighty powers before us, and we shall be seen like we were upon the first day of our births, innocent and free.

I ask you all; "Can you hear your name called out by our fathers from above where they sit and smile down upon us as it is announced to the peoples of this kingdom your soul brings good to where once it was seen to hold strong promising of the bad spirits? I remind you all, that it was the call to war by the bad spirits that drew our peoples before their wanting arms. As we journeyed to those lands where only Pish Pish and Lolo walked alone, we soon heard great mourning as it fell harshly from behind our mothers doors as their sons were then lost to our villages.

From high above where only the great herd of stallions run upon our High Spirit's meadow, as they look down upon us, we each must grasp to their fleeting tails as they reign free upon the opened meadow. As our minds gather in the wisdom they will spell upon our lives, this will allow our souls to become free from the disease that men as these Suyapee have been seen to be promised.

As we walk beside the calm waters of our fathers, we too shall walk in the land of our Hyas Tahmahnawis Tyee and see the light of tomorrow as it shares of the good spirit's wish that our people's voice ring out with much force. We shall not walk among them with weapons readied to pierce their dark hearts. As our fathers look down upon us with much favor, they will then announce we are again free to walk across our lands without fear of standing upon the trails that have no beginnings or endings.

That day, we will all be joined together as does Coyote join his spirit with that of the Hyas Tahmahnawis Tyee upon the highest telecasit, and as our villages each gather upon the meadows of the high places, we shall be heard again to shout out to those that come before us; "We are free again!"

May our spirits from that moment live on through the winds that pass across all our lands as they will share of our greatness, and we shall be remembered for all days.

Our worthiness as keepers to this magnificent kingdom will be seen by all those who will come one day and stand where once sat our villages. The lands will prosper and bring new life to the soils through our good spirit.

We must hold faith we will see tomorrow's light and it shall be cast down upon us in all its greatness.

Many peoples will sit beside the waters of En che Wauna as it will bring calm to their souls as it has to our own through all the seasons we have shared of these lands. These people shall look out over the fast waters and dream to what will soon come, and as they rest, they will see what had offered us commitment to our lands as Pish shall rise up from En che Wauna's depths and gather in great numbers beneath their feet. It will be there, just there, where the cottonwoods dance in the warm breeze along En che Wauna's shore, that Pish shall first carry within them our people's song. As Wind travels through our lands, there too will travel our chorus upon it. Both our spirits will then be coupled upon that magical day from the mighty purse of the great Shaman of Wy-East. Those that come to our lands and find peace within their souls will hear our raised voice that promises of both our returns to the lands of our births.

"Nesika Tahmahnawis Winapie Mitlite Halo Elite Kwonesum!"

"Our Spirits Shall Soon Be Free Forever!"

Kwonesum!

Kwonesum!

Kwonesum!"

As I spoke the final word of my vision, those who sat beside me at the great fire looked up to the heaven through the opened roof. Streaking quickly above us as we sat in great amazement came the light of the High Spirit's messenger.

Again, I remembered the day my friend, and Chief of the Wahkiukum, Tsutho's soul had been taken to the spirit world

369

from where he lay. Those that stood beside him in the darkness of the longhouse were heard to mourn the loss of their great leader. Their wail was then lent to the heaven with much sadness. As Tsutho took his final breath and his soul lay emptied to life as he settled softly upon his mat, the High Spirit's messenger crossed the heaven and brought hope to envelope within our souls through Tsutho's passing.

We each new as light was brought from the passing star within the longhouse where Chief Tsutho's soul laid at rest, life would become renewed upon the lands and bring fortune to our kingdom.

We knew of the wise man Tsutho was as he set aside the troubles that was brought before his people. As he walked amongst his village and of those that came to sit with him, he chose to take the troubles within himself so all peoples would not feel of worry, nor of regret for what they do.

From life comes death, and from death life begins anew. This was the lesson the High Spirit chose to share as we gathered at Tsutho's side and bid him our farewell as we honored his great leadership.

Those that sat ringing the fire of our village sat humbled in their silence as we each had then lain question to the passing Stallion above as it crossed the heaven. We had not heard of a brother that had passed on to his spirit world. There were no messages sent across the trails of Wind by the beats of their village's great drums to announce of their passing.

In our question, we had easily become unsettled to what may come before our peoples, or to our kingdoms. There was much we needed in answer to our question, and we were heard to cry out to the High Spirit to settle our souls so we may not walk upon

370

those trails my father had once spoke that offered only our peoples spirit's left wandering upon the travels of Wind.

Those of our village who were seated before the great fire as the spirits cried out were quick to stand. Many were heard to murmur as they did not understand the message of the Hyas Tahmahnawis Tyee. As I was in great admiration for the light of the Hyas Tahmanawis Tyee's Stallion as it streaked across the heaven, great cries rose up from those villages that were near our own. Deep within my soul I felt the coldness of death stained upon our lands with much hurry. From my mat where I was seated I rose up before them and began to speak in words without knowing of what I had been chosen to share. I wailed to the heavens for repentance for what we had accepted as we chose without question what Suyapee had offered through his many gifts in trade that took from us what offered us peace and any hope for tomorrow.

Looking to the the high peaks where our highest spirits live, we see them, each cloaked in cloud. We were surrounded. From where we could not see came the crash of thunder. As I had witnessed in the vision shared by my father, there was threat looming heavily across the lands. The spirits spoke with much force each time their voice took calm from the land. As the ground shuttered with much distress, it was awakened from its long sleep. My peoples stood in fear as fiery spears were cast across the heavens as they pierced the soils of our lands with great force. Each one, alike the sharpened edge of our arrow and spear, each had swiftly executed their mark upon the lands we were surrounded..

High up upon the peaks above En che Wauna, many trees were seen to light up the darkness of the night's long sky. From where night had become day, from the blaze of the land was seen vision of life's nearing end for our peoples. For many long hours there was not silence stilled upon the travels of Wind before us, and as we shook beneath the dispute of our spirit's grievious cries, saddened mourns rose up from the souls of the sticks that rose high above us as they swayed in distress to the confusion now rising beneath their root.

Those that believed in trade with Suyapee and had not chosen to follow in the Hyas Tahmahnawis' words did not understand why the spirits had come upon them with grave threat. As I wailed to the heavens again and again, my heart lie troubled. My spirit was soon emptied of hope for those that chose the ways of Suyapee and traded our way of life for the greed of their own wealth.

There, before me, the vision I was chosen to witness shared of our peoples lying dead from disease brought willfully from within the dark purse of Suyapee to our lands. From behind the Red Cloud as I passed through our kingdom arose visions of many villages that fell emptied of life as Wind pushed Red Cloud across the lands. No more was to be seen pish drying in sweet alder smoke as it shared happiness of the village's catch to all those who sat downwind from where they rested. No more was to be seen women sorting reed and grass to make baskets to carry the huckleberry from the mountains above in the pleasantness of summer's warmth.

Sadly, from beneath the blue sky of heaven, Red Cloud could be seen immersed in its own wake as the death of many of our brothers and sisters, and many of our mothers and fathers followed without pause as they were lain stricken from their spirit by the disease that Suyapee brings to our lands. Much was lost beneath the grievous shadow as it is now marked by the stench of death.

From many has now become few...

No more will their joyous song be heard...

From my eyes could be seen question and fear to what was to come hard upon our peoples. From my mouth rose up my prayer to the High Spirit to save our souls from the grievance that would come from the peoples we had not yet met. These peoples would approach our lands from behind the Red Cloud that had been promised through vision to spill our lands lifeless and lost to our own people's gathering upon them. We, all the brothers of all the nations would then be left homeless and bound by the ways of the bad spirits. Those same bad spirits that would steal from our souls the breaths of our Hyas Tahmahnawis Tyee that offers of life and liberty to reign free across the lands.

Broken, as are the long arms of sticks when Wind comes hard across their highest bows, our peoples shall be seen to walk into lands we are to be blindly led. Lands that do not share of promise we will be led as deer to their slaughter. Lands we have crossed for many snows that have yet proven they offer hope to our peoples so they will survive to witness Otelagh rising above them in any of our tomorrows.

These are the lands where Moolack will be heard calling from atop the far hill as they too will walk with heads bowed from where our peoples gather below them in great shame. Pish will not swim in the waters that run from the heated pools of Wy-East.

We will gather our peoples and huddle together when storm lashes itself upon us as it shall bind us taut through its mighty convictions of our ways. The cold of winter will strike without warning, and many will die and be left without spirit. They too will not be seen to cross the heavens and sit beside their fathers before the great fire of the Hyas Tumtum. It will, with much sadness, be known their spirits shall be swept from the lands, and they shall drift without course and purpose upon the foreboding journeys of Wind.

"May their souls soon settle upon the lands, and may they one day be seated beside their fathers and find peace within their souls once more," I am heard to cry out!

"Father, Hear my plea for our peoples so they may be granted salvation. May they be delivered from the face of evil as storm falls upon us hurriedly from the heaven. May we all walk free of the pestilence that will befall those who choose to sit with Suyapee and unknowingly make trade for their own misled and unguided souls.

Sadly, today, from the trails of En Che Wauna begins the trails of all our sorrows!"

Acknowledgements

Arlita Rhoan, Warm Springs Reservation, Educator, Warm Springs, Oregon

Hannah Allen, Oregon Historical Society, Portland, Oregon

Sharon Abbott Furze, Artist, Vancouver, Washington. Work can be seen on Facebook and on FineartAmerica.com

Stephanie Wendt, Yakima Indian Reservation, Tourism Coordinator, Toppenish, Washington

Valerie Ann Kelley, Artist's work can be seen on Facebook and on FinearAmerica.com

Printed in the United States
By Bookmasters